Pamela Eva[illegible] Hanwell in the borough of Ealing, Lo[illegible] two grown-up sons and now lives in Wales with he[illegible]sband.

Also by Pamela Evans

A Barrow in the Broadway
Lamplight on the Thames
Maggie of Moss Street
Star Quality
Diamonds in Danby Walk
A Fashionable Address
Tea-Blender's Daughter
The Willow Girls
Part of the Family
Town Belles
Yesterday's Friends
Near and Dear
A Song in Your Heart
The Carousel Keeps Turning
A Smile for all Seasons

Where We Belong

Pamela Evans

HEADLINE

First published in 2000
by HEADLINE BOOK PUBLISHING

First published in paperback in 2001
by HEADLINE BOOK PUBLISHING

10 9 8 7 6 5 4 3

ISBN 0 7472 6811 8

Typeset by CBS, Martlesham Heath, Ipswich, Suffolk

Printed and bound in Great Britain by
Mackays of Chatham plc, Chatham, Kent

HEADLINE BOOK PUBLISHING
A division of Hodder Headline
338 Euston Road
London NW1 3BH

www.headline.co.uk
www.hodderheadline.com

To Fred, with love

Chapter One

Two men hurried along the Thames waterfront past wharves, cranes and barges, skirting the lawned public gardens that fringed the bank. It was hard going because of the strong wind that was rocking the moored boats and churning the river's surface into a shifting collage of colour and light, the splintered reflection of Hammersmith Bridge mingling with fragments of winter sky.

But the men were preoccupied with a more urgent matter and paying little attention to the weather, at least not in terms of its aesthetic effect on the water. The new year of 1966 hadn't got off to a good start for them.

'Surely there must be something we can do to get the money that's owed to the firm?' suggested the younger of the two, Ben Smart. Tall, tough and twenty-nine, even he was forced to stoop slightly against the bitter blasts; his mass of blond hair was blown flat to his head, clean-cut features tensed from the buffeting they were taking from the elements.

'There isn't. Not unless someone's invented a way to get blood from a stone,' replied his employer. Chip Banks was in his mid forties and stockily built, with a swarthy complexion, soft dark eyes and greying black hair curling beneath his cap, which he was clutching to his head for fear of losing it to the wind. 'The company that owed us has gone broke and there's no money to pay their creditors. We're not the only ones who'll suffer from it.'

‘I’m sorry for the others, of course, but that doesn’t help us, does it?’ Ben pointed out, blue eyes clouded with worry. ‘I mean, that’s months of work we’re not gonna get paid for.’

‘Course it is.’ Chip finally lost his cap, which scudded along the path before being lifted by an upward gust and blown over the wall into the river. ‘And I won’t be able to recoup any of my losses by claiming the boats back from them because everything will be put into the hands of the receiver.’

Ben pulled the hood of his duffle coat over his head. His fresh complexion was brightly suffused, cheeks and ears stinging from the wind’s sharp bite. ‘Who’d have thought that a long-established firm like that would go bust,’ he remarked.

‘Not me, for one. I’d never have let them run up such a hefty bill if I’d had an inkling that they were in trouble. But as we’ve been making and repairing their boats for years, the owner had become a good mate,’ said Chip. ‘That’s why I carried on taking in work from them even though their account was building up. I thought the money was safe. I trusted the bloke.’

That was no surprise to Ben, who just muttered a noncommittal ‘Mmm.’

Chip Banks was the proprietor of Banks’ Boats, Thames boatbuilders of repute. The company specialised in traditional, mostly hand-crafted, wooden rowing boats, which they made, renovated and repaired, some for racing, others for ordinary use, the latter being sold mainly to companies who hired out rowing boats on rivers and lakes around the country.

As well as being Chip’s assistant cum workshop manager, Ben was also a friend of long standing, which was why Chip was confiding in him about the current crisis. Both men were qualified boatbuilders and watermen, respected in the trade as masters of their craft. Unfortunately, Chip was a better boatbuilder than he was a businessman, and this wasn’t the first time the firm had lost money as a result of his warm heart and trusting nature.

Reaching their destination, the men went into the Blue Anchor, an old-established riverside pub with a Victorian bar fitting, dark décor, solid wooden tables and a fire roaring in the hearth. Crowded, smoky and clamorous with male conversation, the atmosphere was warm and welcoming and just what they needed on this rough January day. Having exchanged greetings with other lunchtime regulars – mostly men who earned their living from the river in one way or another – they settled at a table in the corner for a pint of beer and a plate of shepherd's pie.

'So,' began Ben, removing his coat to reveal a dark blue thick-knit sweater and denim jeans, 'just how bad *are* things for the firm?'

Chip shook his head slowly, puffing out his lips to illustrate the gravity of the situation. 'Bad enough, mate. It's a lot of dough to lose and I've already got the bank on my back.'

'Oh?' Up went Ben's brows.

Chip nodded gloomily. 'Seems to be a permanent state with me because customers are so slow paying their bills,' he explained, knife and fork poised. 'Having so much money outstanding plays havoc with my overdraft. I'm not sure the business can survive this latest setback as well.'

'Won't the bank support you if they know you've got money to come in?' queried Ben hopefully as he started on his meal.

'The outstanding amount won't cover what we've lost,' the other man confessed.

'Even so, it must help the situation,' stated Ben. 'And your bank manager knows there isn't another boatbuilders in west London to touch us for quality of work.'

'It's hard cash that pays the bills, though,' Chip reminded him.

'Reputation counts for something, surely,' asserted Ben.

'It does, of course,' agreed Chip. 'But the standard of work means nothing to the men in suits if it doesn't put money in the account. They've gotta look after the bank's interests.'

'We'll just have to get out there and get the money in that's owed, won't we?' said Ben.

'If only it was that easy,' sighed Chip. 'These people will pay when they're ready and not a moment before.'

'Because they've had the work done so they've nothing to lose,' Ben pointed out.

'I know what you're getting at.' Chip gave him a sideways glance, looking sheepish.

'I really do believe that the only way to avoid this sort of thing happening is to insist on payment on delivery.' Ben knew he could speak his mind to Chip without causing any lasting offence. 'Or at least be firmer about getting the money in, so as not to put the firm at risk.'

'Of course that's what I *should* do,' snapped the other man defensively. 'But most of our customers are as sound as a bell. I mean, you wouldn't dream of doubting any of the rowing clubs, would you? They pay a deposit when they order a boat and there's never any question that we'll get what's owed to us when the job is finished.'

'True enough,' agreed Ben. 'But there's always a certain amount of risk with commercial firms and private individuals.'

'I've never claimed to be London's greatest businessman,' said Chip. 'Boatbuilding is what I'm good at. I set up in business for myself all those years ago so that I could produce good-quality craft to my own high standards, not because I wanted to make a fortune.'

'That's what comes of being a perfectionist,' said Ben with a wry grin.

'Hark who's talking,' joshed Chip, managing to smile even though he was feeling physically ill from the strain of his recent financial worries. 'I've seen young apprentices break their hearts trying to please you with their work.'

'And who taught me such high standards?' Ben asked him lightly.

'I like to think I did a good job in training you.' Chip's

expression became grim again. 'Even if I'm not so hot at the business side of things.'

'You're not bad at it,' Ben was quick to point out. 'You're a bit too trusting, that's all.'

The other man shrugged. 'I know, I know,' he conceded. 'But what sort of a world would this be if we didn't ever take a chance on anyone?'

What indeed? Ben could hardly bear to imagine what kind of life he would be living now if Chip hadn't taken a chance on him sixteen years ago, when he'd been a stroppy, rebellious youth who hadn't deserved a civil word, let alone the chance to make a decent future for himself . . .

The son of a drunken father who'd beaten his wife into an early grave, Ben had joined a gang of yobs in his early teens as a way of escaping his father's fists. He enjoyed the camaraderie and sense of belonging he'd found within the group that had been missing at home. Hell-bent on petty crime and vandalism, the gang would hang about the streets looking for mischief.

One evening, in search of excitement, they'd broken into the premises of Banks' Boats, intent upon destroying the boats in progress in the workshops. Much to his astonishment, Ben had been horrified to see wanton damage being wreaked on such finely crafted things and had turned on his mates. He'd been trying to stop the mindless destruction when Chip had arrived on the scene, having come back to the boathouse to do some extra work. The gang had made a hasty retreat, leaving Ben to take the blame. Fortunately, they'd been interrupted before too much harm had been done.

Not prepared to grass on his mates, Ben had expected to find himself in the juvenile court with a stretch in borstal ahead of him. But Chip must have seen something in him worth nurturing, because he hadn't called the police. Instead he'd given Ben a thorough trouncing, then made him clear up the mess the gang had left behind them.

When the workshop was back to rights, Chip had told Ben

he was free to leave and had set to work on a racing skiff. Fascinated by the older man's skill and dexterity, Ben had asked if he could stay to watch. It was then that his interest in boatbuilding had been irreversibly implanted.

That night had proved to be a watershed for Ben. He stopped hanging out with the gang and started going to the boathouse after school, earning a few coppers sweeping up and running errands. When the time came for him to leave school, with the idea of going into some dead-end job in a factory, Chip had offered him an apprenticeship. Soon after that, when the drink finally killed Ben's father, leaving him homeless at the age of fifteen, Chip had given him a home, too.

He'd lodged happily with Chip for several years until he'd become qualified and could afford the rent on a place of his own. Chip had been like a father to him, and Ben knew that he himself filled a void in Chip's life, too. There was no love lost between Chip and his son Arthur, who had been taken away from his father at a young age by Chip's wife when their marriage broke up and she'd subsequently married someone else.

Now Ben replied to Chip's question. 'It wouldn't be a world worth living in,' he told him. 'So you stay as you are, mate.'

'I wouldn't know how to be any other way,' said the other man, shrugging his shoulders. 'But getting sentimental isn't gonna bring the business through this crisis, is it?' He paused, looking thoughtful, his eyes shadowed and bloodshot from too many sleepless nights. 'Apart from losing all that money, we've also lost the contract, since that boat-hire company has gone out of business.'

'There'll be other contracts,' Ben reassured him. 'There's always a demand for rowing boats. And the clubs send us steady work because Banks' Boats are the best in the business.'

'I do hope so,' sighed Chip. 'That's always been my ambition for the firm.'

Ben knew it would break Chip's heart to lose his business.

He'd started the boathouse with his army gratuity after the war, having trained as a boatbuilder before going into the services. 'You'll get through this,' said Ben, determined to stay positive. 'And I'll be there beside you, to do what I can to help.'

'I'll understand if you want to look for another job,' Chip told him solemnly.

'As if I'd do a thing like that,' frowned Ben.

'I mean it,' insisted Chip. 'You've gotta look after yourself, and things aren't too secure for any of us at my boathouse at the moment.'

'The last thing I would do is look for another job.' Ben was horrified at the suggestion. 'If it hadn't been for you, I'd probably be in prison by now, or living on the streets. I've no intention of deserting you.'

'You wouldn't have any trouble finding another job,' Chip continued. 'Not with your reputation in the trade. You're more than just good at the job. Some people have that extra something, and you're one of those.'

Although Ben wasn't a conceited man, he knew there was some truth in what Chip said. Apprentices would watch Ben with the same sort of admiration as he himself had watched Chip in the early days as he worked with wood, sawing, shaping, building. Most of his skill came from hard work and good training but there was also some indefinable force that gave him the ability to design and produce exceptional work. He couldn't explain it but knew it was there and felt blessed by it. 'It's nice of you to say so,' he said, flattered by the compliment even though he wouldn't embarrass his employer by reacting in a sentimental way. 'But the only reason I would leave the firm is if it ceased to exist, and that isn't going to happen, because, between us, you and I are going to make absolutely sure it doesn't. Right?'

'If we do manage to keep going, I shall have to cut down on staff,' Chip informed him. 'So those of you who are left will have to work twice as hard.'

'No problem,' said Ben.

Chip gave him a close look. 'You're OK, do you know that?' he said.

'I've had a good teacher.'

Ben wasn't just referring to boatbuilding. He'd learned so much more from Chip than that. The older man had passed on his honesty and humanity, his enthusiasm for life. A plain-speaking man with no pretensions, he was popular with everyone. Everyone, that was, except his son, who made it obvious on the odd occasions that he came to the boathouse that he had no time for his father.

It twisted Ben's heart to hear Arthur doing Chip down. He was contemptuous of him in general but particularly cutting about the fact that he worked with his hands, completely disregarding the special expertise of his respected craft. Ben got the impression that integrity didn't play much of a part in Arthur's life; that he found it more satisfying to live by his wits.

Sometimes Ben would sense a profound sadness in Chip, something he suspected went beyond his failed marriage and uncaring son. It wasn't anything definite, just an occasional wistful quietness.

But now they had finished their meal and Chip was saying, 'Drink up, mate, it's time we got back to the grind. We've still got commitments even if the boathouse is hovering on the brink of disaster.'

'Ready when you are,' said Ben, draining his glass and reaching for his coat over the back of the chair.

'The Westford Rowing Club are sending someone to collect their eights boat some time this afternoon,' mentioned Chip. 'I hope she's all ready for them.'

'Don't worry, everything's under control,' Ben assured him, slipping into his coat. 'But I'll give her a final inspection as soon as we get back and make sure she's in the yard ready for collection.'

'Good man,' approved Chip. 'At least they'll pay on the

dot, so that's something to be grateful for.'

'Yeah.' Ben finished doing his coat up and waited while Chip zipped his navy blue anorak, becoming frighteningly aware of the extent of his employer's stress. It was apparent in the grey pallor of Chip's skin, and in his tightly set mouth, and was especially noticeable because he was normally such a cheerful person. If only there was something more Ben could do to help. 'Look, mate,' he said impulsively, 'why don't the two of us get together after work tonight to see what can be done to keep Banks' Boats in business? We'll be better able to apply our minds to it when we've finished for the day.'

'Good idea,' said Chip, putting his empty glass on the table. 'I'd appreciate that.'

Together they walked across the bar to the door, calling out their goodbyes as they went. Stepping outside, they were both nearly knocked off their feet.

'Good grief,' exclaimed Ben, instinctively reaching out to steady the older man. 'There's a ruddy gale blowing.'

The wind had indeed gained in strength. The bare winter trees were swaying against a hectic sky full of dark racing clouds, and the pub sign was squeaking and rattling as it swung from side to side. Finding it difficult to speak against the wind's breathtaking power, the two men headed back to the boathouse.

'Right . . . when you're ready, boys, ease her down . . . gently and slowly,' shouted Ben to the two men on the upper floor of the boathouse as they prepared to lower the racing boat down to the men in the yard. The operation was being severely hampered by the gale, which was now accompanied by driving rain, making it slippery underfoot.

'Steady as you go, lads,' yelled Chip, who'd come to give a helping hand, being very much a working proprietor. 'Mind the wind doesn't take her.'

The boathouse was a two-storey redbrick building with a yard to the front and side. Both floors were used as workshops.

There was a balcony to the upper floor and a flat roof where boats were sometimes stored. Boats constructed in the first-floor workshops left the premises by way of large double doors since the internal stairs weren't sufficiently wide to take the finished crafts.

'Come on, then, let's be having her,' called Ben, his voice muffled by the wind that was rattling the doors, which were roped to metal brackets on the walls to keep them open.

Struggling to stay upright against the force of the blast, Ben reached up to grasp the bow, the rain beating icily into his face. He and a young apprentice managed to get hold of it, but before they could ease the boat all the way down, a freak gust whipped across the yard, unbalancing one of the men on the upper floor, who tried to steady himself but lost his grip on the rope attached to the stern, sending the boat hurtling to the ground and taking Ben and the apprentice with it. Chip tried to save it but slipped and fell awkwardly to the ground.

'Are you all right, mate?' asked Ben shakily, struggling to his feet and helping Chip up.

'Never mind about me,' said Chip breathlessly, rubbing his arm as though in pain. 'What about the boat?'

'I'll see to that,' said Ben, realising that Chip was hurt. 'You go inside out of the wind.'

And because suddenly Chip wasn't feeling well, he did as Ben suggested without argument.

'There's a bit of damage to the side of the boat where she hit the ground,' Ben informed Chip a short time later. They were in his office, hot sweet tea having been administered by Mrs Butler, the boathouse secretary, who'd been with Chip since he started up in business and was now nearing retirement age. 'But there's nothing that can't be put right without too much time being spent on it.'

'Thank God for that,' said Chip, seeming very shaken by his fall. 'We can't afford any more setbacks.'

'I think perhaps you'd better get on the phone to the rowing club, though, to tell them to collect her tomorrow instead of today, just to be on the safe side,' suggested Ben. 'We'll need a bit of time to check her over and make sure she's absolutely right.'

'Yeah, I'll do it now,' agreed Chip, reaching for the telephone with a trembling hand.

'You still look a bit peaky,' remarked Ben, noticing Chip's bilious complexion and the perspiration shining on his skin. 'That fall really shook you up, didn't it?'

'I think it must have done.' He dropped the receiver on the desk with a clatter and clutched his arm to his chest. 'I feel rotten, to tell you the truth.'

'In what way?' enquired Ben, replacing the telephone and trying not to show his fearful reaction to the bluish tinge of the other man's skin.

'I'm not sure,' said Chip. 'Sort of sick and funny, and I've got a terrible pain in my arm.'

'You must have pulled a muscle or bruised yourself when you fell,' suggested Ben.

'I've got a pain in my chest now an' all,' the other man announced.

'I'll take you down to Casualty in my car,' offered Ben at once, alerted by the sinister sound of the symptoms. 'It'll be quicker than trying to get hold of the doctor.'

'I'm not going to any hospital,' objected Chip, who had never had much to do with the medical profession and was rather frightened of it. 'I'll be all right in a minute.'

But no sooner had he uttered the words than his body seemed to crumple and he began to gasp for breath, clutching his chest and groaning.

'I'm taking you to the hospital whether you like it or not,' declared Ben.

Chip was in no fit state to argue as Ben helped him out to his car, assisted by a worried Mrs Butler. Ben put his foot down on the accelerator and headed for Hammersmith Hospital.

* * *

Rachel West could hardly stay on her feet that same evening when she finished her shift at a factory in Shepherd's Bush and joined the long queue for a bus to Hammersmith. The wind was sweeping the rain horizontally across the street, lashing her face and dripping into her eyes from the hood of her sodden red anorak. She felt wet right through to her underwear.

A small, skinny woman of twenty-six, with lustrous green-brown eyes and curly brown hair flecked with golden tones and worn casually with a fringe, she clutched her hood to her head as the wind tried to tear it off. It was completely soaked but at least it took the brunt of the weather. She was cold to the bone, her eyes itching with tiredness from being awake half the night with a fretful three-year-old, her fingers sore from assembling electrical components all day.

Standing there in the wind and rain, water seeping into one of her much-mended boots through a hole in the sole, she tried not to be depressed about the impossibility of being able to buy another pair. New shoes for her children took priority over her own needs and she didn't even know how she was going to find the money for theirs, let alone a pair for herself. It was just as well she wasn't overly burdened with vanity, because the shabby clothes she was forced to go about in weren't exactly flattering.

She was still wrestling with the problem of footwear for the children, and taking comfort in the hope of overtime sometime soon at the factory, when the bus arrived and everybody surged forward, pushing and shoving in their eagerness to get out of the weather.

The lower deck of the bus was full, so she climbed the stairs into a pungent mixture of cigarette smoke, wet raincoats and stale perspiration, her clothes feeling cold and damp on her skin as she sat down. Through all of this ghastly discomfort, one light burned bright inside her – the thought of seeing her sons Tim and Johnnie, aged four and three respectively.

As she thought about them, her eyes felt hot and moist with sheer gratitude for their existence. How their father could have turned his back on them was completely beyond her. But he had, two years ago. He'd met someone he preferred to his wife – a woman he worked with at the salt factory – and had moved in with her, somewhere in north London as far as Rachel knew, though he'd been careful not to put an address on the goodbye note he'd left on the kitchen table for her to find when she got back from the shops on that terrible Saturday. Presumably he'd been afraid she might hound him for maintenance money, which he'd said in the note he'd send to her every week and never had – which was why she'd had to find a job immediately.

Looking back on how broken and wretched she'd felt in the immediate aftermath of his departure, she thought the suffocating sense of helplessness had been the worst part. She'd always taken security and self-esteem for granted until she no longer had either. Life had become a minefield of uncertainties. As well as the pain and humiliation, there was also the huge responsibility of parenthood, which she now had to bear alone. Jeff had never been what you could call a participating parent, but at least he'd shared the same roof. She'd felt fragile to the point of feebleness at times, unable to survive another day.

It hadn't happened overnight. But gradually, from the wreckage of the person she had once been – a wife with a husband to support her financially and give her a place in society – another woman had emerged, someone far more resilient than she'd ever imagined herself to be. Not that she didn't still feel vulnerable, even now. But she was managing. With two little boys relying on her, she couldn't let herself go under.

No matter how bad she'd felt, she'd been determined that their childhood wouldn't be wrecked by the selfishness of their father. Being just babies when he'd left, they didn't remember him, especially as he'd always taken a background role. He'd not been at ease with babies, and had never involved himself with them.

The heartbreak of being betrayed by the man she'd loved had eventually turned to anger and then to dull resignation interspersed with bursts of outrage at the sheer callousness of what he'd done, though coping with a full-time job and bringing up the children took most of her energy.

Jeff had always been irresponsible and self-indulgent and had made no secret of the fact that he felt restricted by the ties of a wife and children. She'd hoped he would become more settled as he matured. Never in her worst nightmare had she thought he would just walk away from his responsibilities. Her intellect told her she was better off without him, but her heart had said otherwise for a long time afterwards. She couldn't just wipe her mind and emotions clean of someone she'd once shared her life with.

As she got off the bus, depressing thoughts of Jeff were pushed aside by the joyful anticipation of seeing her sons. She hurried towards the home of her sister Jan, whose moral and practical support had been a lifeline to Rachel this past two years.

'Mumm . . . eee,' whooped Tim, his rosy little face wreathed in smiles, as Jan opened the door of her terraced house to her rain-soaked sister, and ushered her into the narrow hall.

'Hello, darling,' Rachel beamed at her son.

'Guess what?' he said.

'I can't guess, so tell me,' she grinned.

'We had fish fingers and chips for our tea,' he informed her proudly.

'And we had some lovely strawberry mousse that Auntie Jan got from the supermarket for afters,' added his chubby-cheeked younger brother, Johnnie.

'Well, aren't you the luckiest boys?' enthused Rachel, peeling off her wet anorak and hanging it on a coat-hook before going down on her knees to hug them both, smothering them with kisses. 'You can't possibly guess how pleased I am to see you.'

'Anyone would think you hadn't seen them for a month,' smiled Jan, a warm-hearted, forthright woman with a penchant for homemaking.

'It feels like a month,' confessed Rachel, feasting her eyes on her children. 'I've missed you two fellas so much.' She looked at her sister. 'Have they been good?'

'Yeah, course they have,' Jan assured her.

'Johnnie spilt milk all over the sofa,' came the triumphant cry of their four-year-old cousin Kelly, a plump child with blue eyes and ginger hair worn in bunches.

'I didn't mean to,' said Johnnie, turning scarlet.

'It was an accident,' supported his brother.

Standing close to her mother with a proprietorial air, Kelly sent a withering look in the general direction of her cousins. 'And Tim scribbled on my crayoning book and Mummy was cross and told him he was very naughty,' she reported jubilantly.

'All right, Kelly, that's quite enough tales from you, thank you very much,' admonished her mother mildly. 'You children go in the other room while Rachel and I have a cup of tea.'

As they trailed noisily into the living room, Rachel turned to her sister. 'Sounds as though you've been having a fraught time,' she said.

'Take no notice of Kelly,' said Jan. 'She's just looking for attention.'

'She resents having to share her mother with her cousins all day, I expect,' suggested Rachel with concern.

'Maybe she does sometimes,' agreed Jan. 'But it certainly doesn't do her any harm. She needs other kids around, it teaches her to mix and to share . . . and she'd miss the boys like mad if they weren't here. She loves them to bits even if she can't wait to drop them in it as soon as you get here. It's just a bit of childish rivalry.'

'Yeah, I know. But you would tell me if minding them is

too much for you, wouldn't you?' asked Rachel, sensitive, as ever, to other people's feelings.

'I'm surprised you even have to ask that question, since I've never been known to hold back,' her sister smilingly assured her. 'Stop worrying. You're nothing more than a bag of bones as it is.'

Rachel had always been slim but never as thin as she was now, mainly because she regularly skipped meals to feed the boys. She always made sure that they had nourishing food, albeit from the inexpensive end of the market: cheap cuts of meat, plenty of vegetables, bread and jam instead of the sweets she used to be able to afford.

On weekdays, when she was out working, they had their main meals at Jan's, which were covered by the money Rachel insisted on paying for childcare. Jan wouldn't take the going rate and only accepted a token payment so that Rachel didn't feel awkward. She said that as she was at home with Kelly anyway, she was glad to help out. Their mother also did what she could within the limitations of her own part-time job. Rachel was constantly thankful for her supportive relatives.

'Thanks for the compliment,' she said now with irony.

'Take no notice of me,' grinned her sister, who was plump to say the least. 'I'm just jealous 'cause you can get into a size ten while I'm pushing it to get into a marquee.'

'Oh, Jan,' laughed Rachel. 'You're not that big.'

'Big enough.'

'That's what contentment does for you,' remarked Rachel lightly. Her sister had been happily married for several years to a man she'd known since she was a teenager.

Two years older than Rachel, Jan was taller and bigger altogether, with a large round face, bright blue eyes and a shock of auburn hair. Of a contented nature anyway, she enjoyed her life as a housewife and had no hankering for anything else at the moment. 'I've got the kettle on,' she said. 'Come and have a cuppa.'

Rachel followed her sister into the kitchen, which was in

the process of refurbishment, with stripped walls and cupboards half built. Jan and Pete had bought this old house with the idea of modernising it gradually. The smell of their evening meal filled the room with a delicious aroma: vegetables cooking on the stove and something savoury in the oven.

'I mustn't stay long,' mentioned Rachel, who kept to a strict routine on weekdays. 'I don't like the boys to be late getting to bed as they have to be up so early.'

'Another ten minutes won't hurt, and if Pete gets home before you're ready to leave, he'll give you a lift in the van.'

'That won't be necessary,' insisted Rachel, who was fiercely independent. 'It's only a few minutes' walk.'

'Far enough for the three of you to get soaked to the skin,' Jan pointed out. 'I know that *you* already are, but there's no sense in letting the boys get wet when you don't have to.'

'I was thinking of Pete,' explained Rachel. 'He's been out working all day. It doesn't seem fair to drag the poor bloke out again on a night like this.'

'He won't mind,' Jan said. 'You know Pete.'

Rachel nodded. Pete Todd was well known for his easy-going nature.

A rush of noise and activity in the other room heralded the arrival of Jan's husband. The children had obviously seen his van draw up and the house was suddenly filled with excitement and the sound of small feet thundering to the front door. Tim and Johnnie usually joined Kelly in welcoming her father, because they were very fond of their Uncle Pete. Rachel felt a lump rise in her throat at this touching picture of family life in which, by the very nature of things, she and her children could only take a peripheral part, no matter how welcome Jan and Pete made them feel in their home.

While Jan joined the reception party at the front door, Rachel poured the tea and took it into the living room, which was comfy and traditional, with a fire burning in the hearth, a well-worn three-piece suite in red and a television set in the corner.

'How are things with you then, Rachel?' enquired her brother-in-law, a large man with a friendly nature and a wild profusion of curly brown hair on both his head and his chin. He was a self-employed washing-machine repairman, and was wearing a pair of blue overalls.

'Not so bad, thanks.' She passed him a cup of tea. 'Have you had a good day?'

'Mustn't grumble,' he said, and Rachel knew he wouldn't even if he'd had a hellish one, because he was the most patient and uncomplaining of men.

'You'll run Rachel and the kids home, won't you, love?' said his wife with the casual confidence of someone who was in a happy and secure relationship. 'It's such a shocking night.'

'Course I will,' he told her.

'Thanks, Pete,' said Rachel.

'No problem.'

His daughter climbed on to his lap and her cousins tried to do the same until they were restrained by their mother, who told them they were going home soon. They were miffed at this but cheered up when they learned they were going in Uncle Pete's van. It was the nearest they ever got to going in a car, since their father had left with the family motor, an old banger but transport none the less.

All three children got a bit wild and excited then, tearing around the room, screaming and giggling, which meant the adults couldn't hear themselves speak until the threat of an early bedtime quietened the trio down.

The telephone rang in the hall. 'I'll get it,' said Jan, rising.

'If it's a customer, tell them I'm fully booked tomorrow, will you, love?' Pete said to her retreating back. 'The day after is the earliest booking I can take.'

'Will do,' replied Jan obligingly.

Rachel gave her brother-in-law a friendly grin, observing how the warmth of his presence seemed to fill the room. 'You're doing well, then,' she said, getting up with the idea of collecting the coats from the hall ready to leave. 'Fully booked sounds good to me.'

He nodded, finishing his tea. 'There's a growing demand for someone like me, with so many people getting automatic washing machines,' he said. 'The automatics have more machinery to go wrong than the old twin-tubs.' He gave her a wicked grin. 'And you won't hear me complaining.'

'You'd be a fool if you did,' smiled Rachel, who hadn't yet joined the élite band of owners.

'It's just as well there's plenty of work about because doing this house up uses money quicker than I can make it,' Pete told her, glancing around the room, which hadn't yet had the benefit of refurbishment.

'I know the feeling,' she said with a sympathetic look. 'Feeding and clothing the boys has much the same effect on me. They grow out of everything so fast I can't keep up with it. It's lucky for me that they're both boys. At least I can pass things down. And they're not old enough yet to complain about it.'

They were still chatting idly when Jan came back into the room, her face ashen.

'Who was it, love?' Pete enquired.

She didn't reply but sank into an armchair as though her legs had given out on her, her eyes staring unseeingly ahead.

'What's happened?' asked Rachel. 'You look as though you've had a shock.'

'It was Mum,' Jan said absently.

'Mum?' Rachel was immediately concerned. 'Is something wrong with her or Dad?' she wanted to know.

'No, not with them – well, not directly anyway,' said Jan, her hand pressed to her head. 'But they've just had a visit from Ben Smart – you know, the bloke who works for Uncle Chip.'

'I know the one,' said Rachel quickly, her heart beginning to pound as there was obviously something the matter. 'But what's he got to do with anything?'

Jan shook her head as though unable to believe her own words. 'He went round to tell them that . . .' She paused, unable to continue. 'To tell them that Uncle Chip died this afternoon,' she finished at last in a bemused tone.

'Blimey,' gasped Pete.

'Died!' exclaimed Rachel, shocked to the core. 'He can't have!'

'He has,' said Jan dully.

'But he wasn't old or ill or anything,' Rachel pointed out.

'No, he wasn't,' agreed Jan grimly.

'Was it some sort of an accident?' enquired Rachel, whey-faced and shaky.

'No. They think it was a heart attack,' explained Jan dully. 'He came over poorly this afternoon after he'd had a fall. Ben rushed him to the hospital. But he was dead on arrival, as they say. There was nothing anyone could do.'

'How dreadful,' said Rachel.

'Terrible,' echoed Jan. 'Apparently Ben went to Mum and Dad's place because he didn't know how to contact Arthur.'

'Poor Uncle Chip,' murmured Rachel sadly. She'd been fond of her mother's younger brother, who'd been a regular visitor at the house when she was a child. 'Poor Mum, too. I bet she's in a terrible state.'

'She didn't sound too good,' Jan confirmed.

'Her and Uncle Chip were always close – and Dad and he were good mates, too,' Rachel continued. 'We'd better go over to their place right away, just to give them some moral support.' She put her hand to her throbbing head. 'I should get the boys home to bed, though.'

'It won't hurt them to be late for once, not at a time like this,' said Pete, getting up in a purposeful manner and taking control. 'We'll all go to your mum and dad's place in the van and I'll run you home afterwards, Rachel. Come on, let's go. Get your coats, everybody.'

'I'd better turn things off in the kitchen,' said Jan vaguely. 'I won't be a minute.'

With coats hurriedly donned, they all went out into the torrential rain and piled into the dilapidated van, Jan and Kelly in the front with Pete, Rachel and the boys in the back among the tool boxes and spare parts. Tim and Johnnie thought it was great fun and Rachel took pleasure in that, but she was still chilled from her earlier soaking and shivering inside her damp anorak and wet boots, the shock of her uncle's death making her feel sick and out of sorts.

When Rachel finally got home that night, the boys were cold, overtired and tetchy. Their poky third-floor council flat on the Perrydene Estate in Hammersmith felt like a refrigerator, the sour smell of damp permeating everything. The curtains in the living room were moving from the force of an icy draught that was finding its way through the closed windows.

'I'm cold, Mum,' said Tim, shivering.

'So am I,' whined Johnnie, looking utterly forlorn. 'And I'm hungry too.'

'I know you are, my darlings. But you'll be as warm as toast once I get the place heated up,' said Rachel in her usual positive manner, though her nerves jangled at the thought of the cost of having the gas fire on. 'I'll get you ready for bed then make us some supper and we'll have it by the fire.'

She lit the gas fire and the boys sat in front of it on the floor. She removed their wet clothes and wrapped blankets around them, then went to the kitchen and put the kettle on for hot-water bottles. The two-bedroomed flat had no other heating besides the money-eating gas fire in the living room.

'Can we have the telly on?' asked Tim.

'It still isn't working, love,' said Rachel. The TV had packed up several weeks ago and she was still trying to find the money to get it fixed.

'Auntie Jan's telly works,' said Johnnie accusingly.

'Yes, well, ours doesn't at the moment,' she told him.

'Not fair,' he huffed.

'Maybe not, but it's the way it is.' She had to be firm about things she couldn't afford. Jeff hadn't earned a huge amount, but at least he'd brought home enough to keep the household running, whereas her wages covered only the basic expenses, which meant that extras had to be saved for.

'Why can't we have strawberry mouse like we have at Auntie Jan's?' asked Johnnie.

'I'll get some at the weekend,' Rachel told him.

'I want some now,' he said, in truculent mood.

'We'll have it as a treat on Sunday,' said Rachel.

'Kelly has it all the time.' His expression was mutinous.

Johnnie was a darling but an absolute pain when he was tired. Being exhausted herself and depressed about her uncle's death, Rachel's patience wasn't at its best. 'Well, it's a treat for us and that's that,' she told him.

'Humph,' he groaned.

'Don't be a misery, love,' she admonished gently. 'You can't have everything you want.'

'Humph,' he snorted again.

'You're being a baby,' accused Tim. 'Baby baby bunting . . .'

'I'm not a baby,' objected Johnnie.

'You sound like one to me,' said Tim.

'Shut up, you,' retorted Johnnie.

'Now then, stop it, both of you, *this minute*,' Rachel intervened.

The tone of her voice rendered the room silent.

'Sorry, Mum,' said Johnnie meekly.

'Sorry, Mum,' added Tim.

'All right,' she said in a forgiving tone. 'Now, let's all calm down, shall we?'

Hurrying back into the kitchen, she filled the hot-water bottles, which she then placed in the beds. When she went back into the living room the boys were playing with their toy cars on the floor. She stood at the door. 'Right, you two. Who's first to get washed?'

'Not me,' they said in unison.

'One of you has to be first,' she pointed out.

'It's too cold in the bathroom,' said Tim.

'Yeah,' agreed Johnnie, shuddering at the thought. 'I'm not going in there.'

She couldn't blame them. The bathroom was the flat's own Arctic region. 'Just a quick wash tonight,' said Rachel, who was tempted to give the ritual a miss but thought she'd better not lower her standards just because she was tired, in case it got to be a habit. 'You're not going to bed filthy just because it's cold in the bathroom. So come on, one of you, *hurry up*.'

In the absence of a response, she marched across the room and gathered Johnnie into her arms, carrying him to the bathroom kicking and screaming. Making a game of it, she tickled his tummy, singing his favourite nursery rhyme. By the time she'd finished washing him he was shrieking with laughter, whereupon she took him back to the fireside and got him changed into his pyjamas.

Having adopted the same tactic with his brother, she made them all some milky cocoa and peanut butter sandwiches, which they ate by the gas fire's glow. When she'd tucked them into their warmed beds, she was dead on her feet but still found the energy to read them a story, something she did every night.

As soon as they were settled, she went into the bitter kitchen to wash the supper things and lay the table for breakfast, then she braved the bathroom for a quick wash and set the alarm clock for six thirty. Although it was still only nine thirty, she went to bed to save the cost of having the gas fire on. Curling into the foetus position and hugging the hot-water bottle in the bed she had once shared with Jeff, she pulled the covers up over her ears. It seemed so long ago since Jeff's warm body had been here beside her.

Although she was desperately tired, sleep evaded her. Her mind was racing with thoughts of her uncle's sudden death. She thought of her mother, and how devastated she was by it, despite her attempts to put on a brave face.

Empathy for her mother was almost stronger than Rachel's own grief for her uncle, because she adored her mum. Dad was great too, but she didn't share the same closeness with him, probably because like so many other men of his generation, he'd taken a less personal role than his wife in the upbringing of his daughters.

Dad had been more of a background security figure, the breadwinner and, allegedly, the head of the household, though Mum had usually made the decisions. As Rachel and Jan had grown into adults, they had been drawn to their mother by the mutual interests of their gender. Their father being outnumbered by women in the household had been a family joke for many years, until his daughters had balanced things up by getting married.

Rachel and Jan had had a childhood rich in love and laughter, mostly due to their mother's warm heart and sense of fun. Rachel remembered the games Mum had played with them, the outings she'd arranged, the avid interest she'd taken in everything they did.

They'd never had much money because their father was only a factory worker. But they'd never felt deprived. Why would they when they knew nothing else? No one in their street had been any better off in those austere days of the forties and early fifties. The high standard of living that many ordinary people enjoyed today had been unheard of then. It was a different world now in more ways than one, with the pill, pop culture and a more liberated attitude towards class and sex.

Her mother was Rachel's role model. If she herself was half as good a mother as Mum had been to her, she'd count herself a success. She thanked God she had inherited her mother's indomitable spirit which made her determined that her boys would have happy childhood memories to take into adulthood, despite their father's departure.

As a single parent, making ends meet was a constant struggle, but she considered herself privileged to have two sons. A sudden death in the family certainly put things into perspective. Finding the money for the gas bill and the children's shoes was trivial in comparison. She was thinking about this when exhaustion finally took over and she fell asleep.

Chapter Two

The home of Marge and Ron Parry, a small house in Wilbur Terrace, Hammersmith, was crowded with mourners after the funeral of Chip Banks. People were packed into the living room, standing in the hall, sitting on the stairs. There had been a large crowd at the cemetery too.

'Good grief, this is like feeding the five thousand,' Rachel remarked smilingly to her mother and sister as they worked companionably together at the kitchen table, making yet another batch of sandwiches. 'They might be mourning, but by God can they eat!'

'Cold weather sharpens the appetite,' commented her mother.

'It's certainly put a voracious edge on theirs,' grinned Rachel. 'Not that I'm complaining. I think it's lovely that so many people came to pay their last respects to Uncle Chip.'

'The turnout says more than we ever could about his popularity,' commented Marge. 'Though I must admit, I didn't expect quite such a crowd at the cemetery. It's lucky I got extra food in just in case.'

'And it's a good job they didn't all accept the invitation to come back here or we'd be entertaining them in the street,' said Rachel good-humouredly. The black sweater and short dark skirt she was wearing suited her – emphasising the light tones in her hair and making the colour of her eyes stand out.

'Isn't it just typical of Arthur to get someone else to host his father's funeral instead of doing it himself?' Jan was fiercely disapproving. 'You'd think he could have done this one last thing for his dad since he did bugger all for him when he was alive.'

'To be fair to Arthur, he did know I wanted to do it,' pointed out Marge. She was an older version of Jan, with the same blue eyes and auburn hair, though heavily peppered with grey. Like her elder daughter, fifty-year-old Marge was the homely type, though now that her children had left home she mixed housewifery with a part-time job in a newsagent's shop. 'I was only too pleased of the chance to give my brother a good send-off.'

'I know you were happy to do it, Mum,' persisted Jan. 'But Arthur took advantage of your good nature. All that man ever did for his father was break his heart. It really wouldn't have hurt him to see to his funeral.'

'Oh well, never mind,' said Marge dismissively. 'It's done now and it's just as well we did have it here seeing as so many people turned up. This house is small enough, but there's more room here than there is in Arthur's little flat.'

'Even so . . .' began Jan.

'He did pay for it all, dear,' interrupted her mother in an effort to defuse any rising resentment. Marge hated arguments and didn't want any to erupt here today.

'I should think so too,' put in Rachel.

'It's a wonder he didn't try to wriggle out of *that*,' was Jan's opinion, 'knowing how our cousin likes to hang on to his money. Still, I suppose he's feeling flush on account of what he's about to inherit.'

'That's quite enough of that sort of talk,' admonished Marge in a quiet but firm tone. 'Your uncle's funeral is no time for backbiting and talk of material gain.'

'Sorry, Mum,' apologised Jan. 'But Arthur really makes me mad.'

'You're not alone in that,' said Rachel supportively.

'There's some good in us all, so they say,' Marge reminded them.

'If there is, Arthur keeps his well hidden,' replied Jan.

'I admit that he isn't the most likeable of people, and it's true that he didn't give his father the respect he deserved,' agreed Marge, pouring boiling water from the kettle into two large teapots on the worktop. 'But he did have a very troubled childhood, you know, with his parents breaking up and his mother constantly turning the boy against his father.'

'Why did she do that?' It had never occurred to Rachel to delve into her uncle's past life before. 'What exactly did she have against Uncle Chip?'

'He wasn't stylish or ambitious enough for her,' explained Marge.

'He was ambitious enough to have his own business,' Rachel pointed out.

'Yeah, but it was hard going when he first started. They had to watch every penny and his wife didn't like that,' Marge told her daughters. 'She reckoned he'd never get rich working with his hands and was annoyed that he wouldn't consider the idea of doing anything else. She was always nagging him about it. She didn't understand how much a dedicated craftsman values his work.'

'Poor old Uncle Chip,' said Rachel.

'I expect there were faults on both sides – there usually are when a marriage breaks down. But they were never really suited,' Marge continued. 'She married a real spivvy type after she and Chip got divorced, so it isn't all that surprising that Arthur's turned out as he has.'

'I suppose not,' agreed Rachel.

'You can't blame everything on his childhood, though,' disagreed Jan mildly. 'I still think he could have made more of an effort with his father.'

'I agree with you, as it happens,' said Marge in her quietly determined manner. 'But today isn't the time for bad feeling between relatives. So I'd appreciate it if you could grin and bear your cousin's company for the next couple of hours. Just for my sake.'

'Don't worry, I won't cause a scene,' Jan assured her.

'Thank you, dear,' said Marge. 'I know I can rely on my girls not to let the side down.'

Noticing how strained her mother was looking, her pallid countenance emphasised by her black clothes, Rachel said, 'You won't be sorry to see the back of today, will you, Mum?'

'I certainly won't,' she said emphatically. 'But having my daughters around has helped. And I feel better now that the actual burial is over.' She paused in what she was doing, setting out cups and saucers on the worktop. 'Still very sad but better.' Tears filled her eyes and she heaved a sigh. 'It's a comfort to know that he was so well loved.'

Her daughters nodded.

Rachel's father entered the room in search of something more potent than tea for some of the guests. 'Let's hope a drop o' booze will cheer things up a bit,' said Ron Parry, a stockily built white-haired man with a square face and small, deep-set eyes which created a misleadingly tough look. 'It's all a bit heavy out there.'

'Funerals aren't supposed to be laugh-a-minute occasions,' his wife reminded him in a tone of affectionate admonition. 'A solemn atmosphere is normal.'

'It's the last thing Chip would have wanted, though,' he said, pouring whisky into some glasses.

'True enough,' his wife agreed.

His little brown eyes rested on her. 'Are you all right, love?' he enquired.

'Yeah, course I am,' Marge assured him.

'That's my girl,' he said, winking at her.

'We've nearly finished here,' she said, biting back the tears his caring attitude made her want to shed. 'As soon as we're done, we'll come and help you entertain the guests.'

'Arthur's doing that at the moment,' Ron said. 'He's playing the bereaved son to the nth degree.'

'Not you as well,' Marge tutted. 'I've told the girls not to be unkind about Arthur, and that goes for you too, Ron. The lad's probably feeling genuinely distressed. Just because he wasn't much of a son to Chip doesn't mean he isn't affected by his death.'

'OK, love.' Ron didn't believe his nephew had a sincere bone in his body but he wasn't prepared to upset his wife by saying so. Not today, when she already had more than enough to cope with. He turned to his daughters and changed the subject. 'Pete is looking after all the children, then?'

Jan nodded. 'He offered to take some time off to be baby-sitter,' she said. 'He'll do some calls later on to make up the time.'

'Are you going in to work later on, Rachel?' enquired her father conversationally.

'No.' She really ought to, because she was paid by the hour and got nothing when she wasn't there. But her mother needed her today. She would try and get some overtime to make up her money. 'I thought I'd make a day of it.'

'Me too,' he said.

Rachel arranged a pile of sandwiches on a plate and heaved a sigh of relief. 'Right. Let's see how long these last, shall we?' she said, picking up the plate and heading for the door.

'I understand that you were with my father when he died,' said Arthur Banks, a chunkily built man with the same dark colouring as his father but without Chip's warmth in his eyes.

'Yes, that's right.' Ben Smart and Arthur were standing by the window in the crowded living room. Both were sombrely dressed in dark suits. Arthur was smoking a cigar and drinking whisky, while Ben, his face pale and shadowed from the strain of the last few days, had a glass of beer in his hand.

'It must have been a hell of a shock for you,' said Arthur, taking a swig of whisky.

'Not half.' There weren't any words to describe how Ben had felt on that terrible afternoon, seeing Chip slumped in the seat of the car when they'd arrived at the hospital. He'd never forget the awful helplessness of not being able to revive him.

'Thanks for doing what you could to help him, anyway,' said Arthur.

'I'm just sorry it wasn't enough,' replied Ben.

'You did your best, mate,' Arthur told him with the studied congeniality he'd affected throughout the funeral proceedings. 'None of us can do more than that.'

Ben nodded. He wasn't feeling particularly sociable and was planning to leave as soon as it was politely possible. He had work to do at the boathouse, which he was managing on the instructions of Chip's solicitor, who had power of attorney until the will was read and the firm legally made over to Chip's son and heir. Ben didn't intend to stay on at Banks' Boats in the long term. He had no wish to work for someone who had no knowledge of or interest in boatbuilding.

Not that Arthur would run the place himself, of course. Ben guessed that he'd put a manager in and sit back and enjoy the profits. He'd still be the boss, though, the one making the decisions, and Ben didn't fancy that at all. But he'd stay on to keep things ticking over until Arthur officially became the owner, because he knew that was what Chip would have wanted.

'You've been working for Dad a long time, haven't you?' remarked Arthur, finishing his drink and looking around as though hoping someone would offer him another.

'That's right.'

'How are things going at the boathouse at the moment?' asked Arthur, who hadn't been near the place since his father's death, much to Ben's surprise. He'd expected him to have made his presence felt to the staff by now.

'Not too bad. We're managing to keep going despite the financial problems,' Ben replied.

'Financial problems?'

So he obviously didn't know. 'That's right. A bad debt

caused your dad some bother with the bank,' he explained. 'He was worried sick about it, actually. I reckon that contributed towards the heart attack, that and the shock of the fall.'

'He always did worry too much about the business,' commented Arthur, seeming surprisingly unconcerned about the firm's money problems.

'I'm doing what I can to keep things going until you take over,' mentioned Ben. 'I'm booking in as much work as I can to keep the place buzzing.'

'Oh.' Arthur didn't sound impressed.

'If the firm is to survive we need to keep busy,' Ben was keen to point out. 'A full workshop is the only thing that's going to get Banks' Boats out of trouble.'

Arthur mulled this over for a moment. 'A word to the wise, mate,' he said, lowering his voice and leaning his head closer to Ben's. 'Don't book work in too far ahead.'

'Why not?'

'Isn't it obvious?'

'Not to me.' Ben was puzzled.

'Surely you don't seriously think that I'd hang on to a boatbuilding firm,' Arthur said in a pitying tone, his caring attitude forgotten, 'when I don't know one end of a boat from the other.'

'I just assumed you'd put a manager in to run it for you,' said Ben.

'Not likely,' Arthur declared. 'I've no intention of getting saddled with a load of worry.'

'You're planning to sell, then,' assumed Ben.

'Too right I am.'

'I see.' Ben's heart lurched because he knew Chip would have wanted the business to stay in his family.

'There's no need to look so miserable about it,' said Arthur lightly. 'I'm sure you won't have any trouble getting another job.'

It seemed odd to Ben that Arthur hadn't suggested the

possibility of his staying on for the new owners; also that he didn't want work booked in. The busier the job book, the better price he'd get for the business as a going concern. 'No, that won't be a problem.' He sipped at his beer, giving Arthur a shrewd look. 'I'm puzzled as to why you don't want work booked in, though, since a healthy work flow will get you a better price for the place.'

'Don't need it, mate,' Arthur informed him brightly. 'I've already got a buyer and the deal is agreed in principle.'

'The new owner will need work, though,' insisted Ben. 'A full work book is invaluable to any boathouse owner.'

'Not to my buyer.' Arthur paused, looking very pleased with himself. 'Oh, well, you've got to know sometime, so now's as good a time as any to tell you.'

'Tell me what?'

'The new owner is gonna clear the site, knock the boathouse down.'

'What!' Ben couldn't believe it.

'He's planning to open a nightclub there,' Arthur explained cheerfully. 'Riverside clubs and discos are all the rage these days – the swinging sixties as they're calling 'em. The boathouse site is valuable. So I'll be able to pay off Dad's debts and still be well in pocket.'

'Your dad will turn in his grave,' exclaimed Ben, horrified at this news.

'Rubbish,' scoffed Arthur. 'Dad's dead. Nothing can touch him now.'

'Even so . . .' began Ben.

'I don't know why you're getting so het up about it,' snapped Arthur. 'You've just admitted that you won't have any trouble getting another job.'

'I'm not bothered for myself,' Ben was keen to point out. 'But your father put everything into the boathouse, and he didn't do that just to have it knocked down.'

'Your concern for my father's interests is all very touching,' said Arthur scornfully, 'but Dad's gone and his business has had its day. I have to look to the future.'

'Your father isn't even cold in his grave and you've already sold his business,' said Ben.

'What's wrong with that?' demanded Arthur. 'There's no point in hanging about. You can get as sentimental as you like but you can't alter the fact that Dad won't be coming back.'

'You're a heartless bugger,' said Ben.

'There's nothing wrong with being quick off the mark,' insisted Arthur, puffing at his cigar. 'I know a lot of people. I've got a lot of contacts. A few phone calls was all it took to find a buyer once I knew Dad was gone.'

'You could at least have waited until after you'd buried him,' said Ben.

'I don't see why,' objected Arthur.

'No . . . I don't suppose you would,' said Ben coldly.

'There's no need to take that tone with me,' hissed Arthur. 'What I do with *my* boathouse, and when I choose to do it, is none of your business.'

'I'm fully aware of that.'

'I'm glad to hear it.' Arthur was miffed. 'Anyway, I've no intention of making my plans public here today. I just thought you ought to know what's gonna be happening, so that you can make other arrangements.'

'I shall certainly do that,' said Ben, moving away from him in disgust.

'Excuse me, Mrs Parry,' said Ben, waylaying Marge on her way to the kitchen.

'Yes, Ben?' she said, turning to him.

'I have to leave now,' he explained, 'and I just wanted to thank you for your hospitality.'

'Aah, do you have to go so soon?' She looked genuinely disappointed.

'I'm afraid so.' He put his head to one side, spreading his hands to indicate that the decision was beyond his control.

'I've things to do at the boathouse.'

'It can't be helped then, and I'm glad to hear that you're carrying on the good work,' she approved. 'That business was everything to my brother.'

'Yes . . . yes, it was.'

'I hope Arthur will be as diligent as you are when he takes over,' she remarked.

Ben guessed that she would be as devastated as he was about Arthur's plans. But it wasn't his place to pass the information on, especially not at such an emotional occasion as this. So he just said, 'Yes, I hope so too.'

'Thanks ever so much for coming, dear,' she said warmly. 'It's very much appreciated. I know how highly my brother thought of you. He talked about you a lot.'

'We were good mates,' he said. 'I don't quite know what I'll do without him.'

'Me neither.'

Tension drew tight in the atmosphere. Ben didn't know what to say to comfort her. 'But he'll always be here and here,' he blurted out, pointing to his head and his heart, then giving her a brief, embarrassed hug. 'Someone like Chip will never be forgotten.'

The words brought tears to Marge's eyes. 'I know, Ben, I know,' she said thickly.

'I'd better be going then.'

'Thanks again for coming.' Marge turned as her younger daughter appeared at her side. 'Ben has to go now, Rachel. Be a dear and see him out.'

'Sure,' she said.

'You're going back to the boathouse then?' said Rachel at the front door as Ben buttoned his dark overcoat. She'd had a passing acquaintance with him for years through calling at the boathouse to see her uncle. It was something she'd done as a child with her parents and more recently with Tim and Johnnie when she took them out walking by the riverside.

Ben seemed to have been there for ever and had been almost as much a part of the place as her uncle.

'Yeah, I've got a lot to do so I must get on,' he explained.

'I ought to go to work too,' she confided, 'but Mum would be hurt if I did, even though she wouldn't say so because she knows I need the money.'

He gave her an understanding nod. 'On a sad day like this it isn't easy to be practical,' he said. 'But life does have to go on.'

'Yes.' She made a brave attempt at a smile, her huge eyes swimming with tears. 'A walk by the river won't ever be the same again now that Uncle Chip has gone.'

'I'm sure it won't be,' he agreed politely.

'The boys will miss calling in at the boathouse to see him, too,' she told him.

'Are they fit and thriving?' he asked.

Her mood lifted visibly at the mention of them. 'Yeah, they're fine,' she told him. 'Full of life and mischief. What one doesn't think of, the other does, so they keep me on my toes! But they're great fun. I expect they're running rings around my brother-in-law as we speak. He's baby-sitting.'

'He's probably having a whale of a time,' said Ben, who liked children but didn't have any of his own. 'They're smashing kids. I used to enjoy seeing them when you brought them in to the boathouse to see Chip.'

'Maybe I'll bring them in to see you if we're out walking around that way,' she mentioned casually.

She was surprised at the look of alarm in those amazing blue eyes. 'I won't . . .' he began, his words faltering.

'Don't look so terrified,' she cut in with a grin. 'I know they're a bit exuberant, but they're not that bad, surely?'

'I didn't mean to suggest that they were bad,' he corrected hastily. He was on the point of telling her that the imminent disappearance of Banks' Boats was the reason for his guarded response to her suggestion, but managed to restrain himself. 'Take no notice of me. I'm not with it today.'

'I don't think any of us are.' She touched his arm lightly, giving him a half-smile. 'I knew you didn't mean that. I was just teasing you.'

'Oh, right.' He managed a watery smile. 'Well, I'd better be going,' he said, opening the door to a blast of cold air.

'Thanks for coming, Ben,' she said warmly. 'All the family appreciate it.'

'If I was to say that it's been a pleasure, I'd be lying,' he told her with a wry grin. 'But it was nice to see you again, anyway.'

'You too.'

'See you then,' he said, stepping through the doorway.

'Yeah. 'Bye for now.'

He turned to go, then swung back quickly. 'It *would* be nice to see Tim and Johnnie again sometime,' he said impulsively.

'Perhaps when the weather gets better we'll call in at the boathouse,' she responded. 'Though I'm not sure if the new owner will approve of visitors.'

'New owner?' For a moment he misunderstood her, thought she was referring to Arthur's buyer, then realised almost at once that she wouldn't be talking about visiting the boathouse if that was the case.

'My cousin Arthur,' she reminded him. 'He doesn't have such a friendly nature as Uncle Chip, but I'll chance it anyway.'

Because he wasn't at liberty to tell her the truth, he blurted out, 'I'll look forward to it then,' and hurried out to his Ford Consul, parked in the narrow street of old-fashioned terraced houses.

Because he'd changed into his suit at work that morning, he didn't have to go home to get into his working clothes, so now he headed straight for the boathouse. Driving through narrow streets flanked by tightly packed houses and flats, he wondered why he'd made that comment to Rachel about wanting to see her little boys again when he knew there would be no boathouse for them to visit. Perhaps he was trying to stay in touch with a member of Chip's family so that all ties with the man and the boathouse wouldn't be severed with his passing. Whatever the reason, it had been a stupid and deceitful thing to do. Slowing down in the heavy traffic around Hammersmith Broadway, he realised that it bothered him to have misled her.

He'd known Rachel vaguely since he was an apprentice and she a schoolgirl. He'd seen her change from a skinny kid into a lovely young woman, vivacious and full of fun but with a warmth and generosity about her too. He'd watched only from a distance and from the detached perspective of someone deeply immersed in their own affairs, but he'd always liked what he'd seen of his employer's niece.

Memories of the boathouse during Chip's reign brought a now familiar lump to his throat. He just couldn't handle it. Coming to a standstill in the traffic, he sniffed, blew his nose and pulled himself together. The loss of Chip was far greater than that of his own father, because Chip had been much more of a father to him.

Remembering the grief in Rachel's lovely eyes, he felt stirred by it and knew that they were of one mind. Her slight build gave her a look of fragility but there was a strength about her too. He knew from what Chip had said that she hadn't had it easy, but she struck Ben as the type who wouldn't be defeated without a fight.

Ben knew all about the pain of a failed marriage. He and his wife Lorna had separated two years ago, after a long period of sniping and indifference towards each other. It had hurt him deeply at the time, but he later realised that his pain was mostly derived from hurt pride and the loss of the illusion that first love would last for ever.

He and Lorna had started going steady as teenagers. Marriage had been the only recognised successor to courtship back in the fifties, so they'd done it almost automatically when he'd turned twenty-one. But the shared interests and enthusiasms of youth had faded as they'd matured. As time passed they seemed to have nothing left in common, and had become irritated with each other.

Lorna had claimed that their problems had been exacerbated by the fact that he held back from her, didn't communicate as he should. Although he'd defended himself with the argument that men tended not to talk about their feelings in the same way as women did, he accepted the fact that he was at fault. It wasn't a deliberate thing. He simply didn't find it easy to express his feelings. He bottled things up instead of talking about them, a legacy of his tough childhood, perhaps.

Some good had come from the break-up, though. After all the acrimony was over, they had managed to become friends. That meant a lot to Ben, because he and Lorna went back a long way and he was fond of her. From what Chip had said about Rachel's broken marriage, Ben doubted if she was on such friendly terms with her husband.

He was still thinking about Rachel as he drove down a side street to the riverside and turned into the boathouse yard. The weather was still cold but the violent winds of last week had moderated to a fresh breeze. Pale sunshine filtered through the clouds, lightening the bleak landscape and shimmering on the gently undulating waters.

Getting out of his car, he stood where he was for a moment, listening to the everyday sounds from inside: the tap of a hammer and the whine of an electric saw; the sound of a radio playing in the background; and a couple of the men singing along loudly and tunelessly to Sonny and Cher's *I Got You Babe*. Most of the staff had been at the cemetery this morning but had gone straight back to work, after the burial.

His gaze lifted almost involuntarily to the sign on the front of the building, where *Banks' Boats* was written in large black letters on a white board. It was hard to imagine it not being there any more. It would be strange and very, very sad. With a heavy heart, he walked slowly across the yard and into the building.

Rachel was thinking about Ben as she washed some crockery at the sink in her parents' kitchen. She was guessing that her uncle's death had been as much a blow to Ben as it had been to the family. He was a smashing bloke, strong and good-looking in an outdoor sort of way, with the most gorgeous blue eyes she'd ever seen. She hadn't noticed with such clarity before how deep and rich his voice was, or the athletic way he moved with long, easy strides.

His wife must have found him lacking, though. Rachel remembered her uncle mentioning something about his marriage breaking up. That was a couple of years ago, though, so he'd probably found someone else by now.

His reaction when she'd mentioned taking the boys to see him at the boathouse had been a bit odd. What had that been all about? she wondered. It hadn't been fear she'd perceived in his expression exactly, more a look of anxiety and regret. Of course, that was it. He wouldn't be at the boathouse because he wasn't planning on staying on when Arthur took over, and he hadn't wanted to admit it to her because he'd thought she might see it as a desertion.

The boathouse wouldn't be the same without Ben, she thought wistfully, as she stacked the cups and plates on the draining board.

'So what are you doing these days, Arthur?' Rachel enquired of her cousin a while later. People were beginning to depart and he was in the kitchen, helping himself from the whisky bottle.

'Oh, this and that, you know,' he told her, spreading his hands expressively.

'No, I don't know actually, Arthur,' she said. 'That's why I'm asking you.'

Two years younger than Rachel, he was handsome in a

greasy, flashy sort of way, she thought. His dark wavy hair was fashionably cut with sideburns; his fingers were adorned with rings. Although it was generally known that Arthur was a chancer, he never made clear how he actually earned his living. Rachel knew he'd dabbled in second-hand cars at one time, and someone had once seen him selling watches from a suitcase in Oxford Street.

But while he boasted about his brain being more profitable than his hands, he never expanded on the subject. Probably because he handled dodgy gear or didn't keep proper accounts for the Inland Revenue, Rachel guessed. She'd never been on close cousinly terms with him and saw him only on rare occasions, but he'd always struck her as being a bit of a loser, despite his substantial ego.

'I'm into amusement machines at the moment,' he informed her now.

'Fruit machines, you mean?'

He nodded. 'And pinball machines and juke boxes, all that sort of thing.'

'Selling them?'

'No. Hiring them out.'

'To pubs?' she assumed.

'And clubs and cafés,' he explained. 'Anywhere where people go to relax.'

'How does that system actually work?' she enquired conversationally.

'Initially I persuade the owner or manager of a pub or club to have a machine on their premises, then I go round emptying the money every few weeks,' he explained. 'It puts their takings up by bringing more punters in, and they also get a percentage of what I collect, so everyone's happy.'

'Will you continue with that when you take over at the boathouse?' she asked.

'I haven't decided yet,' he lied. He wasn't ready to divulge his plans to his relatives and, annoyingly, his father's people had the power to make him feel uncomfortable about the way he lived. Although he was careful not to show it, his self-esteem plummeted when they were around. Tediously respectable, they weren't the sort to be impressed by his high ambitions and the fact that he had a good head for business which would one day make him rich while their lives remained drab and insignificant. He'd always felt like an outsider among his paternal relations and couldn't stand the sight of any of them.

'Never put on a pair of overalls, son,' his mother used to drum into him when he was a boy. 'Nobody ever got anywhere working with their hands. Your brain is what'll get you on in life. You've gotta learn to use your loaf or you'll end up like your father, slaving all hours for a pitiful return.'

Arthur had grown up believing his father to be a failure, and had never tried to hide his contempt for him. He'd never got on with Chip; even when Arthur was a lad, they hadn't hit it off. More recently, Arthur had been tempted to cut all ties, but had deemed it wise to suffer the odd visit just to remind the old man of the existence of his son and heir.

Dad had always been boringly faithful to the straight and narrow when it was a recognised fact that that was the road to nowhere. Arthur himself would be forced to live a lot more frugally if he didn't slip some of the money he collected from the machines into his own pocket. Despite giving Rachel the impression that he owned the gaming machines, he actually only worked as a collector for the man who did.

Still, all that was about to come to an end. When he sold the boathouse site, he'd have enough money to get into buying and selling in a big way. With his wife Ella beside him, he couldn't go wrong. Cast in the same mould as his mother, his darling Ella believed in him and knew he had it in him to succeed. She wasn't the sort of woman to be fazed by dishonesty.

In fact, she was likely to encourage it if it meant his getting hold of some decent money and rescuing her from the shoe-shop where she worked as an assistant. She was worth more than a job pushing people's sweaty feet into shoes all day. She wanted a healthy portion of the good life and trusted him to get it for her. It was Ella's hunger for better things that had first attracted him to her – that and her sexiness, of course. She was the light of his life and the mere thought of her cheered him and gave him confidence.

'I suppose you'll put a manager in to run the boathouse for you, won't you?' Rachel was suggesting now.

'We'll see.'

There was a silence. 'Your wife couldn't make it to the funeral, then?' she remarked to keep the conversation flowing.

'No. She couldn't get the time off from work,' he explained. 'She hardly knew Dad anyway.'

'There is that,' Rachel agreed.

'You still on your own?' he asked, having heard from his father what had happened to Rachel's marriage.

She nodded.

'Shame,' he said sympathetically, though his compassion was entirely false. He was positively jubilant, in fact. His cousin's failed marriage made him feel superior because his was rock solid. Rubbing Rachel's nose in it was immensely satisfying. 'It must have been a real blow for you, your old man walking out like that. I dunno what I'd do if Ella did that to me.'

'It was awful at the time,' she was forced to admit. 'But I've got used to it now. Me and the boys are getting along just fine.'

'Onwards and upwards, eh?' he said, sipping his drink.

'Well, onwards anyway,' she said with a wry grin, and her infuriating lack of conceit deflated his own efforts to go one better.

Marge bustled on to the scene, requesting that Rachel go and say goodbye to some departing relatives.

'See you then, Arthur,' his cousin said, relieved to get away, and went to do as her mother asked.

* * *

The solution to Rachel's problem regarding the children's new footwear came a week or so later when she was offered the chance of some overtime at the factory. Her mother was willing to look after the boys while she did the extra hours, but Jan said there was no point in unsettling them by moving them from place to place, and they could stay with her until Rachel got home.

Immersed in the punishing routine of late evenings and working through her dinner break, Rachel was even more exhausted than usual. But it was such a relief to be earning extra money, she wasn't about to complain.

About the last thing she needed at this hectic time was a letter from a solicitor's office, asking her to contact them as soon as possible. She assumed that Jeff wanted to start divorce proceedings.

'This is something I can really do without,' she told Jan on the morning she got the letter. She had just dropped the boys off and was about to leave for work.

'I can understand that,' sympathised Jan. 'Still, at least you'll find out where Jeff is now, and once you know that, you can get some maintenance money out of him.'

'Mm, there is that.' Rachel heaved a sigh. 'Who would have thought it would come to this between Jeff and me, communication through a solicitor and my hoping to get money out of him?'

'He is the boys' father and he ought to be supporting them,' Jan reminded her.

'I know, but . . .' Rachel looked wistful, and her words tailed off.

'I think I know what you mean,' Jan cut in. 'It's sad to think that something that started off so happily and romantically can come to such a horrible end.'

'Exactly,' said Rachel. 'When you've loved someone and shared your life with them, you don't expect them to be so callous towards you.' She paused. 'It hurts, you know, Jan, that Jeff's chosen to do it this way. You'd think he would have taken the trouble to contact me personally to let me know of his intentions before putting it in the hands of a solicitor.'

'Nothing that man does would surprise me,' said Jan. 'Not after him walking out on you like that.'

'I didn't think he'd do anything as mean as that either,' Rachel confessed.

'Anyway, now that he's going to make it official, he'll have to pay you something to help support the boys,' Jan pointed out. 'It's the law.'

'He'll get out of it if he possibly can, I expect,' remarked Rachel glumly.

'You'll just have to make sure he doesn't, won't you?' lectured her sister. 'So . . . when are you going to see the solicitor?'

'A good question,' replied Rachel. 'They're closed by the time I finish work.'

'Why not give them a ring in your dinner break to get something arranged?' suggested Jan. 'You'll probably feel better once things get started.'

'I'm working right through my dinner hour at the moment,' explained Rachel worriedly.

'I should make sure you find the time to pay attention to this if I were you, kid,' Jan advised her. 'The sooner you find out where that bugger is, the sooner you'll get some money out of him. Then perhaps you won't have to work every hour God sends to pay for the children's clothes.'

'I can't afford to take any more time off work,' Rachel pointed out. 'Not after taking a day off for the funeral.'

'Then you'll just have to persuade the solicitor to see you after normal office hours,' Jan suggested. 'If you explain your difficult circumstances, they might be willing to co-operate.'

'You're right, I ought to deal with it right away,' agreed Rachel, opening the front door and stepping out into the cold January morning. 'I'll nip out to the phone box this dinner time.'

'It's the best thing.'

'Must dash or I'll miss my bus,' said Rachel. 'I'll see you tonight.'

And she hurried down the street to the bus stop, breaking into a run when she saw the bus coming.

Because Rachel was annoyed about having to spend precious time in a solicitor's office after a long day at the factory instead of going straight to Jan's to collect the boys, she wasn't feeling particularly gracious towards the tall, thin man in the dark pinstriped suit who was waiting for her when she got there.

'It's good of you to see me so late,' she said politely as he ushered her into his office and offered her a seat. 'I can't afford to take time off during the day, not with two children to support on my own.'

'I quite understand,' said Mr Brayford, a softly spoken man of about fifty with spectacles and greying hair.

'I hope my husband can afford to have you work overtime on his behalf,' she remarked.

He peered at her over the top of his glasses, his mild brown eyes registering a look of surprise. 'Your husband?' he queried.

'Well, yes,' she said wearily. 'I presume he's the reason that I'm here.'

The man frowned, tapping the end of his fountain pen on the desk and studying the papers in front of him. 'You are Rachel West, formerly Rachel Parry?' he said, looking up.

She nodded.

'According to our information, you are the niece of the late Christopher Banks, not his widow,' he informed her.

'*Christopher* Banks?' she echoed blankly.

'More usually known as Chip.'

'Oh, Uncle Chip,' she said, her tone softening. 'Yes, that's right. He was my uncle. Why, what's he got to do with it?'

'Everything, as a matter of fact.' Mr Brayford's manner was pleasant but formal. 'He's named you as a beneficiary in his will.'

She was touched. How sweet of Uncle Chip to leave her

some little knick-knack to remember him by. 'So I'm here because of my late uncle and not because my husband wants to start divorce proceedings?'

'That's right,' the solicitor confirmed.

'I'm *so* sorry,' she said with an embarrassed grin. 'I just assumed . . . I mean, I couldn't think of any reason a solicitor would want to see me other than because of my marital problems.'

'It's perfectly all right,' he said patiently.

'So, what little thing has Uncle Chip left me?' she asked, her cheeks flushed with pleasure at being remembered in this way by her uncle. 'Is it that little old clock he had on his mantelpiece? It was always a favourite of mine.'

'No, it isn't a clock,' he told her.

'Oh, well, it doesn't matter what it is so long as it reminds me of him,' she enthused. 'I'm very honoured that he thought of me at all in this way.'

Mr Brayford gave her a studious look. 'It's something rather more substantial than a knick-knack,' he told her solemnly.

'Really?' Her tone was puzzled, eyes bright with interest.

He nodded. 'Your uncle has left you his business,' he informed her.

She was too stunned to speak. 'The boathouse,' she muttered at last.

'That's right.' The solicitor lowered his gaze and began to read from a paper in front of him on the desk. 'Banks' Boats Limited in its entirety, the boathouse and everything in it, all equipment and goodwill is to go to my niece, Rachel West, née Parry.'

'There must be some mistake.' It was such a huge bequest, she couldn't believe it. 'The boathouse is surely to go to my cousin Arthur. Uncle Chip's son.'

'Not according to Mr Banks' last will and testament,' Mr Brayford explained in a serious tone.

'But it's Arthur's by law, isn't it?' she murmured, anxiously combing her fringe with her fingers.

'If there was no will, it would go to the next of kin,' Mr Brayford informed her. 'But since Mr Banks did leave a will, a proper legal document made with this firm and witnessed by myself, clearly stating that he wants his business to go to you, this is what will happen.'

'But I can't understand why he would leave it to me,' she queried, brushing her hair from her face in a distracted manner.

'Affection is the most common reason for people to make bequests, other than those to their immediate family,' he told her. 'Your uncle must have been fond of you.'

'Yes, I suppose he must have been to do something like this,' she agreed, thrilled, despite all the complications, that Chip had chosen her. 'Me, the owner of a business! Wow!'

'I can understand your being pleased, it's very nice to be remembered in such a way.' Mr Brayford's expression became frighteningly grim. 'But I feel that I must point out to you that . . . Well, your uncle made this will when his business was doing well.'

She looked up sharply. 'You mean it isn't doing well now?'

He leaned back slightly, looking at her thoughtfully. 'Your uncle had a cash-flow problem recently because of the bankruptcy of one of his regular customers.' He paused, making a pyramid of his long thin fingers and resting his chin on it. 'I'm sure your uncle wouldn't mind my telling you that he was a good man and a brilliant boatmaker but rather too soft-hearted for business.'

'People took advantage of his good nature, did they?'

'Exactly,' the solicitor said. 'And this time the loss was substantial. He met me for a drink and a chat about it a couple of days before he died, as a friend. This firm has acted for him for many years, so I got to know him personally.'

Rachel listened as Mr Brayford continued.

'Your uncle was a relatively young man,' he went on. 'His death was most untimely. He would have expected the business to be flourishing by the time you took over. He wouldn't have wanted to leave you with trouble.'

'Trouble?' She already had quite enough of that.

'Yes, I'm afraid so,' he confessed. 'But there is a solution to the problem.'

'Thank God for that.'

'It's something that your uncle wasn't prepared to consider, but I think you must.'

She didn't much like the sound of that. 'What is it?' she asked nervously.

'If you were to sell the business,' he began slowly, 'you'd be able to pay off the firm's overdraft and still have a little money left for yourself.'

'Sell it! But it wouldn't be right for me to do that, would it?' she pointed out. 'If Uncle Chip wouldn't even consider it, he didn't want it done.'

Mr Brayford inspected his manicured fingernails for a moment. 'Your uncle was a romantic, Mrs West,' he explained. 'He thought that to produce excellent work was enough to keep him in business.'

'Isn't it?'

'Good Lord, no,' was his answer to that.

'Then it should be,' suggested Rachel, who had no experience of business and was, therefore, naïve. 'Or a major factor, at least.'

'I agree with you. Unfortunately financial institutions see things in terms of balance sheets.' He paused again as though choosing his words carefully. 'You might find you have no choice in the matter of whether or not to sell the business. The bank are letting things go on as they are only as a temporary measure, with Mr Smart running the boathouse and us overseeing things. But once the business becomes yours formally, they'll probably insist that you sell so that they can get their money back.'

Her thoughts were racing but her heart was like lead. It was so disappointing to find that she'd inherited her uncle's business only to lose it. 'I see,' she said dully.

'As I've said, you wouldn't come out of the sale empty-handed,' he reminded her. 'There should be some cash left when everything is paid off. And even if you were to sell to someone who just wants the site, you shouldn't have any trouble getting rid of it. There's plenty of scope for development on that stretch of the river.'

'End its days as a boatbuilders, is that what you mean?' She was horrified.

'Well, yes, if it means a quick sale,' he confirmed.

Rachel knew nothing about business or bank overdrafts; she didn't even have a post office savings book, let alone a bank account. But she *did* know that her uncle wouldn't have wanted her to sell the boathouse.

'I'd really rather not sell the business if there is any other way around the problem,' she said.

Mr Brayford stroked his chin, frowning. 'But surely it would be the most sensible thing for you to do anyway,' he suggested. 'Even if you didn't have to.'

'What makes you say that?'

'Well . . .' He scratched his head. 'You wouldn't want to run that type of business, would you?'

'Because I'm a woman?' she suggested defensively.

'Because you're not a boatbuilder,' he corrected in an even tone.

'Oh yes, of course,' she said sheepishly.

'And as you've said,' he continued, 'you have two children to bring up on your own. Surely a little money in the bank would be more than welcome?'

'I can't argue with that,' she agreed.

'Anyway, it's my job only to advise. You must do as you see fit.' The solicitor looked at his watch to indicate that he wished to conclude the interview.

'So what happens now?' she wondered.

'In a few days the paperwork will be complete and the business will be yours,' he informed her.

'I still can't believe it,' she said, shaking her head wonderingly.

He glanced at the papers on his desk. 'One thing I would like to suggest is that you get an appointment with your uncle's bank as soon as possible.' He handed her a business card. 'That's the man you need to see.'

'I'll do that,' she told him. 'Thank you for seeing me so late.'

'A pleasure,' he said. 'I'll be in touch with you again when the paperwork is ready.'

She left his office and walked to Jan's in the cold night air. Her head was spinning but she was exhilarated too. Despite the problems she seemed to have inherited, and her lingering sadness at her uncle's death, she felt quite light-headed with excitement at this unexpected turn of events. It was immensely heart-warming to know that someone had cared enough about her to leave her their most prized possession.

One thing did seem certain. Whatever happened about her legacy, she should have enough money to get the boys the shoes they needed. And a few other things for them besides, she hoped.

Chapter Three

'Cor, stone me,' exclaimed Rachel's father after hearing the news later that same evening. 'What a kind thing for Chip to do. It's about time you had a bit o' luck.'

'I'm thrilled to bits and very honoured to have been entrusted with the boathouse,' she said. 'But one aspect of it worries me.'

'What's that?' her mother wanted to know.

'Well, it doesn't seem fair to the rest of you. I mean, why choose me?' she queried, spreading her hands expressively. 'If he wanted it to go to someone other than Arthur, why not one of you?'

'That's easily explained.' Marge didn't seem to be in any doubt. 'You're the one in most need of it, being on your own with the boys to bring up. Your uncle obviously had that in mind.'

'No doubt about it,' agreed Jan.

'I think so too,' added Pete.

'So take it in the spirit it was given and enjoy it without any qualms,' advised her mother.

'Yeah, you're right,' said Rachel, though she still seemed a little uncertain.

They were all gathered in Marge and Ron's living room. It was small and cosy, with a coal fire crackling in the hearth, well-worn furniture and a television set in the corner around which the children were clustered, watching *Bonanza*, and enjoying the fact that everyone seemed to have forgotten about bedtime.

When Rachel had got to Jan's place bursting with the news, the natural thing had been to pile into Pete's van and head for Wilbur Terrace to share it with Marge and Ron. No one in the family had ever inherited anything of any significance before, so it was a momentous occasion.

'We're all gutted that your uncle's gone, and he'll be sorely missed,' said Ron. 'But having his business coming into this family is a real compliment. It'll help keep his memory alive.'

Rachel made a face. 'It isn't that simple, I'm afraid, Dad.' She went on to explain that there were problems and the boathouse would probably have to be sold.

'That's awful,' cried Marge, looking shocked. 'Chip put his heart and soul into that business.'

'He certainly kept quiet about the fact that he was in trouble,' commented Ron.

'Didn't want to worry you, I suppose,' suggested Pete.

There was a general murmur of agreement.

'Thinking about it, though,' remarked Ron thoughtfully, 'it might not be such a bad thing for you, Rachel, if it does have to be sold, in as much as you don't have the knowledge or experience to run a boathouse. Money in the bank will be a lot more useful to you than a struggling business.'

'I don't think Uncle Chip left it to me with the idea that I'd sell it, though,' she said, frowning.

'No, I don't suppose he did, especially as the solicitor told you that he made this will when the business was doing well,' agreed her father. 'But it's in trouble now and you have to consider what's best for yourself and the boys.'

She couldn't deny that, so she just nodded.

'Anyway, you wouldn't want a big responsibility like that around your neck, would you?' Ron continued.

Articulating her instincts, she said, 'I'd quite enjoy the challenge, I think. Though obviously I don't have the faintest idea how to set about running a boatbuilding business. Or any other kind of business, come to that.'

'It's a nice idea to keep the boathouse in the family, and I'm sure it's what Uncle Chip wanted,' put in Jan. 'But I don't think it's wise for you to hang on to something that's going to cause you problems, Rachel. You want less of those, not more. Frankly, I think it would probably be best if the bank were to give you no choice about selling it. At least that way you can't worry about whether you've done the right thing.'

'There's something in what she says,' added Pete supportively.

'And the money you'll have left over will come in very handy,' Jan went on. 'It'll give you a bit of security – for as long as it lasts, anyway.'

'I can certainly do with that.' Although she knew that what they were saying made sense, Rachel still didn't feel able to commit herself to selling the boathouse. 'But I'll just have to see what the people at the bank have to say.'

'Whatever happens, it was a very nice thing for Uncle Chip to do.' There was not a hint of jealousy in Jan's tone. She wanted better things for her sister and she and Pete couldn't afford to help her financially. 'We're all dead chuffed for you.'

'Thanks.' Rachel bit her lip. 'I know one person who isn't going to be pleased, though.'

'Arthur,' they chorused.

'Exactly,' said Rachel, looking troubled. 'I thought the boathouse would automatically be his, but apparently not, according to Mr Brayford.' She paused in thought. 'Still, he'll get everything else of his father's, his house and stuff. Won't he?'

'Chip's house was rented,' mentioned Marge.

'Oh, really?' said Rachel.

'He couldn't afford to buy a place, the amount of money his wife stung him for after their marriage broke up,' Marge went on to explain. 'Even when she got married again he was still ridiculously generous in his support of Arthur, right up until he left school. Anyway, Chip was of a generation accustomed to renting, like me and Dad. It's different these days, with ordinary people getting mortgages and buying their own places.'

'So the business was all Uncle Chip had,' mused Rachel, feeling even more honoured by her bequest; she was also conscious of an increased sense of responsibility for its survival.

Marge nodded. 'Apart from his car, his furniture and a few other bits and pieces,' she said. 'None of it worth very much.'

'Oh dear,' said Rachel. 'Now I feel even worse. Perhaps I should hand the business over to Arthur, or give him a share in it or something.'

'After the way he treated his father, don't talk daft,' said Ron.

'No! Don't even think about it,' advised Jan.

'Chip obviously didn't want Arthur to have it or he wouldn't have gone to the trouble of changing his will in favour of you,' Marge pointed out wisely. 'And no one can blame him, the way that boy was with him.'

'Arthur won't see it that way, though, will he?' Rachel pointed out. 'He'll think he's been most unfairly treated.'

'I expect he will,' agreed Ron. 'But that isn't your problem. He's brought this on himself.'

'Course he has,' Jan endorsed heartily.

'Anyway, that's enough talk about Arthur,' said Ron with a lift to his voice. 'I know that this is basically a sad occasion, but what do you say to us having a drink to celebrate what Chip's done for Rachel? I think he'd approve.'

'No doubt about that,' enthused Marge. 'Chip always enjoyed a bit of a knees-up.'

'I'll pop down the off-licence and get a few bottles,' Ron told them, getting up and heading for the door.

'I'll come with you,' said Pete, rising and following him. 'We'll go in the van.'

Sensing a promising change in the atmosphere, the children

deserted the goings-on at the Ponderosa Ranch and joined the adults.

'Can you get us some lemonade, please, Grandad?' asked Tim excitedly.

'And some crisps,' Kelly chimed in.

'Cheese and onion, please,' said Johnnie eagerly.

'I think we might manage something nice for you little 'uns,' said Ron, smiling indulgently at his grandchildren.

Seeing her son's faces glowing with pleasurable anticipation, Rachel was reminded of how few treats they'd had since their daddy went away. They wouldn't be quite so rare in the future, thanks to Uncle Chip.

'Looks as though this is going to turn into a bit of a party,' said Rachel when the men had departed.

'Any excuse is good enough for me,' laughed Jan. 'We can do with a lift after all the gloom of the funeral.'

Rachel nodded thoughtfully. 'I think I'll go in to work late in the morning so that the boys can have a lie-in,' she said. 'Just in case you might wonder where I am.'

'You can afford to be a lady of leisure now,' joked Jan.

'Don't make me laugh,' grinned Rachel. 'I've inherited a failing boathouse, not the Dorchester.'

She would have to take some time off work, though, she thought. There were things she'd have to attend to, a visit to her uncle's bank being the main priority. Having never been inside a bank in her life, she was extremely apprehensive, especially as they were almost certainly going to force her to sell the boathouse. But a defiant part of her still couldn't accept this as inevitable.

Because it was so cold everywhere in Rachel's flat except in the immediate vicinity of the gas fire in the living room, that was where she and the boys had their breakfast the next morning. Having got up much later than usual, it was mid morning by the time they were ready to eat.

Wrapped in thick sweaters and trousers, they were all

tucking into porridge and toast when there was a loud, insistent knocking at the front door. 'All right, all right, I'm coming,' Rachel muttered as she hurried to answer it.

It was Arthur. In a state of simmering umbrage, he pushed past her and marched into the living room without uttering a word. As he was obviously on the warpath, she ushered him into the kitchen because she didn't want the children upset.

'I take it you've heard, then,' she said, folding her arms and slipping her hands inside the sleeves of her jumper. It was freezing out here.

'Oh, I've heard all right,' he grunted, his voice rough with fury. 'I've just come from Brayford's office.'

'Oh dear,' she said, biting her lip and bracing herself for the flak she knew would come.

'You may well say "Oh dear",' he exploded. 'A poxy car and some old furniture that's only fit for the rubbish tip, that's what my loving father left me.'

Naturally, she didn't feel good about this. She didn't say anything, just waited for him to get it all off his chest.

'I get that load o' junk while you cop the only thing he had that was worth anything,' he ranted. 'I couldn't believe it when the solicitor told me.'

'I knew you'd be upset,' she said.

'Upset!' he bellowed. 'I'm more than just upset, I'm bloody well steaming.'

'Keep your voice down and watch your language,' she warned. 'There are children in the other room.'

'I couldn't care less if there's a whole nursery of 'em in there,' he barked. 'I'm gonna have my say.'

'That's typical of you,' she retorted. 'You've never had any consideration for other people. Well, you can watch your language or leave. I won't have that sort of talk here.'

'Don't you dare judge me,' Arthur ordered, dark eyes blazing, face ugly with rage.

'I'm speaking as I find,' she told him.

'I couldn't care less what you think of me,' he bawled. 'I haven't come here to listen to your views.'

'You're here to have a go at me for something for which I'm not responsible,' she protested.

'I'm here to make sure you've started to get things under way,' he corrected.

'Under way?' Panic gripped her, though she struggled to hide it. Arthur was dangerous in this aggressive mood and there were two defenceless children in the other room. 'Have I missed something here? What, exactly, am I supposed to be getting under way?'

'The formalities to transfer ownership of the boathouse to me, of course,' he announced.

She should have anticipated it but she hadn't. 'Oh, so that's what you're expecting to happen, is it?' she said.

'Naturally,' he confirmed. 'As his son and next of kin, the boathouse is mine by rights.'

'But he left it to me,' Rachel pointed out.

'God knows what got into him,' he said. 'He must have been senile.'

'He was only forty-five,' she reminded him.

'Mm, well, it must have been some sort of premature thing,' he muttered. 'Some geezers do go funny before they reach old age.'

'Your father didn't,' she protested.

'How do you know?' he demanded. 'You didn't live in his pocket, did you?'

'No, but I did see him from time to time and my mother saw him quite often. There was nothing wrong with his brain.' Rachel shook her head. 'You won't get anywhere by suggesting that he wasn't in his right mind, because people who knew him know that isn't true.'

'Oh, come off it. He must have had a screw loose.' Arthur was standing near the cooker with his arms folded. He was wearing a beige-coloured sheepskin coat with a fur collar and he looked huge and very threatening. 'If he'd had all his marbles, why didn't he leave his business to his son, like any normal person would.'

'I don't know the answer to that,' Rachel confessed. 'I was as surprised as you are when I heard about it.'

'So you admit it isn't right?' He was trying to put words into her mouth.

'I said I was surprised.' She hugged herself against the cold, rubbing her hands up and down the arms of the red sweater she was wearing with black trousers and thick socks. 'I didn't say it wasn't right,' she corrected. 'It's all legal and above board and it's what he wanted, so it must be right. I admit to being puzzled myself at first, though.'

'And you're not puzzled now?'

'No, I'm not. Everyone seems to think he left it to me because I'm the only one of his relatives who is struggling,' she explained. 'And that makes sense, don't you think?'

'You're struggling!' he raged. 'What about me, scratching about to earn a living?'

'I meant with my being on my own with the boys to bring up,' she explained. 'Your father must have had that in mind when he made his decision.'

'But I'm his son,' Arthur persisted, his voice distorted with anger and frustration. 'It's me he should have looked after.'

'I suppose he must have been disappointed because you showed no interest in the boathouse,' Rachel suggested reasonably. 'You must admit that's true. You were always putting it down as far as I remember. How was he to know you wanted it?'

'I don't want the boathouse, you silly cow,' he growled. 'It's the site that interests me, or rather the dosh it will bring in when it's sold.'

'It might not have to be sold,' she answered instinctively. 'There might be some other way around the problems.'

'I'd get rid of it even if it didn't have problems,' he informed her briskly. 'In fact I already have a buyer lined up.' He went on to tell her about his plans.

'You jumped the gun, didn't you?' she said with blistering disapproval. 'Getting a deal under way before you even knew if the boathouse was yours to sell.'

'It was only a question of waiting for the formalities to go through.' His manner was complacent now. 'I knew the boathouse was mine and I'd rather have the cash in my pocket than a business that's riddled with problems.'

'You seem to have it all worked out,' she remarked coolly.

'Of course I have,' he confirmed. 'I'm not a fool.'

'It's rather unfortunate that you didn't inherit the business, then, isn't it?' she said.

His eyes seemed to protrude momentarily and she perceived him to be disconcerted. But he soon recovered his arrogant persona. 'A mere technicality,' he announced with confidence. 'I don't like you but you've never struck me as the sort of person who would take something that doesn't belong to you. So I'm sure you'll do the decent thing and have the business transferred to me.'

Any compunction she might have had about her inheritance was eliminated by the sheer callousness of this man. 'I won't be doing that,' she stated, her mind made up. 'And I don't believe that you seriously thought I would.'

He scowled at her. 'But you must do it,' he demanded. 'There's no question about it.'

'Why?'

'Because the boathouse is mine and you very well know it,' he roared. 'I'm the man's son, for God's sake, the whole of his estate should come to me.'

'And if you'd been a decent son to him it probably would have,' she said.

'My relationship with my father is none of your business,' he objected.

'It is when you're accusing me of stealing something from you,' she retorted. 'Had you treated my uncle decently, I probably would have felt that you deserved to inherit his business and signed it over to you. But you had no time for him when he was alive and all you care about now is making money out of his death. Well, I'll tell you this much, Arthur, there is absolutely no way you are going to get your hands on that boathouse.'

'But it's mine.' He moved towards her in a menacing manner, his dark eyes hot with fury.

Expecting him to hit her, she dodged to one side, mouth dry, heart pumping. 'You lay a finger on me and I'll have you done for assault.'

'I wasn't gonna touch you,' he snarled, staying where he was. 'I don't want to catch anything.'

'Get out of here,' she ordered.

'I'm not going anywhere until you agree to sign the boathouse over to me.'

'You can stay here all day and I won't agree to give you what you want.' She was determined to stand her ground. 'Anyway, I have to go to work soon, so if you stay, you'll be on your own.'

His hatred was overwhelming as he narrowed his eyes on her. 'You so-called respectable types are all the same. You'd think butter wouldn't melt to look at you,' he sneered. 'But underneath the halo you're as hard as nails.'

'Look, Arthur, if you really do believe that the boathouse should come to you, why don't you contest the will properly?' she suggested wearily. 'Let the lawyers sort it out.'

'I will if I have to, don't worry,' he threatened. 'But I shouldn't have to go to those lengths, and if you had a shred of decency in you, I wouldn't.'

'Arthur,' she began in a softer, more persuasive manner, 'your father left the boathouse to *me*, he wanted *me* to have it. Why can't you accept that with good grace?'

'Because it isn't fair,' was his answer to that.

'Oh well, if you want to take that attitude, it's up to you,' she said. 'But it won't change anything.'

'Why *did* he leave it to you?' he rambled. 'That's what I'd like to know.'

'I've told you why,' she replied. 'Because I'm the only one in the family who's struggling.'

'I don't believe that load of rubbish.' Arthur squinted at her, as though mulling something over, then lunged forward suddenly and grabbed her arm roughly. 'You scheming little cow. What did you do to persuade him, or was it a question of what you let *him* do?'

For a moment she was too shocked to react; she couldn't believe what he was implying. But when the full force of his insinuation registered, her instincts took over and she smacked his face so hard it stung her hand. 'You disgusting pervert,' she hissed, watching him cower away, clutching his cheek. 'How could you even think such a thing?'

'It's either something like that or he did it just to get back at me,' he mumbled, still holding his face.

Rachel felt sick. 'Can't you get it into your head that it's neither of those things? Uncle Chip wasn't the type to want to get back at anybody, and he certainly wasn't into incest. Only someone with a sewer for a mind could conjure up such an insulting suggestion.'

'Such things do happen,' he mumbled.

'Not to me or your father. Why don't you just accept the fact that you and he never got along, which is why he didn't see why he should leave his business to you? After all, he was perfectly entitled to leave it to someone he knew would really appreciate it.'

'The man was unhinged.'

'Honestly, Arthur, it's no wonder your dad didn't have any time for you.'

'The feeling was mutual, I can assure you,' he said. 'He was a loser.'

'Not so much of a loser that he didn't leave behind something you would give your right arm to get your hands on,' she pointed out.

He didn't seem to have an answer to that. 'I'll get what's mine one way or another,' he seethed, gripping her by both arms and shaking her violently. 'Make no mistake about that.'

'Mum-eee, mum-eee,' came a cry from the kitchen door, and Tim came hurtling into the room followed by his brother, their eyes wide with horror. 'What's happening? Why is he fighting with you?'

Arthur let go of her, curbing his temper, she guessed, because he didn't want a couple of hysterical children on his hands. 'Just mucking about, kids,' he assured them with feigned joviality. 'Nothing for you to worry about.'

'He's just going,' Rachel told them in a reassuring tone. 'You go and finish your breakfast.'

'We've finished,' announced Tim.

'Go and wait in the other room in the warm,' she said. 'It's cold out here. I'll be with you in a minute.'

They trotted into the living room and she closed the door behind them, then led Arthur down the hallway.

'I wouldn't bother making any plans for the boathouse,' he said in a warning tone at the front door. 'Because it won't be yours for long. I can promise you that. I'm going to see a solicitor to get the will contested.'

'You do whatever you feel you must,' she signed wearily.

When the door had closed behind him, Rachel leaned against it trying to calm herself. She didn't want the boys to see her trembling. How horrible it was to be arguing over something that had been left to her by a good man with her interests at heart. She'd sooner not have the boathouse at all if it was going to cause someone else such resentment. But how could it be wrong for her to have it when it was what her uncle had obviously wanted? Her stomach churned as she thought about her cousin's evil suggestion. How could a son be so different from his father?

Deciding suddenly that she had something important to do before she went to work, she hurried into the living room to collect the breakfast things and get the children ready to go to Jan's.

* * *

'It's beautiful,' said Rachel, watching Ben Smart lacquering a skiff, its lines sleek, the new wood rich with colour.

'Hello, Rachel,' he said, turning to her, having been unaware of her presence in the workshop. 'We don't usually see you in the middle of the week. You skiving off work?'

'Something like that.' Her gaze lingered on the craft: the clean-cut outline, the veneered wood strips fitted together to make up the boat's body. Having an uncle who was a boatbuilder, she'd always known of the skill that went into making a boat but had never been quite so aware of the craftsmanship as she was at this moment. Inheriting the boathouse had given her new eyes.

'What sort of wood is it?' she found herself wanting to know.

'Cedar-faced ply,' Ben informed her.

'How do you fix the strips together so neatly?' she wondered.

'We glue them, then use copper nails and rivets – copper to avoid rusting,' he explained.

'Fascinating,' she said.

'All in a day's work.' He looked beyond her. 'Are the boys not with you?' he asked, putting his brush down on the workbench with the bristle end resting on the lid of the lacquer tin.

'No, not this time,' she told him. 'They're with my sister because I'm on my way to work.'

Ben's thick brows rose. 'So, to what do I owe the honour?' he asked.

She glanced around the workshop, where several men were busy working on different crafts, sawing, nailing, planing the wood. 'I need a private word,' she replied, looking at him.

'Sure.' He gave a young lad who'd been standing nearby instructions to carry on with the lacquering and turned back to her. 'Come through to the office.'

She followed him across the workshop through a carpet of wood shavings. The air was filled with the amalgamated scents of new wood, paint and varnish, and a radio pumped out pop music in the background. He led her into the manager's office at the back and offered her coffee, which she politely refused because she didn't have time to linger.

'Excuse the chaos,' he said, moving an untidy pile of papers from a chair so that she could sit down, and parking himself on a seat behind the desk. 'I don't have the time to be tidy since I inherited the job of running the place single-handed.'

'No, I don't suppose you do,' she said in an understanding manner.

He pointed towards the glass panel through which the next-door office could be seen. A woman of advanced years was busy at a typewriter in there. 'Mrs Butler plays hell with me over the state of this office. I'm sure she won't be sorry to see the back of me when she leaves.'

'Mrs Butler is leaving?'

'Aren't we all?' he replied.

'All of you leaving?' She was puzzled.

'Haven't you heard? This place is going to be knocked down and made into a nightclub as soon as your cousin has sold it,' he said grimly. 'We're all looking for other jobs, since boatbuilders aren't exactly in demand at a nightclub.'

'But . . .'

'Mind you, Mrs Butler has been wanting to retire for ages,' he went on before she could continue. 'She stayed on longer than she intended because she's worked for Chip since he started the place and he relied on her to run the office. So leaving won't be any hardship for her. She can't wait to get some time to herself.'

'Actually, Ben,' she managed to get a word in at last, 'the boathouse isn't my cousin's to sell.'

'Not yet, maybe,' he said, 'but as soon as everything has gone through . . .'

'No, that isn't what I mean,' she tried to explain. 'Arthur won't ever be in a position to sell it because my uncle didn't leave it to him.'

'Didn't leave it to Arthur!' he exclaimed, looking bewildered. 'I don't believe it.'

'It is hard to believe, I know,' she said. 'But it's true.'

'Well, good for Chip,' he blurted out impulsively. 'I never did think Arthur deserved it.' He gave her a sheepish look. 'Sorry, I suppose I shouldn't be making derogatory comments about one of your relatives.'

'Don't worry about that,' she assured him, noticing his long fingers as he combed his hair back with them. 'I agree with you, as it happens, along with the rest of my family.'

'That's all right then.' He stared into space for a moment. 'So who does the place belong to now?'

'Me.'

'You!' He gave her a disbelieving grin. 'You're having me on.'

'Is it really *that* surprising?' she asked.

'Well, yes, it is, as it happens,' he admitted frankly. 'Probably because I just automatically assumed that the place would go to Arthur.' He looked regretful. 'But I suppose you'll be selling it anyway?'

'Why would you assume that?' she wanted to know.

'Because you're not a boatbuilder and the firm is in trouble,' he explained with candour. 'So it would be the most sensible thing for you to do.' He gave her a questioning look. 'Would you mind if I stuck my neck out for a moment?'

'Go on.'

'Well, if you were to sell it to another boatbuilder – and one of the established firms would probably be interested because they know they could bring it through this crisis – some of the staff might be able to keep their jobs. It isn't quite so crucial for me because I've been in the business a long time and I've built a reputation for myself. But we've a couple of young lads who won't find it quite so easy to get another job.'

'Mm.' She was thoughtful.

'I'd buy the place myself if I had the money,' he said

wistfully. 'No two ways about that.'

'You really think a good boatbuilder could turn things round, then?' she asked.

'Oh, yeah, with a lot of hard work and a bit of initiative, it could be done,' he told her.

'The staff would have to be reduced, though,' she said thoughtfully.

'Oh, yes. Your uncle had already decided on that,' he said. 'We were due to have a chat about it the evening he died, as a matter of fact. We were going to see what could be done to save the business. There are a couple of blokes who have already found jobs elsewhere, so they'll be leaving anyway.'

Rachel was silent, her confused thoughts beginning to slot into place. 'Look, I don't know if I'll be able to persuade the bank to let me keep the boathouse and try to get it back on its feet,' she told him eventually. 'But if I was able to talk them into letting me give it a try, would you stay on as manager?'

He shook his head, letting out a soft whistle. 'I don't know about that.' He wanted to be truthful with her. 'I'm used to having a free hand around here. Your uncle trusted me to do the job and he let me get on with it without interference.'

'So would I.'

'But with you not being a boatbuilder, I'm not sure if it would work,' he told her, leaning back in his chair, looking thoughtful. 'I mean, you'd have to take an awful lot on trust, wouldn't you, as you don't know the job.'

'I take your point, and I know it's a crazy idea for me to even think of keeping the place on.' She paused, meeting his eyes. 'But to be quite honest, I feel as though I would be letting my uncle down if I don't at least *try* to turn the business round and keep it going. This place meant so much to him, I just know he wouldn't have wanted me to sell it.'

'I understand how you feel,' Ben said. 'Similar feelings have made me stay on here even though I thought your cousin was selling up. I've been trying to keep things going for as long as I could because I know Chip would have hated the idea of it going out of existence. He was good to me and I owe him.'

'As I've said, I don't know if I'll be able to talk the bank into letting me keep the place,' she said. 'But I think I'd stand much more of a chance if I could tell them that you are staying on as manager, you being experienced in the job.'

'Yes, I think you would, too,' he agreed.

'So before I put the idea to them, I need to know if I can rely on you to back me up,' she said.

He still seemed doubtful.

'Look, I'd let you get on with your job of running the boatbuilding side of things, I promise,' she assured him. 'And you'll have to lead me by the hand through everything else until I get to know what's what, as I've no business experience at all. You have my word that I won't interfere.'

'In that case, you can rely on me,' he said, fired with new hope for Banks' Boats. 'I'll be here for as long as you need me. I owe your uncle that much.'

'I'm *so* pleased.' As daunting as the idea of running a boathouse was, it did seem possible with Ben beside her. She was even beginning to feel excited by the challenge.

'Yeah, me too,' he said. 'So, fingers crossed that you can talk the bank into it.'

Rachel smiled and he thought how pretty she looked, her face becoming bright and animated, just as he remembered her before her broken marriage had taken its toll.

'I think I will have that cup of coffee after all, if it's still on offer?' she grinned.

'Sure.'

'I've a few ideas I'd like to talk over with you,' she explained.

'I'll go and organise the coffee, then,' he said, rising and walking to the door. 'Shan't be a minute.'

The only thing that got Ella Banks through the long, tedious days at the shoe-shop in Shepherd's Bush where she worked was knowing that it wasn't for much longer. She just couldn't wait to tell that creep of a manager what to do with his job.

A pert, blue-eyed blonde with no shortage of physical blessings, she believed that she was meant for better things than selling shoes. How she loathed running up and down ladders, searching through endless boxes and working her socks off to convince members of the general public that the footwear they had chosen to try on suited them, only to have them say they'd go away and think about it.

If a customer left without making a purchase, she had the manager on her back, blaming her for a shortfall in his weekly sales target. She was longing to see the back of all this and took comfort in the thought that that time was imminent.

So when she got home that evening to be greeted with the news that her days at the shoe-shop were not numbered after all, because her husband hadn't inherited his father's business as they'd expected, she was livid.

'You're telling me that he left it to that snotty cousin of yours?' she said to him in their bitterly cold cupboard of a kitchen.

'That's right,' confirmed Arthur woefully. 'I'm ever so sorry, love.'

'Not half as sorry as I am,' she raged, unwrapping a package of fish and chips and slamming it down on to two plates.

'It isn't my fault,' he whined.

'Course it isn't,' she agreed. 'It's that rotten father of yours. I can't believe he would do something as mean as that to his own son.'

'Neither can I, and I'm gutted.'

'You must be, babe.' She was sympathetic. It was her and Arthur against the rest of the world.

Having anticipated the end of his days as an employee, Arthur had become careless with his 'little earner' and suspected that his boss was on to him. He was afraid it was just a matter of time before he lost his job, so he was doubly concerned. 'Of course, Rachel will be laughing all the way to the bank.'

'You're right about that, the cow. I think it's shocking that she won't do the right thing and hand the business over to you,' Ella said, setting two plastic trays down on the narrow home-made worktop with a heavy thud, eyes glinting with fury, large bosom heaving beneath her tight black sweater.

'So do I, but she was very definite about it,' he explained.

'Oh, was she now?' said Ella. Her disappointment was almost a physical pain, but she saw no point in taking her bad temper out on her beloved Arthur. 'We'll soon see about that.'

'I told her she won't get away with it,' he said. 'I'm not letting her walk all over me.'

'That's the spirit, Art,' Ella approved. 'That boathouse is yours and no scheming tart is gonna steal it from us.'

'Too right she isn't,' he declared.

'We'll have to work out our next move,' she told him.

'I'm thinking of contesting the will legally,' he informed her.

'What a good idea.' She sprinkled salt and vinegar liberally on the food then put the plates on to the trays. 'That bitch won't stand a chance once we get the lawyers on to it. She'll soon see what we're made of.'

'The snag is,' he began doubtfully, 'the old man made a proper will, so it's all legal and above board.'

'Don't matter.' Ella wasn't to be deterred.

Arthur bit his lip. 'Er . . . I did actually manage to speak to a solicitor for a few minutes today, and he said that we don't stand much of a chance of overturning it.'

'There's more than one solicitor in London, you know,' she reminded him spiritedly. 'We'll just have to find one who *is* prepared to get it overturned then, won't we?'

'Yeah, you're right.'

She marched into the tiny living room carrying her tray. Arthur followed and they sat down in armchairs by the electric fire to eat their food, trays balanced on their laps.

'It's gotta be done, Art,' she continued firmly. 'We need the cash from the sale of the boathouse so you can get some decent business deals under way. I don't wanna work in a rotten shoe-shop and live in a poky flat like this for the rest of my life.'

'And you won't have to, babe.' He intended to keep his promise to her; that he would make his fortune and raise her to higher things. 'I'll get it sorted.'

'You'd better had.' She dug her long fingernails into her heavily lacquered beehived hair and scratched her head. 'Your dad must have been off his rocker to have done what he did. You'll have to explain that to the lawyers.'

'Will they believe me, though?' he said. 'I'm always uneasy when it comes to dealing with the law.'

'You're not used to being on the right side of it, that's why,' pronounced Ella, who thoroughly approved of the way Arthur had been cheating his employer. 'On this occasion you will be, because that boathouse is yours by rights.'

'I know.'

'And if the lawyers can't pull it off, we'll just have to try something else.' With grubby fingers she plucked a chip from the pile and munched it with relish. 'Because we're gonna get that boathouse site one way or another.'

'Yeah, course we are, love.' Ella's positive attitude restored his hopes, which had been somewhat dashed by the negative attitude of the solicitor he'd seen that afternoon. 'I'll make sure of it, don't worry.'

'We're a team, you and me, Art,' she said affectionately. 'There's nothing we can't do as long as we stick together.'

'Nothing at all,' Arthur agreed, fired with enthusiasm and planning to get an appointment with another solicitor as soon as possible.

Chapter Four

The bank manager made his position dauntingly clear in the early stages of the interview. 'The boathouse *must* be put up for sale right away, Mrs West,' he stated categorically. 'The overdraft has exceeded the limit by an unacceptable amount and the bank isn't prepared to let this situation continue now that new ownership has been established.'

Unaccustomed to dealing with someone of his eminence, Rachel was naturally a little overawed by him. But having been given a few tips by her brother-in-law, who had been successfully persuasive with bank officials when he'd set up in business for himself, she wasn't about to be frightened into defeat. She was determined not to leave here until, at the very least, she'd been given the opportunity to put forward the plans that had been fermenting in her mind ever since her conversation with Ben Smart a few days ago.

'But if I were to keep the business going, the bank would get their money back eventually, and in the meantime you'd be earning interest from the overdraft,' she pointed out bravely. 'All I'm asking for is a little time, a chance to get the business back on track. If things don't improve within a time specified by you, *then* I go ahead and sell.'

He gave an eloquent sigh, looking at her with a bemused expression. 'But surely it would be easier for you just to sell up and keep any money that's left over after all the debts have been paid, wouldn't it?' he suggested.

'Yes, that would be easier,' she agreed. 'But it isn't what I want to do.'

A large, well-dressed man of about fifty, with grey eyes observing her through rimless spectacles, and immaculate silver hair and eyebrows, he leaned back slightly in his chair with his arms folded. 'Unfortunately, personal choice isn't really an option in this case,' he informed her in an even tone. 'You've already admitted that you know nothing about boatbuilding and have no business experience. I'm sure you'll understand that the bank can't afford to take a risk on someone as unqualified as yourself, especially as the boathouse is already in trouble.'

'There would be an experienced workshop manager running the boatbuilding side of things.' It wasn't easy to stay confident given his negative attitude and the fact that he held her future in his hands. But she had to give this her best shot. 'He's a man who worked for my uncle for many years and knows the business of boatbuilding inside out. So the standard of work and the reputation of the firm are assured.'

'But the overall responsibility would be yours, wouldn't it?' he reminded her gravely.

'Well, yes.' She couldn't deny it. 'But if I could just give you an outline of my proposals . . .'

Glancing at his watch, he raised his cautious grey eyes to meet hers. 'Very well then,' he agreed with more than a hint of impatience. 'But I do have other people to see, so I'd appreciate it if you could be brief.'

She nodded. 'What I have in mind is for me to give up my current job in a factory and take over in the office at the boathouse,' she explained, remaining staunchly positive. 'The secretary wants to retire anyway so there'll be a need for a replacement.'

He didn't look impressed.

'The idea,' she continued swiftly, 'is for me to take on the managerial duties that were my late uncle's as well as the routine office work once I've got to grips with how the business works. And all for the same salary as we pay the current secretary. Two jobs for the price of one, in fact.' She decided to confirm her faith in herself by adding, 'Until things improve and the firm can afford to pay me the proper rate for a management position.'

'You say you work in a factory,' he said slowly, his eyes resting on her unnervingly. 'Does this mean that you don't have any office experience?'

Reminding herself that he was only doing his job and there was no personal malice in this grilling he was giving her, she met the challenge in his steely gaze. 'No, it doesn't mean that,' she was able to inform him. 'I did work in an office for a while before I got married.'

'In a position of responsibility?' he probed.

Actually she'd only been a junior filing clerk, but she lowered her eyes and said, 'It wasn't a senior position but it gave me a basic grounding in office routine.'

'Can you do shorthand and typing?' he wanted to know.

'No,' she was forced to admit. 'But I've established that shorthand isn't essential for the boathouse office and I'm planning to do a crash course at Pitman's to learn typing because I will definitely need to be able to do that.'

Up shot his brows. 'May I ask how you can be running the office if you're out learning how to type?' he enquired.

'I'd only be out for a few hours a day, and I'd take the most basic typing course, so I would be competent to the level I need in a matter of weeks,' she replied. 'I've already made enquiries about it and am assured that that is the case.'

'But that sort of tuition is expensive and the firm needs to cut down on expenses, not create new ones,' he pointed out in a warning tone.

He's determined to make an obstacle of every suggestion, she thought. 'I agree,' she said, 'but this would be money well spent because the results would be fast. Much more beneficial to the firm than my just picking it up as I go along, or going to evening classes once a week.'

An eyebrow was raised in irritation. 'Oh, really!' he said with a hard edge to his voice. 'The bank is only interested in serious proposals.'

'These *are* serious proposals,' she was at pains to convince him. 'I've given the matter a lot of thought and I *know* I can make it work. I would, of course, ask the current secretary to stay on until I've learnt the job and have finished the typing course.'

'So that would mean two salaries being paid for one job,' he pointed out.

'Only for a very short time, and after that the situation would be reversed,' she explained.

'Hmmm.' He still didn't seem convinced.

'I'm also planning on getting out and about to promote the boathouse once I know the ropes,' she went on. 'Visiting existing and potential customers with the idea of keeping the work flowing in and bringing in more. I'll do anything to put the business back on its feet.'

'Tell me,' he began thoughtfully, 'is your husband supportive of you in this venture?'

She'd hoped he wouldn't ask about that, because she knew her answer would go against her. 'My husband and I aren't together,' she admitted, feeling hot under his steady gaze.

'Oh.' His expression was predictably disapproving. 'Do you have any children?'

'Yes, I have two,' she informed him proudly.

'May I ask if your husband supports them financially?' he enquired. 'I realise it's a personal matter, but I need to know all the facts if I am to give proper consideration to your proposals.'

She was tempted to lie because the truth would be so damning. But in her experience, even the smallest fib usually backfired and led to complications. 'No,' she told him straight. 'He left us and I don't have an address for him so I can't get any money from him.'

He leaned forward, drumming his fingers on the desk. 'So

. . . how are you expecting to run a business when you have two children to look after and no back-up support?' he enquired wisely.

'In the same way as I cope with a full-time job now,' she informed him frankly. 'My sister looks after the children while I'm at the factory. I have to go out to work anyway, to keep them. And as things are at the moment, I often have to work overtime to make ends meet. So working long hours will be nothing new to me.'

'That's all very well. But running a business is a serious commitment,' he lectured. 'It isn't like having a job in a factory where you can go home and forget all about it when you've finished for the day.'

Credit me with some intelligence, you arrogant bugger, she thought, but said, 'I'm fully aware of that, and I'm not expecting it to be easy. But I really do believe that I'm capable of making a success of it.'

'Hmm,' he grunted again, picking up a pencil which he held loosely, tapping the stump end thoughtfully on the desk. Something in his attitude made Rachel wonder if there might perhaps be a compassionate human being in there somewhere beneath all that officialdom.

'One of the biggest advantages of my plan is that I'd be working towards a definite goal,' she continued, eagerness growing as she realised he still hadn't actually rejected her idea. 'I aim to build something solid for myself and my sons for the future. And, of course, the bank would benefit from this too.'

'Your motives aren't in question, Mrs West,' he said, putting the pencil down and lowering his eyes. 'But the bank is a commercial concern. We can't afford to take such a risk.'

Rachel decided that she had nothing to lose by sticking her neck out good and proper. 'It wouldn't be that huge a risk, though, would it?' she declared boldly. 'Not if you were to give me a definite time limit. If I haven't showed signs of turning things around by then, I sell the business and no arguments. Even if I wasn't able to sell it as a going concern, the site alone should raise enough to pay off the overdraft, if nothing else.'

'And if it doesn't work out as you hope, you'll be even more in our debt and therefore have less cash, if anything at all, left over after the sale,' he reasoned.

'But . . .'

'Contrary to what you're probably thinking, Mrs West,' he interjected firmly, 'I *am* trying to do what's best for *you* as well as the bank.'

Oddly enough, she believed him. 'Yes, of course, I realise that.' Deciding to appeal to his human side, and grovel if she had to, she leaned forward and said ardently, 'And I believe you'd be doing what's best for us both by giving me a chance.'

'I admire your courage, my dear,' he said, 'but . . .'

'Please,' she begged. 'The bank will get its money back one way or another.'

He met her appealing eyes and she suspected that he might be weakening. He looked down at his notes again and was silent for a long time, mulling it over, while her heart did somersaults. 'All right. I'll give you three months and not a day longer,' he said at last, looking at her sternly.

She didn't have the guile to be businesslike about it. 'Oh, thank you,' she burst out, giving him a beaming smile.

'But I must warn you, we shall be monitoring the account *very closely*,' he told her solemnly.

The gravity of his manner indicated that he regretted allowing himself to be persuaded against his better judgement but wouldn't go back on his word. 'I understand,' she said, her joy at having won him over slightly tempered by the enormity of the responsibility she was taking on.

'And if things aren't looking healthier by the three-month deadline, the business goes up for sale *right away*.' He wanted her left in no doubt.

'If it does come to that, you'll get no argument from me, I

promise you,' she assured him, rising to leave. 'Thank you again, very much indeed.'

His plump face creased into a half-smile. He looked at his watch again. 'I'm over-running now, but if you'd like to make another appointment with my secretary on your way out, we'll go over the details.'

'I'll look forward to it,' she said, walking to the door.

'Oh, Mrs West,' he began.

'Yes?' She turned to look at him.

'Good luck.'

'Thank you very much,' she said again, and left his office, smiling.

She was still smiling when she got off the bus and walked along the riverside to the boathouse. The weather was cold but dry, with watery sunshine beaming intermittently from a cloudy sky patched with fragments of blue. The tide was on its way out and the river was a greenish-brown in this light, a muddy strip of the riverbed visible by the bank. Ducks climbed on to the driftwood, preening their feathers, while a crowd of pigeons strutted and pecked on a wooden jetty. There weren't many people about on this midweek winter morning, just a few walking their dogs, an intrepid runner, the odd cyclist, a woman with a small boy trying to fly a kite on the grass in Furnival Gardens. An occasional barge or motorboat drifted by and a lone sculler sped his craft through the water.

It wasn't until she got near to the boathouse and saw the oarsman walking up the slipway carrying his craft on his shoulders that she realised it was Ben.

'My word, someone's feeling brave this morning,' she remarked lightly, noticing that he wasn't wearing a coat, just a thick blue sweater and jeans.

'You soon get warm when you're rowing,' he explained.

'Is it yours?' she asked, because she thought she remembered that he had a rowing boat.

He frowned at the suggestion. 'Of course not. I wouldn't

dream of going out rowing for my own pleasure during the working day,' he explained sharply, his defensive attitude reminding her of her position as his employer.

'I wasn't suggesting you were skiving or anything,' she was quick to amend, her cheeks flaming with embarrassment. 'It was just a casual comment.'

'Oh, I see.' His tone softened as he realised she wasn't being critical. 'It's a customer's boat, actually. We've had her in for repairs and I just wanted to double-check that there were no problems before they take delivery. I just managed to catch the tide.'

'I didn't realise it was you skimming through the water,' she remarked chattily, the awkward moment over. 'You seem to be very good at it.'

'I ought to be: I've been rowing since I was a lad,' he said. 'It was your uncle who first got me interested. He used to do a bit of rowing himself when he was young.'

'Do you compete in races?' she enquired.

'I used to. Now I just do it for my own pleasure,' he explained, walking beside her towards the boathouse. 'But I love handling boats of all kinds and I am a qualified waterman.'

'What's that?' she wondered.

'It means I'm qualified to take people out on the river, in both rowing boats and powered craft,' he explained.

'I didn't realise you had to be specially qualified to do that,' she said.

'On the tidal Thames there are strict regulations,' he informed her. 'On non-tidal waters it doesn't matter.'

'I had no idea there was so much to it,' she told him.

'I don't suppose many people do,' he commented. 'You wouldn't have cause to know about these things unless you're involved with the river.'

'Which brings me to the reason I'm here,' she announced with a note of victory in her voice. 'From now on I'm going to be very much involved with the river.'

He gave her a cautious look. 'You got the bank to agree to give you a chance?' he suggested hopefully.

'Yes, I did,' she confirmed. 'I don't have to sell the boathouse, not yet anyway.'

'Oh, well done,' he congratulated her heartily, halting in his step to give her a warm smile. 'That's the best bit of news I've heard in ages.'

She smiled back. 'I knew you'd be pleased,' she said as they entered the yard of Banks' Boats.

'Pleased is an understatement,' he informed her. 'But let's go through to the office and you can tell me all about it.'

'That's exactly what I had in mind,' she said and followed him into the boathouse, still buoyant from her success with the bank manager.

Jan's reaction to the news was rather more circumspect. Rachel told her all about it later that morning when she arrived at her sister's just in time for lunch.

'It's a huge task you've taken on,' Jan pointed out as they served out beef casserole in the kitchen together, the children playing in the other room. 'Are you sure you've done the right thing?'

'No, I'm not,' confessed Rachel.

'It isn't too late to change your mind,' said Jan, straining some boiled cabbage through the colander at the sink. 'If you pull out now, before things get under way, nobody will be inconvenienced by it.'

'I haven't changed my mind,' stated Rachel.

'But if you're not sure about it, wouldn't it be best to forget it?'

'How can I possibly be sure about something that's uncharted territory to me?' asked Rachel, spooning mashed potato from the saucepan on to the children's plates.

'You can't, I suppose.'

'But just because I'm not one hundred per cent certain, it doesn't mean that I think I'll fail,' she said.

'You'd be safer selling up and keeping what's left of the money.'

'Do you think I don't know that, Jan?' emphasised Rachel. 'I've thought about it until my head aches. But despite all the potential problems, I still want to try to put the business back where Uncle Chip wanted it – in profit.'

'We all know how much the boathouse meant to Uncle Chip, but you have to think about yourself,' her sister said. 'You've two kids to feed and clothe. They must be your first priority.'

'And they are – *surely* you don't doubt that?' replied Rachel, her voice rising.

'Of course I don't,' Jan was quick to assure her. 'I'm just trying to keep your feet on the ground.'

'They're practically cemented to it, I promise you. This isn't just a whim.' Her sister's approval would have been nice, but it wasn't essential to Rachel's confidence in her own decision. 'I've given it a lot of careful thought.' She paused with the potato scoop in her hand. 'It's a chance to make something of myself, Jan. I'm not doing this just because it's what Uncle Chip wanted, I'll also be doing it for the boys and myself, which is what I believe Chip wanted too.'

'But if it doesn't work out, you'll have lost some of the money *and* given up your job,' Jan pointed out.

'Getting another factory job won't be too much of a problem,' Rachel told her.

'I suppose not,' agreed Jan.

'And I've never had any money, so if I lose it I won't miss it,' Rachel went on. 'But for the first time in my life I have the opportunity to build something solid for my little family, like Pete is doing for you and Kelly. If the business does well – and if I work hard and learn from Uncle Chip's mistakes, there's every chance that it will – I'll be able to draw a decent salary in time, a damned sight more than I could ever earn slogging in a factory for the rest of my life. It's a chance of a lifetime, Jan, and I'd be mad to let it pass me by.'

Jan put the colander down on the draining board and turned to her sister, noticing the sparkle in her eyes, the vitality exuding from her. 'Put like that, I think you would be too,' she told her. 'Anything that can make you this excited is worth a chance. I haven't seen you look this cheerful since before that scumbag Jeff walked out.'

'I've got a really good feeling about it,' Rachel said, 'and I can't wait to get started.'

'All that and you get to work with the gorgeous Ben Smart too,' her sister laughed, injecting a more light-hearted note into the conversation.

'Yeah, there's that too,' smiled Rachel, adding more seriously, 'but I really want to do this.'

'If it's what you really want to do, then good luck to you,' Jan said wholeheartedly. 'Truth be told, I'm rather glad Uncle Chip's boathouse is going to stay. The riverside around there wouldn't be the same without it.'

'Thanks, Jan,' Rachel said, giving her a hug.

'Come on then,' said Jan purposefully, moving away and piling cabbage on the plates. Let's get these children fed.'

Rachel turned her attention back to the potato. 'As soon as I've had my lunch, I'll have to go in to the factory to give in my notice.'

'No regrets about that, I assume,' remarked Jan.

'Not likely,' Rachel confirmed.

'When are you going to tell Mum and Dad what you've decided?'

'Tonight. I'll call in to see them when I've collected the boys from here.'

'They'll probably have a fit at the idea of you taking on something as masculine as a boathouse,' Jan commented lightly.

'Mum will be pleased because it'll be staying in the family,' predicted Rachel. 'But Dad will definitely think it's no job for a woman.'

'He will, yeah,' agreed Jan.

Rachel smiled, her voice soft with affection for her parents. 'Still, they always want the best for both of us, even if their ideas don't always match ours.'

'They always do.' Jan put the plates out on the kitchen table, then went to the door and emitted an authoritative yell. 'Kids! Dinner's ready, so go and wash your hands, then come out here . . . right away, please.'

'So what do you think about Rachel trying to make a go of the boathouse instead of selling it, Ron?' enquired Marge that evening after Rachel and the boys had left.

'I think she must be off her head.' Ron's warm brown eyes were full of worry. 'As I told her, it would be much more sensible to sell it, for her own sake.'

They were sitting in their living room having a quiet cup of tea in the aftermath of their grandsons' noisy ebullience, the sound on the TV turned low so that they could discuss Rachel's news. 'It probably would be more sensible,' agreed Marge, brushing her untidy red hair from her brow with her hand. 'But you have to admire her guts for being willing to have a go when she's never done anything like that before.'

'Oh, not half,' he agreed wholeheartedly. 'And it was what Chip would have wanted.'

'I'll say.'

'It's a pity he's left her with a load of trouble, though.'

'If he hadn't had that bit of bad luck, it would have been a thriving business, some security for her and the boys,' Marge pointed out.

'Instead of which he's left her with an uphill struggle,' commented Ron.

'Maybe it will be a struggle for her at first, but at least he's given her the chance of better things.' Marge was defensive of her late brother. 'And surely a chance is better than nothing?'

'I'm not saying it isn't,' argued Ron. 'But Rachel has quite enough on her plate bringing those lads up on her own without taking on more responsibility.'

'I'm not so sure about that,' countered Marge. 'It could work out very well for her. After all, she'll have a job with decent prospects, and she'll be doing something a darned sight more interesting than working on the assembly line at the factory.'

'But she's no experience of business,' Ron reminded her.

'She'll soon learn. She's a bright young woman.'

'Yeah . . . *woman* being the operative word,' he retorted, finishing his tea and disposing of the cup on a small table by his chair. 'It doesn't matter how intelligent and capable she is, running a boathouse is man's work. Most women just don't have the physical build for it.'

'I can't argue with you about that. But she isn't going to be involved in the actual boatbuilding, remember,' Marge told him. 'She'll have Ben and his team to do that. It isn't as though she'll be lugging great lumps of wood about.'

'No, I suppose not,' Ron conceded. 'But she'll still be working in a male environment.'

'They've had a woman working in the office for years,' Marge reminded him, 'and she doesn't seem to find it a problem.'

'But Rachel is going to be the boss,' he argued, his voice rising in concern.

'So?'

'So that's a whole lot different to just working in the office,' he said. 'She'll be in charge of men who are doing a job that she can't do. They won't respect her.'

'It won't be like that at all, Ron. The men will be working directly under Ben, the same as they do now.' Marge was getting quite heated about it. 'Rachel has made it very clear that she's going to give him a free hand with all of that. So as far as the men are concerned, Ben will be their boss, not Rachel.'

'Yeah, I suppose you're right,' he agreed reluctantly. 'I

suppose I'm old-fashioned but it just doesn't seem right to me. Women stepping into men's shoes. I don't want her to have a hard time, that's all.'

'I know you're only thinking of her, love,' Marge told him. 'But she's obviously made up her mind and she'll go ahead whatever we say about it.'

'She's got a mind of her own all right.' Ron couldn't quarrel with that.

'Anyway, I think it's up to us to be behind her whatever our own doubts about it,' she pronounced. 'She deserves that.'

Some small inflection in her voice made him look up sharply. 'We've both done everything we possibly could for her,' he said, meeting his wife's eyes.

'Yes, I know we have,' she agreed, her tone becoming deadly serious. 'Everything except one thing.'

'There's no point in dwelling on that now, Marge,' he muttered, looking at the floor.

She stared thoughtfully into space for a moment. 'No. You're right, there isn't,' she agreed with a sigh of resignation. 'So let's concentrate on giving her all the support we can in her new venture.'

'That goes without saying,' he said.

Chapter Five

At the end of Rachel's first day at the boathouse, she felt sure she would never get the hang of things; at the end of the second, she was convinced she'd made a terrible mistake in keeping it on at all.

Completing the typing course seemed beyond her, the office telephone sent her into a panic because she didn't have the knowledge to answer the queries, and the filing system was a foreign country to her.

'You're feeling a bit confused by it all, I expect,' remarked Ben as they left together and walked across the yard.

'Baffled is more the word,' she corrected.

'It'll soon fall into place,' he said encouragingly. 'It's bound to take time to get used to it.'

'I seem to be running around in circles getting nowhere at the moment,' she confessed, confident that anything she said to him wouldn't go any further. 'I don't know where anything is and it takes me ages to file things away. And as for the typing course . . . Well, my fingers turn to sausages the minute they get anywhere near the keyboard. I'm like a fish out of water and it's doing terrible things to my confidence.'

'It isn't my place to tell you how to tackle the job in these early days, of course,' he said cautiously. 'But I do have one suggestion, a way to get your confidence back and do the firm some good at the same time.'

'I'm listening,' she told him.

'Well, instead of trying to learn the office routine all at once, why don't you spend some time going out and seeing people who are important to the firm,' he suggested. 'Introduce yourself as the new owner to regular customers and suppliers.'

'That sounds a bit drastic for a beginner,' she responded.

'It would be throwing yourself in at the deep end but I should think it would make you feel more a part of things.'

'Kill or cure, eh?'

'It might work.'

'I was intending to do what you're suggesting later on, when I'd learned the office routine,' she explained. 'That seemed to take priority.'

'You've a bit of time to get to grips with that as Mrs Butler is willing to stay on until you feel able to cope,' he reminded her. 'Personally, I think it's more important that you go to see people on boathouse business. There's been a lot of uncertainty in the trade about the future of Banks' Boats. Rumours in the pubs around here have been rife, about it being sold and knocked down.'

'And you think customers might have been looking elsewhere?' she suggested.

'Exactly,' he confirmed. 'That's why it's vital that they know the firm is staying in business. And what better assurance than a personal visit from the new proprietor?'

'I think you might have something there, Ben,' she said approvingly.

'You could make a start by going to visit one of our wood suppliers, if you like.'

'Oh?'

'The bloke stopped our credit when the cash flow was dodgy and he had to wait for his money,' he informed her. 'Having to pay for everything in cash is a hell of a nuisance because it means someone going to the bank specially. He won't even take our cheques.'

'Are you saying that you want *me* to persuade him to reopen our account?' she exclaimed.

'That's right.' He didn't seem to have any doubts.

'You really think I can do it?'

'Sure I do,' he assured her. 'Just because you haven't yet become office worker of the year doesn't mean you won't make a brilliant ambassador for the boathouse. You managed to talk the bloke at the bank into doing what you want, so I'm damned sure you can get our credit back with suppliers.'

His confidence in her was very inspiring. 'OK, I'll give it a go,' she agreed. 'You give me all the details and I'll see if I can get an appointment tomorrow afternoon.'

'We'll have a look at the file together in the morning,' he suggested.

They were standing chatting by his car, parked in the corner of the yard, a strong breeze gusting across the river whipping colour into their cheeks and blowing their hair about. The days were beginning to lengthen so it wasn't yet dark.

'Can I give you a lift?' he offered pleasantly. 'This wind is a bit sharp for standing about in a bus queue.'

'It's kind of you to offer, but I don't want to take you out of your way.'

'I'm not bothered about that,' he said, unlocking the car door. 'So jump in.'

'OK, you've twisted my arm.' She was glad she'd confided in him about the difficulties she was having with the job. It was comforting not having to pretend to him that she was in complete control, as she felt obliged to do with the other men. Despite Ben's faith in her, however, she still felt unequal to the responsibilities she had taken on.

'Well, well, it didn't take you long to get yourself on cosy terms with him, did it?' was Jan's jovial greeting when she opened the door to Rachel.

'With who?' Rachel was still deeply preoccupied with the problems of the day.

'The hunky hired help, of course,' her sister laughed as Rachel stepped into the hall. 'I saw you out of the window, getting out of his car.' She cocked her head, a wicked gleam in her eye. 'Two days into the job. Not bad going.'

Rachel raised her eyes and tutted but she was grinning too. 'We just happened to be standing talking near his car after work and he offered me a lift,' she explained. 'I wasn't likely to refuse the chance of getting home quicker, not after a day in that ruddy madhouse.'

'What's this?' Jan teased her gently. 'Fed up with the job already?'

'Not fed up with it,' Rachel corrected. 'Just completely out of my depth. Honestly, Jan, I haven't got a clue.'

'Oh, for heaven's sake,' admonished Jan lightly. 'You've only been there two days.'

'I'm being pathetic, I know,' she said, frowning. 'But it isn't like anything I've ever done before and I feel completely incompetent. I'm exhausted with trying not to look like an idiot, as I'm supposed to be the boss.'

'No one would expect you to know what to do right away,' Jan pointed out.

'Probably not, but the staff need to have confidence in me, since their jobs rely on my making a success of things,' she explained. 'And how can they have confidence in someone who doesn't know what the hell they're doing?'

'You'll just have to bluff it out until you're feeling more on top of things,' suggested Jan.

'I wouldn't admit this to anyone else,' Rachel confided gravely, 'but I'm not sure I'm up to the job. Maybe I just don't have what it takes up top.'

Anyone else might have tended towards an 'I told you so' attitude. But that wasn't Jan's way. 'Now you really are being stupid,' she said.

'But the situation is ludicrous,' Rachel went on. 'I mean, the success of the business lies entirely with me and I'm fumbling around like a fool. The whole thing's a ruddy farce.'

Jan giggled.

'It isn't funny,' warned Rachel.

'It is the way you're telling it.' She composed herself. 'Anyway, I don't go along with your idea that the whole thing depends on you. The workshop is Ben's responsibility. And the boatbuilding *is* the business.'

'It's my name over the door, though,' Rachel pointed out. 'It was me who pleaded with the bank manager to give me a chance to turn things round. I can't think what possessed me to do such a thing. I must have been stark staring mad.'

'Ask yourself, though, would you rather be back at the factory?' Jan said firmly.

'At least I knew what I was doing when I was working there,' replied Rachel.

'I bet you wouldn't want to go back, though?' Jan persisted.

'I might have to if I don't get the hang of things at the boathouse,' said Rachel gloomily.

'Answer my question,' ordered Jan. 'Would you want to be back on the assembly line?'

Rachel remembered the long, boring days in an enormous room full of machines, the repetitiveness, the noise. She thought of Ben's confidence in her, recalled what she had committed herself to do tomorrow at his suggestion and felt weak with nerves. But she was suddenly infused with determination, too. 'Not likely,' she said. 'And I'm going to make sure I don't have to go back.'

'That's more like it,' cheered Jan.

In the next instant Rachel's worries melted away as her offspring realised that she'd arrived and came tearing down the hall to give her a rapturous welcome. 'Hello, you little terrors,' she said, sweeping first one and then the other into her arms and kissing them. 'It's so good to see you.'

'Have you been to work at the river?' They had both been given brief details of Mummy's new job.

'That's right.'

'Can we come with you tomorrow?' asked Johnnie.

'Not tomorrow,' she told them. 'But if the weather's nice at the weekend I'll take you down to the river to see the boats, and show you where I work.'

'Goodee!' they whooped.

She was imbued with warmth and clarity of thought. Her children were what mattered most to her. The boathouse was a serious responsibility and she would spare no effort to restore it to its former glory. But if it didn't work out, Tim and Johnnie would still be here, needing her, and she would be there for them. That was the most important thing.

The following afternoon, Rachel entered the male-dominated territory of a local wood yard to a lusty chorus of wolf whistles. Some of the men were cutting wood, others loading it on to a lorry. Guessing that any other female visitor would receive a similar noisy reception, she wasn't particularly flattered. She certainly wasn't dressed to encourage it, wearing as she was a red coat that was in its fourth winter and long boots which she'd just had mended for the umpteenth time. At this early stage in her career she couldn't afford to splash out on clothes for herself.

Ignoring the attention, she headed towards the office, where she told the receptionist that she had an appointment with the proprietor, Syd Merrick. After a while she was shown into a room and confronted by an enormous man seated behind a desk littered with paperwork, an overflowing ashtray, a half-eaten cheese roll and an empty coffee mug. His plump face was surrounded by wild ginger hair, his thick lips were tinged with purple, and he had a bright red boozer's nose. He wasn't dressed in a businesslike way, instead wearing a chunky-knit blue sweater.

He offered her a seat. 'You're from Banks' Boats then,' he said pleasantly.

She nodded, offering her hand. 'Rachel West, I'm pleased to meet you.'

'Sending the office girl out on business now, are they?' he grinned, shaking her hand.

'I'm the new owner actually,' she informed him. 'Just

thought I'd come and introduce myself personally, since I understand our two companies have had dealings with each other for many years.'

'*You're* the new owner?' he said with such disbelief she might have just claimed to be a personal friend of the Beatles.

'That's right,' she affirmed. 'Why? Is there something wrong with that?'

'A woman running a boatbuilder's?' he said in a critical tone. 'Seems a bit iffy to me.'

'Why is that, exactly?' As if she didn't know.

'I should have thought that was obvious,' he replied. 'Boatbuilding is a man's trade.'

'Cutting wood and loading delivery vehicles is your business but you're not actually out there doing it, are you?' she said pointedly.

'I pay people to do it for me,' he explained.

'Exactly,' she said, standing her ground.

'Ah, but I could do it if I needed to,' he said, wagging his finger at her and grinning. 'That's the difference.'

'OK, point taken,' she said, because it wasn't in the interests of the boathouse to be at war with this man. 'But I do have Ben Smart running the workshops.'

'He's working for *you*?' Merrick sounded surprised.

'That's right.'

'Phew, you wouldn't catch me taking orders from a woman,' he said.

'Let's hope you never have to if you feel that strongly about it,' she replied, determined not to lose her cool over his attitude. 'Anyway, I don't give Ben orders. He knows what he's doing and he gets on and does it.'

He shrugged his shoulders as though bored with the subject. 'I heard that Chip Banks had died,' he mentioned chattily, 'but I didn't realise his business had been sold yet.'

'It hasn't,' she explained. 'Chip Banks was my uncle. I inherited the boathouse from him.'

'Oh, I see.' His attitude changed instantly. 'Your uncle was one of the best. I was sorry to hear he'd died. Very sorry.'

'Most people were,' she said. 'He'll be much missed.'

'You can say that again,' he agreed.

'Anyway, as well as coming to introduce myself, Mr Merrick,' she said, her confidence rising, 'I'm also here to ask if you'll consider reinstating our account now that our cash-flow problem has been sorted.'

'Ooh, I dunno about that,' he said, breathing out and shaking his head. 'Your uncle was a good bloke, but business is business.'

'It just isn't practical for us to pay for our materials in cash, especially when there's a large order being delivered, or when we send someone to collect small stuff that's needed urgently,' she told him. Ben had briefed her well. 'As well as the inconvenience of having to go to the bank to draw cash, the men aren't keen on having the money on them in case they lose it. It would be much simpler for us if we could have a monthly account again. I understand from Ben that we had an arrangement with you until quite recently, when the boathouse got into difficulties and you were kept waiting for payment.'

His brow furrowed. 'I liked your uncle and was sorry he got into a bit of financial bother and we had to close the account,' he said gravely. 'It was nothing personal; he knew that and there was no bad feeling at all over it. You can't afford to be soft when you're in business.'

'Of course you can't,' she agreed wholeheartedly. 'But you'll get paid regularly from now on, I promise you. Banks' Boats is on the way up again.'

'Mm . . . maybe it is, but surely you can see this from my point of view,' he began.

'Yes, I can. But if you could look at it from our side for a moment, I'd be very grateful,' she requested firmly.

He looked at her, waiting for her to continue.

'The fact of the matter is . . . with the amount of work we've got booked in, we're going to be needing a lot of wood,' she informed him, hardly able to believe she was asserting herself in this way. 'But if you can't see your way to giving us an account, we shall have to think about looking elsewhere for our supplies, because it really isn't convenient the way things are at the moment.'

Merrick met the challenge in her eyes and she saw anger, then a hint of amusement. 'Is Ben Smart staying on permanently?' he enquired. 'Or just until you get used to things?'

'Permanently,' she told him. 'And as you probably know, he's one of the best boatbuilders in west London.'

'Probably *the* best now that your uncle has gone,' he amended.

'Which is why I'm so hopeful for the future,' said Rachel in a definite tone. 'He could have got a job anywhere but he's chosen to stay with us.'

Merrick's stubby fingers stroked his chin as he considered her ultimatum. 'OK, you win,' he told her with a fat grin. 'We'll reopen your account. But if payment is so much as a day late, I'll be on your back so fast you'll wonder what's hit you.'

'I understand that,' she said, rising. 'And I'll make sure it doesn't happen.'

They chatted for a few minutes more, then she said she had to go. 'It was nice to meet you, Mr Merrick,' she said politely.

'You too,' he said, rising and walking to the door with her. 'The best of luck to you.'

'Thank you.'

As she crossed the yard to another outbreak of male appreciation, she heard a shout from the office window. 'Pack that in, lads,' came Syd Merrick's rough, booming tones. 'Show a little respect for the lady.'

Instant silence fell over the yard but Rachel was too buoyant with triumph to pay much attention. It was as much as she could do to stop herself leaping for joy when she stepped through the gates. She felt that she had won the account on her own merit and not just because Chip Banks was her uncle. Her confidence was so high, she went straight to one of their other suppliers from whom they brought such things as glue, paint and lacquer, and got their account reinstated there too.

Then she caught the bus to Putney, where she visited a regular customer, one of the larger rowing clubs, just to introduce herself and make sure they knew that Banks' Boats were still very much in business and likely to remain so in the future.

On both occasions she received a similar reaction to her gender to the one she had got from Syd Merrick. It made her even more determined to prove that a woman could run a boatbuilding business successfully.

By the time she got back to the office, yesterday's doubts were forgotten. She was under no illusions; she knew she still had a great many obstacles to overcome, but she was now confident that she had it in her to head this company. She felt like an intelligent woman with a job to do, rather than a gormless office junior with no hope of staying the course. The office routine she would learn in time. Now that she'd proved to herself that she had it in her to hold the reins of the firm, she knew the rest would come eventually.

'Sounds as though you went down a storm,' remarked Ben when she told him about her afternoon.

'I think I managed to convince them of our credibility,' she said cheerfully. 'You were right to suggest that I go out and introduce myself. It's made me feel a whole lot better. Thanks, Ben.'

'A pleasure,' he said, giving her a melting smile.

Over the next few weeks, Rachel made several more personal calls in her role as proprietor, though not all with such a successful outcome as the first ones.

One evening in April she went to an address in Barnes to see a man about an unpaid bill, leaving her visit until after working hours to make sure that he was home. The house was an ordinary semi in a quiet street.

'Mr Smith?' she said when the door was answered by a dark-haired man in a business suit.

'Yes,' he said enquiringly.

'Oh, good. My name is Rachel West. I've recently taken over from my uncle at Banks' Boats . . .' she began.

'Never heard of 'em,' he cut in quickly, in a tone that didn't invite argument.

'Oh, really? Well, you had a boat restored by us last year,' she continued, 'and our records show that we still haven't received the payment of fifty-five pounds.'

'You've got the wrong man,' he stated categorically. 'Boats aren't my thing.'

'But you definitely had work done on one by us last year,' she insisted, looking at her notes. 'I have all the details here.'

'Not me,' he said with cutting indifference.

A woman's voice drifted out from inside the house. 'Who is it, Brian?' she shouted.

'Just a canvasser, love,' he replied.

'Well, get rid of 'em,' she yelled. 'Your meal's on the table.'

'You heard what the lady said,' he told Rachel with a hard look. 'I've just got in from work after a hard day and I want my dinner. So piss off.'

'If you've a problem with the amount,' said the indomitable Rachel, 'perhaps we can come to some arrangement for it to be paid over a period of time.'

His dark eyes blackened with fury and he stepped out into the porch, pulling the door to behind him. 'What's the matter with you, have you got cloth ears or something?' he said in a rasping voice which he kept low so as not to attract the attention of his wife or the neighbours. 'I've told you, I know nothing about any boat, and I mean it. If you come round here pestering me again, I shall call the law.'

'And I'll tell them about the money you are cheating us out of,' she retorted.

'Oh, bugger off,' he said, then went inside and shut the door, leaving her with no option but to do as he said, feeling angry and frustrated and powerless to do any more.

'He said he'd never heard of Banks' and didn't know anything about any work on a boat,' Rachel reported back to Ben the next day, showing him the paperwork.

'He would say that, wouldn't he?' said Ben. 'The lying toad. I remember that job well. It stuck in my mind because the customer wasn't a boating type. He obviously wanted it restored so that he could sell it at a profit.'

'How come he got away with it at the time?' Rachel wanted to know.

'That was the way your uncle operated,' Ben explained. 'He took people on trust. Expected everyone to live by the same rules as he did. I don't know the details because it was Chip's job to get the money in. But the bloke probably promised to come back and pay another time and Chip believed him. Even if Chip had chased him for the money, he would have given him some excuse. Now that he's denying all knowledge, we'll have the devil's own job to get anything out of him.'

'That isn't right,' Rachel was appalled.

'No, but it happens in business if you let it,' he said. 'I was always telling Chip to be firmer with customers. But he did things his way and it wasn't my place to be too critical.'

'So what do I do now?' she asked.

'Some people are genuine and will pay the bill eventually if you keep on at them,' he told her. 'But I think it's probably best to employ a debt-collecting agency for people like Mr Smith.'

'The best way of all is not to let any work leave these premises until payment has been made and the cheque cleared,' she suggested.

'You're learning fast,' he told her.

'Seems as though I need to,' was her reply to that.

* * *

As the trees came into leaf along the riverside and the bitter winds turned to light spring breezes, Rachel continued to promote the boathouse with her personal visits. As well as visiting all the rowing clubs in and around their area, she also used public transport to go to places further afield, calling on boat-hire firms in areas as far out as Richmond and Windsor. She even went to the council parks department of various London boroughs with a view to getting a contract to supply and repair boats on boating lakes in the municipal parks.

She also finished her typing course and got to grips with Mrs Butler's filing system, as well as PAYE so that she could do the staff wages every week. When Mrs Butler did eventually retire, Rachel felt able to manage, though it did mean she had a very full day. But now that she could see the wood for the trees, she enjoyed the job enormously.

Despite her punishing work schedule, she wasn't in such a state of exhaustion when she collected the boys from Jan's in the evening as she had been after a day at the factory. On the contrary, the job revitalised her and she had enough energy left at the end of the day to enjoy her children.

Her meeting with the bank manager at the end of the three-month deadline was far less harrowing than the first one had been.

'Well,' he began, looking up from the file he'd been studying and smiling at her, 'I'm not usually glad to be proved wrong, but in this case I'm delighted.'

She smiled politely, waiting for him to go on.

'It wasn't that I doubted you personally, you understand,' he continued. 'But it seemed such an impossible task for anyone to take on, let alone someone with no business experience, that I questioned my own judgement in letting you do it.'

'I've been a little daunted myself at times,' she confessed.

'But you've succeeded,' he beamed, and she could hardly

recognise the stern man she had faced across this same desk three months ago. 'You've put Banks' Boats back into the black.'

'Yes, I know,' she said. 'I've been keeping a close eye on the account.'

'Well done,' he congratulated her.

'Thank you.' Although she felt a strong sense of personal achievement, she was very much aware of Ben's contribution. 'But it isn't all down to me. We work as a team at the boathouse.'

'Delighted to hear it, my dear,' he said, closing her file with a satisfied smile. 'Keep up the good work.'

'I intend to,' she said, rising to leave.

Because of the children, Rachel made it a rule never to work at weekends unless there was a crisis. But she did sometimes call in at the boathouse when she was out walking with Tim and Johnnie because Ben usually went in for a few hours on a Saturday and the boys thought he was terrific. Like most small boys they were keen on boats, especially Tim, who was mad about the river and anything to do with it.

When they discovered that Ben was the owner of the small blue and white motor boat called *Nipper* that was moored at the boathouse moorings, they wouldn't rest until he showed them inside the tiny cabin. Rachel had a look too. There was just enough room for a stove big enough to boil a kettle, a little sink, a bench seat and some shelves containing books about boats. The children loved it and Rachel thought it was sweet. Predictably the boys wanted to go for a trip in *Nipper*, and Ben didn't need much persuading.

It was on a sunny Saturday afternoon in early summer that Rachel and her sons, forced by Ben to wear lifejackets, went on a cruise into greener, leafier stretches of the river. They chugged past the wonderfully conspicuous Chinese Pagoda at Kew and the glorious trees of Syon Park, following the Thames' winding course out to Richmond, where they glided under the oldest bridge on London's river with its five arches and elegant balustrade. Ben moored the boat and they stopped for refreshments at a tea garden on the bank, Johnnie clutching the football he took everywhere with him in the hope of a game.

On the way back to Hammersmith, Johnnie asked Ben if he could help to steer the boat.

'Course you can't,' said his brother, who was standing next to Ben at the rudder.

'Why can't I?' persisted Johnnie.

'Because you're not big enough,' declared Tim with some authority. 'Little kids aren't allowed.'

'Come on, little 'un,' said Ben patiently, taking Johnnie's hand. 'You can hold the rudder with me for a minute.'

'Can I have a go next?' asked Tim.

'Yeah, go on then,' agreed Ben.

Sitting at the side of the boat by the rail, casually dressed in denim jeans and a white T-shirt, the sun feeling warm on her face and the breeze ruffling her hair, Rachel watched the three of them together. She was impressed by the patient way Ben dealt with her sons' relentless exuberance as well as the way he handled the craft with such a sure touch. There was something powerfully attractive about a man who was so physically capable, especially when he was tall and tanned with a mop of thick blond hair.

'You handle the boat like you've been doing it for ever,' she called to him.

'Not quite for ever, but I have had her for years,' he explained.

'Really?'

'Yeah. I got her cheap from a bloke who used to rent a mooring from Chip,' he explained. 'He wanted to get rid of her when he got too old to bother, so I snapped her up. She's just a water buggy really, but I enjoy having her.'

'She's handy for business too,' remarked Rachel.

'That's right,' he agreed. 'If I need to go to one of the

other boathouses to borrow some special tool or materials, it's quicker to go on the water.'

When they got back to the boathouse, Ben didn't go straight back to work and Rachel and the boys didn't go home. Instead they went for a walk along the riverside as far as Chiswick Mall, then came back and sat on a bench in Furnival Gardens eating ice creams. When they'd finished, Ben had a kick-about on the grass with the boys, who then played on their own while Rachel and Ben sat chatting, completely at ease in each other's company.

'I suppose I ought to be getting back to work.' He gave her a wicked grin. 'Or I'll have the boss after me.'

'On a Saturday afternoon? You're joking!'

'I was actually.'

'I should hope so too,' she said, smiling. 'Anyway, I hope you don't regard me as the boss. I prefer to think of us as two people who work alongside each other: a team.'

'That's nice of you to say so,' he told her. 'But when all is said and done, you are paying me to do a job.'

'Yeah, and you get on and do it without any sort of supervision from me,' she said lightly. 'Being on a manager's salary, you don't even get paid overtime.'

'I do get an annual bonus if the firm does well, though,' he reminded her. 'That's a good enough incentive to make me put in extra hours.'

She turned to him, looking serious. 'Is that really why you put in such a lot of hours?' she asked.

He shook his head. 'Not really, no,' he said, leaning back on the bench with his arms along the back and his long legs sprawled out in front of him. 'The bonus is more than welcome, of course. But I'm never happier than when I'm messing about with boats. I don't know if it makes me a workaholic, but I do enjoy working.'

'It's lucky I don't pay you by the hour,' she laughed, 'or I'd be bankrupt in no time.'

Something came into his eyes that she recognised because

she herself had experienced it many times since Jeff left. 'I've nothing much else to do at weekends, so I might as well do a bit at the boathouse.'

'Weekends can be difficult when you've been married and you're not any more, can't they?' she said impulsively, sensing that he wouldn't be offended by the personal nature of her comment. 'I know that only too well.'

'Yes, they can,' he agreed. 'Not so bad for you, though, because you have the boys for company.'

'Oh yes,' she said with great enthusiasm. 'And I love to be with them.'

'You have your family too,' he mentioned.

'Yes, I'm very lucky in that way.' She turned to him. 'Do you not have any family?'

'Chip was the nearest thing I had to it,' he said. 'And my wife, of course, before she left.'

'Am I allowed to ask if you and your wife parted on bad terms?' she enquired.

'Of course you're allowed to ask,' he said amiably. 'And the answer is, yes, we did part on bad terms. But we're good friends now. We get on better now than we ever did when we were married.'

'I suppose that's because the struggle of trying to make it work is over so you can be more relaxed with each other.' She paused. 'Are you divorced?'

'No, just separated,' he told her. 'We haven't got around to taking that final step yet.'

'Do you see much of each other?' she wondered.

'No,' he told her, 'but we keep in touch on the phone. We don't have any children to tie us together so we don't talk very often. But I'm glad we're on good terms. It's much more civilised that way.' He turned to look at her. 'How about you? Do you keep in touch with your ex?'

'Chance would be a fine thing,' she replied. 'I don't even know where he is. I haven't had so much as a postcard since he left.'

'You mean he doesn't even get in touch to find out how the boys are?' he said in astonishment.

'That's right,' she told him. 'He walked out of our lives nearly two and a half years ago and hasn't been heard of since. No contact, no financial support, nothing.'

'That's terrible.' Ben seemed genuinely concerned.

'Yeah, I think it's pretty disgraceful too,' she agreed, 'for someone to just turn their back on their responsibilities like that.'

'The man must be insane,' he opined.

'It was Cupid's dart, apparently,' she explained with a lingering hint of bitterness. 'A woman he worked with.'

'Ah, I see.'

'I was desperate for a long time after he went,' she confessed. 'But I've got used to being without him now. It still breaks my heart that he left his kids, though.'

'It's fortunate they weren't older and didn't have longer memories,' he said.

Rachel nodded. 'I console myself with that thought. I don't think they remember him at all. He wasn't the sort of dad to have much to do with his kids.'

'He's missing out on something very precious, in my opinion,' Ben commented.

'That's what I think,' she said. 'Still, that's people, isn't it? We all have different values, and Jeff's obviously aren't the same as mine.'

'Mm.'

'And having the business has made things a lot easier for me financially,' she went on chattily. 'At least I'm not struck with panic any more every time one of them needs some new item of clothing. I don't take a big salary out of the business, but I do pay myself enough to cope.'

'Sounds sensible.'

'If things go on as they are, it will get even better,' she predicted. 'If the firm does well, I can give myself a rise in salary.'

'We're holding our own then?' he said.

'Yes, we are.' She still kept a very close eye on the accounts and didn't allow any work to leave the premises without payment, except in very special circumstances. 'Things are beginning to come together nicely. Thanks to you.'

'Only doing my job,' he said modestly.

'No, Ben,' she corrected, leaning towards him without even realising she was doing it. 'You do a lot more than just your job. As well as working more hours than any employer could reasonably expect, you're always there for me with advice and moral support. You are the backbone of the company and this will be reflected in your bonus.'

'Thank you,' he said.

'Thank *you*,' she replied, touching his hand in a friendly gesture. 'And thanks, too, for this afternoon. It's been lovely, a real treat for the boys . . . and me.'

He gave her a broad smile. 'I've enjoyed it too,' he said. 'The boys are great fun.'

Returning his smile, she spoke on impulse. 'Maybe we could do it again some time,' she suggested.

A look passed between them. She recognised wariness in his eyes and guessed that he was reminding himself that she was his employer. 'I'm usually at the boathouse for part of the weekend anyway. So you know where to find me if you're out for a walk,' he told her, keeping it casual.

'OK,' she said, taking his lead. 'I'll keep that in mind.'

'Anyway,' he said, raising his arms in a long, lazy stretch, 'I really had better get back to work now.'

She found herself wanting to invite him to supper that evening. They were both on their own, so why not? But would he want to spend the evening in a cramped council flat with his employer and her two children? A good-looking bloke like him probably liked to hit the town on a Saturday night. And she wasn't in a position to join him in that. Having had the boys minded during the week while she was at work, she wouldn't leave them at the weekend unless there was an emergency. And Ben might be afraid to decline in case he offended her. So it was best not to encourage anything beyond a working friendship. It could cause all sorts of complications.

'Yes, I'd better be going too,' she said. 'I usually take the boys to Mum and Dad's place on a Saturday afternoon for tea. Jan and co. will be there, I expect. There's usually a gathering of the clans at Wilbur Terrace of a weekend. It's a bit hectic, but it's good fun.'

'Sounds nice,' he remarked, and she thought she detected a hint of wistfulness.

'See you on Monday, then,' he said as they stood up to go.

She paused, tempted again to invite him round for the evening. But good sense finally prevailed. 'Yes,' she said, already looking forward to it. 'See you on Monday.'

He said goodbye to Tim and Johnnie and walked towards the boathouse, a tall, athletic figure with a long, purposeful stride.

'He's very good at driving boats,' remarked Tim as they walked to Wilbur Terrace.

'Yeah,' agreed Johnnie enthusiastically.

'He's gonna teach me to drive the boat when I'm bigger,' announced Tim with a boastful air.

'And me,' said Johnnie.

'He's quite good at football, too,' said Tim.

'I know.' Johnnie was practically reverent.

'When are we going to see him again, Mum?' Tim asked Rachel, who was walking in between the two, holding each one firmly by the hand.

'I'm not sure,' she said.

'You could ask him if we could go out on his boat again,' he suggested hopefully.

'Yes, I could do that,' she said, drawing pleasure from the feel of their small hands clutching hers so trustingly. 'I'll speak to him about it next week.'

'I hope he says yes,' Johnnie chimed in.

'So do I,' added Tim.

'Depends how busy he is.' She didn't want to take anything for granted. 'But I'll see what I can do.'

'Thanks, Mum,' said Tim.

Since Jeff had left, Rachel had become an expert at simulating happiness for the boys' sake, but she didn't normally spend time studying her own feelings. She did know, though, that she hadn't felt this happy and positive in a very long time. And who wouldn't in her position? she asked herself. She had two fine, healthy boys, and a job she enjoyed within a business that was heading for success. She'd even put on a little weight now that she could afford to eat properly.

Things were so much better for the children now, too, because she wasn't so tired and fraught with financial worry the whole time. Now she didn't have to pretend to be cheerful because she really was, and she could feel this reflected in her offspring's behaviour. And to add to all of that, she had the friendship of a man she liked and admired. Was there, potentially, something more too? She couldn't be sure, but found herself liking the idea.

Apart from anything else, it was such a relief not to dread going to work on a Monday morning, she thought, heading towards Wilbur Terrace through the back streets behind Hammersmith Broadway. She could enjoy the weekend without the dark shadow of the factory hanging over her. She'd never thought she would ever look forward to going to work. But she did now. Life was good indeed.

Then, on Monday morning, she got a letter that threatened to change everything.

Chapter Six

'You don't seem your usual chirpy self this morning,' observed Ben when he went into Rachel's office with an estimate to be typed and found her staring gloomily into space. 'Everything all right? The boys OK?'

'The boys are fine,' she muttered, still preoccupied with her own thoughts. 'Thanks for asking, though.'

He replied with a shrug, putting the estimate form down on her desk. 'Well, you know where I am if you need someone to talk to,' he said, keeping it casual so as not to be intrusive.

'Actually, Ben, there is something I have to speak to you about.' She was alert now, and his eyes widened in concern at her serious tone of voice. 'But I think you'd better shut the door. This isn't for the staff's ears, not at this stage anyway.'

'Sounds ominous.'

'It is rather.'

Closing the door, he parked himself on a chair opposite her. 'So, what's the matter?' he enquired, noticing how strained she looked, the green tones in her eyes heightened by her pallor, which was all the more noticeable because she'd been looking so much happier and healthier lately.

'My cousin Arthur is legally contesting his father's will,' she announced without preamble.

'No!' Ben was shocked.

'Yeah, he's taking me to court to try and get the ownership of the boathouse transferred to him.'

'Why, the evil bugger!' His face was dark with disapproval. 'I've never thought much of Arthur, but I didn't think he would stoop so low as to go against his father's last wishes.'

'Me neither,' she confessed. 'He made it clear to me at the time that he wasn't happy about my inheriting the boathouse. Tried to make me agree to sign it over to him, and was livid when I refused. But as I didn't hear any more about it, I thought he must have accepted the situation.'

'He doesn't stand a chance of winning the case, does he?' Ben suggested tentatively.

'I shouldn't think so, as my uncle made it clear in his will that he wanted me to have it. But you can never tell with these things, can you?' she said. 'Arthur does have the advantage of being Uncle Chip's son, and he'll play that card for all it's worth. And – knowing him – he's probably cooked up some devious plan, too.' She paused, biting her lip. 'I want to be honest with you, Ben, because I can't completely rule out a victory for him, and if the worst happens the boathouse will go and all our hard work will have been wasted.'

'I'm sure it won't come to that,' Ben reassured her, but he couldn't hide his concern entirely.

'Arthur must think he has a good chance or he wouldn't have taken it to a solicitor,' Rachel pointed out. 'He isn't the sort of man to spend money lightly.'

'Mm, you do have a point. But why has he waited this long?' Ben wondered. 'Why didn't he do it at the time?'

'Perhaps it wasn't easy to find a solicitor willing to take the case,' guessed Rachel. 'Seeing as Uncle Chip's will was all legal and above board.'

'That's probably it,' agreed Ben. 'Bearing that in mind, I don't think he's got a leg to stand on.'

'Arthur's dead crafty, though,' she informed him. 'He'll have cobbled together some highly convincing story from a pack of lies.'

'I don't know much about these things,' Ben admitted, 'but in cases like this, don't people usually try to prove that the deceased wasn't in his right mind when he made the will?'

'I think so,' she said. 'But I've never had experience of anything like it before, so I'm not sure.'

'He'll be on to a loser if he tries that one, because everyone knows that Chip was as sound as a bell,' he pointed out.

'Yes, so he'll probably take the line that I used some sort of pressure to persuade my uncle to leave the boathouse to me,' Rachel told him. 'He's already made some pretty disgusting suggestions along those lines.'

'There's no shortage of people who will vouch for your character,' Ben assured her, deeming it polite not to ask exactly what Arthur's suggestions might have been. 'And I'll be willing to stand up in court and say that Chip and Arthur didn't get on, and anything else that might be helpful to you.'

'That's really good of you,' she thanked him warmly. 'But I don't want to drag you into it unless it's absolutely necessary.'

'It's in my interests to help.' He sounded very keen. 'Since my job's at stake.'

'That's why I thought you ought to know about it, especially as you're so closely involved with the firm. But I don't think it's worth unsettling the staff at this time,' she explained. 'They'll only need to know if Arthur does win the case. You can't be sure what might happen when you're dealing with someone as cunning as he is, especially if he's got a good solicitor.'

'Have you contacted yours?' he asked.

'I haven't had a chance yet,' she told him. 'I only got the letter this morning.'

'I should get on to that sharpish if I were you,' he advised her gravely.

'That'll be my first job when we've finished our chat,' she informed him.

'If there's anything I can do, anything at all, you only have to ask,' he offered. 'As I've already said, I'll be quite happy to speak up for you in court.'

'Thanks, Ben, that's worth a lot to me,' she said.

'Your family will give you plenty of moral support, too.' He was doing everything he could to keep her spirits up.

'By the bucketload, I should think,' she confirmed. 'They don't know anything about it yet. I was too gutted by the letter to mention it to Jan this morning when I dropped the boys off.'

Ben seemed thoughtful. 'Is it worth your going to see Arthur?' he suggested. 'To try to persuade him not to go ahead?'

She shook her head. 'Not unless I'm prepared to sign the business over to him,' was her firm belief. 'That's the only thing that will stop him going through with it. He wants this site and is determined to get it.'

'I expect you're right.'

'If I thought he should have the boathouse, I'd give it to him like a shot,' she confided. 'I wouldn't want to keep something I didn't truly believe was mine.'

'Course you wouldn't.' He was wholly supportive. 'So you just stick to your guns.'

'I intend to,' she assured him. 'It's a bit scary, though, the idea of having to go to court. I've never been inside one of those places in my life.'

'When does the case come up?' he asked.

'Not until August, unfortunately,' she informed him. 'Although I'm dreading it, I'd rather get it over with instead of having it hanging over me for the next three months.'

'I think I would too,' he said. 'You'll just have to try to put it out of your mind and concentrate on the job.'

Heartened by his positive attitude and the lack of any suggestion of their slowing down in case they lost everything to Arthur, she said, 'You're right. I'm not going to let this development affect my attitude towards the boathouse. I'm absolutely determined that Arthur isn't going to steal it from me.'

'That's the spirit,' Ben encouraged, full of admiration for

her. 'Don't forget to let me know if there's anything I can do.'

Because she'd been made to feel particularly vulnerable by this latest blow, his heartfelt kindness and support moved her unbearably. 'Thanks, Ben,' she breathed, lowering her eyes so that he wouldn't see that they were brimming with tears. 'I'll keep you posted.'

'I'd appreciate that,' he said, and rose to leave.

Rachel was more worried about the court case than she was letting on, Ben thought, as he went back into the workshop and checked the work of an apprentice who was working with copper rivets on a fours boat.

Arthur Banks was big trouble and always had been as far as Ben could see. He'd watched Arthur hurt and humiliate his father over the years. Now he was about to do the same thing to his cousin, a woman Ben liked, admired and instinctively wanted to protect. If he wasn't so certain that any intervention from him would make matters worse, he would pay Arthur Banks a visit himself.

Her parents' reaction that evening to the news of the court case was stronger than Rachel had expected.

'But Arthur can't do that,' protested Marge, facing her daughter across the kitchen table, out of earshot of the boys, who were kicking a ball about in the garden. 'The boathouse was left to you legally. He can't reverse that.'

'He thinks he can, apparently,' Rachel told them. 'He believes it should have gone to him as a matter of course because he's Chip's son.'

'If he'd treated his father decently it probably would have,' was Marge's answer to that. 'But we all know that he didn't, so he doesn't deserve it.'

'He's prepared to cast doubt on his father's judgement in a court of law just to get his own way,' said Ron in disgust. 'He always was a greedy little devil, even as a boy.'

'Mm,' agreed Rachel.

'Why can't he just respect his father's wishes and leave things be?' questioned Marge.

'That isn't Arthur's way, is it?' Rachel reminded them. 'He's determined to get what he thinks is his by right.' She paused. 'When he was giving me a hard time about it, I told him to contest the will if he wasn't happy. I never dreamed he would actually go ahead and do it.'

'Well, I shall have a thing or two to say to him about it, don't worry,' proclaimed Marge, anxiety blotches suffusing her face and neck.

'Don't do that, Mum,' Rachel advised her. 'You'll only upset yourself and you won't achieve anything. He's obviously set on doing this, and a dressing-down from you won't stop him.'

'I don't see what he can achieve,' said Ron. 'I mean, the will was done properly and witnessed by the solicitor.'

'I went to see Mr Brayford today,' Rachel informed them. 'He thinks that Arthur will try to make out that I deliberately persuaded Uncle Chip to leave the boathouse to me.' She didn't go on to tell her parents about Arthur's perverse suggestions, because she knew it would upset them even further.

'That's terrible.' Marge looked stricken. 'As if you'd do a thing like that.'

'Such a thing would never even have occurred to me.' She spread her hands expressively. 'I was very fond of Uncle Chip but I was never that close to him. I was bowled over when Mr Brayford told me I'd inherited the boathouse.'

'We know that, dear,' her mother assured her sympathetically.

'There's no need to look quite so worried, Mum.' Rachel gave her mother's hand a reassuring squeeze across the table. 'Arthur won't get away with it. I'll make damned sure he doesn't.'

'Win or lose, you'll still be dragged through the courts,' Marge pointed out. 'That's what's upsetting me.'

'Me an' all,' muttered her father.

'I'm not thrilled about it either,' admitted Rachel. 'But at least this way it'll get it settled once and for all. Once the court has made its decision, Arthur will have to accept it and leave me alone. It'll be worth going to court just for that.'

'It's not right, though,' grunted Ron.

'No, it isn't,' his wife agreed hotly.

'Calm down, you two,' intervened Rachel, feeling guilty now for worrying them. 'I wouldn't have told you if I'd known you'd get so steamed up about it.'

'I hope you don't mean that,' admonished Marge. 'We're a family; we share the good and the bad things.'

'Yeah, course we do, and I didn't really mean it.' Rachel stood up. 'But I'd better be going. I have to get those boys of mine home to bed.'

'I'll go and fetch them from the garden.' Marge seemed very preoccupied as she disappeared out of the back door.

Watching her retreating back, Rachel could tell from the rigid set of her shoulders that she was really suffering over this. That was the caring mother she was. Her children were everything to her, even though they were grown up.

As soon as the door had closed behind Rachel and the boys, Marge turned to her husband and said, 'We can't let Arthur do this to her, Ron.'

'No, we can't,' he agreed, following her into the living room and sitting down heavily in an armchair.

'He's not going to get away with it,' she declared in a fiery tone, absently picking up the mugs and plates the children had been using.

'I could go and see him . . . try to make him see sense,' suggested Ron.

'Do you think he'd take any notice of you?' Marge's face was pinched with worry. 'Of course he wouldn't.'

'I s'pose not,' he sighed, scratching his head and frowning. 'But I don't know what else to suggest.'

'There's only one thing we can do to get this court case stopped,' she announced, becoming suddenly decisive. 'And we both know what that is.'

'Oh, Marge.' Ron's brow was deeply furrowed, his eyes full of dread. 'There must be some other way.'

'There isn't.' She was adamant about it. 'Unless we are prepared to let Rachel go through the trauma of court proceedings and maybe lose her business, we simply don't have a choice.'

He sat in silent contemplation for a few moments. 'You're right,' he agreed at last.

'Why have we been invited to Mum and Dad's on Friday night without the children?' Jan asked her sister a few days later.

'Search me,' replied Rachel. 'I thought you might know. It's all very mysterious, especially the children not being invited.'

'Mum says it's an adult thing,' said Jan. 'She suggested that Pete look after the kids. It isn't imperative that he's there, apparently. Tim and Johnnie can stay overnight at our place to save you dragging them out late at night, if you like.'

'OK, that'd be great, thanks,' said Rachel.

'There isn't some special occasion we've forgotten, is there?' queried Jan, looking puzzled. 'A birthday or wedding anniversary or anything?'

'I've already thought about that,' Rachel told her. 'And I don't know of anything.'

'I've never known their beloved grandchildren to be excluded from a family occasion before,' mentioned Jan.

'It isn't like Mum at all,' agreed Rachel.

'When I asked her why, she muttered something about it being too late for them to be up,' said Jan.

'It's never mattered before,' Rachel pointed out.

'That's what I thought,' agreed Jan. 'It's really weird.' She gave her sister a wicked grin. 'They must be planning on telling us something that isn't for little ears.'

'You don't think one of them has got some illness, do you?' suggested Rachel anxiously.

'No, we'd have noticed something, seeing them as often as we do,' Jan pointed out.

'That's true.' The relief of that fact inspired Rachel to lighten the mood. 'Perhaps Mum's having a menopausal baby,' she suggested jokingly.

'Or maybe she's found out that Dad's got a mistress,' grinned Jan.

'And as both those things are about as likely as the wedding of the Pope, what on earth can it be?' Rachel wondered.

The atmosphere was fraught with tension when the two sisters arrived at their parents' home on Friday evening. Both Mum and Dad seem very het up, Rachel thought, and was even more curious as to what could be causing them so much stress.

'Thanks for coming, girls,' said Marge, who was ashen-faced, though her neck was red and blotchy. She handed round coffee and biscuits.

'Well, don't look so doom-laden, Mum,' said Rachel in an effort to lighten the mood. 'A night out without the kids is no hardship to us.'

'We are wondering what it's all about, though,' said her forthright sister.

'Well, it isn't exactly a social gathering,' Marge informed them in a high-pitched voice as she sat down on the edge of an armchair, her husband perching on the arm.

'Oh dear,' said Jan. 'This is beginning to sound serious.'

'It is,' confirmed Marge.

'Don't keep us in suspense then,' urged Rachel, who was ensconced on the sofa with Jan.

Marge studied her fingernails for a moment, her hands trembling slightly. 'We've asked you both here because we have something to tell you,' she said, looking up. 'And we want you to hear it together because it affects you both.'

'Get on with it then, for goodness' sake, Mum,' urged Jan, sipping her coffee.

Clasping her hands tightly together, Marge began to speak in dry worried tones. 'This dreadful business of Arthur contesting his father's will has made it necessary for certain facts to be made known to you both,' she informed them. 'Facts that I shall reveal to Arthur once you've been told so that he will realise that he simply doesn't have a case and will stop the whole thing.'

'What facts?' asked Rachel, beginning to get really worried now.

'Yeah, what's going on?' added Jan.

'Arthur is angry and embittered because his father left the boathouse to his niece rather than his son,' Marge continued. 'He sees the boathouse as his right.'

'It suits him to think that,' Rachel put in.

'And you were both very surprised when Rachel inherited the boathouse from her uncle, weren't you?' Marge continued.

They both nodded. 'Of course,' replied Rachel. 'It was a shock to us all.'

'Yes, it was, but although Dad and I weren't actually expecting it, we weren't quite as surprised as you were about Chip's choice of beneficiary.' She paused, swallowing hard and looking at Rachel. 'Because . . . you see, we know the reason why my brother chose to leave his most valuable possession to you, Rachel.'

'Yeah, you told me. Because I was the only one in the family struggling to make ends meet,' Rachel reminded her.

'I only said that because I didn't have the courage to tell you the real reason,' Marge confessed, her eyes heavy with shame.

'What *are* you getting at, Mum?' Rachel wanted to know.

'I think my brother would have left his business to you whatever your circumstances,' she said grimly.

'Why?' asked Rachel.

The older woman stared at the floor, her breathing loud

and erratic. 'Chip wasn't your uncle,' she said, fixing her gaze on Rachel. 'He was your father!'

Into the horrified silence that followed, Rachel heard herself say in a broken voice, 'Incest?'

'No, no, of course not,' Marge hastened to make clear.

'But if your brother is my father and you're my mother, how can it be otherwise?'

Marge put both hands to her head, looking tortured. 'Isn't it obvious, dear?' she asked.

'Well, no . . .' For a moment Rachel was too confused to work it out. 'Not unless you mean . . .'

'That's right,' Marge blurted out in an agonised tone. 'I'm not your mother, not in the biological sense anyway.'

Reeling from the shock, Rachel felt sick and disorientated, a cold sweat seeming to suffuse her whole body. She looked from one to the other of the people she had always believed to be her parents. 'You mean that neither of you . . .' She paused, hardly able to get the words out. 'You're telling me that you're not my parents at all.'

Her equally stunned sister put a comforting hand on her arm. 'Steady on, sis,' she said.

'But I'm not your sis, am I? Not according to them,' snapped Rachel, bewildered and distraught. 'We don't have the same parents, so we're not sisters.'

'Technically you're cousins,' explained Marge. 'But you're sisters in every other way.'

Rachel combed her fringe back from her brow with her fingers, closing her eyes with the horror of it all. 'So this makes me Arthur's sister,' she whispered.

Marge and Ron gave a simultaneous nod.

'I can't believe this is happening to me,' groaned Rachel, pressing her fingers to her throbbing temples. 'I came here tonight believing I was part of a family . . .'

'And you *are* part of a family!' Marge burst out, desperate to ease the pain she knew her belated confession had caused.

'You're still our daughter, whatever the biology of it.'

'Oh, please,' snapped Rachel, too deeply hurt to consider Marge's feelings. 'Don't insult my intelligence by coming out with that sort of claptrap. Facts are facts. No amount of pretty words will change them.'

'In our hearts, I mean,' Marge told her in a small voice.

'There's more to being a parent than giving birth,' added Ron, slipping a comforting arm around his wife's shoulders. 'As you very well know, being a mother yourself.'

The fact that they were both in pain registered with Rachel, but she didn't have the emotional reserves to help them at this moment of great trauma to herself. 'So, if you're not my mother,' she said, looking at Marge, 'who is?'

'Her name was Doris Dunn,' Marge informed her.

'Doris Dunn,' repeated Rachel through dry lips. 'And how come I've lived for nearly twenty-seven years without knowing of her existence?'

'It's a long story,' said Marge.

'The sooner you start telling it the better, then.' Her tone was sharp.

'Now then, there's no call to be rude,' admonished Ron, tightening his hold on his wife protectively.

Marge raised her hand to him in a halting gesture and began speaking to Rachel. 'Chip was nineteen when his girlfriend got pregnant with you and her father threw her out,' said Marge. 'She was only sixteen and she didn't have anywhere to go, so Ron and I took her in.'

'Uncle Chip didn't want to marry her, then?' Rachel interrupted in a dull voice.

'He was away fighting for his country by the time she realised she was pregnant, so he didn't know anything about it,' she explained.

'Surely she could have written to him,' Rachel pointed out.

'She was just a kid herself,' said Marge. 'The poor girl didn't know which way to turn. She didn't want Chip to feel he had to marry her when he came back, *if* he came back. He couldn't have got home in time to save her reputation anyway, and they hadn't been planning to get married at that time. She left it to us to tell him about the baby after she'd gone away.'

'She went off . . . ?'

'Hear me out, please, Rachel,' requested Marge, feeling braver now that the truth was actually out. 'Had the circumstances been different, I've no doubt that Chip would have married her and we wouldn't be having this conversation now,' she continued. 'Chip wasn't the sort of man to let a girl down. But, as I've said, your mother was very young, and neither of them were ready for marriage.'

Rachel looked from Marge to Ron, waiting to hear the rest of the story.

'Whereas Ron and I had a home and a stable family life . . . well, as stable as anything could be back in those wartime days,' Marge continued. 'Ron had some sort of fault with his eardrum so didn't pass the medical to go into the services and was working in a munitions factory quite close to home. I couldn't have any more children because of complications when I had Jan, but I wanted another child very much. So we made an arrangement with Doris to bring you up as our own so that she could go off and get on with her life.'

'Very cosy,' said Rachel bitterly.

'Don't be like that, dear,' urged Marge. 'We did what we thought was right. And times were very different back then.'

'So, what happened to my . . .' Rachel couldn't bring herself to utter the word. 'What happened to Doris Dunn?' she managed at last.

'I've no idea,' replied Marge. 'She left as soon as she was strong enough after the birth.'

'Did she never get in touch?' Rachel's sense of rejection was hardly bearable. 'Not even to find out how her child was getting on?'

'We'd agreed that she wouldn't,' explained Marge. 'A clean

break was best for us all, especially you. They insist on that in legal adoptions and we thought it sensible to follow their guidelines. If we were to be good parents, we needed to be able to get on with the job without interference. We couldn't risk having you unsettled later on by a change of heart on Doris's part.'

'Uncle Chip couldn't cut himself off from me, though, could he?'

'No, he couldn't,' Marge admitted frankly. 'When he came home and we told him who you were, he was shocked, naturally, but glad that you were in good hands. It must have been hard for him to take a back seat, but he did so because he thought it was the right thing for you. Although to you he was your uncle, I believe he always thought of you as his daughter. Leaving his business to you was obviously his way of showing that.'

'In a nutshell, then,' said Rachel in a sour tone, 'my real parents had their fun and left you holding the baby, literally.'

'I know that's how it must seem to you, but it wasn't like that at all,' Marge contradicted. 'We loved and wanted you. I was older than Chip, with a home and a good husband. I truly believed that Ron and I could give you a better life than Doris and Chip could have done at that time. Doris wouldn't have stood a chance in those days, the way people were about that sort of thing.'

Rachel's thoughts were in chaos. There were so many questions she had to ask even though she dreaded the answers. 'How did you . . . I mean, I remember seeing my birth certificate when I got married. It had your names on it as my parents.'

They both looked sheepish. 'We registered you as ours,' confessed Ron.

'But that's illegal,' she exclaimed.

'Course it is,' admitted Marge. 'But it didn't seem as though we were doing anything wrong at the time.'

'It was easier to get away with things like that in those

days,' Ron put in. 'People solved their problems in their own way.'

'Yeah,' added Marge. 'With the chaos of war and people coming and going and wondering if they'd live to see another day, things like that weren't noticed so much as they are today. The only person besides us who knew the truth was the midwife, and she turned a blind eye. As I've said, we all thought it was the best thing.'

'It was the best thing for Doris, you mean,' said Rachel. 'She just wanted shot of me.'

'No, Rachel,' corrected Marge, her tone more admonishing now. 'It wasn't like that at all. Ask yourself, how could she have kept you under the circumstances?'

'Plenty of women manage it,' Rachel pointed out. 'She wasn't the first woman to get herself knocked up. They don't all just dump their babies on to someone else to bring up.'

'She didn't just dump you. She handed you over to us because we wanted you,' insisted Marge, her eyes now brimming with tears. 'And we couldn't have loved you more if you were our own.'

'I'm not your own though, am I?' said Rachel. 'I'm not your flesh and blood.'

'No, you're not,' Marge was forced to admit, wincing with the pain of speaking the truth she had kept locked away for so many years.

'We've always thought of you as our own, though,' added Ron.

'And you made sacrifices for me, I know that,' said Rachel emphatically. 'But that only makes me feel worse.'

'Why?' asked Ron.

'How do you think it makes me feel knowing that I wasn't your responsibility yet you still had to do all those things for me?' she asked, her voice breaking.

'You *were* our responsibility,' persisted Marge. 'And a welcome one at that.'

'Oh, God.' Rachel put her hand to her head. 'I'm not sure

what I feel about anything at the moment,' she said. 'Everything's changed. You're not my parents, Jan isn't my sister.' She looked at Marge and Ron through a blur of tears. 'You're not even my sons' grandparents.'

'Calm down, Rachel,' intervened Jan, who had been quietly listening up until now. 'Can't you see how upset Mum is?'

'I'm not about to dance a jig myself,' said Rachel, who wasn't normally sarcastic.

'I'm sorry we've had to hurt you in this way,' Marge went on. 'But the truth had to come out to stop Arthur going ahead with the court case. As Chip's eldest child, you have more right to the boathouse than Arthur, and would have even if it hadn't been left to you. So that squashes Arthur's claim altogether.'

'Thank God for Arthur, then,' was Rachel's response to that. 'I might never have got to know otherwise.'

'Would that have been such a terrible thing?' Marge suggested tentatively.

The enormity of the situation overwhelmed Rachel. 'Of course it would. Don't you think I had a right to know?'

'Chip didn't want you to be told,' explained Ron. 'And we felt we had to respect his wishes.'

'Too ashamed to have his dark secret come out into the open, I suppose,' she said harshly.

'No, it wasn't that,' corrected Marge. 'I think he would have loved to claim you as his daughter, especially when his wife left him and took their only child with her. But he believed you'd be better off if things were left as they were. You were happy as our daughter and he wanted it to stay that way.'

'He certainly put the cat among the pigeons leaving the boathouse to me, though,' Rachel remarked.

'He wasn't to know that Arthur would take things this far,' Marge pointed out.

'I should have been told as soon as I became of an age to understand such things,' proclaimed Rachel. 'Surely everyone has the right to know who they are.'

'I quite agree,' said Marge mildly. 'And I often said as much to Chip. But he wouldn't hear of it. "If it ain't broke, don't fix it" was his motto. When you were little it didn't seem to matter, but when you grew up I had many a sleepless night worrying about it and often thought we should tell you. After Chip died, I thought I should say something, but couldn't quite find the courage.'

'Well, now you have told me, good and proper,' declared Rachel, standing up, her legs weak and shaky. 'And it feels like hell. I shall have to go home.'

'Don't go like this,' begged Marge. 'Not while you're still so upset.'

'I have to go, I need to be on my own for a while, Mum.' Rachel stopped, looking at Marge through narrowed eyes. 'But I suppose I shouldn't call you that now, should I?' She was hurting and wanted to hurt back. 'Should I call you Auntie Marge?'

'That's enough, Rachel. There's no call to speak to Mum like that,' said Jan, fiercely protective of her mother. 'I realise that you've had one hell of a shock, and you've every right to be upset. But Mum and Dad have always done what they thought was right for you, for us both, you know that.'

Rachel brushed a tired hand over her damp brow. She felt like an outsider, as though they were all against her. She was vaguely aware that she was behaving badly but seemed to have lost control. 'Look, it's best if I go home now before I upset you all even more.' She looked at Jan. 'Is it still all right if I leave the boys at your place for the night? I need to be on my own.'

'Of course,' affirmed Jan.

Turning to Marge, Rachel spoke emotionally, her eyes wet with tears. 'Look, I don't want to hurt you, and I know I'm not handling this as well as I might. But all I can think of is that you haven't been honest with me, and it's tearing me apart. That's why I have to go home now.'

'At least let's talk about it,' Marge implored her.

'I can't, not now,' sobbed Rachel, shaking her head. 'I really have to go.'

'If you must, then go,' sighed Marge dejectedly.

'I'll see you all tomorrow,' said Rachel, and fled from the house.

'She'll come round, Mum,' said Jan, breaking the terrible silence that followed Rachel's departure.

'Will she, though?' said Marge, holding her head and pacing the room.

'Course she will,' Ron assured her. 'Don't worry, love. She'll be round here tomorrow as always on a Saturday.'

'She'll come round here, I don't doubt that,' Marge told him. 'But will it ever be the same again? Will she feel the same way about us now she knows the truth?'

'I don't know much about these things, but I should think she's bound to be traumatised for a while,' suggested Jan. 'It's been a shock for her – for me as well, to be honest. It's an odd feeling to know she isn't really my sister at all. And if I feel like that, just imagine what she must be going through.'

'You don't feel any different towards her, though, do you?' said Marge.

'I'm not sure how I feel,' was Jan's honest answer to that. 'I don't love her any the less. But I do feel kind of disappointed that she isn't my sister.'

'Oh dear,' sighed Marge, sinking into a chair with her head in her hands. 'What have we done, Ron?'

'Nothing we can't put right,' he said reassuringly.

'We should have insisted that she was told the truth as soon as she was old enough,' Marge muttered worriedly. 'We should have forced Chip to let us tell her.'

'There's no point in going over what we should have done,' Ron observed wisely. 'We have to concentrate on the situation as it stands, and work out what we can do to put things right.'

'I don't think there's anything you can do, not at the moment,' Jan told them. 'This is something she'll have to come to terms with herself. If she's the woman I think she is, she'll forgive you for not telling her because she loves you and knows what good parents you've been to her.'

'I hope she doesn't turn away from us,' said Marge fearfully. 'I couldn't bear to lose her.'

'You won't lose her.' Jan was confident. 'Rachel wouldn't let a thing like that happen. She's upset, that's all. She isn't heartless.'

The flat felt empty and lifeless without the boys when Rachel got home. Although she'd wanted to be on her own, now she regretted the fact that they weren't here. If it wasn't for the fact that it wouldn't be fair to drag them out of bed, she would have gone to Jan's this minute and brought them home. She wanted them with her, to hold them and feel close to them. They, at least, were true blood relations.

Of course, she reminded herself, she was actually related to Marge by blood, albeit much further removed than she'd always believed, though there was no blood tie between herself and Ron, who was just related by marriage. She made herself a mug of coffee and sat in the armchair, staring into space and trying to crystallise her perception of the revelations, without success. Maybe it was the shock, but the whole thing seemed unreal. The woman she had known as mother was her aunt, and her sister was her cousin. It was bizarre!

She tried to be objective. Did it matter who had actually given birth to her? she asked herself. Her intellect told her that it didn't. It was the caring that mattered. And in all honesty, she couldn't recall a time when she'd ever been made to feel different from Jan. She'd certainly never felt any the less loved. Family life had always been so normal, a mixture of laughter and tears and the boringly ordinary, like most other families.

Maybe that was why it was so painful to find out that she wasn't really one of them, because they had always been so close. Yes, that was what really hurt, the fact that she wasn't one of them. Ironically, the one thing in her life she'd always taken for granted was something she could never have. She wondered how Marge and Ron had managed to keep things so evenly balanced between herself and Jan, for surely it was nature's way for a mother to love her own child more than someone else's.

She could only put it down to their strong sense of commitment. They weren't the sort of people to do anything by halves. They must have conditioned themselves from the start to think of her as their own daughter. But she wasn't, and, try as she might, she couldn't make it hurt any the less.

That she owed them everything, she was in no doubt. By all accounts, she wouldn't have had much of a life if her real mother had kept her. But at least things would have been as nature intended. And that was at the heart of her anger – the rejection by Doris Dunn.

No matter how justified or how right for Rachel it had been, the fact that she had been given away hurt to the depths of her consciousness. She couldn't help it. As a mother herself, she simply couldn't imagine such a thing. The mere thought of doing that to Tim or Johnnie was unthinkable.

Recalling the wounded look in Marge's eyes earlier when she herself had rushed off, she loathed her own self-pity, and knew in her heart that she wasn't being fair to the people who had done so much for her. They were wrong not to have told her the truth a long time ago, there was no doubt in her mind about that. But what was one mistake weighed against a lifetime of loving care? Her filial feeling for Marge and Ron had never been more poignant than it was at that moment, and she wanted to weep with love for them.

Although she knew she wouldn't sleep, she went to bed and lay staring into the dark, trying to calm herself and make some sense of it all. But there was too much raw feeling for rational thought. She felt ravaged by events, and unable to cope with this huge emotional upheaval.

Then, suddenly, through all the agonising complications

that now filled her life, she knew one thing for certain. No matter how bad she might feel tomorrow, there was something she must do. The night seemed endless as she waited, wakefully, for it to pass.

Chapter Seven

Seeing the signs of a sleepless night on Jan's face when she opened the door to her the next morning, Rachel's compunction was exacerbated. She shouldn't have stormed off like that, leaving everybody upset.

'Sorry I rushed away last night.' The two women managed to snatch a few minutes on their own in the kitchen, Rachel having greeted the boys and left them with Kelly and Pete in the living room.

'It was understandable.' Jan noticed the dark shadows under Rachel's eyes. Her face was almost as pale as the white T-shirt she was wearing with a short summer skirt. 'You don't look as though you've had any more sleep than I have.'

'I don't think I'll ever sleep again after a revelation like that,' Rachel told her.

'I'm still reeling from it myself.' Jan spooned instant coffee into some mugs and got the milk out of the fridge. 'Who would have thought that a family as mundane as ours would have such a steamy secret hidden away?'

'It would be a nice juicy bit of scandal for us to chew over if I wasn't the subject of it,' said Rachel wryly.

'Yeah.' Dressed in a pale blue candlewick dressing gown, her hair still tousled from bed, Jan looked at Rachel. 'Look, kid, I don't know what to say . . .'

'Don't worry about it.' She pushed her fringe from her brow, sighing. 'There isn't much you can say, really. It's a weird feeling to discover that everything you've always believed in isn't true; that your whole life has been a lie.'

Jan made the coffee and they sat at the table drinking it. 'Does it really matter so terribly much, though?' she wondered. 'After all, Mum and Dad brought you up, cared for you.'

'That isn't in question,' Rachel affirmed quickly.

'They are your parents and I'm your sister, whatever the biological truth of the matter,' Jan continued.

'The truth does exist, though,' Rachel reminded her. 'I can't just forget about it.'

'No, I don't suppose you can,' agreed Jan in a thoughtful tone. 'But I've been awake most of the night thinking about it, and I honestly can't remember either Mum or Dad ever treating the two of us any differently. Can you?'

'I've never been aware of any favouritism,' admitted Rachel. 'But it must have been a conscious thing on their part not to show it. It would have been there, it's only natural.'

'Not necessarily,' Jan disagreed. 'They say they always loved you like their own, and I believe them.'

'Maybe they did. That isn't really the issue.' Rachel sipped her coffee. 'Whatever their true feelings, they *did* make a good job of bringing me up, and I owe them. So the first thing I must do is go and make my peace with them, after some of the hurtful things I said last night.'

'They'll be pleased about that,' approved Jan.

'I'm going to push my luck now as your sister,' began Rachel with a wry grin, 'and ask you if you could do me a favour and hang on to the boys for a bit longer while I go and sort things out at Wilbur Terrace.'

'Course I will.' Jan didn't hesitate. 'Anything that'll help get things back to normal is fine with me.'

'I don't think it can ever be normal again, not in the same way as it was,' stated Rachel.

The lack of sleep caught up with Jan suddenly and she yawned heavily. 'I don't see why not,' she uttered drowsily.

'Life'll be pretty miserable for us all if it isn't.'

'Face the facts, Jan,' urged Rachel in a tone of mild admonition. 'How can anything be the same when I'm not the person we thought I was?'

'You're making more of this than there actually is,' warned Jan, shaking her head worriedly. 'OK, so your parents aren't who we thought they were, but you're still the same person, still the woman I've shared my life with for nearly twenty-seven years. The fact that you didn't actually spring from Mum's womb doesn't make any difference to what you and I have, what we all have as a family.'

'But I'm not actually one of the family now, am I?' Rachel insisted.

'Oh, don't be so ridiculous.' Jan was impatient now. 'It'll take more than some technicality to alter your place in the family. It's the person you are that matters, not where you came from. You're overdramatising the whole thing.'

As Jan's attitude registered fully, Rachel realised that no one else could be expected to share her own perception of this matter or understand how discarded and displaced she felt; not even her soul-mate, Jan, the person who probably knew her better than anyone else. No matter how supportive the family tried to be, she was on her own with this one. And it wouldn't be fair to constantly seek reassurance from them or let them know how awful she was feeling. 'We're still sisters, then?' she said with false levity.

'Still sisters,' confirmed Jan, reaching across the table and taking her hand. 'Mates as well as sisters. It's what you feel inside that counts.'

Like any normal siblings, they'd had their ups and downs, with no shortage of rivalry, especially in their teenage years. Even now they didn't always see eye to eye. But there was a strong bond between them and Rachel couldn't bear the idea of losing that. 'I'm glad you feel that way,' she said, struggling to hold back the tears.

The atmosphere was tense and delicate, the air fraught with

raw emotions. 'If you think I can do without a sister after all this time, you can think again,' said Jan thickly.

With one accord they stood up and rushed into each other's arms in a tearful effusion.

Jan blew her nose. 'There is one good thing about your not knowing the truth when you were little,' she said in an effort to lighten the mood with humour.

'Is there?' sniffed Rachel.

'If you'd known that Arthur was your brother, it might have ruined your childhood,' she said through a mixture of laughter and tears. 'That's enough to give any sane person serious psychological problems.'

Rachel managed a brave attempt at a smile. 'At least he's only my half-brother,' she hastened to point out.

'You don't feel differently towards him now that you know the truth, then?' queried Jan.

'Of course not.'

'Which proves my point,' Jan wanted to emphasise. 'Bonding comes from mutual affection and respect over a long period, which is why you and I will always be sisters and you and Arthur will never be siblings in any emotional sense.'

'I know all that.' Although Jan's homespun philosophy was a comfort, it couldn't repair the damage to Rachel's self-esteem that the knowledge of her abandonment had caused. She didn't believe anything could.

'Sorry about last night, Mum,' Rachel blurted out, giving her mother a warm hug as soon as she opened the door to her. 'I shouldn't have gone off in a huff like that.'

'You were upset.' Looking pale and tired, Marge plodded along the hall to the kitchen with Rachel following. 'It must have been a terrible shock for you.'

'I can't remember having a worse one,' was Rachel's candid reply.

Marge put the kettle on for coffee, explaining that Ron

had had to go to work at the factory because of a rush job. Rachel was rather glad they were on their own. Although Ron was a part of all this, the emotional side was primarily a mother and daughter thing. As long as she put things right with Marge, he would be happy.

'I really am very sorry we didn't tell you the truth before,' confessed Marge, standing stiffly by the cooker waiting for the kettle to boil while Rachel sat down at the table. 'I wish to God I'd been firmer with Chip about it.'

'I'd be lying if I said I think you were right not to tell me when I reached an age of understanding,' Rachel said frankly. 'But I realise that you had your reasons. Anyway, there's no point in my going on about it, as we can't turn the clock back.'

'No.'

'Some little part of me wishes I'd never found out,' Rachel told her.

'I feel like that too, if I'm perfectly honest,' admitted the older woman. 'It would have been a lot less painful for you that way.'

'Coming at this late stage, it's harder to take than if I'd grown up knowing about it,' Rachel tried to explain. 'And I can't just blank it out and pretend that nothing's happened.'

'It doesn't have to change anything between us, though, does it?' said Marge fearfully. 'I really have always thought of you as my own daughter, you know.'

'Yeah, I know.' Rachel's tone was warm. 'I've been thinking back to when Jan and I were children . . . all the happy times.'

'There were plenty of those,' said Marge mistily. 'I'm glad this hasn't clouded your memory of them.'

'Nothing could ever do that.' She paused. 'But tell me . . . why didn't you go through the proper channels when you took me on?' she asked. 'Surely you could have registered me with the truthful facts and then adopted me legally.'

'We thought we might run into complications if we did that,' Marge explained. 'We were afraid you'd get taken into care while they sorted out all the red tape.' She paused, looking grave. 'We didn't want to risk losing you.'

'I see.' Rachel was deeply moved.

'It was a frantic time back then,' Marge went on, her eyes glazed in thought. 'We lived for the moment. I know what we did was wrong, and it seems primitive by today's standards, with health visitors and the like going around to check up on the welfare of new mothers and their babies. But it didn't seem wrong then; it seemed like the only decent thing to do. I think we were more inclined to follow our instincts during the war. Doing things by the book didn't seem nearly as important as looking out for each other when we were all struggling so hard to survive, and living from day to day.'

Rachel fiddled with her fingernails, inwardly trembling as she uttered the words she could hold back no longer. 'What . . . what was my mother like?' she asked, looking up.

There was a pause while Marge cast her mind back. 'Similar to you in appearance, from what I can remember of her,' she pondered. 'She was a pretty girl, small like you are and with the same big greenish-brown eyes. That's one thing I'm never likely to forget.' She looked blankly ahead, remembering, a smile touching her lips. 'Because Chip always used to be going on about her great big saucer eyes.'

'But what sort of person was she?' Rachel was eager to know. 'Was she quiet, outgoing or what?'

'Outgoing.' Marge had no doubt about that. 'She was a friendly sort of a girl. Very up-to-date and she loved to go out dancing. She knew all the steps and all the latest songs.'

'Where was she from?' asked Rachel.

'Fulham.' Marge thought for a moment. 'She was a bit rough and ready but she had a warm heart. She thought the world of Chip an' all.'

'It wasn't just a fling, then?' suggested Rachel.

'It didn't strike me that way,' said Marge thoughtfully. 'They seemed to get on very well.'

'Why didn't they make plans to stay together after the war, then?' asked Rachel.

Marge shrugged. 'Who knows? Maybe because they hadn't been going out together for all that long and hadn't got round to making plans yet. And, of course, they were very young, especially her.' She gave Rachel a shrewd look. 'I know what you're probably thinking. But I don't think she was flighty or anything. Chip was going away . . . and, well, these things happen.'

Nodding in agreement, Rachel waited for Marge to continue.

'Anyway, after he went away and she found out she was pregnant, I suppose the romance went out of it a bit for her. She was left in the cart and he wasn't around to help her. I don't know the details because neither of them confided in us about their feelings for each other.'

'And you really don't know what happened to her?' enquired Rachel.

'I honestly don't,' confirmed Marge in a serious tone. 'I expect she met someone else and settled down later on. She was a good-looking girl and not the sort to stay single. But after Chip got married, no one ever mentioned Doris.'

'She just disappeared?' asked Rachel.

'From our lives, yes,' Marge confirmed. 'It's easily done in a place like London. If someone moves to another neighbourhood and uses different shops and bus routes, they soon get lost in the crowd.'

'She could have been killed in the bombing, though,' suggested Rachel.

'Yes, that is a possibility,' agreed Marge, frowning. 'Many people did lose their lives.'

'I know,' muttered Rachel, finding herself ardently hoping that Doris was still alive.

The kettle boiled and Marge made the coffee and sat down at the table opposite Rachel. 'Are you thinking of trying to find her, then, love?' she asked.

Despite the ostensibly casual nature of the enquiry, Rachel guessed there was fear in Marge's heart. She would see any such action on Rachel's part as a threat to their own relationship. 'No,' she said, keen to reassure her and take that worried look out of her eyes. 'I'm not going to do that. Why would I want to find someone who didn't want me?'

'Curiosity?' Marge suggested.

'I'm curious about her, of course,' Rachel admitted. 'It's only natural. But even if I did want to see her, which I definitely don't, I doubt if she would want to see me. She's hardly likely to want some kid she thought she'd seen the last of turning up in her life now and disrupting things.'

'I think it's probably best to leave things as they are,' advised Marge diplomatically.

In spite of what she'd said, Rachel was imbued with a profound longing to find her birth mother. She wanted to see her, to talk to her and ask her how she could have given a child away, just literally turned her back on her for ever. As well as the ache of rejection, there was also fury towards the woman who had brought her into the world but not cared enough to stay around to bring her up. 'There's no point in dragging up the past after all this time, is there?' she went on to say, partly to ease Marge's mind but mainly to try and convince herself that she must banish all notions of finding Doris because it would only lead to more pain and trouble for them all.

'Not really.' Marge was visibly relieved, her eyes softening, the rigid stance of her shoulders loosening. Rachel was again reminded of the love Marge had given to her in such abundance over the years.

Steering the conversation to another aspect of the same subject, Rachel said, 'I suppose Arthur will have to be told the truth as soon as possible.' Although she was relieved that the ordeal in court would not now be necessary, she was too hurt and confused about her own identity to feel any sense of triumph.

'Your dad and I will take care of that,' Marge informed her. 'We're planning to go and see him tomorrow. We're more likely to find him at home on a Sunday.'

'Would you like me to do it?' offered Rachel. 'Since I'm the one at the centre of all this, and anyway, he is my . . .' She swallowed hard. 'My half-brother.'

'No, that's all right, love,' Marge assured her. 'It's our mess, our job to put it right.'

'If you're sure, then,' said Rachel, finishing her coffee and standing up to leave.

'Quite sure, dear.'

'Arthur isn't going to be a happy man, though,' commented Rachel. 'I hope you're prepared for the flak.'

'That doesn't worry me.' Marge was quite definite about it. 'But I am hoping that he'll accept the facts now, that you are Chip's first-born child and therefore entitled to the inheritance, even without the terms of the will. I shall make it quite clear to him that I'm prepared to stand up in court and speak the truth if he still intends to go ahead.'

'He's not that much of a fool,' opined Rachel. 'He won't want to spend money on legal fees on a hiding to nothing.'

'There is that,' Marge agreed.

'Anyway, I really must go,' said Rachel, moving towards the door. 'I have to relieve Jan and Pete of my offspring.'

Marge gave Rachel a cautious look. 'Will you be round for tea as usual this afternoon?' she enquired.

'Where else would we go for Saturday tea?' replied Rachel, smiling.

'I'm sorry you've been hurt, dear,' said Marge.

'And I'm sorry I hurt you.' Rachel flung her arms around her and held her tight. 'Thanks for taking me in and looking after me for all these years. God knows what would have happened to me if you hadn't. I'll see you later.'

And before Marge could say another word, Rachel fled from the house, tears streaming down her cheeks. But these weren't tears of anger and resentment; this outpouring was born of affection and relief at having put things right with the woman she would always think of as her mother.

'Did you have a nice time this afternoon at Gran's?' enquired Rachel that evening as she soaped Tim's back with the sponge. The boys were in the bath together, bright-eyed and pink-cheeked from playing in their grandparents' garden in the sunshine.

'Yeah, it was good,' said Tim.

'It's smashing at Gran's because we can play football in the garden,' added Johnnie.

'Which reminds me,' said Rachel, her expression becoming sterner. 'You must learn to play without kicking the ball over the fence into Gran's neighbour's garden.'

'It's not me,' denied Johnnie. 'It's Tim.'

'It is *not*,' argued Tim, frowning darkly at his brother and smacking the water in front of him so that it splashed into his face. 'You're the one who kicks it too high.'

'No I'm not.'

'Yes you are,' insisted Tim. 'You're always doing it. It'll be your fault if we lose our ball. Grandad says if it goes over there again, the man next door will keep it.' He whacked the water again as though to make his point.

'Shut up,' retorted Johnnie, retaliating in a similar manner and sending water everywhere.

'That's enough of that, both of you,' scolded their mother, who had got caught in the spray and was soaked all down her front. 'Honestly, there's more water on me and the floor than there is in the bath.'

'It's *his* fault,' they chorused.

'And that's enough of that, too. I don't want to hear any more of your silly bickering,' she said, wiping the floor with a cloth. 'You're giving me a headache.'

'Sorry, Mum,' said Tim.

'Me too,' added his brother.

Rachel held the towel out. 'Right. Who's coming out first?'

By some strange quirk of nature they didn't quarrel over this and agreed it would be Tim. She wrapped the towel around him, enjoying the smell and feel of him, the smoothness of his skin, his eyes and hair colouring very similar to hers.

'Anyway,' continued Johnnie, who hadn't quite finished with the subject, 'if we do lose our ball, we can play on the bikes.' He was referring to the small, rather shabby second-hand bicycles her parents had bought them for Christmas and which they kept at Wilbur Terrace because there was nowhere to ride them here.

'Yeah, we could do that,' said Tim in another rare moment of agreement.

'I wish our bikes were here,' wailed Johnnie.

'Yeah, that'd be good,' Tim was keen to add.

'Can we bring our bikes home, Mum? Can we? Please?' begged Johnnie.

'But where would you ride them, darling?' she commented, sitting Tim on the toilet seat to dry his feet.

'Out the front . . . down in the street, anywhere,' Tim intervened hopefully.

'We could easily find somewhere,' announced Johnnie, who was using the plastic soapdish as a warship and bombing it with the soap.

The 'out the front' to which they were referring was a concrete walkway leading to steps which were extremely dangerous for children of their age. And they certainly weren't old enough to play in the street three floors down, especially as there were so many hooligans roaming this estate.

'You're not big enough to play outside,' she announced firmly, buttoning Tim's pyjama jacket, and turning her attention to Johnnie, whom she helped out of the bath and into the towel she was holding up ready for him.

'Why haven't we got a garden?' enquired Johnnie, who was darker in appearance than his brother and had the look of his father about him.

'Because we live in a flat and flats don't have gardens,

stupid,' said Tim with all the worldly authority of an elder child. 'People with houses have gardens. Everyone knows that.'

'I forgot,' retorted Johnnie as Rachel finished drying him and helped him into his pyjamas.

'Why don't we live in a house, Mum?' Tim enquired.

'Because we don't have enough money,' she told him.

'I could give you my money box,' he said with a solemn expression. 'There's quite a bit in there 'cause I've been saving the pocket money I get from Gran and Grandad.'

She gulped at the poignancy of his innocence. 'I'm afraid we'll need a lot more than the contents of your money box before we can have a house with a garden,' she said gently. 'But it was a kind thought, Tim. Thank you.'

'Will we ever have a garden?' asked Tim with childish persistence.

'I hope so,' she told him. 'It's what I'm working for.'

'Is that why you go to work then?' he asked with interest. 'So that we can have a garden?'

'It isn't the only reason. I go out to work to pay for things like food and clothes. But I hope that one day we might be able to have nice things like a garden.' She eased Johnnie's feet into his slippers. 'In the meantime, you two go and choose your bedtime story while I clear up here.'

'Can we watch the telly for a little while before we go to bed?' asked Tim predictably.

'Only for a little while, and no arguing when I say it's time for bed. Promise?'

'Promise,' they agreed in unison and scuttled off, pushing and squabbling about whose turn it was to choose the story. She certainly had an incentive to make a success of the boathouse in those two, she thought, gathering the dirty clothes and putting them in the washing basket in the corner.

Optimistic thoughts of the future took her mind off the pain of the past twenty-four hours. She made two mugs of milky cocoa then took them through to the living room and sat between the boys on the sofa, feeling a moment of such bliss she wished she could somehow preserve it. Moments like this were what life was really all about.

This was real, this was what mattered, loving her sons and doing her best for them. Compared to that, everything else was incidental, even her dubious parentage.

If it was humanly possible, she would provide them with some of what was on offer for those who could afford it in these affluent times. New bikes for instance, and a garden to ride them in. But if, for some reason, it didn't happen, they would still have her devotion, which was surely the most important thing.

Monday morning at the boathouse was so frantic Rachel didn't have time to dwell on her personal problems. The workshop was inundated with repairs to racing boats entered in the various rowing events taking place on the Thames during the summer. The secretary of one of the rowing clubs came in to talk to Ben about a new craft they were having made for a big race in the autumn; a private customer wanted details on the phone about the restoration of a boat; and Rachel got an important telephone call from one of the boat-hire firms she had visited when she first took over. They were asking if someone could go and see them with a view to giving them an estimate for a fleet of boats they wanted to commission.

Her typing tray was overflowing and the phone didn't seem to stop ringing. It was hectic but invigorating and she enjoyed the bustling atmosphere. She had just come off the telephone and was putting a sheet of paper into the typewriter ready to do an estimate when two unwelcome visitors arrived unexpectedly.

'I suppose you put your mum and dad up to this latest scam,' accused Arthur, marching into her office, his scowling wife at his heels.

'It isn't a scam and I haven't put them up to anything.' Her parents had told her that Arthur had been infuriated by the news, so she'd been expecting a visit from him sometime. He'd obviously chosen the boathouse rather than her flat to avoid any interference from her children.

'Don't give us that,' came Ella's vociferous contribution. 'Surely you don't expect us to believe that load of baloney.'

'You can believe what you like,' replied Rachel. 'But it does happen to be true.'

'Do you think we're thick or something?' Ella demanded. 'Do you think we're so green that we can't see through a ridiculous story like that?'

Rachel got up and closed the office door. 'We don't want the entire workforce to know about our personal affairs, do we?' she said coolly.

'I couldn't care less who knows about it,' roared Arthur.

'It's a pack of lies anyway,' Ella chipped in.

Rachel took a deep, calming breath. 'I didn't want to believe it either, but for very different reasons to you,' she told them, sitting back down at her desk, feeling weakened by this attack despite her bold front. 'But as it is obviously true, I have to get used to the idea, and so do you.'

'Oh, do us a favour,' said Ella in a pitying tone. 'You suddenly becoming Chip Banks' daughter at the same time as we're taking you to court over the ownership of the boathouse? Even you must see that it's a bit too convenient.'

'I realise it might look that way,' she couldn't deny. 'But it is actually the truth and has come out into the open *because* of the court case. There's nothing coincidental about it.'

'You'll go to any lengths to keep this place, won't you?' accused Arthur, his dark eyes full of spite.

Rachel looked at him levelly. 'I'm prepared to fight for what's mine, sure I am,' she wasn't afraid to admit. 'But I certainly wouldn't tell lies to that end.'

'Don't make me laugh. You cooked up the story because you hoped I'd drop the case,' he shouted. 'Well, I'm not going to, and that's that.'

'No he isn't,' confirmed Ella, her blue eyes bright with

temper. 'You don't put us off that easily.'

'It's up to you what you do,' Rachel told them. 'But surely you can see that you don't stand a chance of winning in the light of the facts as we now know them.'

'Facts my arse,' snorted Ella. 'Lies, more like.'

'What your parents claim to have done is illegal anyway,' Arthur announced smugly.

'It was also an act of enormous humanity,' Rachel pointed out.

'Sentimental twaddle,' he scoffed. 'Not that it happened anyway. No one in their right mind would believe a tale like that. It's like something out of some daft storybook.'

'Do you think they would be prepared to stand up in court and admit to something like that if it wasn't true, knowing that they've broken the law?' she asked.

This seemed to leave both her visitors temporarily lost for words. 'Yeah, I think they'd do anything at all to deprive me of my inheritance,' Arthur blustered after a while. 'They've always hated the sight of me.'

'That's hardly surprising, is it, the way you treated your father?' Rachel said. 'He *was* my mother's brother.'

'You watch what you're saying,' interrupted Ella in a warning tone. 'My husband's relationship with his father has nothing to do with you.'

'No, it hasn't. And even if what you're saying is true, I'm still his legal son,' mumbled Arthur, changing tack as he began to realise that there might be something in the story after all.

'Yeah, that's right, my Arthur isn't some bastard his father didn't want,' Ella hastened to add.

Rachel winced from the cruelty of her words but managed to stay in control. 'I can't deny that,' she said evenly, though she was quivering inside.

'I'm the legal heir to the boathouse, the rest is just your word against mine,' Arthur declared. 'You know we've got you whichever way you play it.'

'If you think you have a chance of winning, then please go

ahead with the case,' Rachel advised him wearily.

'We intend to, don't worry,' Ella made it clear.

'That's entirely up to you,' said Rachel. 'But do bear in mind that I'm the one named in the will. And the fact that the reason has now become clear as to why your father . . .' she looked at Arthur meaningfully, '*our* father . . . chose to leave the boathouse to me will weaken your already feeble case. If you continue, it could work out very expensive for you.'

'Don't listen to her, Art,' urged Ella. 'She's just a jumped-up little chancer.'

'You won't get away with this,' seethed Arthur.

'No, you won't, you scheming cow,' added Ella, throwing Rachel a vicious look.

Arthur fell silent suddenly, obviously having serious doubts now. 'OK, maybe I don't have a case to take to court,' he admitted grudgingly, his eyes narrowed on Rachel with malice. 'And maybe I can't get back what you've stolen from me. But I'll make you pay somehow, make no mistake about that. You'll wish you'd never done this to me, I can promise you that.'

'What you choose to do is your business,' said Rachel, meeting the chilling hatred in his gaze with an anxiety she managed to conceal. 'But now that you've said what you came here to say, will you please leave.' She stood up, her cheeks flaming, looking from one to the other. 'Go on. Get out of here, the pair of you.'

'We're going, don't worry,' he told her. 'But don't think you've seen the last of us.'

'That would be too much to hope for,' she sighed, wearied by his threats.

'People who muck me about don't get off lightly,' he ranted on.

'I'll take my chances,' said Rachel, going to the door and opening it. 'You can see yourselves out, can't you?'

'We'll go when we're ready,' he told her. 'I'm not having you order me around.'

'Don't you dare try to push us out,' Ella chipped in.

'Bloody cheek,' added Arthur, fired up by his wife's support. 'Trying to order us off what would be my premises if you had a scrap of decency in you.'

At that moment Ben appeared at the office door, clutching some papers. 'Sorry, I didn't realise you were busy,' he said to Rachel. 'I'll come back later.'

'It's all right, Ben, come on in,' she said, giving Arthur an expressive look. 'Arthur and Ella are just leaving.'

While Arthur looked ready to explode, his wife's mood seemed to change and she took his arm in an uncharacteristic show of sang-froid. 'Come on, love, let's go,' she said, leading him to the door.

'But . . .' began Arthur.

'Don't waste your breath on the heartless bitch.' Ella threw Rachel a parting look. 'But you'll hear from us again, I can assure you of that.' She paused, brows raised, eyes resting on Rachel unwaveringly. 'One way or another.'

As the door closed behind them, Rachel let out a long, slow breath.

'Sounds like problems,' said Ben.

'You can say that again.'

'Serious ones?'

She nodded briefly. 'Let's just say there have been some developments about Arthur's claim on the boathouse that haven't pleased him,' she told him.

'Bad news in the enemy camp is good news for us, though, isn't it?' he assumed.

About to confide in him, she paused, considering their heavy workload, and decided that now wasn't the time. 'Are you doing anything at lunchtime?' she asked.

'Nothing special.'

'Let's have a bite to eat together somewhere and I'll tell you all about it,' she suggested.

'OK.'

'The Dove?'

'Suits me,' he endorsed warmly. 'And in the meantime, I have some typing that needs doing.'

'More?'

'Yep,' he said, smiling. 'Business is booming.'

'That's the way we want it to stay,' she said, managing a rather bleak smile. Although she'd hung on to her composure, she'd found the incident with Arthur very upsetting. He and his wife were dangerous, she had no doubt about that; they were the sort of people who would actually carry out their threats.

'We'll get our own back on 'em, Art,' declared Ella as she and Arthur walked across the yard in the sunshine to his pale green Austin Cambridge. 'Don't you worry your head about that.'

'I'm sorry, Ella,' he said, his tone noticeably subdued. 'But I don't think we're gonna get the boathouse after all. I think we've lost it to her.'

'I know that,' she confirmed in a surprisingly agreeable manner. 'That cow has got it all neatly sewn up.'

'Sorry, I've let you down, love,' he told her sheepishly.

'It isn't your fault.' She was completely supportive. 'You'll just have to find something else that'll bring in some decent dough.'

'I daren't fiddle on the machines as the boss got suspicious before,' he reminded her.

'You've left that alone for long enough now, though,' she pointed out. 'It should be safe to start again, as long as you're careful and don't overdo it.'

'It won't bring in enough to make up for losing the cash we'd have made on this place, though,' he said, looking gloomily towards the boathouse.

'You'll soon find something else,' she chirped. 'A smart bloke like you will always find a way to earn a few quid on the side. And you'll just have to keep your ear to the ground for that special little job that will put us on a different level.'

'Mm. But until I do, you'll have to stay on at the shoe-shop,' he reminded her.

'Not necessarily.' She pondered for a moment. 'I might look for something else while I'm waiting for you to get into the money. Something a bit more interesting. A job in a ladies' dress shop or a boutique would suit me, and there's plenty of those about.'

'Once I get into something tasty, you won't have to work at all,' he reminded her.

'That's what's keeping me going, babe,' she told him. 'Knowing you'll get there eventually.'

'You're a real diamond, you know that, the way you've taken it,' he complimented her as they got into the car.

'No point in moping about it, is there?' she said. 'That'll get us nowhere.'

'I know that,' he agreed. 'But I wasn't quite sure if you'd see it that way.'

'I'm not happy about it, of course,' she let him know. 'But there's always the satisfaction of getting our own back on that cow to look forward to.'

'There is that,' he said. 'But I'm buggered if I know how we're gonna do it.'

'We're gonna bide our time, that's what we're gonna do,' she told him with authority.

'We are?'

'That's right. We're gonna wait for the right opportunity before we make our move. There's no hurry,' she explained, taking control of the situation. 'We'll let that bitch think she's sitting pretty before we shake the ground beneath her feet. It'll have more of an effect then.'

'But what can we do to make that happen?' he wanted to know, turning to her in the passenger seat and looking at her with unveiled admiration. He adored everything about Ella. Her sharp tongue and streetwise manner, her tarty make-up and skirts so short they took your breath away. Most of all he loved her for her unstinting loyalty to him. A woman like

Ella could have any bloke she wanted, and yet she'd chosen him. He was the luckiest man in London.

'You're gonna make it your business to get to know some of the blokes who work at Banks' Boats,' she informed him.

'Am I?'

'You are.'

'How, exactly?'

'How do you think?' She was full of confidence. 'You go to a few of the pubs around here and find out where they go for a pint after work of an evening.'

'And then?'

'Then you get talking to them, matily, like men do in pubs,' she explained. 'Find one who fancies earning a few quid on the side with no questions asked. Get him to tell you what's going on in the firm, what boats they're making, that sort of thing.'

'Then what?'

'When we see the right opportunity, we'll go for it,' she explained.

'But Ben Smart probably drinks in the same pubs,' he pointed out.

'So what? A pub is a public house, a place where anyone can go. He won't know you have an ulterior motive for being there,' she pointed out. 'Anyway, he's their boss. The blokes won't want to drink with him after hours. They'll have had quite enough of his face all day.'

He gave her a quizzical look. 'What actually do you have in mind in the way of an opportunity?' he wondered.

'I'm not sure yet, Art, but we'll recognise it when it comes along,' she said with a slow smile. 'Just use your loaf and keep us up to date with what's going on inside the boathouse. When the right time comes, we'll both know it.'

'You're a bright girl,' he said with awe.

'I'm no dimwit,' she readily agreed. 'Come on, Art, let's go home.'

'OK.'

'As you've phoned the shop and told 'em I'm sick so that I could go with you to sort that bitch out, I might as well make the most of the day and relax at home,' she told him.

'You deserve a day off after the way you stood by me in there,' he said.

'Let's get out of here,' she suggested eagerly. 'We don't want to waste any more of our time hanging around this place, do we? Not for the moment, anyway.'

'I'll drop you off at home then go straight to work,' he told her, starting up the engine. 'I'm quite looking forward to getting back to my fiddle again.'

She nodded, looking with a purposeful gleam in her eye out of the window at the boathouse as the car swept out of the yard. 'Here's to revenge, eh, Art?' she said.

'I'll second that,' he agreed with a malevolent smile.

Chapter Eight

Rachel and Ben had lunch on the outer terrace of The Dove in the sunshine. Because the pub was so popular, they couldn't get a table in the glazed-over section, which was a pity because tender green vine leaves flourished beneath the glass there, bringing a touch of the Mediterranean to this traditional English inn, which had first opened as The Dove coffee house in the 1740s. It was famed for its literary patronage, so Rachel had heard.

But eating al fresco was no hardship on a lovely day like this. It was easier to talk out here, anyway, away from the noise and bustle inside. They both chose a ploughman's lunch, which was delicious, the bread freshly baked, a generous portion of moist mature cheddar, the pickles nice and tangy.

'It's certainly the right weather to be outside,' remarked Rachel, glancing towards the river. The sun was glinting on its undulating surface, and a warm breeze stirred the air and rustled through the trees on the opposite bank.

'Not half,' Ben agreed, breaking some bread and looking idly upriver towards the small willow-covered island known as Chiswick Eyot, a haven for bird life where swans nested and an annual crop of osiers were cut for basket-making.

Lulled into a more relaxed state of mind by the tranquil ambience and a couple of glasses of wine, Rachel told him about the purpose of Arthur's visit and the revelations of the weekend. She'd originally only intended to disclose the fact that the court case would not now be happening, to reassure him that his job at the boathouse was safe. But his unassuming presence was so soothing that the whole thing flowed out in a therapeutic effusion.

'Well, well, you *have* been having a traumatic time,' he responded, looking concerned as he cut a piece of cheese to put on his bread.

'I feel as though I've been turned inside out and given a thoroughly good shaking,' she confessed, breaking some bread and spreading it with butter.

'I should think you do after a thing like that,' he sympathised.

'And the set-to with Arthur this morning didn't help,' she continued. 'Though I knew he wouldn't just fade quietly out of the picture, of course.'

'So . . . you've had a shock and he's had a smack in the eye,' he observed gravely.

'That's about it,' she told him, sipping her wine. 'It's bad enough trying to come to terms with the personal side of things. A battle over the business is about the last thing I need.'

'You won't have to fight for it now, though, will you?' he pointed out. 'Because this changes everything, and there's not a thing Arthur can do about it.'

'There isn't much point in him continuing with the court case, it's true,' she agreed. 'But I'm sure he'll think of some other way to make me suffer.'

'I shouldn't worry about his threats,' he advised her. 'They were just the empty words of a beaten man. People say all sorts of things when they're angry.'

'I'm being made to feel that I've taken something that should be his, though,' she explained.

'You mustn't allow him to make you feel like that, because it isn't true.' He was adamant. 'Chip wanted you to have it and you must know that in your heart.'

'Yeah, I do.' She forked some pickle on to her bread. 'If I wasn't so certain of it, I'd have already handed the boathouse over to Arthur. In fact, sometimes I feel tempted to do it anyway, just to put an end to all the bad feeling.'

'Don't do that.' He was fervent about it.

'I won't, don't worry,' she assured him. 'I'm determined not to let him bully me into doing something that wouldn't be right.'

'Especially as you've turned the business around and are enjoying the job so much,' he said, adding cautiously, 'well, you seem to be, anyway.'

'I am . . . enormously,' she confirmed. 'But the fact that the boathouse has turned into a battleground is spoiling things. I feel so threatened.'

Something about her tone made him say, 'I don't think Arthur would use violence, if that's what's worrying you.'

'It isn't,' she was quick to explain. 'I don't think he'd have the stomach for anything like that. But I do think he and Ella will try to make trouble for me.'

'Would it help if I were to go and see him?' Ben offered thoughtfully. 'To issue a few threats of my own?'

'It's sweet of you to offer.' She gave him a warm smile. 'But that won't be necessary. I'll deal with anything he dishes out when and if it comes.'

'Well . . . I'm here if you need me.'

Looking at him across the table, she noticed how vividly blue his eyes looked against his tanned skin, his hair seeming blonder in the sunshine. 'I really appreciate that.' She paused thoughtfully. 'To be perfectly honest, the other stuff is worrying me far more than anything Arthur can throw at me.'

'The stuff about your parents, you mean?' he suggested.

'Mm,' she confirmed, and went on to tell him how profoundly she'd been affected by the knowledge of her true origins. 'I'm an adult mother of two, and it's probably the height of self-indulgence for me to let something like this matter so much. But it just keeps gnawing away at me.'

'It's bound to take time to get used to something like that.' He was very understanding.

'It's knowing that my parents aren't my parents that hurts so much. Knowing they haven't been straight with me all these years.' She shook her head. 'I feel so betrayed.' She paused. 'And I realise how self-pitying and ungrateful I must sound.'

'No you don't,' he disagreed. 'Why should you?'

'Because Mum and Dad have been great and I'm very grateful to them for everything,' she explained. 'It seems wrong to feel bad when they could easily have just let me go into care instead of taking me in and bringing me up.'

'Stop apologising for your feelings,' he cut in. 'You're entitled to have them.'

'But it isn't as though I had a disadvantaged childhood or anything,' she said. 'Quite the reverse.'

'That doesn't make you shockproof,' he pointed out. 'I mean, how could anyone suddenly discover what you did at the weekend and not feel upset by it?'

It was such a relief to talk to someone who could look at the problem objectively and give her an honest opinion; she suspected he had the sort of integrity that would force him to give her that even if it wasn't what she wanted to hear. 'It feels as though everything's changed between us because I'm not their own,' she went on. 'And, of course, it's such a terrible feeling to know that you weren't wanted.'

'But you *were* wanted,' he was quick to point out. 'By the people who matter, the ones who brought you up. It's them who have given you your values and made you who you are today.'

'Yeah, yeah, I know,' she said. 'It's just knowing that my birth mother gave me away.'

'She probably really did think she was doing the right thing for you at the time.'

'It doesn't matter how many times I tell myself that, I still feel rejected,' she said. 'As a mother myself, it's inconceivable to me how anyone could give a child away.'

'Sometimes people just don't have a choice,' he said. 'And at least you grew up in a loving home.'

'Which is why I wish I was their own flesh and blood and everything was back as it was, and I didn't have all these complicated emotions,' she burst out. 'All this self-analysis is driving me up the wall. I'm racked with guilt about my feelings and wondering how I'm supposed to feel. And the worst thing of all is not being able to talk to the family honestly about it, not even my sister, because they get upset and worried and think I'm going to turn my back on them and break the family up.'

'Yes . . . I can see it must be difficult for you.'

'The trouble is, unless something like this has actually happened to you, it's impossible to know what it feels like,' she was at pains to explain. 'I mean, I've read about this sort of thing. But I never dreamed how devastating it was until it happened to me.'

He gave her an understanding nod.

As they finished their lunch and ordered coffee, she found herself recalling something he'd said. 'When you mentioned just now my growing up in a loving home . . .' She hesitated, wondering if she should continue and deciding to take a chance. 'I got the impression that you didn't?'

'That's right,' he said impulsively.

'Oh?' she said in a manner that was persuasive without being intrusive.

Never before had he talked about his childhood to anyone; even his wife hadn't been given the full details. Chip had come the closest to it but even he hadn't had the full story because Ben couldn't bring himself to confide in anyone.

But now, as they drank coffee together, he found himself baring his soul to Rachel as he never had before, talking about the pain and helplessness of seeing his mother beaten, and of how his own attempts to protect her had always resulted in a thrashing for himself. He spoke of his sorrow when she died, of the wretchedness of his father's cruelty and the desperation of having no one to turn to. 'Of course, I didn't realise I was any different to anyone else at the time. I thought it was normal to feel so alone. I didn't find out it wasn't until I became an adult,' he tried to explain.

'As children, we accept whatever we have as the norm, don't we?' she remarked.

'That's right,' he agreed. 'I concentrated on getting through each day as it came, taking refuge in being a yob as soon as I was old enough. As a member of a gang, things like love and caring are so completely beyond the pale, I didn't feel out of things. Being tough was the only criterion and I had learned to be that all right.'

'It's a wonder you didn't turn out to be a gangster instead of the fine, upstanding citizen that you are,' she remarked, her own troubles pushed to one side in concern for him. 'Conditions like that are a breeding ground for villains.'

'I did get into thuggery with the gang for a while, and it could easily have led to my becoming a serious criminal if it hadn't been for Chip,' he said, and went on to tell her how he had first met Chip and how it had changed his life.

'What an amazing story,' she remarked.

'Your uncle was an amazing man in his own quiet way.' He paused thoughtfully. 'Your father, I mean.'

'No, Ben,' she correctly hastily. 'He *was* my uncle. Ron Parry is my father. Nothing can alter that.'

'Yeah. It's what someone means to you that matters,' he said. 'Not who they are.'

'That much I *am* sure about,' she said. 'I just wish all these other new feelings would go away.'

'They probably will once the shock wears off and the dust settles,' he said reassuringly. 'It's still early days.'

'I hope you're right,' she said. 'And if they don't go, I'll have to learn to live with them, because I don't want to hurt the family by letting it show, my mother in particular.'

'Of course not,' he agreed.

'Anyway, it wouldn't be fair to the boys for me to get all moody because of something that happened before they were even born,' she went on. 'They've already lost their dad. They need their mum to be cheerful and uncomplicated. So I'll have to put this whole business to the back of my mind.'

'I expect you've been wondering about your real mother, though, haven't you?' he mentioned.

'Oh, yeah, it's only natural that I would, I suppose,' she admitted. 'It's a really weird feeling to know that she might be out there somewhere.'

'Are you . . . ?' he began.

'No,' she cut in quickly, 'I'm not going to try and find her.'

'No hesitation about that then,' he said.

'None at all,' she confirmed a little too vigorously. 'I don't need any more emotional turmoil.'

'I think you're wise,' he said. 'You've enough to do with those boys of yours.'

'I won't argue with that.'

'They're blissfully unaware of all the drama, I suppose,' he said.

'I hope so. I've certainly tried to make it that way for them,' she told him. 'Children soon sense when something is wrong so I've had to work hard at pretending all is well.'

He smiled at the thought of them. 'They're smashing kids. I think they're great.'

'They like you too,' she told him.

'Really?' He seemed pleased.

She nodded. 'I don't think I'm ever going to hear the last of that boat trip,' she said.

'They enjoyed it, then?'

'They were ecstatic about it. In fact, they've been nagging me ever since to ask you if they can go again.' The instant the words were out, she regretted putting him in a position where he might feel he had to offer. 'Sorry, that was really pushy of me.'

'Why?'

'Because now you'll feel you have to invite us and I'm sure you have better things go do with your time at a weekend than spend it entertaining someone else's children,' she explained.

'I can't think of anything I'd rather do.' Without further ado he added, 'How about Sunday morning?'

'That would be lovely.'

'Great,' he said with a broad smile. 'Let's hope the weather stays fine.'

Rachel had thought she would never feel normal again after the events of the weekend and the stress of Arthur's visit. But sitting here in the sunshine talking to Ben, she was infused with a feeling of cheer and optimism. He had the knack of putting everything so firmly into perspective, his company was just what she needed. Although they were only working colleagues, the atmosphere over lunch had seemed intimate somehow.

'And in the meantime,' she said, picking up her handbag from the floor by her feet, 'as much as I'd like to sit here all afternoon talking to you, I suppose we ought to think about getting back to the boathouse.'

'Of course.' He looked awkward suddenly. 'Thanks for lunch, are you sure I can't . . .'

'No,' she declined firmly. 'As I said earlier, this was a business lunch since its primary purpose was to discuss the future of the boathouse, so it'll come out of petty cash.'

'OK.'

He still seemed embarrassed and she guessed that he was the sort of man who objected to the idea of a woman taking care of the bill. 'You can do the honours next time,' she assured him.

'I'll hold you to that,' he said, in a manner to suggest that he meant it.

Making their way back to the boathouse, he got on to the subject of work. 'I've been meaning to have a word with you about young Brian Miller,' he said. Miller was one of the workshop staff.

'Have you?'

'Yeah. I'm not at all happy with him,' he explained.

'Why's that?'

'He's lazy and arrogant and doesn't seem to have any interest in the job,' he informed her.

'Oh dear, that's not good enough, is it?' she said, frowning. 'He came to us fully trained, didn't he?'

'That's right.'

Around the time Rachel took over the boathouse there had been a small staff reshuffle. Although they'd intended to cut down on the workforce, more men than expected had left because of the uncertainty of ownership, leaving them understaffed. This meant that when the work flow had later increased, they'd had to employ another man – Brian Miller.

'It seems odd that he would have gone right through an apprenticeship if he wasn't interested in the job, don't you think?' remarked Rachel.

'He was probably bullied into it by his father, who's a boatbuilder out at Richmond,' Ben told her. 'It's a trade that's often passed on from father to son. His dad would have encouraged him to go into a good solid trade . . . something that would give him regular employment.'

'That sounds sensible.'

'But I'm not sure if Brian's cut out for it,' Ben went on. 'He seemed keen enough when I interviewed him, but it's a different story now that he's actually doing the job. I think he'd be happier doing something that's less like hard work and pays better than boatbuilding. He's always saying he's overworked and moaning about the money.'

'But we pay the going rate, don't we?' Rachel relied on Ben to decide on the amount they paid the men.

'Yeah, course we do. We pay more in certain cases, when someone really deserves it,' confirmed Ben. 'But boatbuilding is something you do because you have a feel for it and enjoy it. Not because you want to earn big money. Brian just doesn't seem to have an interest in the job.'

'Why does he stay on, I wonder?' she commented.

'Wouldn't it be better for him to go into something that does interest him?'

'Again, he's probably under pressure from his father,' suggested Ben. 'He's only nineteen and living at home, so he'd still be under his parents' influence to quite a large extent.'

'So . . . do you think we should consider letting him go, then?' she wanted to know.

'Well, we can't afford to keep him on if he doesn't start to pull his weight,' he informed her gravely. 'And he certainly isn't doing that at the moment. The last thing I want to do is sack anyone – but when they become a liability to the firm, there isn't really a choice.'

'I'll leave you to deal with it as you see fit,' she said. 'Given that the workshop is your domain.'

'I just thought you ought to be aware of the situation,' he mentioned.

'I appreciate that, Ben, but I'll support you whatever you decide to do,' she told him.

'Good. I'll keep an eye on him for a week or two, and if things don't get any better, I'll have a few strong words with him,' he said as they approached the boathouse yard.

'You'll give him a warning?'

'Yeah. I'll tell him that he'll have to shape up if he wants to keep his job,' he explained. 'See what he has to say about that. If he wants to stay on, I'll give him a few weeks to show us what he can do. If there's no improvement after that . . . then he'll have to go.'

'Let's hope it doesn't come to that,' she said hopefully. 'But I trust your judgement whichever way it goes.'

'Thanks.'

They walked across the yard and paused outside the entrance to the building, their eyes meeting. She felt a strong sense of mutual liking and trust between them, and it was warm and sweet. 'I hope this afternoon is a bit calmer than this morning was,' she remarked.

'With Arthur and his wife off the premises it can't fail to be!' he said as they went inside together.

The weather was fine on Sunday; the sun sparkled on the water and gently warmed Rachel's face and bare arms. They all clambered aboard *Nipper* and Ben gave them a change of scene by heading into central London, cruising past built-up banks as far as Westminster Bridge, with the architectural magnificence of the Houses of Parliament gleaming in the sunshine on the north bank.

The boys weren't quite old enough to fully appreciate the beauty of London's old buildings and were more interested in the boat and the variety of craft around them on the busier reaches of the river – little sailing boats, working barges, pleasure craft.

Watching her sons having a wonderful time, Rachel was imbued with gratitude to Ben, who teased them and talked to them and never tired of answering their questions. Tim's curiosity about the workings of *Nipper* was endless, but Ben seemed to enjoy his interest, allowing him to steer the boat.

The boys' insatiable appetite for fun and pleasure was fully evident when they got back to the jetty at Hammersmith and Ben moored the boat.

'Can we go for another ride . . . now?' asked Tim.

'Yeah, can we?' echoed Johnnie.

'Oh, come on, chaps, give us a break,' Ben told them cheerfully. 'We'll do it another day soon.'

'Don't push your luck, you two,' admonished their mother. 'And don't you have something to say to Ben?'

They both looked mildly sheepish, then, 'Thank you very much, Ben,' they chimed in unison.

'It's a pleasure.' He looked thoughtful, as though trying to make a decision, before turning to Rachel. 'I suppose you have Sunday lunch with the family?'

'Sometimes,' she told him. 'But not today, because Mum and Dad have gone to Brighton on a day trip, and Jan and

Pete have gone to Pete's parents.'

'How about joining me for a pub lunch then, my treat?' he suggested. 'We can sit outside as it's sunny.'

'Yeah,' shrieked the boys excitedly.

Rachel smiled at Ben. 'It seems as though senior management have made the decision for me,' she said wryly.

'Thanks, chaps.' He ruffled their hair in a friendly manner.

The rest of the day took on a holiday atmosphere for Rachel. After steak and chips on the terrace of the Old Ship, Ben drove them to Ravenscourt Park, calling in at Rachel's place first to collect the boys' football.

All four of them had a kick-around on the grass, then Rachel and Ben left Tim and Johnnie to it, watching from the bench as they teamed up with some other little boys.

'I love to see them playing in the fresh air,' she told him.

'It helps to use up some of their excess energy,' he commented.

'Yes, and they certainly need to do that. You appreciate your kids being outdoors when you live in a flat and they can't run in and out of doors as they like.'

'They'll sleep well tonight,' he remarked, watching them run, jump and shout.

'I think we all will,' she said, turning and smiling at him. Casually dressed in an open-necked shirt and light cotton trousers, he was sitting with his arms spread along the back of the bench and his legs sprawled out in front of him. 'It's been a lovely day, Ben. Thanks for taking such trouble with the boys.'

'It's no trouble,' he assured her.

'Even so, it's a treat for them to have a man to play with them and make a fuss of them,' she said. 'Pete's very good with them but his daughter is the apple of his eye, naturally. And my dad's a bit past playing football.'

'There's no need to thank me, honestly, because I've enjoyed every moment,' he smiled. 'They give me an excuse to kick a ball about and play sailors. It's like a second childhood for me, and I can take any amount of that.'

'That's really nice.' She was suddenly achingly aware of him, his short hair blowing lightly in the breeze around his finely carved countenance. There were times when she thought perhaps he fancied her, other times she felt as though he regarded her merely as a work colleague and a friend. It was an odd situation, almost as though they spent time together outside of work only because of his rapport with her sons. He and Rachel liked each other, certainly, even admired each other, but she didn't know if it would ever progress beyond that. But anyone who made Tim and Johnnie this happy was a star in her book, and that was enough to be going on with.

The boys came tearing towards them, Johnnie emulating an aeroplane with his arms outstretched and emitting a terrible roaring noise. 'Can we go to the swings, please?' he asked breathlessly.

Rachel looked at Ben, who nodded and stood up. 'Come on, then, I'll race you there.'

'Yippee!' said Tim.

Watching Ben's lean form race forward at a gallop with the boys trailing after him, then slow his pace to even things up, she felt such a rush of warmth towards him, it brought tears to her eyes. After her recent traumas it was so good to feel this carefree again. Rachel found herself hoping most ardently that there would be other occasions like this in the future.

Because the boathouse currently had a heavy workload, everybody had to pull together to meet deadlines. Not only did late delivery upset the customer and damage the firm's reputation for good service, it also cut their profits.

So when Brian Miller's indolence continued for another week or so, Ben was forced to have him in his office for a serious talk. He tried his best to be understanding, to find out if the man had a problem. But all he got in return was rudeness.

'I'm doing my best,' defended Brian, a spotty, ginger-haired young man with sleepy blue eyes and an unfortunate attitude. 'What more do you want? Blood?'

'No, but I do expect a decent day's work from the people who the firm are paying,' proclaimed Ben, sitting at his desk with his arms folded. 'The jobs are estimated on the labour as well as the materials, and if someone is using double the hours they should on a job, it reduces our profits as well as upsetting the customer, who's kept waiting longer than he expected. The firm just can't afford to lose money in this way.'

'I'm not using double the hours that I should,' denied Brian sulkily.

'OK, maybe that was a slight exaggeration,' admitted Ben. 'But you are taking longer than you should. A good bit longer.'

'I earn my money,' objected Brian.

'If that was true, we wouldn't be having this conversation,' Ben told him gravely.

'I do my best,' said Brian again.

'If that really is your best, then there's no point in your pursuing a career as a boatbuilder,' said Ben, stroking his chin thoughtfully. 'But I don't believe it is. I think you could do a whole lot better if you put your mind to it.'

Brian's reply was a nonchalant shrug.

'Don't you like the job, son?' asked Ben, his tone softening and becoming more understanding. 'Is that the problem?'

'The job's all right,' replied Brian without enthusiasm.

'You don't behave as though you enjoy it,' said Ben. 'Only, if you're not happy working here, perhaps you might be more suited to doing something else.'

'Are you trying to get rid of me?' demanded Brian sulkily.

'No,' Ben denied evenly. 'I'm just trying to get this matter sorted out in everyone's best interests.'

'Your interests, you mean,' was Brian's insolent reply.

Ben took a deep, calming breath, determined not to lose his temper. 'You watch what you're saying,' he rebuked.

'Whether you like me or not, I am the workshop manager here, and I'd appreciate a little respect.'

The other man didn't reply; just stared at the floor.

'I'll be straight with you,' said Ben, spreading his hands expressively. 'This boathouse isn't a charity. We can't afford to carry passengers, so if you want to stay on here you'll have to buck your ideas up.'

As Brian looked up, Ben noticed that his eyes were burning with resentment. He expected the younger man to resign there and then. But instead he said, in a surprisingly subdued manner, 'OK.'

'Have you listened to what I've said about the consequences if you don't make more of an effort?' asked Ben, thinking perhaps that Brian's sudden compliance meant he hadn't realised the seriousness of the situation.

'Yeah, course I have,' he confirmed.

'We'll see how it goes then,' Ben told him. 'But if I don't see an improvement, you're out.'

'Right.' His tone was expressionless, his eyes lowered.

'You'd better get back to work now, mate,' said Ben, uneasy about Brian's attitude. 'Before any more time is lost.'

'Sure.'

As the young man swaggered from the office, Ben was sorry the interview hadn't had a happier outcome. Brian was obviously very discontented with his lot.

Brian Miller was, indeed, very discontented as he stood at the bar of the Blue Anchor that evening, drinking a pint of beer and staring gloomily into space. Of a saturnine nature anyway, he was mulling over the trouncing he'd had from Ben Smart and remembering how much he'd wanted to put his fist in the workshop manager's face. If it hadn't been for the fact that he hadn't got anything else fixed up, he'd have told him to stuff his job. But he'd only have the old man on his back if he became unemployed and couldn't pay his way at home.

'Evening,' said someone standing next to him at the bar.

'Evening,' replied Brian, turning and vaguely noticing the dark-haired man he'd seen in here a few times lately. Judging by the suit he was wearing, Brian guessed he was some sort of a businessman or sales rep, but they'd never done more than pass comment about the weather.

'Cor, I needed that,' said the man, knocking back a whisky. 'After the day I've had.'

'It couldn't possibly have been as bad as mine,' muttered Brian miserably.

'I wouldn't bet on it, mate,' said the man.

'I would,' replied Brian. 'Mine's been an absolute pig.'

'Still . . . nothing seems so bad after a livener, does it?'

'S'pose not,' agreed Brian.

'Do you work round here?' asked the man.

'Yeah,' Brian told him. 'I work at Banks' Boats. But not for much longer, I hope.'

'Got something else lined up then, have you?' enquired the man, looking at Brian with interest.

'Not at the moment, but I soon will have,' Brian informed him, his anger rising at the thought of the unjust way he'd been treated. 'I'm not staying there to be treated like dirt when I could earn more money doing something else.'

'Why should you?' agreed the man supportively. 'There's plenty of work about. You don't have to put up with bad treatment, not these days.'

'The guv'nor gave me a right rollicking today,' Brian said miserably.

The man tutted sympathetically. 'That isn't right, is it, mate?'

'They think they can say what they like to you just 'cause they're paying your wages,' Brian complained bitterly. 'Never a word about how much money you're making for them to put in their own pocket.'

'It's terrible the way they carry on, I know,' sympathised the man. 'Have a drink with me to cheer you up.'

'Oh.' Brian brightened considerably at this. 'Thanks very much. I'll have a pint of bitter, please.'

'I'm Arthur, by the way,' the man informed him as the barman served their drinks.

Brian introduced himself, looking at Arthur more closely. 'Have I seen you somewhere before?' he enquired.

'You may well have done,' said Arthur. 'I was at your firm quite recently.'

'Are you a rep, then?'

'No. My old man used to own the place,' he explained.

'Chip Banks?'

'That's right,' confirmed Arthur.

'I've heard of him, of course, but he was before my time,' Brian explained without a great deal of interest. 'The woman who took over is his niece, so I've heard.' He thought about this for a moment and gave Arthur a sharp look. 'But . . . if you're his son, you must be related to her.'

'That's right.'

Brian narrowed his eyes on Arthur suspiciously. 'I hope you're not gonna go and tell her what I've been saying about the job,' he said anxiously.

'Relax, mate,' Arthur assured him. 'There's no love lost between me and her.'

'Are you sure?' Brian wasn't convinced.

'Positive.'

'I hope that's true, because I don't want them at the boathouse knowing my plans until I'm ready,' he declared. 'I wanna leave there in my own time, not theirs.'

'That woman stole my inheritance from me, so I'm hardly likely to be on friendly terms with her, am I?' Arthur pointed out.

'Oh.' Brian looked at Arthur cautiously, as though he still wasn't entirely sure of him. 'You'd better not be having me on,' he said with an accusing look.

'Why would I do a thing like that?' Arthur asked.

'Dunno, but you might.'

'I've got no reason to lie to you,' he assured him.

'I suppose not . . . not if she really did do the dirty on you,' commented Brian.

'I'm on your side, believe me,' Arthur said persuasively. 'Your plans are quite safe with me.'

Brian was thoughtful for a moment. 'I wouldn't put it past her to do a thing like that, steal what belongs to someone else,' he said, looking at Arthur. 'She seems like a right greedy cow to me.'

'She is,' nodded Arthur. 'You wouldn't believe what some people will do for greed.'

'Bosses are all the same,' pronounced Brian. 'They're all out for themselves.'

'You can say that again.' Arthur paid for the drinks. 'Actually, mate,' he began, 'I think you and me might be able to do each other a bit of good.'

'Oh? How's that?'

'How would you like to earn yourself a bit of extra dough as well as the chance to get even with your bosses?' he enquired. 'Doing a little job for me?'

Brian's eyes lit up. 'What do *you* think?' he said in an affirmative manner.

'It'll mean your having to stay on at the boathouse for a while longer, though,' Arthur explained. 'Because I'll be needing information from inside the firm.'

'Ooh, I don't fancy that.' Brian looked disappointed. 'I can't wait to get out of there.'

'Surely it wouldn't be too hard to bear if you were getting a good few extra quid in your back pocket, would it?' Arthur pointed out. 'And it wouldn't be for very long.'

'Put like that, I reckon I could just about manage it,' said Brian with a slow smile.

'If you do agreed to do it, though, you mustn't give the guv'nor any reason to get rid of you,' Arthur instructed, his expression becoming hard. 'Because I'll need you inside that boathouse. So you'll have to work hard and not give him any lip. Not until you've finished the job for me; then you can do whatever you like.'

'Count me in,' said Brian, feeling more cheerful than he had in ages.

'Good man. Let's drink to it then, shall we?' Arthur was beaming as he raised his glass. 'Cheers.'

'Cheers,' said Brian, lifting his pint pot.

Arthur swallowed his whisky, congratulating himself on his good work. Ella would be delighted with him for finding such a perfect candidate for the job. 'Now, listen to me, Brian,' he began. 'This is how the plan will work . . .'

[illegible]

[illegible]

[illegible]

[illegible]

There [illegible] who [illegible] with [illegible] between [illegible] what [illegible] attraction [illegible] together [illegible] they [illegible] just [illegible]

Chapter Nine

Arthur's threats slipped to the back of Rachel's mind as the summer galloped along at a hectic pace. She was so busy, even the trauma of learning about her true origins began to lose its grip, and her relationship with the family more or less reverted to normal.

Things were going extremely well at the boathouse. The diligent expertise of most of the boatbuilding team, added to her own newly acquired administration skills – in particular with regard to keeping a tighter rein on customer payment – was really paying off.

Life was good outside of work, too. Much to her joy, Ben's interest in Tim and Johnnie continued, and the four of them enjoyed regular outings together at weekends. There were Sunday-morning boat trips, afternoons at the park, rides into the country in Ben's car. It was lovely. The boys adored having him around and usually managed to secure the promise of his company in the future by means of a little artful presumption. 'Next weekend can we have a game of cricket for a change, Ben?' they'd say, or, 'Please, will you let us steer the boat next week?'

They got no opposition from Ben, who seemed to thrive on their company. Rachel was pleased because an active male influence was just what the boys needed. She became increasingly attracted to Ben as they spent more time together, but they remained just friends, despite her sister's impatient suggestions to the contrary.

'Are you telling me that it's still just a pally thing?' Jan asked with a mixture of disbelief and disapproval.

'That's right,' confirmed Rachel.

'Surely you're not expecting me to believe that you don't feel a good healthy dollop of something other than friendship for him, though?' probed Jan.

'No, I'm not saying that,' admitted Rachel. 'But at the moment we're just friends.'

'"At the moment" meaning that things could change?' Jan persisted.

'Who knows?' Rachel didn't want to speculate on something so important.

'A nice steamy romance is just what you need to bring the colour back to your cheeks,' observed Jan.

'The boathouse has already done that,' Rachel pointed out. 'It's given me a new lease of life.'

'There are other things in life besides work and motherhood, you know,' Jan was keen to remind her.

'They'll do me for now,' smiled Rachel. 'I've no cause for complaint.'

'Having a man in your life would make things even better,' suggested Jan. 'And the boys need a dad.'

'Rest assured,' Rachel told her lightly, 'if anything changes in that direction, you'll be the first to know about it.'

'I'd better be,' cackled Jan. 'Anything more than a handshake, I want to know about it.'

'You'll know,' laughed Rachel, who valued her sister's interest even though she wasn't ready to confide in her fully about the depth of her feelings for Ben. 'It would be more than my life's worth to tell anyone else first.'

'I'll say it would,' Jan confirmed with a grin.

There was a lot of excitement at Banks' Boats when the Westford Rowing Club ordered a boat which was to make its public début in the Big River Race, an international river marathon on the Thames in October.

Most exciting of all was the fact that the rowing club had given Ben a free hand to vary the basic design and produce something that would give their crew more speed. The fact that they were given short notice, added to Ben being a perfectionist in his work, meant that there was a mad rush to get it finished in time, with Ben spending most of his evenings working.

However, the craft was ready for delivery by the agreed deadline. This gave the crew a chance to get the feel of it before the race, having been practising in one of their other boats.

'It's a lovely job, a veritable work of art.' Rachel was standing with Ben and the other men who'd been involved in the boat's production, admiring the finished product, a sleek, elegant craft, fifty-six feet long and built for speed. 'Well done, all of you! You've done yourselves proud.'

The men from the rowing club who came to collect it were equally impressed. 'Your boys have excelled themselves, Mrs West,' complimented the club secretary, a slim, athletic man of middle years who'd been a brilliant oarsman in his day and was still an enthusiast.

'I hope the members will be as pleased as you are,' said Rachel, idly chatting to him in her office while he wrote out a cheque for the full amount.

'You can take it from me that they will be,' he predicted confidently, handing her the cheque with a smile. 'And this race could do you a lot of good, too.'

'We're fully aware of that,' she told him. 'It's the perfect opportunity to promote the boathouse. If the Westford crew do well, people will want to know who made the boat.'

'Course they will,' he agreed heartily. 'And anybody who's anybody in boating circles will be at the river for the race. Those who aren't competing will be watching.' He threw her a look. 'I hope you'll be there to cheer us on.'

'Try keeping me away,' she grinned. 'And as I have two

little boys who are just mad about boats, I wouldn't be allowed to miss it anyway.'

He laughed. 'Glad to hear they've got their priorities right at an early age.'

After chatting to him for a while longer, she gave him a receipted invoice, then the boat was loaded on to a trailer attached to a van and driven away.

'Another satisfied customer,' she remarked to Ben as they saw them off.

'Yeah, I think we can definitely count that one as a success,' he agreed.

'And it's all thanks to you.'

'Oh, no,' he denied with characteristic modesty. 'I can't accept all the praise. It was very much a team effort.'

'Only up to a point,' she insisted. 'You designed it and did most of the work on it, so most of the credit goes to you, and I'm full of admiration.'

He was more touched by her praise than she could possibly imagine. 'Thanks very much then,' he conceded in a more gracious tone.

'Now . . . are you sure you've sussed the place out properly and know exactly what you've got to do?' enquired Arthur of Brian Miller when they met in a Hammersmith pub two weeks later.

'Course I know what I've got to do,' growled Brian defensively. 'I ain't thick, you know, and we've been through it enough times.'

'All right, all right. There's no need to be so touchy,' warned Arthur, paying for the drinks and leading the way to a table in the corner, out of earshot of the other punters. 'You take offence too easily, that's your trouble.'

'What do you expect me to do when you treat me like an idiot?' As usual, Brian was aggrieved.

'No one's treating you like an idiot,' Arthur firmly denied. 'All I'm doing is trying to make absolutely sure that nothing goes wrong. For both our sakes.'

'Nothing will,' Brian insisted, taking the top off his beer.

'We've only got one chance and that's tonight,' Arthur reminded him. 'We can't have another go at it tomorrow or next week if it doesn't come off.'

'Stop going on about it, will you?' snapped Brian with seething impatience. 'I've got everything under control. How many more times must I tell you?'

'Make sure you don't get caught, and don't leave any sign that you've been there,' instructed Arthur, undeterred by the other man's irritation. 'That's absolutely imperative.'

'What do you take me for?' objected Brian.

'Just making absolutely sure there are no slip-ups,' he explained, taking a large swallow of whisky.

'There won't be,' sighed Brian.

'OK, I'll take your word for it,' said Arthur. 'Now, is there anything you want to ask me?'

'Yeah, there is, as it happens, mate,' Brian told him. 'Where's my money?'

'Don't worry, I hadn't forgotten.' Arthur took a furtive look around the bar, then dipped his hand into his pocket and took out some notes, which he handed to Brian under the table.

Brian bent his head, counting the money, then looked up, scowling fiercely at Arthur. 'That isn't the amount we agreed,' he said accusingly.

'You'll get the rest when the job is done,' Arthur told him. 'You can't expect to have it all up front.'

'How can I be sure that I will actually get it, though?' enquired Brian aggressively, slipping the notes into his pocket.

'You'll get what's owed to you,' Arthur assured him.

'I'm the one taking all the risks,' whinged Brian.

'You're getting well paid for it an' all,' Arthur reminded him with an edge to his voice.

'But I've got no guarantee that I will get the final payment, have I?' Brian complained. 'You could do a runner once I've done the job and you don't need me any more.'

'I could but I won't,' said Arthur unequivocally. 'You'll just have to trust me on that one. I'm a man of my word.' Arthur drew hard on a cigarette to steady his nerves, because Brian was making him tense. 'Meet me in here tomorrow night at seven o'clock and you'll get the final payment.'

That wasn't enough to satisfy the other man's suspicious nature. 'But will I, though?'

'If the job is done – and I shall know by tomorrow night if it has been – you'll get your money,' Arthur told him, his patience wearing thin. 'You have my word.'

'Um . . . well, you'd better be here,' warned Brian in a threatening manner.

'I'll be here.' Brian's attitude was really beginning to annoy Arthur, especially as there was still a look of suspicion in those mean little eyes of his. 'There's no need to look at me like that,' said Arthur irascibly. 'Obviously I can't give you the money before the job's done, now can I?'

'I don't see why not,' Brian said.

'In that case you don't have the brains I gave you credit for when I asked you to work for me,' grunted Arthur, his temper rising. 'You could take the money and not do the job if I did that, couldn't you? One of us has to take the other on trust, and as I'm the one who's dishing out the dough, it's bound to be you.'

'And I just have to hope for the best,' whined Brian.

'Oh, for God's sake,' said Arthur, his patience finally snapping. 'If you don't want to do the job, just say so and have done with it.'

'I didn't say I didn't wanna do it,' denied Brian. 'I'm just being cautious.'

'Cautious, my arse. You're nothing short of paranoid,' growled Arthur, struggling to control his temper. 'Half on account, the other half on completion of the operation. That's the deal we agreed when we first started working together. Remember?'

'S'pose so.'

'You can trust me.' He spread his hands to emphasise his point. 'You think about it, mate. Have I seen you go short since you've been supplying me with information?'

'No,' Brian was forced to admit.

'Right, so are you gonna do the job, or shall I have the first instalment back?' said Arthur, confident that Brian's greed wouldn't allow him to drop out.

'Of course I'm gonna do the job,' said Brian. 'I never said I wasn't.'

'Good man,' said Arthur.

Brian shrugged indifferently and guzzled his beer.

'You'd better make that your last drink until after you've done the business,' instructed Arthur forcefully. 'You'll need to keep a clear head.'

'OK,' said Brian, finishing his beer and rising. 'I'll see you in here tomorrow night.'

Arthur nodded and lapsed into thought as the other man left the pub.

The last of the evening sunshine was filtering through the French doors into the living room of Ben Smart's terraced house in Fulham, patching the wall with small squares of light. The nights were beginning to draw in, he observed, standing by the doors and looking out across the tiny paved garden – barely more than a terrace really, with a few pot plants dotted about here and there. It would soon be time to turn the clocks back.

He'd bought this place very cheaply before property prices had started rising so dramatically in London. He'd used his half of the money from the sale of the marital home to pay the deposit. It was very small, but it was big enough for him and convenient for work. It was furnished in a very contemporary style, and had a fitted kitchen he'd built himself. His training stood him in good stead for DIY.

But now he was faced with the gloomy prospect of Saturday evening alone. It was the loneliest night of the week when you were unattached. He'd had a couple of short friendships since splitting up with Lorna, both with nice women whose company he'd enjoyed. But in neither case had the chemistry been sufficient to sustain a long-term relationship.

Generally speaking, he was content with his lot. He came and went as he pleased, with no one to answer to. If he wanted to work late or go out for a few pints with his mates in the evening, he could. But weekends were always a poignant reminder that there was a hole in his life that couldn't be filled by male company and work.

Lorna had a new man in her life, apparently; a sales rep from Wembley. She'd been telling Ben all about it on the phone earlier today, and seemed very happy about it, too. It sounded serious so she'd probably broach the subject of divorce before too long. He wished her well but the thought of making their failure official exacerbated his loneliness.

Oh well, there was no point in getting morose about it, he thought, washing some dishes that had been left in the sink from the beans on toast he'd had for his tea. He'd go down the pub for a pint later on, rather than stay in on his own. He could usually find someone to have a game of darts with in his local. And at least he had tomorrow to look forward to.

A feeling of joyful anticipation washed over him at the thought. He always enjoyed the Big River Race, and this year it would be especially exciting because of the new boat's début appearance. Is it really the race you're looking forward to, he asked himself, or the fact that Rachel and the boys will be with you?

Rachel! What *was* he going to do about her? He couldn't let things drift on as they had been, being a surrogate uncle to her children and a friend to her, when he wanted so much more than that. He wanted to be part of her life; to be with her, to love her, everything.

But making the transition wasn't an easy thing when you'd established a pattern. And how could he be sure she wanted the same thing? She was his employer, after all. If he'd misjudged the signals and she turned him down, it would make things very awkward for them both. Not only with regard to his friendship with the boys but also at work, because something like that would obviously cause tension between them. That was a scenario that didn't bear thinking about. He'd probably have to leave the firm, which would disappoint him and make things very difficult for Rachel, because she relied on him quite heavily.

Her reliance on him was the reason he didn't feel inferior to her in their working environment, even though she paid his salary. Her need for his expertise gave him a certain equality, especially as he was extremely proud of his skills. His staying on at the boathouse under her ownership wouldn't have worked without such an even balance.

So . . . he'd established that she needed him at the boathouse. But did she want him at a personal level, as the man in her life? That was the question he had spent an increasing amount of time pondering lately. At times, when they'd been out with the boys and he'd felt very close to her, he'd almost followed his heart and blurted out the truth about his feelings for her. But caution had always prevailed in the end.

Now he smiled, lingering on a vivid mental image of her, her lovely eyes, her wide smile, the way she made every occasion feel special, and the tender way she behaved towards her sons, who were everything to her. Maybe to the exclusion of all others, it occurred to him suddenly. Perhaps there wasn't room left in her heart for love of the romantic kind, especially after she had been so cruelly let down by her husband.

Drying the last plate and putting it away in the cupboard, he looked at the clock and saw that it wasn't even seven o'clock yet. It seemed like for ever to wait until it was time to collect her and the boys in his car tomorrow morning to take them to the starting point of the race near Ham House, from where the competitors would row the twenty-two miles to the Isle of Dogs.

What would she be doing this evening? he wondered, longingly. She didn't go out much at night because of the boys, so she'd probably be at home. Why didn't he give her a ring . . . ask if he could call to see her? Keep it casual. She'd had the phone put in recently; a genuine business expense, she'd told him, as though she still had to justify spending any money on herself, even though the boathouse was now out of trouble.

Under what pretext could he invite himself round to her place, though? His usual reason for spending time with her outside of working hours was Tim and Johnnie, who would both be in bed.

Why not dispense with any sort of excuse and go to see her as a man who was falling in love with a woman? Why not bring his feelings out into the open? After all, he couldn't fudge the issue forever. How much longer was he going to get away with pretending to be only an avuncular figure for the children and nothing else, as fond as he was of the boys?

Telling himself not to be so pathetic but to get on and do something about the situation he found himself in, he walked purposefully to the telephone.

'How long is it now until Ben comes to take us to the race, Mum?' asked Tim as she dried him after his bath that evening. His brother was already in his pyjamas.

'A very long time,' she told him, hoping to discourage a countdown at this early stage or they'd be wanting an update every two minutes.

'How long, though?' he persisted.

'It's much too soon to start watching the time, darling, so I'm not going to work it out in hours and minutes,' she made it clear. 'You've got a whole night to get through yet, so try to forget about it until then.'

'How long will it be till the race when we wake up in the morning?' he persevered.

'Depends what time you wake up,' she said patiently.

'But it won't be quite so long then.'

'Will it be about ten minutes by then?' came Johnnie's hopeful suggestion.

'No . . . much longer than that.' She was beginning to feel jaded by their relentless questions on the subject. 'But I want you both to stop asking me, until tomorrow morning at least. I'll go mad if you keep on about it.'

There was a short silence, then Tim asked, 'How long is it until tomorrow morning?'

'A long, long time,' she said, her nerves jangling at their dogged persistence. 'Now, neither of you are to mention it again before you go to bed.'

'But . . .'

'I mean it, boys, honestly.'

'All right,' Tim agreed reluctantly. After a brief period of quiet, he announced, 'I like Ben.'

'I know you do,' she said.

'He can do lots of stuff,' put in Johnnie, breathless with awe. 'He can drive a boat, drive a car, play football . . .'

'He's a good swimmer too,' added Tim; they'd all been going to the local baths on a regular basis recently because Rachel thought it was important the boys learn to swim, and Ben was helping her to teach them.

'Do you like him, Mum?' enquired Johnnie casually.

'Yes, I think he's great, I like him very much.' Her heart lurched, because she had grown to do a lot more than just like him; she was well on the way to being head over heels in love with him. But she wasn't sure how he felt about her. Increasingly she sensed romantic vibes, but he'd never made any actual moves in that direction, had never shown any sign of wanting to be anything other than a pal for the boys. How she wished he would.

'How long till he comes for us for the race?' asked Johnnie, chancing his luck.

'What have I just told you about that?' She was feeling really harassed now.

'Sorry,' he said.

'I should think so too,' she said. 'Don't start that again, for goodness' sake.'

'How long do we have to wait until we can ask?' asked Tim with infuriating stubbornness.

'Aaah!' she shrieked. 'You little tykes are driving me up the wall with your questions, and I'm not answering any more of them.'

'You're driving Mummy up the wall,' Johnnie admonished his brother.

'So are you,' retorted Tim.

'You both are,' she said. 'So button your lips or there'll be no bedtime story.'

This had the required effect, for the moment anyway. When she'd helped Tim into his pyjamas and slippers, they trotted off into the other room. She was sorting out their clothes for the next day when the phone rang.

'Hello, Rachel.'

'Ben, hi,' she said, delighted to hear his voice.

'How are you?'

'I'm fine,' she said. 'Yourself?'

'Pretty good, thanks.'

'The boys have started the countdown to the race tomorrow, and they're driving me nuts,' she told him. 'So I hope you're not calling to tell me that it's cancelled.'

'No, nothing like that,' he assured her.

'Thank goodness for that,' she said, detecting some slight difference in his manner. He seemed a little tense and not quite as chatty as usual. 'I think I'd have had a mutiny on my hands if you had.'

Silence echoed down the line as she waited to learn the reason for his call. When nothing happened she decided to give him a nudge. 'So what can I do for you?' she asked in the studiously casual way of someone with hopeful expectations.

'Actually,' he began, pausing to clear his throat, 'I was

wondering if you're doing anything this evening?'

That sounded extremely promising, but she didn't want to take anything for granted. 'No. Nothing special. I'll be doing what I do every Saturday night,' she said lightly. 'Putting the boys to bed, watching the TV. I might go mad later on, though, and have coffee instead of cocoa.'

His rich, throaty laugh that she found so appealing resonated down the line. 'You're so funny, Rachel,' he said with a smile in his voice.

'You couldn't survive motherhood without a sense of humour,' she chuckled.

The line went silent again apart from a crackle of interference. She waited in hopeful anticipation.

'I was wondering,' he began hesitantly, 'if I could come round and see you.'

This really was beginning to sound favourable, she thought, but she kept her tone casual and said, 'You're welcome here any time, you know that.'

'That's nice,' he said. 'Thank you.'

'If you can get here in the next half-hour, you'll be in time to say good night to the boys.'

'I'll be there,' he told her.

'See you soon, then,' she said, replacing the receiver and raising her hands in jubilation. This could be the change of course she'd been hoping for.

By the time she answered the door to him, she'd made some effort to look like a civilised, attractive woman rather than a wild, harassed mum; she'd changed into a pair of slimline black trousers and a red overblouse, her hair was freshly brushed, and a dusting of make-up gave her face a glow.

The bottle of wine he was clutching gave her a clue that the essence of their relationship might be about to change. Although buoyant with hope and expectation, she deemed it wise to greet him in the normal way and let things take their course at his instigation.

The boys were in bed but had been told that Ben would go in to say good night to them when he arrived, which he did. 'Phew,' said Rachel, when she and Ben were finally settled in armchairs in the lounge with a glass of wine. 'I'm glad to get those two to bed; they've worn me out today.'

'Yeah?'

'Yeah,' she confirmed. 'They're so wound up about the race tomorrow, they haven't stopped yapping about it all day. And they're so impatient for the time to pass, they keep asking me how long they've got to wait.'

'If they're like that about a river race, what must they be like at Christmas?' he remarked casually.

She almost said she hoped he'd be around to find out this year, but said instead, 'Manic is the only way to describe it.'

He smiled, but seemed a little preoccupied.

'Isn't this nice?' she remarked.

'The wine?'

'The wine's lovely, but I was referring to your being here to share it with me,' she blurted out.

'Now that *is* a nice thing to say.' Ben was looking smart but casual in a V-necked sweater over a white shirt and pale grey, lightweight slacks. His face was freshly shaven and his hair combed neatly into place.

'Cheers,' she said, raising her glass. 'Here's to the race tomorrow, and may the best crew win.'

He lifted his glass. 'Let's hope it's the one competing in a boat made by us,' he said.

'That goes without saying,' she grinned.

An uneasy silence descended as they sipped their wine. She guessed that he had something on his mind and stayed quiet so that he could tell her about it.

'I phoned you on impulse,' he explained at last. 'I was on my own at home and thought I might as well . . .' His voice tailed off.

'You thought, Rachel is sure to be at home on a Saturday night because of the kids, so I was a safe bet,' she finished for him, keeping things light so that he'd feel able to continue.

He responded defensively. 'No, it wasn't like that at all.'

'Just kidding,' she laughed.

'Of course.' He tutted, making a face. 'I'm a bit slow on the uptake tonight.'

The atmosphere was alive with sexuality. Rachel restrained her urge to leap on him, partly because of female modesty and partly because of her maternal conditioning, which made her expect to be interrupted at any moment by the demands of a child.

'Is there something special on your mind, Ben?' she prompted.

'No.' He gulped his wine.

'No?'

'Well . . . yes, there is actually,' he burst out.

'And am I going to get to know what it is before my hair turns white?' she enquired.

He gave a nervous laugh, then blurted out, 'The fact of the matter is, Rachel . . . Well, I love the boys to bits and everything, but well . . . I'm not sure how to put this. You and I have got into a bit of an odd routine.' He scratched his head. 'It's awkward. I'm not certain how you'll take it.'

'You won't know unless you try me, will you?' she advised him in an encouraging tone.

'Oh, what the hell,' he said, standing up and looking at her. 'The truth is, I'm falling in love with you.'

'Well, isn't that the most amazing coincidence?' she smiled, putting down her drink and going into his arms.

Some time later, when the wine bottle was empty and they were ensconced together on the sofa, he said, 'You must have thought I was very slow.'

'I did wonder if you were ever going to get around to it,' she confessed.

'It wasn't so much a question of my not getting around to it,' he corrected. 'It was more that things were set into a pattern and I didn't know how to break out of it. We'd got caught up in a peculiar situation. If you hadn't felt the same, it would have made things very awkward.'

'I know,' she agreed. 'And I must admit that I didn't know what to do about it either.'

'All sorted now, though,' he said.

She snuggled more closely to him. 'Oh, yes, it's all sorted now,' she agreed happily.

Sunday was a perfect autumn day, hazy sunshine making an appearance around mid morning and shining on the crowds along the south bank of the Thames near Ham House, Richmond. The stately home, which dated back to Jacobean times, was screened from the river by glorious elms and sycamores. It was a lovely spot.

A carnival atmosphere prevailed on this stretch of the river this morning, coloured bunting lining the riverside at the starting point, ice cream vans and hot dog stalls doing a roaring trade as the crews and spectators waited for the cannon to indicate the start for the flotilla of rowing boats of varying sizes lined up and waiting to go.

'They're taking a long time to start, aren't they?' said Tim impatiently.

'Yeah,' agreed Johnnie. 'We've been here for ages. Why don't they start the race?'

'They have to wait for the tide,' explained Ben. 'But I think they'll be away very soon now.'

'Come on, Westford!' shouted Johnnie, getting into the spirit of the thing.

'You're not supposed to cheer until the race has started, dumbo,' rebuked his brother.

'Just practising,' said Johnnie.

They all laughed. They'd done a lot of that this morning, in between eating hot dogs and drinking coffee and cold drinks. Rachel was so happy to be here with her children and the man she loved, and who she now knew loved her.

'It must have been very hard to make that boat,' mentioned Tim, craning his neck to see the Westford craft, which was at the front of the flotilla.

'It took a lot of work but it wasn't hard because I knew what I was doing,' Ben explained. 'I was taught the job properly by a man who was very good at it.'

'I'm gonna be a boatmaker when I grow up,' announced Tim categorically.

'Why are some of the boats in front of the others?' asked Johnnie with interest.

'There's too many of them to have them all in one line,' explained Ben.

'But that isn't fair,' said Tim. 'The ones at the front will have more chance of winning.'

'That's all taken account of at the finish,' explained Ben. 'They're judged on their time.'

'Oh. That's all right then.' The explanation seemed to satisfy the boy.

'Hey up, everyone,' said Ben, looking towards the starting point and shading his eyes with his hand. 'I think they're about to start now.'

They fell silent, listening for the sound of the cannon which would set the race in motion. The explosion boomed into the air and the boats were off, cutting through the water. Westford got off to an excellent start.

Rachel and the others ran along the riverside cheering and shouting. It was so exciting to see the crew they were supporting moving at a fast, even pace. Rachel was yelling with such enthusiasm, her throat ached.

But suddenly something seemed to go wrong. The Westford boat slowed dramatically, even though the oarsmen were still rowing frantically. Other craft were overtaking them; they were being left behind.

'Come on, Westford, put a spurt on!' bellowed Ben. 'What's the matter with you?'

'What's happening, Ben?' asked Rachel, her eyes glued in

astonishment to the Westford craft as it began to wobble slightly, then rock violently, the valiant efforts of the oarsmen seeming to have no effect on the performance of the wayward craft.

'I'm blowed if I know,' Ben confessed, looking bewildered. 'The boat shouldn't be rocking like that.' He chewed his lip anxiously, raising his hand to his head. 'If I didn't know better, I'd think she was about to turn over.'

'That wouldn't happen, would it?' Rachel said.

'It certainly shouldn't do,' he told her.

'The crew will probably settle her in a minute,' suggested Rachel hopefully.

'I hope so,' he said, but he didn't sound convinced and the boat continued to lose speed.

'Oh, Ben!' Rachel cried with a sob in her voice, her gaze fixed firmly on the river. 'Look . . .'

'I don't believe it,' he gasped in amazement.

'Me neither,' muttered Rachel, clutching her sons' hands as they stood bewildered by her side.

They all stood rooted to the spot as, in full view of a large crowd of spectators, boating officials and enthusiasts, the boat that had been so lovingly crafted by Ben and his workmates rocked violently, then overturned, leaving the crew floundering in the water and the reputation of Banks' Boats in ruins.

Chapter Ten

'We don't know for certain that it was an act of sabotage on Arthur's part,' Rachel pointed out to Ben in the early evening of the same day. He had arrived back from the rowing club convinced that he knew who was to blame for the accident.

'Oh, come on, Rachel,' he said. 'I think we both know that it was.'

'But you've told me before that sabotage does sometimes happen between rival crews in big races.' She wanted him to be sure of his facts before any accusations were made, because Arthur would leap on the opportunity to claim slander. 'Could it have been something like that, perhaps?'

'That sort of thing does go on,' he admitted. 'Unscrupulous competitors sometimes slip someone a few quid to pierce a hole in a rival boat at the starting point. But the damage to our boat was done by someone who wanted to harm our reputation rather than that of the rowing club. It was made to look as though the boat overturned because of shoddy workmanship.'

She tutted, shaking her head. 'What was actually done to the boat?' she asked.

'The bolts on several of the oar support frames had been partially loosened so that the fault wouldn't be noticed until the race got under way and the rowing got into a steady rhythm,' he explained. 'Then, of course, the supports collapsed, upsetting the balance and making the boat wobble and turn over. It was definitely planned to look as though we hadn't done our job properly.'

'So it must have been done by someone who knows something about boatbuilding,' she suggested.

'Absolutely,' he confirmed with emphasis. 'The saboteur knew exactly what he was doing.'

'That rules Arthur out then, doesn't it?' she pointed out. 'He knows nothing about boats at all.'

'A detail like that wouldn't stop a man like Arthur,' Ben declared heatedly. 'He'll have paid someone to do the job for him.'

'Of course he would,' she agreed. 'I hadn't thought of that. It does sound more like Arthur's style. He wouldn't want to get his own hands dirty.'

'Exactly,' Ben affirmed.

They were sitting at Rachel's kitchen table having a cup of tea together; the boys were busy with their crayons and colouring books in the other room. The day had been a huge disappointment for them. Not only had the team they were supporting failed so spectacularly, but Rachel and the boys had been deprived of Ben's company too. He'd had to spend the rest of the day trying to convince the officials at Westford Rowing Club – who, understandably, blamed the boatbuilder for their humiliating demise – that it was an act of sabotage and not bad workmanship. By way of compensation, Rachel had taken the children to the park and then to Wilbur Terrace to see their grandparents. But they'd missed being with Ben, who'd only got back to the flat about ten minutes ago, convinced of Arthur's guilt and incandescent with rage. She had never seen him so angry.

'Have you got any idea when the damage was done?' she wondered.

'It must have been either last night or early this morning,' he informed her. 'It couldn't have been before then because the crew had been using the boat for practice and would have noticed something then. It must have been done when the boat was in the rowing club's boat store.' He stroked his chin meditatively. 'The strange thing is, there's no evidence of a break-in. That's why the club officials are putting it down to bad workmanship. And I suppose you can't blame them.'

'It must have been an inside job, then,' Rachel assumed.

'Most unlikely,' pronounced Ben. 'No one at Westford would want to ruin the chances of their own club, no matter how much of a financial incentive they were offered.'

'Looks as though we have a mystery on our hands, then,' she told him.

'Not for long, though,' he declared forcefully. 'I'll soon get to the bottom of this lousy trick. No danger.'

'In the meantime, what do we do about keeping Westford's goodwill?' she asked.

'I've told them I'll have the boat in first thing tomorrow morning for a thorough overhaul at no cost to them,' he explained. 'It might take a bit of persuasion, but I'm hoping to make them see that the cause of the accident wasn't shoddy workmanship on our part. Once they've got over the disappointment, they'll be more receptive to what I have to say.'

'How can you prove it to them, though?' she wondered.

'I can't actually prove it,' he admitted. 'But I can point out a few technicalities to them. I shall tell them that if we hadn't fixed the bolts properly, the crew would have noticed something wasn't quite right when they were out on the river training before the race. The fact that the supports actually collapsed within minutes of the start is a strong enough indication that the bolts were tampered with.'

'That makes sense to me,' Rachel said.

'And I hope it will to them when they've calmed down. They were too angry to be reasonable today, needing to blame someone, not willing to listen. The maker of the boat was the obvious target for their fury.'

'I do hope you can convince them, Ben,' she said with a worried shake of her head. 'We've only just got the business back into profit. The last thing we need now is a slur on our reputation.'

'Leave it to me,' he reassured her. 'I'll get it sorted. I might not be able to prove who it was who set us up but I think I can make the officials at Westford see the truth of what happened, without seeming to pass the buck. They know the standard of our work. We've been making their boats for yonks.'

'There is that,' she said, his positive attitude raising her own optimism.

'In the meantime, do you have Arthur's address?' he asked. 'I've some business to do with that bloke.'

'It's my job to sort him out,' she told him. 'I'm the one he's trying to get at, not you.'

'If he hurts you, he hurts me too,' he said simply, his tone becoming tender.

She was imbued with warmth for him. 'Oh, Ben, you say the nicest things,' she said, reaching for his hand across the table and squeezing it.

'I'm only saying what I feel,' he uttered softly, taking her hand in both of his. 'Anyway, even apart from my feelings for you, he's put my reputation as a boatbuilder on the line and I'm not having that. So you leave Arthur to me.'

'However you deal with it, you have my blessing,' she said. 'But be careful. He's not a nice man.'

'Don't worry about me. I'm a match for the likes of Arthur Banks. And there's no time like the present.' He stood up, giving her a melting smile. 'When I get back, perhaps we can take up where we left off last night.'

'That would be lovely.' She gave him an intimate smile. 'This awful business has put a damper on what was otherwise a wonderful weekend.'

'There'll be others,' he said gently. 'Lots of others.'

'Yeah, I know,' she replied softly.

'And this one isn't over yet,' he reminded her.

'Not quite,' she smiled.

'I'll go and say good night to the boys while you find

Arthur's address for me,' he said.

'OK,' she replied, going out into the hall to fetch her address book.

Ella answered the door to Ben. 'Yeah?' she said, scowling at him. 'What do you want?'

'Is Arthur in?' he asked.

She narrowed her eyes on him, as though trying to place him. 'You're the bloke from the boathouse, aren't you?'

'That's right.'

'Arthur's not here,' she informed him briskly.

'Don't give me that,' he challenged.

'He's not here,' she said again with emphasis, opening the door wider and waving her arm towards the hall. 'Come in and have a look if you don't believe me.'

He believed her. 'I need to see him as a matter of urgency,' he told her.

'You can't see him if he's not here, can you?' she sighed, rolling her eyes impatiently.

'Where is he?' asked Ben. 'Do you know?'

'Whether I know or not is none of your business,' she snapped.

'He's in some pub or other, I bet,' guessed Ben.

'So what if he is?' She wasn't prepared to co-operate. 'There's no law against it.'

'Which one?'

In reply she tapped the side of her nose with her finger, looking at him with disdain.

Ben's face was sheer granite. 'OK,' he said, his tone hardening. 'You can take your choice. Either you tell me where I can find him *now* or I'll come back later on, when the pubs are shut, and bang on your door until you let me in. I'll stay here all night if I have to, and I won't pass the time quietly.'

Ella thought about this. She supposed it couldn't do any harm if she was to tell him where Arthur was, since the job was done and he couldn't prove that Arthur was involved. And it would save having a ruckus here later on, which would give the narky neighbours grounds for complaint.

'He's in the Fiddler's Arms, Hammersmith,' she informed him. 'The big pub at the end of King Street.'

'I know the one,' he said, and hurried away from the block of flats towards his car.

'It tipped over exactly as you said it would, leaving the crew in the water and out of the race,' said Arthur, roaring with laughter as he recounted the tale to Brian at a corner table in the Hammersmith pub where they'd arranged to meet that evening. 'So much for the reputation of Banks' boathouse now, eh? You certainly know your boatbuilding, mate . . . you did well.'

'I wish I could have seen the look on Ben Smart's face when the boat turned over,' grinned Brian in a rare cheerful mood. 'But I thought it best to keep away as I don't usually take an interest in river races. Didn't want anyone wondering why I was there and putting two and two together afterwards.'

'Wise man,' approved Arthur. 'A mate of mine went on my behalf because I didn't want to risk going myself, in case they spotted me and got suspicious. Seeing as I've never watched a rowing race in my life.'

'It's best to be on the safe side,' agreed Brian. 'But there's nothing at all to connect either of us with it, I can promise you that.'

'Did the job go smoothly?' enquired Arthur, eager to know the details.

'Sweet as a nut,' Brian told him, brimming with self-satisfaction. 'As we arranged, I went into Westford's club bar on the pretext of having a drink . . .'

'It was lucky for us that Banks' Boats staff members are allowed to drink in the Westford clubhouse,' interrupted Arthur. 'Some sort of special arrangement, you say?'

'Yeah, it's because of Banks' long-term connections with

the club, apparently. Heaven sent for us, 'cause it meant I didn't have to break in.'

'So you stuck to the original plan, did you?' prompted Arthur eagerly.

'That's right. I knew the office wouldn't be locked while the bar was open because staff are in and out for various reasons,' he explained. 'So I kept slipping out to the Gents', which is near the office, until there was nobody around, then I nipped into the office and got the key to the boat store. I went in, did the business, put the key back in the office and was back in the bar before you could say "Man overboard". Job done and no sign of forced entry, just as we planned, mate.'

'Well done.'

'I enjoyed teaching that Ben Smart a lesson,' said Brian gleefully. 'The big-headed git.'

'And I've settled my score with *her*,' mentioned Arthur, feeling hugely pleased with himself.

'So now that we're both happy,' said Brian, 'I'll have the final payment.'

'Yeah, of course,' said Arthur, reaching into his pocket, far too high on success to exercise caution. 'It's been a pleasure doing business with you.'

'Yeah, you an' all,' smiled Brian.

The instant Ben saw Arthur and Brian together he knew exactly how the sabotage had been done so neatly and without any sign of a break-in. Until that moment it hadn't occurred to him that one of their own staff would be so lacking in scruples as to use his position to make trouble for the firm.

Sitting at a table with their heads close together, the two men were deeply immersed in conversation. Ben watched them for a while, gradually edging towards them unobserved, choosing his moment to make his presence known. They were far too engrossed to notice him.

When he saw Arthur take some paper money out of his pocket and hand it to Brian, he made his move. 'I'll take that,' he said, swiftly snatching the notes from Brian's hand and putting them into his own pocket. 'It'll go towards the damage to the boat.'

Both men were stunned into silence. But not for long. 'Here, give that back to me,' said Brian, 'or I'll call the law.'

'I don't think you'll do anything as silly as that,' Ben told him evenly, sitting down and speaking *sotto voce* so as not to attract attention. 'Not after what you've been up to.'

Brian didn't bother to deny it. 'You can't prove anything,' he said with a nonchalant shrug.

'That's quite true, I can't. But I'm sure you wouldn't want me to have a word with the local police about it, just in case they start sniffing around, and upsetting your dad.'

'I'm not worried about him,' was the scornful reply.

'I'm sure you're not,' agreed Ben in an even tone. 'But you're going to have quite enough problems at home without adding police harassment to them.'

'I'm not the one with problems,' Brian retorted, giving Ben a meaningful look.

'You will be without a pay packet to look forward to every week,' Ben informed him. 'Your dad won't like that one little bit.'

'I wasn't gonna stay on at Banks' Boats anyway,' Brian scoffed. 'I've just been biding my time.'

'You won't get a job at any boatbuilding firm,' declared Ben. 'I'll make sure of that.'

Despite Brian's unconcerned manner, Ben guessed he was shaken by this turn of events. He might not enjoy boatbuilding but at least it was something he knew how to do, and he was aware of Ben's influence in the trade.

'You don't scare me,' he blustered.

Suddenly sickened by his noisome presence, Ben said, 'Oh, get out of here so that I can talk to the organ grinder. Go on, get lost!'

'I'm going,' he said but didn't make a move.

'And count yourself lucky that I'm not a violent man,'

added Ben. 'Go on, before I change my mind.'

Looking aggrieved, Brian got up and left without another word.

'Right,' said Ben, looking at Arthur coldly. 'Outside.'

'What?'

'You heard,' said Ben, standing up. 'We'll finish our business outside.'

'I don't have any business with you,' said Arthur, who was wishing he'd made his escape while Ben had his attention focused on Brian. Ben was a bit too fit and nifty for Arthur, who was fully aware of his own limitations in that department. It was only greed that had kept him here, the thought that he might, somehow, be able to retrieve his money.

'Maybe not, but I have business with you. So . . . are you going to come outside of your own accord or shall I drag you out?' threatened Ben. 'And don't think I wouldn't do it, because I would. Causing a scene has never bothered me.'

Whey-faced, Arthur got up. Outside, Ben grabbed his arms and dragged him round the back to the small car park.

'Here, what's your game?' Arthur gasped as Ben pushed him against the wall and held him in an iron grip.

'This isn't a game,' Ben informed him gruffly. 'Oh no, this is deadly serious.'

'You've got nothing on me,' growled Arthur. 'You can't prove a thing and you know it.'

'I caught you paying Brian off,' Ben reminded him. 'That's good enough for me.'

'It's only your word against mine,' Arthur pointed out breathlessly. 'Surely you don't expect Brian to back up your story, do you?'

'I'm not that stupid,' replied Ben, holding the other man's arms tightly. 'I may not have the proof but I know that you set it up.'

'All right, so what if I did? What was I supposed to do when that bitch of a woman stole my inheritance?'

'Don't you *dare* speak about her like that – and she didn't steal it from you,' said Ben, pulling him forward then pushing him back against the wall.

'As good as.'

'It was left to her fair and square,' continued Ben. He knew from Rachel that Arthur earned his living from amusement machines. His common sense told him that owners of such machines wouldn't live in dingy accommodation such as he'd just visited, and that mere collectors couldn't afford to wear flash clothes and pay people to work for them. He decided to use this to emphasise his point. 'And if you ever make trouble for her again, not only will I break all your limbs, I shall also make sure that your guv'nor gets to know that you've got plenty of money to throw around, paying people like Brian to do your dirty work. I'm sure he'll be very curious about that.'

'I dunno what you're getting at,' denied Arthur, but Ben could see the fear in his eyes.

'Don't make me laugh,' said Ben, his breath coming fast with the physical strain of retaining his hold on the other man. 'You don't make enough from emptying amusement machines to be able to afford to dish out dough to losers like Brian Miller. And don't tell me the machines are yours, because I won't believe you.'

'All right, so they're not mine,' admitted Arthur, groaning under the pressure of Ben's bruising grip.

'Which means that you're taking a slice that your guv'nor knows nothing about,' he accused.

'You've got no proof,' bluffed Arthur, but he was worried. The boss had been suspicious once before, and Arthur daren't take any risks because he couldn't afford to lose the job until he'd found something to replace it. Played straight, the job wasn't worth much, but it was fertile ground for fiddling and it provided him with contacts who might be useful in the future.

'I don't need proof,' Ben pointed out. 'A word in your guv'nor's ear about the scam you've just pulled with Brian, and, more importantly, the fact that you could afford to give him a wad of notes, would be enough to make him keep a closer eye on you. You'll be out of a job before you've got time to catch your breath.'

'You wouldn't,' challenged Arthur.

'I will, if there's so much as a hint of trouble for Rachel from you *ever again*,' he said, squeezing Arthur's arms even tighter to make his point. 'Do I make myself clear?'

'OK, OK,' wailed Arthur. 'I get the message. Now for God's sake let go of me, will you? You're breaking my arms.'

'I'll break more than that if you don't give me your promise that you'll keep away from her,' Ben persisted.

'I will, I will,' said Arthur. 'I wanted to get back at her, that's all. It's done and finished. I won't trouble her again.'

'You'd better not,' warned Ben, letting him go at last. 'You'll regret it if you do.'

'I've told you I won't and I meant it,' said Arthur, rubbing his arms and sucking in his breath. 'So now that we've got that sorted, you can give me my money back.'

'You're joking.' If it hadn't been such a serious matter, Ben might have laughed.

'Let's split it fifty-fifty then,' Arthur suggested. 'It was my money in the first place.'

'That money is going to Rachel so that the firm can put right the damage to the boat,' said Ben. 'Anything left over will go into a charity box.'

'Oh well,' sighed Arthur gloomily. 'You can't win 'em all, I suppose.'

'You won't win anything at all if you don't change your attitude to life,' advised Ben.

'Spare me the lecture,' muttered Arthur, before turning and going back into the pub to drown his sorrows, while Ben got into his car and drove back to Rachel's.

'You won't have any more trouble from Arthur,' Ben stated categorically. He and Rachel were sitting on the sofa together and he'd given her a full report of events at the pub.

'Thanks, Ben.'

'My pleasure.'

'He must have been beside himself with rage when you got the money,' grinned Rachel.

'That was an extra bonus for us, I must admit,' he laughed. 'The timing couldn't have been more perfect if I'd planned it that way. But it was just chance that I happened to walk into the pub at exactly the right moment to find out who the saboteur was and to appropriate the money in one fell swoop. I was pushing my luck in taking the money, but I didn't see why they shouldn't pay for the damage they caused.'

'Arthur's face must have been a picture,' she said.

'Not half.'

'I can't believe he asked you to split it with him,' she said. 'Only Arthur would have the cheek.'

'He's a brave man with his line of patter but he's got no bottle when it comes to anything else,' he told her. 'He was scared witless when I got him outside the pub. It was as much as he could do not to burst into tears. No wonder he has to pay someone else to take risks for him.'

'It's hard to imagine him being Uncle Chip's son, isn't it?' she remarked.

'Or your brother,' he added.

'Don't mention that,' she said quickly. 'I try not to think of him in that light.'

'It just goes to show that character isn't always hereditary, though,' he mentioned.

'Which is just as well, because I should hate to think that either of my boys might take after their selfish father.'

'No chance of that with you bringing them up,' he reassured her heartily.

'I may not always get it right, but I do my best,' she told him. 'Since raising children is something you learn on the job, you have to rely on common sense and trust your instincts. There's plenty of advice around from experts who write books on the subject, like Dr Spock. But in the end you have to get on and do it your way.'

'You're doing a good job, you can take it from me,' he assured her.

'Thank you,' she said, snuggling closer to him.

'I wonder if Arthur will tell his wife what happened,' he mentioned casually.

'He'll probably give her a fictionalised version,' she suggested. 'Something along the lines that he beat you up and sent you scurrying off with your tail between your legs. He wouldn't admit the truth and risk looking a fool in her eyes.'

'Not Arthur.'

'I really am grateful to you for sorting him out,' Rachel told him, taking his hand in a gesture of tender appreciation. 'But I hope you don't think that I'm always going to sit back and let you fight my battles for me.'

'I think I know you well enough to realise that you're your own woman,' he assured her. 'Though I'll willingly do it if you want me to.'

'That's nice,' she said softly.

He slipped his arm around her. 'Without intending to belittle your independence in any way, I think there are times when a spot of male muscle is the best thing for the job; this business with Arthur was one of those times.'

She looked up at him. 'My hero,' she said in a light-hearted, jokey manner.

'I hope I can always be that,' he said, pulling her to him and kissing her.

Unbeknown to them, the door wasn't quite closed and two eyes peered through the gap. Then a small figure padded back to bed and buried himself beneath the covers.

Rachel was thrilled to have her feelings for Ben out in the open. The intensity and excitement of being in love made her feel like a young girl again. Everybody else seemed pleased for her too. Jan said they made a smashing couple; Marge claimed they were made for each other and it was about time Rachel had some fun and romance in her life; and Ron simply said that it was good news.

Inevitably, Ben spent a lot more time with her and the boys; he was at the flat most evenings and at weekends. When her mother included him in the standing Sunday lunch invitation, Rachel really felt as though he'd been accepted as one of the family. They didn't talk about moving in together or divorcing their ex partners at this stage, though Rachel assumed that that would be the next step. For the moment, however, they just enjoyed spending time together and getting to know each other better.

Everything would have been perfect had it not been for the sudden and dramatic change in Tim's behaviour. The sunny-natured little boy everyone loved became moody, rude and downright naughty at times. Although Rachel's patience was stretched to breaking point, her heart ached for him too. She knew he must be very unhappy to behave like this.

'Attention-seeking, that's what it is,' pronounced Marge one day in November when all the family were gathered at Wilbur Terrace for Sunday lunch.

'She's right,' agreed Ron.

The adults were lingering at the table after lunch, discussing an upsetting incident during the meal which had resulted in Tim being banished from the table and sent upstairs to the spare room in disgrace. He had shocked them all by picking up the gravy boat and deliberately emptying the contents on to the clean tablecloth, thereby wrecking the occasion for everyone. Rachel was embarrassed by his appalling conduct and desperately worried as to why her darling child had become such a monster.

'It'll pass,' predicted Marge.

'But why would he suddenly start behaving like this?' said Rachel. She had given the boy a thorough scolding but had failed, as usual, to extract any explanation from him. 'He was such a wonderful child; he's never been the sort of boy to want more than his fair share of attention.'

'They all go through phases,' said Marge, to ease Rachel's worry, though she herself was concerned.

'It's my job to bring him through this and I don't know how,' confessed Rachel. 'I've tried the firm approach and I've tried being kind. I've done my damnedest to find out what's behind it but he just keeps shtoom. It's almost as though he doesn't know himself why he's doing it, and he can't control his actions.' She paused as a powerful surge of compassion for Tim swept over her, despite all her anger and frustration. 'Although he's being infuriating, he seems so sad and vulnerable too.'

'He's obviously feeling wretched about something,' put in Jan, 'or he wouldn't be doing it.'

Rachel nodded, biting her lip.

'Perhaps he's worried about starting school after Christmas,' suggested Jan. 'It could be playing on his mind without him actually realising it.'

'It could be, but I don't think so,' was Rachel's opinion. 'He seems to be looking forward to it so much.'

'Kids don't always show what they're really feeling, though, do they?' Jan reminded her. 'When they're worried about something it often comes out in different ways.'

'I've been wondering if it's anything to do with Ben and me,' mentioned Rachel, glancing at Ben, who was sitting beside her.

'It does seem to have started at about the time we got together as a couple,' he pointed out.

'But the boy thinks the world of you, doesn't he, Ben?' said Marge. 'So it isn't likely to be that.'

'I've always got on very well with both of them, I must admit,' he told her.

'He's Tim's hero,' Rachel put in, looking around the table at them all. 'Which is why it doesn't make sense for it to be that. Surely the fact that Ben and I are together would make him feel more secure, not less. I mean, he can't possibly see Ben as a threat, because they both love having him around and can't get enough of him.' She looked at Ben. 'Isn't that right, love?'

'It always seems that way,' he said. 'Especially Tim, because he's so keen on anything to do with boats.'

'It's probably just a temporary thing,' suggested Pete helpfully. 'He'll get over it.'

'And in the meantime he's spoiling things for the rest of us,' said Rachel, tension knots pulling tight in her stomach. 'Honestly, I don't know what he's going to do next these days.'

'There's one thing for certain,' her father pointed out. 'The more attention it brings him, the more he'll do it.'

'I know that. But I can't ignore it, can I?' said Rachel, at her wits' end. 'He can't be allowed to get away with it.'

'It's easier said than done, but try not to let him see how much it's getting to you,' Jan advised her.

There was general agreement about this and a few more suggestions about how she should deal with the problem before they eventually moved on to other topics.

Ron asked how things were going at the boathouse. 'Did you manage to square things with the rowing club after the trouble Arthur caused?' he said to Ben.

Ben nodded. 'I think I've smoothed things over with them. I told them what had happened without mentioning any names,' he explained. 'I just said it was someone who had a grudge against us and the member of staff involved had now been dismissed. In the end they accepted that it had been done deliberately.'

'Thank God for that,' said Ron.

Marge shook her head gravely. 'Arthur,' she sighed. 'I'm ashamed to call him a relative of mine.'

'Well,' said Rachel, eager to move on from a subject that always reminded her of her true place in the family, 'we'd better start clearing up and get the dishes washed, or it'll be teatime before we've finished.'

There was a ripple of agreement and they all began to make a move.

That night Rachel was awakened with a start by a movement beside her.

'Tim,' she said as he snuggled against her. 'What's the matter, darling?'

'Nothing.'

'Don't you feel well, love?' Illness was the usual reason for the patter of little feet in the night.

'I'm all right,' he said sleepily, cuddling into her.

'That's all right then.'

'I love you, Mummy.'

'And I love you, Tim,' she said, and they fell asleep snuggled closely together.

The same thing happened the next night and quite often after that until it became a regular habit. He obviously needed extra security at the moment for some reason. She was worried sick about him.

If the weather was reasonable, Ben still took the boys for a Sunday-morning trip in *Nipper* even though winter was beginning to take a hold. Sometimes Johnnie didn't want to go so he and Rachel stayed at home.

One Sunday in November, however, the weather was so lovely that they all went out on the river. It was one of those sharp and still winter days with gentle sunshine and a smoky blue sky.

'I can't believe what a smashing day it is,' Rachel remarked casually as they took a stroll along the riverside afterwards, the boys running on ahead swathed in red fur-lined jackets and red and white woollen bobble hats. 'Fog and frost is more what we expect in November.'

'Let's make the most of it,' Ben said. 'It'll probably revert to normal tomorrow.'

They moved at a brisk place to stay warm, arm in arm,

chatting pleasantly and enjoying watching the children ahead of them. But suddenly they both broke into a run as Tim climbed on to the river wall and stood there waving his arms in a deliberate attempt to provoke them. Having grown up near the river, he'd been taught not to go too near the edge and was fully aware that he was breaking the rules.

'You naughty boy,' rebuked Rachel, her voice distorted with fear and anger as Ben lifted the boy off the wall and set him down firmly on the path. 'You know you mustn't go near the river's edge. It's high tide, you could have fallen in and drowned.'

She could hardly believe her eyes when he poked his tongue out at her.

'Tim . . .'

'Don't you dare do that to your mother,' intervened Ben before she could finish.

'Shut up, you,' said the boy, glaring at Ben, his cheeks brightly suffused with temper but his eyes filled with tears. 'It's none of your business.'

'Tim!' Rachel said again, aghast to see her adored and hitherto well-mannered son behaving in such a way. 'Don't speak to Ben like that.' Her heart was thumping and her nerves tingling. 'Now, say you're sorry.' She was very stern. 'This minute.'

'No.'

'Just do it, Tim,' she insisted.

The atmosphere was fraught with tension as they waited for him to do as he'd been told. 'I hate you all,' he said, and broke away from them and tore off along the path.

Rachel hesitated for only a fraction of a second. 'Could you look after Johnnie, please, Ben?' she requested. 'I'll take care of this on my own.'

'Sure,' he said, taking Johnnie's hand while she dashed off in pursuit of her first-born child.

She caught up with Tim on the stretch of the riverside beyond the Dove. She was on the verge of tears but determined not to let him know that. 'You're a very bad boy,' she told him, grabbing him tightly by the hand. 'Very bad indeed. Don't you dare run away from me.'

His eyes were brimming with tears as he stared at her, his bottom lip trembling as he struggled not to cry.

'You know that it's very rude to poke your tongue out at someone, don't you?' she reproved. 'Are you going to say that you're sorry?'

He didn't reply at once but hung his head in shame. 'Sorry,' he mumbled at last.

'Don't you ever let me see you do that again, to anyone,' she ordered firmly. 'Is that clear?'

Silence.

'I'm waiting, Tim,' she persisted.

'OK.' His head was down and his voice barely audible.

Sensing that this was the right moment to bring things to a head, and also suspecting that he was desperate for her to lead him out of the impasse he found himself in, she said more gently, 'I think it's about time you and me had a talk, don't you?'

He shrugged.

She found a bench and sat down, patting it for him to sit beside her. 'So, what's all this about?' she enquired in a subdued tone.

Up went his shoulders again.

'Are you cross with me about something?' she asked, looking at his profile, the small bowed head.

'No,' he muttered, his voice barely audible.

'Has Ben upset you in some way then?' she wanted to know.

No reply.

'You like Ben, don't you?'

He studied his mittened hands, moving them about. 'Yeah, I like him, but . . .'

'But what, darling?' she urged him.

'Everything has changed now, it isn't the same,' he mumbled without looking up.

'You mean now that Ben and I are . . .'

His nod of affirmation came before she'd finished the sentence, and she struggled to find the right words to comfort him whilst remaining honest about her relationship with Ben. 'But I still love you the same as I always have. Being with Ben hasn't changed that. It never would.'

'It isn't that . . .'

'What then?'

'Ben was *my* friend,' he reminded her.

With the utmost gentleness, she turned his face towards her and looked at him intently. 'He still is, Tim,' she told him.

'He's *your* friend now,' he stated miserably.

The penny finally dropped. 'So that's it,' she said. 'You think I've taken him away from you.'

'He kisses you,' he tried to explain.

'Well, yes.' Whilst she and Ben didn't make an exhibition of their feelings in public, they didn't try to hide them either. 'It's what grown-ups do when they like each other a lot. It doesn't mean that he's stopped loving you, or being your friend.'

'I saw him *kissing* you one night,' he went on in a whisper, as though he'd witnessed an act of such horror he daren't say it out loud. 'I got out of bed and went down the hall. I saw you through the gap in the door.'

Scanning her mind for anything else he might have seen, she was confident there was nothing. She and Ben were always aware of the children's presence in the flat and were therefore very discreet. 'Why didn't you tell us you were there?'

'Dunno,' he said.

'The way Ben and I are with each other doesn't make any difference to the way we both feel about you and Johnnie,' she explained. 'Loving you both has brought us together.'

'Will he go away?' he asked, his sudden change of tack

making her realise just how confused he was.

'What on earth has put a thing like that into your mind?' she said.

'Dad went away, didn't he?' he reminded her.

'Yes, he did.' Her thoughts were racing, her head throbbing. Surely he'd been too young to be affected by Jeff's departure? 'But that doesn't mean that Ben will too.'

'Doesn't it?'

'Of course not,' she said, putting her arm around him and holding him close.

'Oh, good.'

'Do you remember your dad?' she probed gently.

'I don't think so,' he confessed. 'I don't know what his face looked like.'

'The thing is, Tim,' she said after a pause, 'if you want Ben to stay around, you'll have to be nicer to him than you've been just lately. Or he'll think you've gone off him.'

'You mean he won't come to see us or take us out on the boat any more?' His voice rose with worry.

'He might get fed up if you're going to be horrid to him like you were just now,' she said. 'And who could blame him?'

'Oh,' he said glumly.

'But you could easily make things right by saying sorry to him,' she suggested hopefully. 'I think he'd really like that.'

'He's cross with me, though, isn't he?' he said nervously, obviously afraid to face Ben.

'Well, he's bound to be, a bit, isn't he?' she suggested reasonably. 'But I'm sure he'll forgive you when you've said you're sorry and promised not to be rude to him, or any of us, again.'

'OK,' he agreed reluctantly.

'Good boy.'

After a long hug and copious tears shed by them both, mother and son walked hand in hand along the riverside to find Ben and Johnnie.

* * *

‘He’s obviously been feeling threatened by the change in our relationship,’ Rachel told Ben that night. She’d waited until the boys were asleep to give him the full story, though Tim had made his peace with Ben earlier on.

‘He doesn’t want to share you with me,’ he said. ‘It’s perfectly understandable.’

‘He doesn’t want to share you with me either,’ she amended.

‘I didn’t realise the emotions of a five-year-old could be so complicated.’ He chuckled. ‘But I’m flattered, I must say, that he cares that much about me.’

‘I suppose he thinks that because we’re paying each other attention, he’s going to lose out both ways,’ she suggested.

‘Mm.’

‘The poor kid has been hurting so badly inside, he couldn’t stop himself from hitting out at us all,’ she said.

‘Poor little chap.’

‘I feel sorry for him too,’ she confessed. ‘Even though he’s been a perfect brat lately.’

‘He seemed more like his old self this afternoon, though,’ Ben mentioned.

‘Oh yes, now that it’s all come to a head, I think he’ll feel better,’ she said. ‘But we’ll have to tread carefully while he’s still in this fragile state of mind.’

Ben nodded thoughtfully.

‘Obviously he mustn’t be allowed to get away with rudeness and tantrums, whatever the reason,’ Rachel emphasised. ‘But until he’s feeling more settled within himself and realises that our relationship isn’t going to change anything for him, let’s make sure he isn’t given the opportunity to get the wrong impression.’

‘Sure, I’ll go along with that,’ he agreed. ‘I could take him out on the boat on his own, if you think it’ll help.’ He was eager to do what he could to help this family he’d grown to love. ‘Johnnie isn’t as keen as Tim anyway in the cold weather.’

'That's nice of you,' she said, looking at him. 'You're so thoughtful.'

'I want to be a part of the whole of your lives,' he told her. 'The serious things as well as the fun bits.'

'All of this domestic stuff must be a real pain for you,' she remarked thoughtfully. 'I mean, having children to consider, their emotional problems cluttering up your love life.'

'It's worth it,' he assured her.

'It isn't every man who would be willing to take on someone else's children,' she pointed out. 'I should think that your average unattached male would much rather be seeing some childless woman with no ties and no complications.'

'I can't speak for other men; I only know that isn't how it is for me,' he told her gravely.

'You are sweet,' she said.

'Oh dear,' he said, making a face. 'You're making me sound very dull.'

'You could never be that,' she chuckled. 'I just want you to know that I realise it might be difficult for you at times. It's a wonder you don't want to back off.'

'Surely you don't think I'm that shallow, do you?' he said, looking hurt.

'It isn't a question of being shallow,' she assured him ardently. 'It's just that I think it must be hard for you, you know, never having any peace.'

'It isn't a problem.'

'There must be times when you wish that we were on our own with no one else to consider, though.' She looked at him tenderly.

'Obviously there are occasional moments when I wish we had nothing else to do but please ourselves, talk about adult things and make love without fear of interruption,' he admitted frankly. 'But they are only occasional fleeting moments. And I don't think I'm any different to any other man in that respect. I should think most married men with kids probably have similar thoughts now and again. It doesn't mean they don't love their family and value their position within it.'

'True.'

'But honestly, Rachel,' he said solemnly, 'I wouldn't have it any other way.' He paused. 'And I'm not just saying that because I know it can't be any different.'

'The boys and I come as a package,' she said. 'That's what you're trying to say.'

He nodded. 'And it's the right package for me,' he said. 'I love you all to bits and I love the way you love them. I don't see them as rivals for your affections. I enjoy sharing you with them and I couldn't be more fond of them if they were my own.'

'Oh, Ben, I'm so lucky to have you,' she said.

'No, I'm the lucky one,' he hastened to correct her. 'I've got you loving me and two little boys to keep me young. How else would I get the chance to kick a football around in the park, play cowboys and Indians or show off my boating skills uncriticised, if it wasn't for them?'

'You are a fool,' she said softly.

Who would have thought her life would take such a turn for the better? she thought. This time last year she'd been slaving away in a factory to keep home and hearth together, terrified that one of the children would need new shoes or some other essential that she couldn't afford to pay for; she'd been completely disillusioned about the male species after Jeff's betrayal, and her confidence in herself as a woman had been non-existent.

Now the love of a wonderful man had restored her faith in herself and she had her own business which enabled her to bring up her darling sons in a decent manner.

'A fool, am I?' he joshed, playfully slapping her arm.

'Don't ever change.' Her manner became deadly serious. 'And don't let anything come between us.'

'That's a promise,' he vowed solemnly. 'On both counts.'

Chapter Eleven

Christmas was very special for Rachel and the boys that year. Ben entered into the spirit of the season with such gusto, it was difficult to tell who was more wound up, him or the boys.

The holiday seemed to flash by, a veritable blur of joy and laughter, all the usual family festivities enhanced by Ben's warm and entertaining presence among them. The fact that Tim was his old self again added to the pleasure too.

Rachel felt quite sentimental when Tim started school in January. And she wasn't the only mother feeling emotional at the school that first morning, either.

'Got time for a quick cup of coffee at my place before you go to work?' Jan suggested thickly. 'If we're both going to be miserable, we may as well do it together.'

'Good idea,' agreed Rachel and they walked back to Jan's house with Johnnie between them, neither saying very much.

'They're both more than ready for school, of course,' Jan pointed out as she made the coffee.

'I'm not sure I'm ready for them to go, though,' said Rachel with a nervous giggle.

'Me neither.'

'They'll be fine,' Rachel said as Jan put a mug of coffee on the kitchen table in front of her. 'They'll be full of it when we collect them later on.'

'Course they will,' agreed Jan. 'I didn't half feel put out, though, when the teacher took Kelly away and shooed all us mums out of there. I felt like saying, "Here, don't you tell my Kelly what to do. She's mine and I do the telling."'

'I felt a bit like that too,' grinned Rachel. 'I suppose our protective maternal instincts are bound to go a bit wild at a time like this. Starting school is a big step.'

'A new stage in their lives,' added Jan.

'We won't be at the centre of their world any more,' said Rachel wistfully. 'They'll have new horizons.'

'It'll certainly seem quiet around here during the day without them.' Jan turned to Johnnie, who was drinking a mug of hot chocolate. 'Won't it, love?' she said.

He nodded gloomily, seeming bewildered by the whole thing. 'I want to go to school with Tim and Kelly,' he announced.

'This time next year you'll be going too,' his mother sighed. 'All three of you off to school every morning.'

'And what will your Auntie Jan do for company then?' Jan asked, smiling affectionately at her nephew.

That one was beyond him. 'When will they be coming home?' he asked.

'This afternoon,' his mother told him.

'Not until after dinner?' He was horrified. 'That's a very long time to wait.'

'It seems like that to me too, son,' confessed Rachel. She was planning to finish at the boathouse in time to collect Tim from school today, and every other day if possible, though Jan had agreed to do it when she couldn't get away in time. 'I'll be dying to know how they got on.'

'So will I,' said Jan. 'Still . . . at least while I'm fretting about Kelly, I can't be worrying about other things.'

Rachel gave her a sharp look. 'Other things,' she repeated, frowning. 'You got problems?'

Jan nodded. 'Things are a bit tight for us financially at the moment,' she explained.

Having been hard up herself, Rachel could empathise. 'But

I thought Pete's business was doing really well,' she said. 'He always seems to be busy.'

'Yeah, he is, but we've had some hefty repair bills for the van lately,' she confided. 'And Pete had to take all that time off when he went down with flu before Christmas, remember. Those things, added to the fact that he doesn't work over Christmas anyway so doesn't get paid, put us in shtook. When you're self-employed, you can't afford not to work.'

'You can't stop illness or public holidays coming, though, can you?' Rachel pointed out sympathetically.

'Neither can you avoid repair bills when you run an old vehicle,' added Jan.

Rachel knew that she pitied her sister at her peril, but she was very keen to assist her. 'I can help out,' she offered, 'now that the boathouse is back on its feet.'

'I wouldn't dream of scrounging off you.' Jan was adamant.

'You wouldn't be scrounging.' Rachel was equally as emphatic. 'I *want* to help. I'm only in a position to do so because of Uncle Chip, and he was your uncle too.'

'No, honestly,' protested Jan, her cheeks brightly suffused. 'We'll get by. Some serious belt-tightening should see us through this bad patch.'

'But Jan . . .'

'Thanks for offering but we'll manage,' she said forcefully. 'I wish I hadn't mentioned it now. It was only a casual comment.'

Deeming it wise not to persist at this stage, Rachel said, 'Well . . . if you're sure?'

'Quite sure. It's nice of you to offer, but it isn't a serious problem, not at the moment anyway. As long as Pete gets a clear run of work with no more unexpected expenses, we should be all right.'

'Well, if you need help, you only have to ask,' said Rachel, rising. 'It isn't just words, Jan, I really mean it.'

'You've quite enough on your plate bringing up the boys,' her sister pointed out.

'Yes, that's true,' Rachel admitted, adding with sincerity, 'But if I can help, I will.'

'That's nice to know,' said Jan.

Saying no more about it, Rachel put her coat on, gave her son a valedictory hug and went to work.

When she got to the boathouse, Ben was waiting for her, looking extremely anxious.

'Well, how did Tim get on?' he enquired, following her into her office.

'He was fine,' she said. 'I'm the one who's a nervous wreck, worrying about him.'

'Did you tell the teacher that he can be quite a sensitive boy at times?' he asked.

She burst out laughing. 'It's school, not a child-minding service,' she pointed out. 'The teachers don't have time to listen to the tiniest details of every new child's personality. They'll get to know them soon enough.'

'I suppose so,' he said gloomily.

'Good grief, you're worse than I am,' she admonished lightly. 'You're supposed to be the one telling me not to be overprotective, not the other way around.'

'Sorry,' he said, absently raking his thick hair from his brow with his fingers. 'But it's a big thing for him.'

'You're as soft as I am about him,' she grinned, shaking her head.

'I admit it,' he conceded. 'He's like a son to me.'

'I know he is,' she said softly, squeezing his hand. 'As I've told you before, don't ever change.'

'I wouldn't know how,' he said.

Time passed and the bleak riverside sprouted and blossomed into spring. The swinging sixties, with their pop icons, uninhibited attitudes towards sex and growing drug culture, were a world away from a hard-working mother of two like Rachel. She loved the colour and vibrancy of everything, though, the feeling that anything was possible now that social barriers were no longer so rigid. Even those who weren't a part of the youth culture couldn't deny the truth of Bob Dylan's song 'Times They Are A-Changin''.

A more serious mood became perceptible during that summer of 1967, though, as the horrors of the Vietnam war were visually transmitted into living rooms via television. The growing popularity of cults and Eastern religions marked a move against rampant materialism. But while the hippie lifestyle suited many people, who headed for communes in their thousands, Rachel wanted a more traditional way of life for herself and her children. And one day in June she made an important decision that proved to be something of a catalyst.

The weather was sweltering that afternoon when she and the boys trudged heavily up the steps to the flat. When she opened the front door a suffocating blast of hot air greeted them. The place was stifling, having been closed up all day. Sometimes it seemed to Rachel as though this flat had the capability to emphasise the extremes of the weather, being arctic in winter and like a greenhouse on warm summer days.

'Phew, it's too hot in here, Mummy,' puffed Johnnie, pulling his T-shirt away from his chest and fanning himself with it.

'I know it is, love,' she said, throwing open all the windows. 'It'll cool down a bit once we let some fresh air in.'

'Can we play outside?' asked Tim, looking uncomfortably hot. 'It's much too warm in here.'

'You know it's too dangerous for you to play out,' Rachel reminded him.

'Can we go to Gran's then and play in her garden?' he begged, his face flushed and sweaty. 'I don't want to stay in here. It's making me feel sick.'

'And me,' added Johnnie.

'Maybe we'll go to Gran's later on.' She hated being driven from their home in this way but didn't have much option.

Even with the windows open, it was still unbearable in here.

As it happened, a telephone call solved the problem. Ben rang to ask if they'd like to go out for a trip in *Nipper*. He said he had to see a potential customer later on but had a couple of hours free, and would leave the boathouse on the dot of five if they were interested. The mood in the flat immediately lifted.

'You saved my life,' Rachel confessed to Ben after the boat trip as they were having a drink on the terrace of the Old Ship. Tim and Johnnie were standing by the balustrade eating crisps and watching some oarsmen bring their skiff out of the water and carry it into the boathouse of a nearby rowing club. 'The kids really needed to get out of that stuffy flat.'

'That's what I had in mind,' he told her.

'Who is it you have to see about business?' she enquired with interest.

'Some bloke in Putney,' he said.

'Why can't he see you during working hours?' she asked, concerned for him.

'He's a well-off businessman and boating fanatic with a love of old traditional craft,' he explained. 'He's got a boat in his garage he wants me to look at with a view to restoration, and he isn't available until about nine o'clock in the evening. If we get the job it'll be worth a few hundred quid so I'm certainly not going to make an issue about going to see him after working hours.'

'Aah, I see.' She was impressed by this further evidence of Ben's loyalty to the firm. 'It was very thoughtful of you to make the time to take us out on the river anyway.'

'I was only too pleased to do it. It was a nice break for us all,' he said. 'And I know how difficult it is for you, with them not being able to play outside.'

'It's getting to be more of a headache now that they're getting older,' she admitted. 'But I can't let them go down into the street.'

'Course you can't.'

'Still, at least they're not cooped up in the flat all day.' She sighed. 'And there are plenty of people a lot worse off than we are. At least I can take them to Mum and Dad's or Jan's for an hour in the evening.'

'There is that,' he said.

'I try not to do it too often because it gets them out of routine and makes them late for bed.' She grinned towards them. 'Not that you'll hear them complain about that.'

He laughed and they fell into a comfortable silence, enjoying being together in such pleasant surroundings. She was cool in a floral-print cotton dress with a short skirt; he was wearing a casual black shirt with light cotton trousers. It was the most glorious evening, the setting sun gleaming orange on the river, which was running cool and green towards Chiswick Eyot, the blue sky flecked with streaky pink clouds. Swans rode the waves from the wash of a passing motor boat, while ducks pecked and preened their feathers around a grassy bank on this verdant stretch without a river wall.

There was a steady flow of people strolling in the soft evening air. Rachel luxuriated in the fresh feeling of the outdoors, a suggestion of tar and mud from the river mingled with the sweet scent of wild roses growing in patches along the riverbank and fragrant honeysuckle here on the terrace.

In thoughtful mood, something she had been contemplating for some time came into her mind with sudden clarity. 'I've made a big decision, Ben,' she blurted out quickly, pushing her hair back from her brow, the sun picking out the golden lights in it as she looked at him intently.

'Sounds serious,' he said with a half-smile. 'I hope you're not about to give me the sack.'

'Don't be daft.'

'So, what is this big decision?'

'I've decided it's time I got the kids out of the flat and into a house with a garden,' she announced.

His brows rose. 'Oh, really?' he said.

She nodded. 'It's been my aim ever since I inherited the

business,' she explained. 'And if I hang on until I'm really flush with money, I may wait for ever. I've heard that property prices around here are shooting up, so it's probably best if I take the plunge before a place of my own gets out of reach. The boathouse is doing well now, so I should be able to find enough for a deposit and the repayments on a mortgage if I go for something small.'

He seemed preoccupied.

'What's the matter?' she asked quickly. 'Don't you think it's a good idea?'

'I have a better one,' he informed her.

'You do?'

'Why don't we get a place together?' he suggested boldly, looking at her with an uncertain smile. 'I'll sell my place and buy a house with you.'

Up shot her brows. 'And me a respectable mother of two,' she said, but her tone was light-hearted.

'Get married, I mean, of course,' he explained.

She eyed him cautiously but with a smile hovering. 'Is that really a proposal?' she asked.

He nodded with a wry grin. 'Not the most romantic one, though, was it?'

'I've heard more romantic railway announcements,' she joked. 'But it doesn't matter. It's what you said that counts.'

'So let's see if I can improve on it.' His eyes met hers as he took her hand in both of his. 'I love you, Rachel, very much. Will you marry me . . . please?'

Her face was wreathed in smiles as she savoured the moment. 'Just try and stop me,' she whispered at last, leaning over and kissing him.

'Of course,' she said later on, back at her flat, 'there is the little matter of us both being married to other people.'

They were sitting in her kitchen having a cup of coffee; the boys were in the other room watching television. 'I hadn't forgotten,' he said ponderously.

'If only we could,' she sighed.

'That's why I haven't brought the subject of marriage up before,' he explained. 'I've wanted to . . . very much. But everything has been so great for us. I didn't want to risk spoiling it with the grim reality of divorce.'

'Mm. I know what you mean,' she said.

'But we can't go on avoiding it,' he stated categorically. 'It's time now to get things sorted out properly.'

'Heaven knows how in my case, though,' she sighed, 'since I haven't a clue where Jeff is.'

'That is a problem, I admit,' he agreed in a serious tone, 'and we'll have to get some professional advice about it. I don't know much about the technicalities of divorce, but the fact that your husband committed adultery and deserted you must go in your favour, I should think.'

'It probably will do, but I don't know what the correct procedure is,' she told him. 'I'll have to get an appointment to see Mr Brayford. He'll soon put us right.'

'I'm certain that I won't have any trouble with Lorna,' said Ben on a more positive note. 'She's seriously involved with someone else so it was only a matter of time before she asked me for her freedom anyway.'

'That's all right then,' said Rachel.

'It makes it so much easier when you can stay on friendly terms,' he remarked.

She nodded in agreement. 'Being realistic, though,' she went on, 'it's going to take time whatever happens. It'll be a while before we're both free to marry.'

'True.'

'The thing is, Ben, I don't want to wait to get a house,' she explained, looking at him intently. 'I'd like to go ahead with that right away. I want to get the boys out of this flat. I can't wait until we're able to marry to do that . . . it'll take too long.'

Although they were lovers and Ben sometimes stayed the night with Rachel at the flat, they hadn't yet discussed the possibility of moving in together on a permanent basis. Unmarried couples living together was a growing trend but not in the circles in which Rachel moved. There had to be a serious commitment on Ben's part before she would even consider it. He had just made that commitment.

'So . . . what do you have in mind?' he asked, meeting her steady gaze.

'We know where we stand with each other now, so I think we should go ahead and find a house,' she suggested.

'Move in together?'

She laughed. 'Well, I wasn't thinking of buying a house with you and then making you live somewhere else.'

'Just making sure,' he grinned.

'We'll get married as soon as we are free to,' she went on to say. 'It isn't ideal but it would be ridiculous, not to mention impractical, to do anything else, keeping two homes going when we'll be spending most of our time together in one of them.'

'Well, if you're sure you're happy with that, it suits me,' he told her.

'That's settled then.'

'But there's one thing we must do before we do anything else,' he said.

'What's that?'

'We must go and choose you an engagement ring,' he said. 'We might not be able to get married yet, but there's no law to say you can't wear my ring.'

'You certainly won't get any objections from me about that,' she said with a twinkle in her eye.

'We'll go shopping at the weekend, then. Would you like that?' he asked.

'Yes, please.'

'Great.'

'I'm so happy, Ben,' she said softly.

'Me too,' he replied, looking into her eyes.

* * *

Driving home from his business appointment in Putney later that same evening, Ben lingered on thoughts of his engagement to Rachel, his joy so overwhelming he could have wept with the wonder of it. Although he might have appeared to be letting things drift along these past months, marriage had been very much on his mind. Ben was the sort of man for whom love and marriage went together, but as marriage wasn't immediately possible, he was happy to accept the next best thing until it was.

Rachel's decision to buy a house had prompted him to act. It had been precisely the motivation he'd needed. Rachel was the love of his life. That wasn't to say that he hadn't loved Lorna, because he had in a youthful way, and was still fond of her now, as a friend. But he had never felt for another woman the same way as he felt for Rachel.

Parking his car and going into his silent little house, he noticed that it didn't seem quite so bleak and lonely now that he knew it wasn't for much longer. He would set things in motion tomorrow by getting an appointment with an estate agent to put the property on the market. He and Rachel had agreed that he wouldn't move in with her while she was still at the flat. They would wait until they found a house they both liked and could move into it together. But he was aching to move out of here and start a new life with Rachel and the boys.

Rachel went into the boys' room to check on them before going to bed herself. She moved silently to the foot of the beds and looked at the sleeping children, one so much like her, the other like his father. Reminded of Jeff, her stomach churned at the thought that his unknown whereabouts would lengthen the divorce procedure. And she so much wanted to be free to marry Ben.

The mere thought of Ben warmed her heart. To make the whole thing even more perfect was the knowledge of how thrilled the boys would be to have him as their stepdad. She had no doubts about that at all. She and Ben were going to tell them at the weekend, just before they told the rest of the family.

She was standing in the darkness, looking at them in the light from the hall. They were growing so fast. Tim would be six next birthday. Another few months and Johnnie would be starting school. Tim was lying on his back with his arms spread out; Johnnie was on his side, his hair dark against the pillow. Tim was still the more sensitive of the two. She reflected on that difficult period he'd had when she and Ben had first become lovers. Thank goodness that was behind them now.

They needed a father and nobody was more suited to the job than Ben. She placed a kiss on each sleeping head and quietly left the room.

Lorna Smart came out of a house in Wembley that same night and stumbled blindly along the back roads towards the High Road. Her cheeks were streaked with mascara, her greyish-brown eyes red and swollen from crying, her thick chestnut-coloured hair damp and dishevelled from scraping her tear-soaked fingers through it in despair.

Force of habit sent her in the direction of the tube station to get a train back to Kilburn where she lived, though she was too distressed to care where she went. All she wanted was to crawl into a corner and die, but somehow her feet kept moving one in front of the other.

She'd been seeing Alan for over a year. He was a good-looking, dark-eyed divorcee who exuded charm – or had done until recently. She'd thought they were perfect for each other. Their chemistry was right, they had a similar sense of humour and they shared opinions about a great many things.

They'd first met at work. She was a clerk-typist at the head office of a confectionery firm in Willesden. He was one of the sales reps. He was out on the road most of the time but came into the office for sales meetings and other administrative matters. They'd got together at one of the firm's social evenings and embarked upon a relationship soon after which had continued after he'd left the company for a job with another firm of confectioners.

He covered a large territory so was often away during the week. But they saw each other most nights when he was at home. She'd thought they had a future together, had expected him to make a firm commitment to her soon. She'd even been intending to speak to Ben about a divorce, she'd been so sure that Alan was about to pop the question.

Fool that she now knew she was, she'd gone round to his place this evening intending to surprise him, armed with a bottle of wine and plenty of his favourite perfume splashed about her person. She should have taken the hint when he'd told her on the phone earlier that he wanted an early night because he was tired after a sales stint on the south coast. But not Lorna. Oh no. She'd thought a spot of her company and a few glasses of wine was just what he needed to liven him up.

But when he'd opened the door to her, his look of brutal hostility had sent shock waves through her. He'd even seemed reluctant to invite her in, and when he had, he'd made it obvious that he was bored and irritated by her company. This wasn't the first time she'd seen the nastier side of his personality; he tended to be moody, especially lately, so she'd put his attitude down to that.

'If I didn't know you better I'd think you were trying to get rid of me,' she'd said girlishly, stretching her powers of self-delusion to the absolute limit.

He'd tutted. 'I told you on the phone that I wasn't feeling sociable,' he'd said impatiently, 'and I meant it.'

'Come on, Alan baby,' she'd coaxed. 'Don't be such an old misery-guts.'

'Grow up, Lorna, for goodness' sake,' he'd said with seething impatience. 'You're old enough to know when a man wants to be left alone.'

A knot of fear that had begun with his icy greeting at the door drew tight in her stomach, making her feel weak and nauseous. 'I hope you're not seeing some other woman,' she'd said, only half joking.

He looked at her sheepishly.

'My God, you are!'

'I've been trying to tell you for weeks . . .' he began.

'Oh, have you?' she'd interrupted bitterly. 'Well, I'm listening now.'

She hadn't even sat down. Just stood where she was in his living room while he told her he'd been seeing a woman he'd met on his rounds. She had a newsagent's shop in Neasden that also sold sweets. They'd got friendly when he'd called there on business and one thing led to another.

'So where does this leave us?' she'd asked.

'Well . . . nowhere,' he'd said with shattering candour, as though the idea of anything else hadn't even occurred to him.

'Nowhere?'

'It's run its course, babe,' he confirmed breezily. 'Time to go our separate ways.'

'You can't do this to me,' she'd said frantically, her voice trembling, a burning flush suffusing her face and neck. 'You can't just drop me after all we've been to each other.'

He looked very peeved. 'I was hoping you'd be adult about it,' he said.

'You can't treat me like this.' She'd been too desperate to notice that she was repeating herself and irritating him even more.

'Don't tell me what I can and can't do,' he'd told her. 'You've no claim on me, you're not my wife.'

'I thought I was going to be, though,' she'd made it clear. 'I thought we had a future together.'

'Well, you certainly didn't get the idea from me,' he informed her briskly. 'I've no plans to settle down, with anybody, and I've never indicated as much to you. I wouldn't do that, Lorna, it just isn't my style.'

'I thought I was special to you,' she'd said, tears unashamedly falling now.

'You are special,' he'd told her in an impersonal manner. 'I wouldn't have been seeing you if you weren't. I wouldn't have wasted my time.' He did have the grace to look a little shamefaced then, she remembered. 'But nothing lasts forever, not for me anyway. I'm not the settling-down type. It's over, Lorna.'

She'd gone berserk then, uttering every expletive she could think of, punching, kicking and scratching him, completely beside herself with anguish.

'Here, lay off,' he'd objected, holding her at arm's-length to avoid her blows. 'There's no call for this sort of thing.'

'You've deceived me,' she accused him.

'No I haven't,' he denied. 'I've never promised you anything beyond what we had in the present.'

'I naturally assumed,' she'd sobbed. 'I mean, the way you've been with me.'

'Dangerous things, assumptions,' he said, still gripping her firmly by the arms.

'What else was I to think?' she'd asked him. 'You were all over me until just lately.'

He sighed heavily and let go of her, eyeing her warily as though ready to ward off another attack. 'Look, I don't want to hurt you, but you're not some starry-eyed young girl, are you? You're a mature woman, you must know how these things work.'

'Turn the knife, why don't you,' she'd spat at him.

'I'm just trying to get you to accept the way things are,' he'd told her firmly.

'Sure.' Her voice was thick with tears.

'You're an attractive woman.' She'd been too upset to worry about whether or not he was patronising her. 'You'll soon find someone else.'

'I don't want anyone else,' she'd screeched at him, her voice rising hysterically. 'I only want you.'

'Look, we've had a really good time, but it's over now,' he'd said, scratching his head. He hadn't expected her to be so difficult. 'Lots of good memories but no hard feelings; let's just leave it at that.'

'I can't turn my feelings off just like that.' She knew she was being feeble but seemed powerless to stop this woeful outpouring.

His manner had hardened. 'I know what you're about,' he'd said cruelly. 'You've got a broken marriage and you're looking for a second husband, or at least something permanent. I don't blame you for wanting that, but you won't find what you're looking for in me.'

She'd left then, managed to drag herself away while she'd still had a shred of dignity left, before she made a complete and utter fool of herself by begging him to carry on seeing her even though he didn't want to.

Now she trudged on through the dark streets in the pale amber glow of the streetlights, the air filled with the poignant scent of a summer evening, tears of fury, frustration and utter despair blurring her vision. Maybe Alan was right. Maybe she was so desperate for a partner she latched on to anyone who paid her attention, seeing him as a potential second husband. Whatever the truth of the matter, she felt wretched – cheap, pathetic and utterly rejected.

Lorna prided herself on being independent. Since she and Ben had split up, she'd made a life for herself. She had a nice flat and a job that paid enough to support her. She didn't need help from anyone at a practical level. But emotionally, the single life wasn't for her. She missed the warmth, the company, the sex. All that had gone now that Alan had dumped her.

Her looks weren't something she deluded herself about. She was no great beauty but she was reasonably attractive and knew how to make the most of her good points. She had her mouse-brown hair well cut and regularly coloured, was clever with make-up and wore clothes that flattered her trim figure.

But what chance did a woman of nearly thirty have of meeting a decent bloke? All the men in her age bracket were married or attached. It was no wonder she'd allowed herself to read more into the relationship with Alan than there actually was. She'd heard it said you could be lonelier with someone who wasn't right for you than you were on your own. But at this moment of desperation that seemed like a load of old codswallop.

Of course, she wouldn't be in this parlous state now if things had worked out for her and Ben, she thought miserably. He was a good man. They'd been right for each other once. But what they'd had was never coming back, that much she was sure of. They were lucky to have stayed friends – lots of couples didn't manage that after they split up. From what she could gather from speaking to him on the phone, he'd got something going with the woman he worked for. She didn't know if it was serious or not, but he'd sounded pleased with himself.

Tears of self-pity were falling in a scalding tide. She couldn't stop them. She longed to be at home in the privacy of her own place, where she could hide away with her pain and humiliation. Not far now, she told herself as she approached the High Road along a side street, breathless from crying.

She was replaying the incident with Alan in her mind and shedding fresh tears as she stepped off the pavement to cross the road, far too immersed in her painful thoughts to check to see if anything was coming.

Turning sharply at the sound of screeching brakes, she was dazzled by headlights; then there was pain so intense she couldn't even identify exactly where it was in her body as the bonnet of the car hit her, the impact lifting her into the air. She fell to the ground with a dull thud and lay motionless in the road, knowing nothing of the shock and chaos that was going on around her.

In all the excitement of becoming engaged to Rachel, Ben couldn't get to sleep that night. One o'clock passed, then two.

It seemed as though he'd just dozed off when he came to with a start, wondering what had woken him. The sound of the doorbell solved the mystery.

Struggling into his dressing gown, he hurried to the front door, alarmed to see two policemen standing on the doorstep.

'Ben Smart?' one of them asked.

'Yes.' He stared at them in a daze, his first thought for Rachel. Something must have happened to her or the boys. 'Why, what's the matter?' he asked, his voice gruff with nerves.

'Are you the husband of Lorna Smart?' enquired the policeman solemnly.

Lorna? She was the last person on his mind. 'Yes, that's right.' He was fully awake now, heart hammering fit to burst, mouth parched. 'Why, has something happened to her?'

'I think perhaps we'd better come inside, sir,' suggested the policeman kindly. 'I'm afraid we have some rather bad news for you.'

Dumbly Ben stood aside to let them in.

Chapter Twelve

Ben was normally at the boathouse before Rachel, so she was surprised to find that he wasn't there when she arrived the next morning. Having spent most of the night in glorious contemplation of their future together, she wondered if perhaps he had been similarly affected and had consequently slept through the alarm.

Getting no reply from his number, she assumed he must be on his way. She hoped he wouldn't be long, because the workshop foreman was waiting to speak to him and calls were coming through for him, his presence very much in demand as the day's busy schedule gathered momentum. She tried his number again several times. Still no reply. She was beginning to worry now, because it was so unlike Ben to be this late for work.

She was about to send one of the men round to his house in the van when the phone rang.

'Rachel.'

'Ben.' Her voice was warm with relief. 'We were just about to send out a search party. I've been worried to death about you. You're never late for work.'

'Sorry about that,' he apologised. 'And I'm sorry I haven't been in touch before.'

'Did you not hear the phone?' she enquired. 'I've been ringing you more or less nonstop since nine o'clock.'

'I'm not at home.' He sounded odd.

‘Oh?’ She waited for him to explain.

‘Look, Rachel, I don’t know what time I’ll get in to work today, if at all,’ he told her.

‘What’s happened?’ she asked, anxiety rising. ‘Where are you?’

‘At a hospital in Wembley.’

‘*A hospital*,’ she exclaimed, her voice shrill with shock. ‘Oh, Ben, what’s the matter?’

‘Nothing with me,’ he informed her with a noticeable anguish. ‘It’s Lorna.’

‘Your wife?’ She couldn’t help feeling threatened, and was immediately riddled with guilt about it.

‘That’s right,’ he said. ‘She’s been involved in a road accident . . . knocked down by a car.’

‘Oh, Ben.’ She was full of concern. ‘Is she . . . is she badly hurt?’

‘Yes, very. She’s unconscious . . . barely alive . . . they’ve told me she won’t pull through,’ he informed her gravely.

Rachel felt for him deeply but was oddly lost for words. ‘I’m so sorry,’ she uttered at last. ‘Poor Lorna. You must be out of your mind with worry. When did it happen?’

‘Last night,’ he said. ‘The police came to my place in the early hours. I’ve been here ever since.’ He paused, adding as though an explanation was necessary, ‘I’m her next of kin, you see.’

‘Yes, I suppose you would be,’ she said.

‘Anyway, I don’t know when I’ll be able to get away from here,’ he went on to say. ‘So I can’t tell you when to expect me.’

‘I understand,’ she said sympathetically. ‘Don’t worry about anything here. We’ll manage . . . the blokes will muck in and do a bit extra.’

‘I’ll get there as soon as I possibly can,’ he was keen to assure her.

‘I know you will,’ she said softly. ‘But you’ll need to go home and get some sleep if you’ve been up for most of the night. So we'll expect you when we see you.'

'It depends when . . .' He sounded very shaky. 'God, this is awful, Rachel . . . just being here waiting for someone to die . . . someone of not quite thirty.'

It was almost a physical pain to her to know that he was suffering. 'Yes, it must be hellish for you,' she said gently.

'There's nothing I can do for her,' he went on. 'Just be here with her even though she isn't aware of it.'

'What about her parents?' Rachel wondered aloud. 'Are they at the hospital with you?'

'They're both dead,' he explained dully. 'There isn't anyone except me.'

'I thought you said she had a boyfriend.'

'Yes, she has been seeing someone but I haven't had a chance to work out how to contact him yet. I've had a look in her handbag but there's nothing in there except her purse and make-up. No address book or anything. Her keys are there, though, so I could get into her flat to have a look . . . but I can't get away from here.'

'Can I do anything to help?' she offered. 'It wouldn't take me long to get to Wembley on the tube. If nothing else, I could give you some moral support.'

'It's sweet of you to offer,' he said. 'But I must do this last thing for her on my own.'

'I understand,' she told him, angry with herself for being hurt.

'I'll be in touch later on,' he said.

'OK.' She paused. 'Love you, Ben.'

There was a heart-stopping silence that seemed to go on for ever. 'Love you too,' he said at last.

Replacing the receiver, she felt the cold hand of fear clutch her heart. The joy of last night had been completely wiped out by this appalling twist of fate. Last night their engagement had filled his world; it would be the last thing on his mind now. She admonished herself for having such selfish thoughts. In a hospital in Wembley a young woman was about to lose her life, and here was Rachel worrying about how it was going to affect her. Ben had shared his life with Lorna once; he had to be with her now. It was only right.

Vowing to give Ben her wholehearted support in this crisis, she turned her attention to work.

That afternoon Ben sat by Lorna's bed, feeling deeply ashamed for wanting to leave. His wife was unconscious and barely recognisable, her face bruised and swollen, her hair dragged back, a large dressing on her forehead. It was like looking at a stranger.

Over the past few hours he had experienced a mixture of emotions – compassion, affection, fear, sadness; also, to his shame, he'd been plagued by a longing to escape. He'd been told he must prepare himself, and was both dreading the moment and wanting it to be over. So he sat by her bed, sick with tension, afraid that every breath she took would be her last and almost subconsciously willing her to take another, trying to keep her alive.

The medical team here at the hospital hadn't expected her to last the night. It was now mid afternoon and she was still hanging on. Watching someone die was the most devastating experience, whoever it was, and you didn't stop caring about someone when you fell out of love with them.

A profound longing to be with Rachel overwhelmed him, closely followed by a surge of compunction. How could he even think of what *he* wanted at a time like this, when the woman he had once loved was about to slip away. But thoughts of Rachel persisted despite his best endeavours, and he was comforted by the memory of what had happened between them last night.

He needed Rachel beside him and wished he could have accepted her offer to join him here; but it wouldn't have been right. He and Lorna had long since gone their separate ways, but his estranged wife's deathbed wasn't the place for his wife-to-be. This was his duty, not Rachel's.

The door opened and the doctor entered quietly. Being such a critical case, Lorna was in a side ward on her own. 'You really ought to try and get some sleep, you know, Mr Smart,' advised Dr Ferguson, a small, bespectacled man with a pale complexion and a quiet, unassuming manner. 'We do have a relatives' room you could use.'

Ben shook his head. 'Thanks, but I'd rather stay with her until . . . well, you know . . .'

'It could be a while.' His attitude was almost matter-of-fact, and Ben was reminded of the fact that human tragedy was something doctors had to face on a daily basis. 'You need some rest. Your being exhausted isn't going to help your wife.'

'I'll stay here if you don't mind,' Ben told him firmly. 'I can always doze off in the chair.'

The doctor studied a chart on Lorna's bed, then stood looking at his patient for a while before he left. On impulse Ben followed him outside into the corridor. 'I was wondering if there's any chance that she might recover?' he asked.

'Very little, Mr Smart,' the doctor told him with necessary frankness. 'Obviously the longer she survives the better her chances, but they are still very slim. I'm sorry, but it would be wrong of me to give you false hope.'

'But she wasn't expected to survive the night and she did,' Ben pointed out. 'It's afternoon now and she's still here.'

'Don't read too much into that,' he said in a level tone. 'Your wife is still very ill.'

'I understand,' said Ben.

'Why don't you go to the cafeteria for a cup of coffee?' suggested the doctor. 'One of the nurses will come and get you if there's any change.'

'No, I'd rather be with her.'

The doctor looked at this whey-faced man who was clearly exhausted. 'I'll get one of the nurses to bring you some coffee then,' he told him kindly.

'That's very nice of you. Thank you,' said Ben gratefully,

and went back into Lorna's room, hating himself for not wanting to.

'You're getting to be quite a stranger outside of working hours,' Rachel said to Ben one evening a week or so later.

'I know, love,' he said with genuine regret, 'and I'm really sorry about it.'

They were cosily ensconced on Rachel's sofa. Ben had spent most of the evening at the hospital so the boys had been in bed and asleep by the time he arrived. Most nights since Lorna's accident he hadn't made it to the flat at all.

'It isn't quite so bad for me because I do get to see you at the boathouse,' she said. 'But the boys miss you. Still, it can't be helped.'

Grey with tiredness, he emitted a weary sigh. 'I miss them too, but as you say, it can't be helped,' he said. 'I have to go to the hospital straight from work and by the time I get away from there, I'm too shattered to do anything but go home to bed.'

He'd stopped spending the whole day at the hospital but went every night and had been at Lorna's bedside for most of last weekend. She was still unconscious, her condition unchanged.

'Do the doctors have any idea how long she's likely to stay as she is?' Rachel enquired.

'They don't seem to,' he replied. 'They didn't expect her to still be with us now. The entire medical team are in a state of suspense about her.'

'They're bound to be.'

He slipped his arm around her. 'I hate not being able to see you as often as usual,' he said, attempting to kiss her but yawning instead. 'And I realise it's miserable for you too.'

It certainly was. Having to share him was bad enough. But even worse was the guilt that plagued her about that tiny knot of fear and resentment that niggled inside her despite her very best efforts to banish it.

'I'm OK,' she reassured him. 'You've enough on your mind without having to worry about me as well.'

'But I do worry about you,' he said. 'And I miss seeing you of an evening.' He paused, tracing her cheek with his finger. 'I'm very sorry we didn't get the chance to go out and get you an engagement ring at the weekend.'

'There's plenty of time for that.' She wanted to make things easier for him, even though she had to force the words out. 'Our plans will just have to be shelved until . . .' Her voice tailed off. She didn't want it to sound as though they were waiting for Lorna either to die or get better so that they could get on with their lives. 'Until things are more settled with Lorna.'

'She doesn't have anyone else but me,' Ben explained. 'Some women friends have been to see her, but they're just mates from work. There's no one close.'

'No news of the boyfriend then?' she asked.

'Ex-boyfriend,' he corrected wryly. 'I tracked him down through Lorna's firm. I remembered her saying he used to work there, so I got on the phone to them and they told me the name of his new company. I got through to them and they gave me his home phone number when I explained the circumstances.'

'And he said it was all off between them?' she prompted.

'He made that very clear,' he told her in a definite tone. 'He said he was sorry to hear that she was so ill, but there was no chance of a reconciliation.'

'Didn't he even go to the hospital to see her?' Rachel asked in surprise.

'He went once, according to the nurses,' Ben said. 'He only stayed a few minutes and he hasn't been back.'

She drew in her breath sharply. 'That's a bit brutal.'

'He obviously doesn't want to know and is afraid of getting involved,' was Ben's opinion.

'So . . . it's all up to you.'

'Seems like it.' He turned her face to his and she could see the strain and tension reflected in his eyes. 'I miss being with you so much,' he said.

'I know,' she said softly. 'I know.'

'Did you manage to see Mr Brayford about your missing husband and the divorce?' he asked.

'No, it didn't seem right to go and see him, not the way things are for you at the moment,' she told him. 'I'd rather leave it until everything's back to normal.'

'OK.'

Rachel could see that he was making a valiant effort to take an interest but was too tired for his heart to be in it. 'If you don't mind, though,' she went on to say, 'I'd like to start getting some property details, to see what's around in our price range. I want to get the kids settled in a house as soon as I can.'

'Good idea,' he agreed. 'You get some stuff from the estate agents and we'll browse through it together.'

They talked about the boys for a while. 'I must find time for them this coming weekend,' he said worriedly, 'or they'll think I've deserted them.'

'They are disappointed not to see you, I can't deny that.' She shrugged resignedly. 'But it's just one of those things . . . they'll have to be patient.'

'Thanks for being so good about it,' he said.

'No need to thank me. I love you and I don't want to add to your burden by complaining because I see so little of you.' She looked into his pinched, pallid face. 'You look terrible,' she said.

'Thanks a bunch,' he said with feigned umbrage in an attempt to lighten the atmosphere.

'Tired, I mean,' she said, feeling extremely loving towards him. 'Exhausted and stressed but just as gorgeous as ever.'

'That's better.' He took her in his arms.

They were just beginning to get passionate when the telephone rang. 'It might be the hospital,' he said, immediately tensing. 'I gave them this number.'

Rachel went to the hall to answer it. 'Yes, it is the hospital,' she said, coming back into the room.

He departed to the hall with a grim expression on his face. Rachel waited with her nerves stretched to breaking point. This must surely be news of the inevitable.

When he reappeared, he looked bewildered. Rachel waited to be enlightened but he just stood in the middle of the room, lost in thought.

'Ben,' she prompted him, 'was it, has she . . . ?'

'No, no, she hasn't died,' he said, still looking bemused. 'Quite the opposite, in fact. They called to tell me that Lorna has regained consciousness. I must go immediately.'

The nurse waylaid Ben as soon as he arrived on the ward. 'Wonderful news about your wife, isn't it, Mr Smart?' she said with a beaming smile. 'You must be so relieved.'

'Yes.'

'We're all so pleased for you both,' she told him.

'Thank you.' He wasn't sure if the latest development was just a temporary thing or an indication of a recovery. 'Does this mean she's going to get better?' he asked.

'Oh, I don't know about that,' the nurse said guardedly. 'You'll have to speak to the doctor about that.'

'Yes, of course.'

'But having her back with us is enough to be going on with, eh?' she smiled.

'Yes, yes, of course it is,' he agreed swiftly. 'Is she awake, do you know?'

'On and off,' she said. 'Go in, see for yourself.'

Lorna was asleep when he went in but woke up almost as soon as he sat down. 'Ben?' she said sleepily with a question in her voice, her eyes taking a while to focus on him. 'Ben, is that you?'

'Yeah, it's me,' he said gently. 'Welcome back to the land of the living.'

'They tell me I've been out of it for quite a while,' she mumbled drowsily.

'That's right.'

'That's incredible. When I came round I felt as though I'd woken up after just a few minutes.' She moved her hand forward, searching for his. 'The nurse said you've been here with me a lot of the time while I've been unconscious.'

He nodded, taking her hand in his. 'Yeah, I have been around a bit.'

'Thanks, Ben,' she said.

'It was the least I could do,' he assured her gently. 'Someone had to be here to make sure you didn't get any silly ideas about leaving us.'

'Thanks anyway,' she said, her lids drooping. 'It's so good that you're here.'

Again he nodded.

'Will you be coming again?' she asked.

'Of course,' he said.

'Good,' she whispered as she drifted off to sleep.

Ben stayed for a while longer and then left. The improvement in her condition was a huge relief, but he felt uneasy without really knowing why.

The next day, while Ben was at the hospital, he managed to exchange a few words with Dr Ferguson when they met in the corridor. 'Does the change in my wife's condition mean that she'll make a full recovery?' he enquired.

The doctor hesitated. 'The improvement in her condition is nothing short of a miracle,' he said after a while. 'But it's still too early to talk in terms of a full recovery.'

'Surely this is a positive sign, though, isn't it?' Ben suggested.

'It certainly is, and we are now certain that Mrs Smart doesn't have any brain damage,' he went on to say.

'That really is good news,' said Ben.

The doctor's expression became grim. 'However, you mustn't lose sight of the fact that your wife sustained multiple injuries in the accident. She has several serious fractures, and her back is quite badly damaged.'

'Meaning . . . ?'

'Meaning she may not be the woman she was before the accident.'

'You're trying to tell me that she could be disabled, aren't you?' Ben suggested.

The other man nodded. 'Exactly,' he said. 'But it's too early to say to what degree.'

'I see.' Although Ben had suspected as much, it was still a shock to have his fears confirmed.

'Your wife has amazing resilience, though,' the doctor continued. 'She must be strong to have come through this at all. But I think it will be best if we give it a little time before we start predicting the long-term effects of her injuries.'

'Yes, of course,' nodded Ben.

Jan looked at her sister across the kitchen table. 'Are you sure you're not imagining things?' she asked.

'I only wish I was.' Rachel had had to work late at the boathouse, so Jan had collected Tim from school. All the children were now playing in the garden while their mothers had a cup of tea and a chat before Rachel took the boys home. 'I'm losing him, Jan. I can feel him drifting away.'

'Remember that Lorna is still his wife even though they're separated.' Jan could see both sides of the question. 'He's bound to feel that it's his duty to visit her. But that doesn't mean his feelings for you have changed.'

'I've been over all that a thousand times, and I know I'm being selfish,' Rachel replied. 'But Lorna's illness is definitely coming between us. There's no doubt in my mind about that.'

'He's in a very awkward position,' Jan reminded her. 'I mean, with her being laid up in hospital and not having anyone else much to visit.'

'But it's been a month since her accident,' Rachel pointed out. 'And she's out of danger. But he seems to spend more time at the hospital now than he did when she was critical, and he was there often enough then.'

Leaning on the table with her chin on her fists, Jan pondered the question. 'That's probably because she's more aware of things now that she's getting better, and he feels sorry for her because her boyfriend dumped her and she doesn't have anyone else to visit her. When she was unconscious, he didn't feel obliged to be there so much.'

'I realise that, and I feel very sorry for her,' Rachel said. 'But even when he does find the time to be with me, he's preoccupied the whole time. He seems miles away.'

'Probably some sort of a reaction to the trauma he's been through,' said Jan.

'Honestly, Jan,' Rachel went on, 'I'm scared of losing him and it's tearing me apart.'

'If you're that worried, why not talk to him about it,' suggested Jan. 'Tell him exactly how you feel.'

'I don't want to add to his problems by going all clingy on him,' she explained.

'Telling him how you feel isn't being clingy,' Jan pointed out. 'I think you've been absolutely marvellous about the whole thing. Now that she's on the mend, you're entitled to know where you stand with him.'

'I love him and want to support him in this,' said Rachel. 'I don't want to nag him.'

'And you wouldn't be nagging,' said Jan. 'You'll be reminding him that you have needs too, that's all.'

'I can't bear to lose him, Jan, honestly.'

'Then talk to him,' said Jan. 'Tell him exactly how threatened you feel.'

'It's a delicate matter,' Rachel pointed out. 'I can't risk driving him away by putting pressure on him.'

'You'll have to do something,' advised Jan. 'You can't go on worrying yourself to death like this.'

'Yes, you're right.' Rachel's mood became positive. 'I shall bring things out into the open . . . and the sooner the better.'

* * *

'I know that you're having a very difficult time, and I've tried to be as patient and understanding as I can, Ben,' said Rachel later that same evening. 'But I really do need to know where I stand.'

'As regards what?' he asked.

'As regards us, of course.' They were in Rachel's living room. Ben had come to the flat straight from the hospital as usual. The boys were already asleep, so Rachel had taken this opportunity to say her piece, sitting opposite him rather than next to him on the sofa so that she could look at him directly and judge his reaction to what she had to say. 'Only just lately I've been feeling as though there is no us.'

He looked shocked. 'Nothing's changed between us as far as I'm concerned,' he said emphatically.

'Well, I feel as though it has.' She was determined not to be fobbed off. 'Lorna's illness is driving a wedge between us. You can't be unaware of it, surely?'

'My feelings for you haven't changed.' He clutched his head, looking troubled. 'Oh God, how could I have been so insensitive? I should have talked to you about it more.' He plunged his fingers into his hair. 'I never seem to get the chance to clear my mind for long enough to talk properly about anything.'

'The last thing I want to do is put any pressure on you,' she was keen to point out. 'But I do feel as though we're drifting apart. And that's the last thing I want to happen.'

He took a slow breath, looking at her so intently that all she could see was the hypnotic blue of his eyes. 'It's the last thing I want too. It's really awkward for me at the moment, Rachel. I feel I have to visit Lorna.'

'I understand that, and I'd be disappointed in you if you didn't.' She was emphatic about this. 'That isn't the issue. What's worrying me is that even when we do manage to get some time together, you're not with me in spirit. I get the impression that you're thinking of her the whole time.'

'No, no,' he denied hotly. 'I'm not thinking about Lorna

as such. I'm thinking about the situation I find myself in because of her.' His tone became deadly serious. 'I'll tell you something I wouldn't admit to another living soul, Rachel, something I'm deeply ashamed of. The truth is, I don't want to go to the hospital at all, I hate going to visit Lorna. I don't want to be with her. In fact, I'm sick and tired of the whole damned situation. But I can't just desert her while she's stuck in hospital with no one to visit her apart from an occasional workmate.'

'Oh, Ben, I feel terrible for going on at you now,' she told him.

'There's no need for you to feel bad. It's perfectly understandable for you to feel neglected and I'm glad you've told me. But I feel I must continue to spend time with Lorna. She's in a lot of pain and very low in spirits. Being chucked by your boyfriend and getting run over on the same night is a hell of a lot to cope with. She thinks that one event was responsible for the other; she was in such a state when she left Alan's that she just stepped out into the road without looking. The driver of the car didn't stand a chance, she's admitted that to the police.'

'I see,' said Rachel in a subdued tone.

'The truth is, I can't wait for her to be discharged from hospital so that she can get on with her life and we can get on with ours,' he said. 'She won't brood so much once she's back home.'

'When do they think that will be?'

'Not for a while, I shouldn't think,' he said. 'She still can't walk on her own because of the injuries to her spine.'

'They're expecting that to improve, though, aren't they?' Rachel said.

'Yes, they're hoping she'll be able to get about on her own by the time she comes out of hospital,' he confirmed. 'With the help of crutches, that is. She won't be able to manage without those.'

'Poor thing,' said Rachel.

'She is a poor thing, all right, at the moment,' he said. 'And I feel as guilty as hell for not wanting to spend time with her. But even apart from the fact that I want to be with you, she's very hard work because she doesn't want to talk. She's lost interest in everything. It's as though she doesn't care what happens to her any more. I'm exhausted when I come away, and I dread going back. Then, of course, I feel terrible about that.'

'Don't be too hard on yourself,' she advised him. 'You're only human.'

'I still feel bad about it, though,' he told her. 'As well as not wanting to be with Lorna, I feel permanently torn. When I'm at the hospital with her, I'm longing to be with you and feeling guilty about that as well as guilty for neglecting you. When I'm with you, I feel as though I'm not doing my duty towards Lorna. My life has turned into a nightmare.'

'Poor Ben,' she said, going over to him, sitting on his lap and smoothing his hair back from his brow. 'Now I'm the one who feels guilty, for nagging you.'

'You've every right,' he was quick to assure her. 'It's no way to treat the woman you've just got engaged to. I should have talked to you, explained the emotional complications.'

'And I should have realised how hard it is for you,' she said. 'So, we'll both have to be more patient in future.'

'I don't deserve you,' he said lovingly. 'You've been really great over this.'

'And then I go and spoil it all by giving you a hard time,' she said. 'We're so lucky compared to Lorna. It must be terrible for her, having to go through all that pain and misery.'

'Yes, it is.' He paused thoughtfully. 'But that's quite enough about Lorna,' he said, his voice lifting. 'Let's talk about us.'

She looked at him, her eyes shining now that she had been reassured. 'Actually I've got some property details I'd like us to have a look at together so that we can sort out those that we think are worth viewing. Perhaps we can find the time to go and look at some of them at the weekend.'

'We'll make a point of it,' he said.

'Oh, it's so good to have you here, Ben,' she said. 'I can't wait to get on with our plans.'

'Me neither,' he said, kissing her.

Dr Ferguson looked across his desk at Ben. 'I understand that you and your wife are separated.' He'd been waiting to see Ben when he arrived on the ward one August evening, and invited him into his office.

'That's right,' Ben confirmed. 'We split up some time ago.'

'Yes, it's all down in the notes in her file . . . but with you having spent so much time with her while she's been in hospital, I was wondering if perhaps all might be well between you again,' the doctor suggested, his hands linked together in front of him on the desk.

'Oh no, we're just friends,' Ben hastened to explain.

'I see.'

'She broke up with her boyfriend on the night of the accident so I stepped in to give her some moral support,' he continued in an explanatory manner.

'Mm.' The man stroked his chin meditatively. 'The thing is, Mr Smart,' he went on in a serious tone, 'she will be leaving here soon, and as you're her next of kin, I need to explain to you the problems she is going to face.'

With a sinking heart, Ben said, 'She isn't going to be as severely disabled as you originally thought, though, is she?'

'In as much as she won't be confined to a wheelchair, no, things aren't as bad as we expected. But she still can't walk without crutches and is still in an awful lot of pain,' the doctor reminded him. 'The thing that concerns me most of all, though, is her state of mind. She's extremely depressed.'

'Yes, I've noticed that.' Ben sighed. 'I'm hoping she'll pick up once she gets home with her own things around her.'

The doctor looked at his fingernails, then raised his eyes slowly to meet Ben's. 'I should think that's most unlikely,' he stated in his quiet way. 'She's going to find it very hard to get about, and in the state of mind she's in at the moment, she isn't likely to make the effort to get better. Being in pain is very draining, you know. That, added to her personal circumstances, doesn't bode well for her recovery.'

'You did tell me that her back was likely to improve in time,' Ben reminded him.

'With intense physiotherapy there should be an improvement, even to the point where she doesn't need crutches, though she'll always walk with quite a severe limp,' he explained. 'We can arrange for her to have the physiotherapy here at this hospital as an out-patient; we can even arrange transport to get her to and from the hospital.'

'That sounds promising,' said Ben.

'But we can't force her to have the treatment,' the doctor continued, his manner becoming stern. 'The patient has to have the will to get better in these cases. Mrs Smart is very depressed at the moment and doesn't want to do anything at all. She doesn't even want to go home because she dreads the thought of being alone.'

'I'll call on her every day once she's at home, to make sure she's all right. I'll encourage her to have the treatment,' Ben assured him eagerly. 'I'll take her shopping in the car, all that sort of thing. I won't abandon her just because she's been discharged from here.'

'I'm sure you won't, Mr Smart.' The doctor stared at the backs of his hands for a few moments. 'Unfortunately I don't think what you have in mind will be sufficient to bring your wife through this,' he said, looking up, 'and I would be failing in my professional duty if I didn't tell you that I think she should not live alone. I think that would be absolutely fatal for someone in her state of mind.'

The nagging worry that Ben had forced to the back of his mind these past months now surfaced with shocking clarity. 'Are you saying that I should have her to live with me?'

'It isn't my job to tell you how to work it out, Mr Smart,' the doctor said. 'But she does need to live with someone,

someone she knows well and feels comfortable with.'

'But Lorna and I haven't been together for years,' explained Ben. 'I'm engaged to someone else.'

'I can understand how difficult this must be for you, Mr Smart,' said the doctor in a quiet but firm tone. 'But my first concern is for the well-being of my patients after they leave here. It's my responsibility to point out to their next of kin the reality of the situation. We've done everything we can for her as an in-patient here; the next step is to send her home. In my professional opinion, she is not in a fit state to live alone. The consequences of such a thing could be grave.'

'Suicide?' suggested Ben.

'That is possible, yes,' he affirmed. 'But a general deterioration is almost certain if she is forced to live alone. What you choose to do about it is up to you. But she needs the security of knowing that she isn't alone.'

'I see,' said Ben grimly.

He found Lorna in the day room, staring blankly at the television screen along with a group of other patients. She was dressed in a pink dressing gown. Her hair was scraped back from her face with slides and her face was plumper than it used to be. Her trim figure had been destroyed by a large daily intake of confectionery which she'd turned to for comfort and obtained from the hospital shop.

'Hello, Lorna,' he said.

'Hi,' she replied, glancing at him briefly.

'Enjoying the programme?' he asked.

'It's all right.'

'It's nice to get away from the ward for a while, I expect,' he suggested hopefully.

'The nurses say it's good for our morale to come down here for a change of scene, and it's easier to do it than argue with them about it.' She sounded completely defeated.

Compassion and a feeling of suffocation invaded him in equal measures, followed by the usual surge of compunction about the latter. 'I expect they know best,' he said.

Admonishing looks from the other patients and reminders that they were trying to watch *The Avengers* prompted them to make a move.

'I've been having a chat with Dr Ferguson,' he told her as they trekked back to the ward. She was leaning heavily on her crutches, her face creased with pain and misery.

'Oh yeah, and what did he have to say?' she enquired without interest.

'He tells me that you'll be able to go home quite soon,' he informed her.

'Oh, that,' she said gloomily. 'God knows what'll happen to me then.'

He couldn't bring himself to utter the words he knew she wanted to hear. 'You'll be all right,' he said encouragingly.

'Will I?' She sounded bitter.

'Course you will,' he said kindly. 'It will all seem different once you get out of here, away from the hospital environment.'

'This is real life, Ben,' she pointed out with a hard edge to her voice. 'Not some soppy, sentimental film with a guaranteed happy ending.'

'I know,' he said, his manner subdued. He wasn't going to insult her intelligence with any more cheery platitudes.

The river was beautiful in the early-morning light, the air still and gentle, the summer sky reflecting on the surface in undulating pastel shades. The birdsong was loud and sweet as Ben sped through the water past Chiswick Eyot, the water lapping gently around the skiff as his oars cut into the river's smooth surface, seagulls swooping and diving, swans resting in their nesting places.

He rowed energetically, hoping the exercise would calm his nerves and soothe his troubled mind. There was a heavy dew on this grassy stretch of the river bank and he could smell that indefinable scent of autumn even though it was still only August – a tangy coolness mingled with mist and woodsmoke, a hint of earthy dampness perhaps.

After thrashing about all night getting tangled in the sheets, unable to sleep under the weight of his dilemma, he'd got up in the pale light of dawn and headed for the boathouse where he kept his skiff. As well as being a source of pleasure when things were going well, the river was also his salvation in times of stress. Its quiet waters comforted him, helped him to think more clearly.

On this particular occasion, however, clarity of thought was not particularly desirable because of the decision he feared his conscience would force him to make. 'What the hell am I going to do?' he asked a seagull that was soaring towards the pale blue sky.

Chapter Thirteen

'So what you're actually telling me is that you're going back to your wife?' said Rachel, hardly able to utter the words for the pain of them.

'Not exactly, no,' he denied.

'Pardon me. Did I hear you wrong or something?' She was driven to sarcasm by her aching disappointment. 'Haven't you just told me that Lorna is moving in with you?'

It was late evening and they were confronting each other in Rachel's living room. Ben had dropped this bombshell on her almost as soon as he'd stepped inside the door. Anxious to get it over with, she guessed

'Yes, that is what I said,' he confirmed stiffly, looking very pale and drawn. 'But we're not getting back together in the way you're making it seem, not as husband and wife.'

'But you'll be living together, for heaven's sake.' Her voice was high-pitched and ragged with emotion, though habit stopped her from shouting in case she woke the boys. 'What's that if it isn't a reconciliation of some sort?'

'She's ill, Rachel,' he reminded her, spreading his hands to emphasise his point. 'I can't let her go back to her own place to live alone while she's like this.'

'Why not?' Rachel was hurting too much to be charitable. 'It isn't as though she isn't able to do things for herself. You said she can walk on her own with crutches.'

'She can only get about slowly and with great difficulty,' he informed her.

'How is she going to manage while you're at work then?' she asked brusquely.

'I'll have to make provision . . . make sure she has everything she needs for the day before I leave in the morning, I suppose,' he told her. 'Fortunately she can see to the basic essentials herself and make herself a cup of tea, that sort of thing. But not much else.'

'You've got it all worked out then?' she said accusingly.

'No, not really,' he contradicted. 'You asked so I gave it some thought.'

'I see.' She was very cool.

'She's in a lot of pain and it's making her even more depressed than she is already,' he went on.

Rachel was about to lose the man she loved and her natural human instinct for self-preservation had come to the fore, overshadowing her more worthy qualities. 'Forgive me for being selfish enough to ask, but where do I come into all this?' she enquired harshly.

Ben lowered his eyes for a moment. 'All I can say is, I love you, Rachel,' he said solemnly, raising his eyes to meet hers. 'Nothing has altered that.'

'But we were going to get a house together, get married as soon as we're both free,' she reminded him, her voice breaking with the frustration of her blighted hopes.

His face tightened. 'Obviously I won't be able to go ahead with that for the time being,' he confessed guiltily. 'I'll have to stay on where I am, and I can't talk to Lorna about divorce while she's in this low state.'

'So that's it, then.' She was too deeply hurt herself to perceive the full extent of his disappointment. 'It's over for you and me, just like that, finished . . . *kaput.*'

'I don't want it to be over, Rachel, you must know that,' he said in an agonised tone.

'Surely you're not suggesting that we can continue

under such impossible circumstances?'

He spread his hands expressively. 'To be perfectly honest, I don't know what I'm suggesting,' he confessed, looking genuinely bewildered. 'I'm just as miserable about it as you are.'

'I doubt that,' she said, needing to hurt him as he was hurting her.

'Rachel . . .' He was begging now. 'Can you tell me what else I can possibly do but have her to live with me?'

'No, I can't,' she admitted shortly. 'But there must be a better way than this.'

'If there is, I don't know what it is,' he said. 'And don't think I haven't tried to think of an alternative.'

'If, as you say, your marriage really is over, three lives are going to be ruined by this arrangement,' she pointed out. 'Yours, mine and Lorna's. If you couldn't live together before, it will be a million times worse for you both with her being so dependent on you.'

'Do you think I haven't thought about that, over and over?' he said, his voice distorted with emotion. 'But what else can I do? Just tell me that?'

'A live-in companion, perhaps,' she blurted out, clutching at straws. 'Someone who could be with her all day. There are such people who do that sort of thing for a living.'

'Even if I could afford it, she wouldn't agree to it,' he said. 'She'd hate having a stranger about the place. Anyway, the doctor said she needs to be with someone she knows well so that she feels at ease when she's at home.'

'Even if *you* could afford it?' She narrowed her eyes on him quizzically. 'So, you're taking over financial responsibility for her too?'

'I shall have to help her, certainly,' he admitted. 'She won't be able to work so she'll only have the state benefit.'

Hating herself for being callous enough to query this side of things when Lorna was in such a bad way, Rachel sank wearily into an armchair, her manner becoming milder as she began to accept the inevitable. 'Yes, of course you must help her in that way,' she said dully. 'But what will happen to her place?'

'She'll have to give it up, I suppose,' he told her. 'She won't be able to afford to keep it on, and it would be pointless anyway as she's going to be living with me.'

Rachel's spirits took even more of a dive. 'So you're thinking in terms of this being a permanent arrangement, then, since she won't have a place of her own to go back to.'

'She'll look for somewhere else when she's well enough to live on her own again, I imagine.' He shook his head. 'But I'm going to take it one day at a time and live in hope. It's the only thing I can do if I want to keep my sanity.'

'Does she know about me?' Rachel enquired.

He nodded. 'She knows I'm seeing someone . . .'

'But you haven't told her that we are actually engaged in case it upsets her?' she surmised.

'I haven't mentioned it because I don't want to make her feel even worse than she probably does already about having to give up her own place and be reliant on me.' His tone was firm.

'*Probably does?*' she queried in astonishment. 'Has she not made her feelings known on the subject?'

He scratched his head distractedly, his blue eyes clouded with sadness. 'She's become very introverted,' he explained. 'She isn't keen to talk, and on the rare occasions we do have a conversation, she doesn't seem able to see outside of herself and her own problems. Other people don't really exist for her at the moment. The doctor said it's all part of the depression.'

'Surely there must be some sort of treatment,' Rachel suggested. 'Something to help her.'

'She's on anti-depressants,' Ben told her. 'And they're hoping that regular physiotherapy will eventually ease her pain and get her more mobile, which will in turn improve her mental state. So there is light at the end of the tunnel.'

'Too far off to be of any help to you and me, though,'

Rachel stated gloomily, her initial rage having turned to a mood of grim resignation.

He sat down with his hands to his head. 'I'm in a trap, Rachel. I can't turn my back on her even though our marriage is over; she's too vulnerable, too frail.'

'Yes.'

'I know this is a terrible thing to say, but I felt that trap begin to close around me the minute the police came to my door on the night of the accident,' he went on. 'I know that, strictly speaking, she isn't my responsibility but I feel as though she is and it's been weighing heavily on me ever since that dreadful night. I've been trying to blot it out, telling myself that she'd get better and get on with her own life without me. But when the doctor spelled out the reality of the situation I knew in my heart that I'd been expecting it.'

Now that the fire had gone out of her fury, Rachel's senses were more attuned to his feelings; she knew she expected nothing less of the sort of man he was than to put what he saw as his duty before his own happiness. There was nothing she could do but accept the painful fact that they didn't have a future together. 'I've been feeling threatened ever since the accident too,' she now felt able to admit. 'I've been living in fear and dread because I could see events taking you away from me.' Her tone was softer but she couldn't bring herself to physically comfort him because her own pain was still too intense. 'The trouble is, Ben, I'm caught in your trap too, and being only human, I don't like it. I know it isn't your fault, it isn't even Lorna's fault.' There was a sob in her voice even though she was trying to be brave. 'But my life is being ruined and it's breaking my heart.'

'Oh, Rachel, I'm so sorry . . .'

'It isn't your fault . . . I've told you.'

'Perhaps we could see each other when we can,' he suggested lamely.

'We both know that wouldn't work.' She saw no point in them deluding themselves. 'When Lorna moves in with you, your life will revolve around her even though you don't have plans to revive your marriage. How can it be otherwise when she is going to be so dependent on you?'

'But you and I could still . . .'

'I want us to be together *properly*, Ben,' she cut in quickly. 'I want us to live as a family. You me and the boys sharing a house . . . sharing our lives.'

'It's what I want too.'

'But we can't have that, can we?' She felt compelled to be realistic no matter how much it hurt. 'And I'm just not prepared to settle for an odd hour of your company on the rare occasions when you can get away from your wife. That wouldn't be fair to either of us or the boys.'

'No, of course not.' He looked very downhearted.

'Thank goodness I didn't tell the boys that you were going to be their dad,' she said. 'At least they'll be spared that disappointment.'

'I just can't bear the idea of it being over between us,' he told her fervently.

'Neither can I,' she said thickly. 'But we both know that we can't continue.'

He sighed heavily. 'I suppose I knew that when I decided to give in to my conscience and offer Lorna a home with me,' he confessed miserably. 'But I just didn't want to face up to it.'

'The boys are going to be upset.' She was thinking aloud rather than trying to make him feel worse. 'They hadn't been told that you were about to move in with us, but that doesn't alter the fact that they are going to miss you.'

'Maybe I could still see them now and again,' he suggested weakly.

She shook her head forcefully. 'Definitely not. That would be much too upsetting for us all,' she declared. 'It will have to be a clean break. If we can't have you properly, it's best if we don't see you at all.'

'What about work?' he enquired gloomily.

'You'll have to look for another job and I'll have to find another manager, I'm afraid,' she told him. 'It will be too painful for both of us to have to work together.'

He knew she was right. 'Yeah, I'll go along with that,' he sighed.

'Obviously you must stay on until you find something else; I don't want to put you out of work,' she hastened to add. 'But finding a job won't be a problem for a man with your reputation.'

'I'm not worried about that side of it,' he assured her. 'But I'll stay on until you've got someone to replace me. I know several blokes who might be interested in the job. All good boatbuilders who won't let you down. I'll put the word around if you like.'

'Thank you. That would be a great help.' She held her fingers against her temples. 'Oh, Ben. How are we managing to be so civilised about this?'

'Needs must when the devil drives, I suppose,' he said miserably. 'I certainly don't feel very civilised.'

'Me neither.' She stood up, her legs weakened by the shock of events. 'The thing I'm dreading most is telling Tim and Johnnie that they won't be seeing you again.'

'Leave it to me,' he offered. 'I'm the one causing the problem so I'll be the one to break the news to them. I'd rather they heard it from me anyway.'

'I think that would be the best thing,' she agreed.

'I'll do it tomorrow night.'

'OK,' she said sadly.

'Are you going away to live in another country?' asked Johnnie, his big dark eyes resting on Ben solemnly.

'No,' replied Ben. 'I'm not going abroad.'

'Why can't we see you then?' the boy demanded.

Ben struggled for the words he had been rehearsing in his mind all day. But nothing came. This was the hardest thing he had ever had to do.

'Because he's leaving us, like Dad did,' said Tim, on the verge of tears.

'No, Tim, I'm not walking out on you like your father did.' Ben's heart ached as he looked at the two little boys sitting unusually close together on the sofa while he delivered his farewell speech from his knees in front of them so as to be on their level. Rachel had retreated to the kitchen so that he could have centre stage. 'It isn't like that at all. I'm not stopping seeing you because I want to. I'm doing it because I have to.'

'Why?' Tim wanted to know.

He swallowed hard in an effort to clear the choking sensation in his throat. 'Because the lady I used to live with needs me at this time,' he explained. 'She isn't very well so she's coming to live with me.'

'Has she got measles?' Johnnie enquired. 'Does she think we'll catch it off you?' He paused for only a moment then went on before Ben had a chance to reply. 'That's all right, because measles doesn't last long. We'll see you when she's better.'

'She doesn't have measles,' said Ben.

'Chickenpox then,' suggested Johnnie helpfully. 'That's catching too.'

'No, it isn't chickenpox,' said Ben, unbearably moved by his childish logic.

'She doesn't have anything with spots then?' said Johnnie, looking mystified.

'Will you stop going on about stupid spotty illnesses,' ordered Tim, glaring at his brother through tear-rinsed eyes. 'He means he's not going to be seeing us ever again, not just while this woman's got some silly illness like measles.'

'She got hurt in an accident,' Ben informed them.

'Why will that stop you seeing us?' asked the irrepressible Johnnie. 'Doesn't she like children?'

'It isn't that.'

'Why then?'

'It's a grown-up thing,' he struggled to explain. 'Because I have to live with this other person, your mummy and I can't be together as we want to be.' He cleared his throat. 'You see, boys, there are times in a grown-up's life when they can't do what they would like to do, times when they have to put someone else first, like your mum always does with you. A man can't have two women in his life because it wouldn't be fair to either of them, so it's better if I don't come round here at all.'

'Do you love this other woman more than you love our mum?' asked Tim gravely. His face was paper-white and he was much more subdued than his brother.

'No,' said Ben. 'I love your mum more and I love both of you very much too.'

'If you really loved us you'd still want to see us,' said Tim, his eyes dark with accusation.

'Yeah,' agreed Johnnie, united with his brother against this bearer of bad news. 'It's not fair.'

'No, it isn't fair,' agreed Ben. 'And I'm just as upset as you are that I won't be seeing you again.' He paused to compose himself. 'But we'll just have to get used to it.'

'You won't be taking us out on the boat any more, then?' said Tim miserably.

'I'm afraid not,' said Ben.

'Or to play football in the park?' Johnnie added.

Ben couldn't trust himself to speak so he just shook his head.

'Oh,' said Johnnie.

Tim just looked at Ben with silent enmity.

'Look, chaps,' Ben said, getting up and opening his arms to them, 'it's important that you know I love you and I'm not deserting you because I want to. So can we still be friends?'

'You can't be our friend if we never see you,' Tim stated categorically.

'No, you can't,' added Johnnie.

'I hate you,' rasped Tim and rushed from the room, followed by his brother.

Listening from the kitchen door to what was being said, Rachel hurried into the other room to see Ben looking stricken.

'Children are very resilient, you know,' she said compassionately. 'They'll get over it, Johnnie sooner than Tim, I think. He seems to feel everything that bit more than his brother.'

'I'm so sorry to do this to you all, Rachel,' Ben said in a strangled voice. 'If there was any other way . . .'

'But there isn't, is there?' she said, wiping her eyes with the back of her hand. 'We've been over it, and this is the only way.'

'I love you,' he said simply.

She stood there with tears running down her cheeks. 'Yes, I believe you do,' she muttered. 'And I love you, but it just wasn't meant to be.'

He took her in his arms and she was too distressed to resist. He kissed the top of her head, stroking her hair.

'This is goodbye, then,' she murmured into his chest, 'even though we'll see each other at work for a little while longer.'

He didn't reply, just held her closer.

She dragged herself away. 'I have to go to my children now, they'll be needing me,' she choked out. 'Can you see yourself out?'

'Sure.'

As she got to the boys' bedroom door, she heard the dull thud of the front door closing behind Ben for the very last time. She wiped her eyes, took a deep breath to compose herself, then went in.

Tim was sitting on the edge of his bed, staring at his feet, which were swinging to and fro. Johnnie was playing with his toy cars on the floor.

'Now then, you two,' Rachel said, sitting beside Tim on the bed. 'We all have to be very brave about this.'

'I told you he'd go away, didn't I?' announced Tim. 'And you said he wouldn't.'

'Yes, I remember all that,' she said, recalling how upset he'd been when she and Ben had first become lovers. 'But it isn't Ben's fault, honestly. This is something that happened through no fault of his. He really does love you.'

'Well, I don't love him,' was Tim's vehement reply. 'I *hate* the sight of him.'

'So do I,' announced his brother predictably and with much less venom.

'I know you're upset, but that isn't a nice attitude,' she said. 'Being horrible about Ben isn't going to change anything. I shall miss him too, you know.'

Neither of them said anything. When Rachel tried to give Tim a hug, he turned away. 'Come on, Tim,' she coaxed. 'You're not cross with *me*, are you?'

He kept his head lowered for a moment, in a sort of protest against adults in general, she guessed. But eventually the thought of his mother's comforting arms proved too much and he nestled against her. Not to be left out, Johnnie joined them and the three of them sat on the edge of Tim's bed in shared sorrow.

'I hope he *never* comes back,' said Tim, struggling to hold back the tears.

'Yeah,' cried Johnnie supportively. 'I hope so too.'

Aware of the profound hurt that these young boys had suffered, and knowing that it wasn't something that would simply disappear after a night's sleep, Rachel vowed that she would not allow them to be hurt in this way again while they were in her care. Their father had done it; now Ben. But never again.

Ben couldn't bear the idea of going home to the house he'd thought he'd be leaving to make a new life with Rachel. So he went in search of comfort of the liquid sort, heading almost automatically for the river.

Parking the car in a side street, he made for the river walkway, which was well lit at night. The lights of

Hammersmith Bridge poured shafts of gold on to the black water, and from where he was standing, out of earshot of the traffic's roar, a steady stream of cars seemed to sail over it.

He walked past the public gardens and carried on to the boathouse, staring at the silent dark building, acutely aware of the fact that this was the end of an era. He'd worked there man and boy; he'd seen it almost go under and rise again under Rachel's supervision. And yes, maybe he had made a contribution towards its success.

It was all over now, and he was desperately sad. But his sorrow at cutting his ties with Banks' Boats was as nothing compared to the pain of losing the woman he loved. He turned and began walking back the way he'd come, turning the situation over in his mind and wondering if there was any other way he could have dealt with it. Was there anything he had overlooked that might have saved his relationship with Rachel and the boys?

One option would have been for him to turn his back on Lorna. But the weight of that on his conscience would probably have ruined his relationship with Rachel anyway. Being completely honest, he knew there was nothing anyone with scruples could have done differently. And Rachel was right to end their relationship here and now. She couldn't be expected to play second fiddle to his wife.

With a heavy heart he went into the Blue Anchor, the roar of laughter and conversation inside seeming oddly distant to him; he was excluded from the warm, pervasive atmosphere by the depth of his spirits. This bar that held so many memories for him, where he'd come with Chip and other workmates so many times over the years, seemed achingly poignant tonight because it wouldn't be his working local for much longer.

It would be a mistake to look for a job on this stretch of the river; he needed a fresh start, well away from Banks' Boats. The further away from Rachel the better if he was to cope with his responsibilities towards Lorna.

* * *

The next day was Saturday, one of those warm, lazy August days made for holidays and outings. The sunshine seemed to exacerbate Rachel's despair. It was a day to be happy, to be out enjoying the weather, and all she wanted to do was stay in bed and nurse her broken heart.

But since that sort of self-indulgence wasn't an option for a single mother of two energetic little boys, she got up, put on a cheerful face and proceeded to get on with the day. Both the children were subdued over breakfast but Johnnie could never stop talking for long and was chatting normally by the time the meal was over.

Tim left most of his cornflakes and refused his usual slice of toast. He was distressingly silent, and Rachel knew it was going to take time for him to get over Ben's departure. It was up to her to help him through it in whatever way she could.

They had to go to the supermarket, but they called in at Jan's on the way because Rachel wanted to tell her what had happened. People had to know sometime, and she'd sooner Jan was the first. She was about the only person on earth Rachel would take sympathy from, and then only in the strictest moderation.

'So you and Ben have finished altogether then?' said Jan, somewhat bemused by Rachel's news. They were drinking coffee in the dining alcove with the French doors open. The children were outside playing in the garden and Pete was busy upstairs finishing off the fitted wardrobes he was building in the bedrooms.

'That's right,' Rachel replied.

'I don't know what to say.' Jan looked very perplexed. 'I knew you were having problems because of his wife's accident. But I didn't dream it would split you up permanently.'

'Well, it has,' Rachel told her.

Jan tutted sympathetically. 'I can see that Ben was put into an impossible position,' she remarked, absently stirring her coffee and staring at the swirling liquid. 'And it's a real bugger because you two are so right for each other.'

'Yes, we are,' agreed Rachel. 'But that's the way it goes, isn't it? Just when you've found something good and think everything's set fair, fate decides to throw a spanner in the works.'

'I know I risk my life if I go overboard with the sympathy,' Jan said in her usual down-to-earth manner. 'But, oh, kid, I'm *so* sorry. You must be breaking your heart.'

'It's in little pieces,' admitted Rachel, tears welling up in her eyes.

'The boys?'

'Shattered,' said Rachel. 'They thought the world of him. First Jeff, now Ben. They'll start to think that father figures are ships that pass in the night.'

'It isn't quite as bad as that,' Jan disagreed mildly. 'But I know what you mean.'

'Anyway, I thought I'd keep them busy over the weekend, to stop them thinking about it and get them out of that stuffy flat,' Rachel went on. 'So I'm planning to go to the park this afternoon. Fancy coming along with Kelly?'

'Yeah, that'll be lovely,' Jan agreed enthusiastically. 'Pete will be busy with his DIY upstairs, so Kelly and I will be glad of the company.'

'Pete must have nearly finished everything you'd planned to do to the house by now,' remarked Rachel.

Jan nodded. 'Everything will be done when he's finished the wardrobes.'

'He's certainly done wonders with the place,' commented Rachel, glancing round at the archway to the lounge, the brick shelves by the fireplace, the strip wooden flooring in this dining alcove. And the shabby old scullery had become a dream kitchen in highest 1960s contemporary style.

'Yeah, he has done well,' Jan agreed heartily. 'Doing the house up has become a bit of a hobby for him, as you know. I don't know what he'll do with his spare time when he's finished upstairs.'

'Knowing Pete, he'll find something about the place

that needs his attention,' said Rachel, managing a watery smile, glad to have her thoughts diverted from her own troubles.

'I've got a horrible feeling that you're right,' said Jan with a wry grin. 'He isn't happy unless he's sawing, hammering or slapping paint or wallpaper around the place.'

'You're not complaining, I hope,' joked Rachel

'No fear,' Jan confirmed. 'I'm thrilled with everything he's done. It's just that I could do with a bit of a break from all the mess and upheaval.'

Rachel glanced towards the garden, where the children were doing handstands on the lawn. 'We'll have to drag him off to the park with us later on to slow things down a bit,' she suggested. 'The weather's too nice to be indoors.'

'We'll never manage it,' said Jan. 'With me and Kelly out of the house, he'll combine his amateur carpentry with watching sport on TV in peace. His idea of a perfect Saturday afternoon.'

Rachel opened her mouth to reply but was suddenly overcome, her eyes filling with tears despite all attempts to stop them.

'Come here,' said Jan, standing up and opening her arms.

'I'm being pathetic,' apologised Rachel, hugging her sister then mopping her eyes with her handkerchief. 'It just came over me. This nice weather makes it worse. It seems to be rubbing it in, somehow.'

'Sunshine can make things worse if you're feeling low,' mentioned Jan. 'And weekends are bound to be worse than weekdays. Being busy at work will take your mind off it. You'll be all right.'

'Once he's left the firm,' agreed Rachel.

'Mm. I suppose this has scuppered your plans to buy a house, too,' remarked Jan, finishing her coffee.

'I'm going ahead with that,' Rachel announced determinedly. 'Getting the boys into a house has been my aim ever since I took over the boathouse, and that hasn't changed just because Ben isn't going to be around. I know that lots of families with kids manage perfectly well in a flat and I would have accepted that as our lot for life had Uncle Chip not raised my expectations by remembering me in his will. But now that the boathouse is doing well, I think it would be wrong of me not to improve our living conditions. Nothing very expensive, just an ordinary little place with a garden.'

'Good for you,' said Jan.

'It'll give us something to look forward to,' mentioned Rachel. 'I shall start sifting through the pile of estate agents' details I've got at home. And naturally I shall want your advice.'

'You'll get that whether you want it or not,' laughed Jan.

Rachel managed to smile. She was far too engrossed in her own problems to hear the falseness of her sister's laughter or see the anxiety in her eyes. Had she been her usual self, she would have realised that Jan had worries of her own.

Although Rachel had thought she couldn't live without Ben, somehow the days passed regardless of her world having fallen apart around her. The sun grew cool, the evenings drew in and autumn mists shrouded the river.

Ben left the firm in mid September to join a company in Twickenham, leaving Rachel's workshops in the capable hands of a man called Ted Barratt, who came highly recommended by Ben. Ted was an excellent boatbuilder with an unassuming personality, a reliable family man with two teenage children.

Rachel and Ben didn't make a performance of his departure. They'd said everything that had to be said that last night at her flat. So she just gave him everything that was owing to him, wished him well and declined the invitation to join him and his workmates in the pub for a farewell drink. A booze-up with a bunch of men was about the last thing she fancied.

As she and the boys faced up to life without Ben, Rachel focused her mind on finding a new home. It didn't prove to be an easy task, because she had so little time to look at property. One of her biggest problems since she'd taken over the boathouse was having to cope with two jobs – her uncle's and his secretary's. She had originally taken this on to save the firm money, but it was a huge workload for one person, especially as her family responsibilities didn't allow her to work late very often.

Through determination and careful juggling of her time, she did manage to look at those houses she thought had possibilities, though this proved to be disheartening since anything half decent was either out of her price range or needed too much done in the way of refurbishment. Much of the property in Hammersmith was old, and anything that had been modernised was too expensive for her.

When a Victorian terraced house opposite Jan and Pete came on to the market in her price range, she thought her search was over. But on viewing it and seeing how much modernisation it needed, she was forced to rule it out. She couldn't afford to have the work done, and the house was barely habitable without some drastic improvements.

She finally found the perfect house for them on a dismal wet day in November, a dear little terraced place with a long, narrow back garden with an apple tree at the bottom. Having been to look at it in her lunch break, she went straight to Jan's afterwards and told her all about it over a cup of tea at her kitchen table, while Johnnie was being entertained by *Watch With Mother* on the television in the other room. Outside a steady drizzle was falling. The windows inside were steamed up and it was so dark in the house they had to have the lights on.

Waiting for her sister's reaction to her description of the house, she was amazed when Jan burst into tears. 'Whatever's the matter?' she asked, astonished.

'Nothing.' Jan buried her face in her handkerchief.

'Come on, love,' Rachel urged her kindly. 'Tell me why you're so upset.'

'You're talking about the house you're going to buy and we're about to lose this one,' she sobbed.

'What!'

'We're behind with the mortgage,' she explained through her tears.

'Oh, Jan . . .'

'Unless we pay the building society the four hundred pounds' arrears, they're going to repossess it,' she went on tearfully. 'Oh, Rachel, I just don't know what we're going to do.'

They'd been struggling with financial problems for months, Jan told Rachel when she managed to stop crying for long enough to articulate the words. She hadn't said anything about it before, partly because she was ashamed and partly because she thought Rachel had enough problems of her own.

'I remember you mentioning that you were a bit worried back last winter.' Rachel had maintained a diplomatic silence after Jan's confession last January because she knew that was what she wanted. 'But I thought you must have come through it when you didn't say any more about it.'

'No, the problem was still there but we managed to keep going, living on a knife edge,' Jan explained. 'But having to buy a new van in the summer made things very tight again.'

Rachel nodded in an understanding manner.

'We're caught in a vicious circle,' Jan confessed, shaking her head. 'We're too overstretched to get any money behind us, so any unexpected expense puts us back in bother. If we could only get back on our feet properly we might stand a chance. But it just seems to be one expense after another. The new van put us in deep trouble but the old one was costing so much money we couldn't afford to keep it, and Pete can't do his job without transport.'

'Of course he can't,' agreed Rachel.

'That slack period he had when people were away on holiday made matters worse,' Jan continued. 'Things just went from bad to worse after that and it's finally led to this.'

'Won't the building society give you some more time?' Rachel enquired.

'They already have,' explained Jan. 'But now they want paying and they're planning to repossess the house if the arrears aren't paid off by the end of the month.'

'Oh dear,' sympathised Rachel.

'The letter came in the second post,' Jan muttered worriedly. 'I don't know how I'm going to tell Pete.'

'He's bound to be upset,' tutted Rachel. 'After all the work he's put into this house.'

'He loves this place and he's got it exactly how we want it,' sniffed Jan, dabbing at her eyes with her hanky. 'And now we'll have to give it up.'

'You can't lose it,' Rachel said with sudden resolution. 'We can't let that happen.'

'I don't see how we can stop it if we don't have the money to pay the arrears,' Jan pointed out.

'You haven't taken me into account, though, have you? Surely you don't think I would stand by and let you lose your home?' Rachel was emphatic.

'Be realistic,' urged Jan. 'You're about to buy a house yourself so you'll have enough expenses of your own, especially now that Ben isn't around to help out. House-owning eats your money like nothing else I know of . . . just gobbles it up.'

'Even so . . .'

'Your first duty is to those boys.' Jan pulled herself together so that her sister wouldn't feel obliged to offer assistance. 'You'll need every penny you earn for your own commitments.'

Rachel chewed her lip anxiously. 'I am going to have an expensive time, I admit,' she told her sister frankly. 'But I can't bear to let you lose this place.'

'Forget about trying to help us.' Jan was adamant. 'If we have to move out of here, we do. People have much worse things happen to them than that. We'll get over it.'

'True. But I still think there must be another way,' persisted Rachel.

'I meant what I said.' Jan's composure was now fully restored for fear of charity being aimed in her direction from someone with two children to bring up on her own. 'It's our mess, mine and Pete's, and we'll deal with it.'

Knowing that it would be a mistake to pursue the matter at this stage, Rachel looked at her watch. 'I have to go back to work,' she said with reluctance. 'Will you be all right on your own?'

'I won't top myself while you're gone, if that's what you mean,' said Jan with a spirited grin. 'So go and look after your business or you'll be in trouble too.'

Rachel went into the other room and gave Johnnie a big hug, then walked back to the boathouse in the rain, deeply worried about her sister and her family.

She was still mulling it over when she got into bed that night, finding herself on the horns of a dilemma. As Jan had wisely pointed out, Rachel's children had to take priority. It was her duty to get them decently housed now that she was in a position to do so. But at the same time, she simply couldn't see her sister and her family lose their home.

There was a limit to her own resources, boathouse or no boathouse. There wouldn't be much left over after the deposit on a house and the moving expenses had been paid, and she daren't overstretch herself with two children to raise and no one to turn to for financial assistance. Even if she could lay her hands on some extra cash, there was still the matter of Jan and Pete's self-respect to be considered. They were fiercely proud when it came to this sort of thing, and she couldn't force them to accept help.

Weary of tossing and turning in search of a solution, she got out of bed and went to the kitchen to make a cup of tea. It was while she was waiting for the kettle to boil that the beginnings of an answer began to form.

Chapter Fourteen

If not the perfect solution, it was, Rachel thought, probably the next best thing, though Jan was rather more circumspect when she tried to tell her about it the next morning.

'So what this idea of yours actually boils down to,' she said, her pride colouring her attitude with scepticism, 'is that you're intending to buy a house you don't want just so that you can give us some money to pay off our mortgage arrears.'

'No, that isn't how it is at all,' Rachel protested. 'You might at least let me tell you about the whole of the plan before you write it off as a handout.'

'Sorry . . . go on then.' Jan still looked wary.

Bursting to explain the scheme she'd been thinking about for most of the night, Rachel had gone to her sister's place after they'd dropped the children at school. They were having a quick cup of coffee in the kitchen before Rachel went to work. Johnnie was playing in the other room, so the two women were able to talk in peace. 'As I've just said,' Rachel went on, 'the idea is that instead of my proceeding with the house I'd decided on yesterday, I buy the one that's up for sale across the road from you.'

'Which you'd already decided against,' Jan cut in.

'Only because it needs such a lot doing to it,' Rachel pointed out. 'It's perfect for us apart from that, being close to you and everything, and there's a lovely garden at the back.'

'Yeah, yeah, I know all that, but what about all the work

that needs doing?' Jan wanted to know.

'The bad state of repair that it's in is reflected in the price, which means it's a lot cheaper than the other one,' Rachel explained excitedly. 'So I could afford the deposit and still help you and Pete out.'

'But you said you couldn't afford to have the place done up.' Jan was beginning to get exasperated now.

'I can't.' Rachel paused, a gleam in her eye. 'But it won't cost anything if Pete does it for me.'

'Ah.' Jan gave Rachel a shrewd look. 'Now it's beginning to sound better.'

'If I were to go for the cheaper house, I could afford to give you and Pete enough to pay off the arrears and a bit extra so that you're not quite so vulnerable until you get back on your feet. And Pete could pay the debt off with his labour, in his spare time, of course,' she told her sister, enthusiasm rising with every word. 'DIY is something he enjoys anyway, and you've been wondering how he's going to fill his time after work now that your place is all but finished.'

Jan's own enthusiasm was beginning to bubble, but she still had a few queries. 'You'd still have to pay for the materials, though,' she pointed out.

'Of course, but without the labour charges my costs would be dramatically reduced, and they'd be spread over a period, so I wouldn't have to find the money all at once. That, added to the fact that the cost of the house is less, would mean I could help you and stay out of trouble myself,' she said. 'So we'd all benefit from it. I get the house I want, all refurbished, and you don't have a debt around your neck or any hang-ups about accepting charity.'

Jan's plump face was flushed with hope, but there was still some doubt in her eyes. 'It does sound feasible,' she admitted, 'but you seemed so keen on the house you found yesterday.'

'Only because I didn't think the one across the road was a viable proposition,' Rachel explained.

'And you really would like that one?' Jan's pride still needed more reassurance.

'I'd love it,' Rachel burst out. 'I was really disappointed when I had to rule it out.'

'It would be nice having you and the boys so near, I must admit,' smiled Jan. 'Kelly will be thrilled.'

'So will the boys,' added Rachel. 'It will be a new start for us.'

'Just what you need,' observed Jan.

Rachel became thoughtful, fixing her gaze on her sister's face. 'And while we're on the subject of new beginnings, I've got another idea I'd like to put to you.'

'You're full of 'em this morning, aren't you?' she grinned. 'So let's have it.'

'You know you've been talking about getting a job when Johnnie starts school after Christmas,' Rachel reminded her.

'Yeah,' nodded Jan. 'I shall have to do something to help out with the finances when there are no kids around for me to mind. But finding something that will fit in with Kelly isn't going to be all that easy.'

'I know of a job with flexible hours and a boss who's very understanding when it comes to the problem of school holidays for working mums,' said Rachel.

'There aren't many of those around.' Jan looked doubtful. 'Where is it?'

'At the boathouse, working with me,' Rachel announced. 'I'm in desperate need of someone to help me in the office.'

'Oh, Rachel,' responded Jan worriedly. 'You haven't created a job just to help me out, have you?'

'Of course I haven't,' Rachel was quick to reassure her. 'I'm not a complete idiot where business is concerned.'

'I wasn't suggesting you are . . .'

'You know that I've been doing the work of two people ever since I took over at the boathouse,' Rachel cut in, eager to make her point.

'Yes, you have mentioned it,' admitted Jan. 'But this job

does seem to have come up suddenly and at rather a convenient time for me.'

'Your needing to go out to work has inspired me to do something definite about getting help, that's all,' Rachel explained. 'I had to do the two jobs to save on the wages bill when the business was in trouble. But it's doing well now and there really is far too much work for one person. I knew I would have to seriously think about taking someone on anyway, now that the firm can afford it, and I'd love that someone to be you.'

'But I don't have any experience of that sort of work,' Jan pointed out.

'Neither did I when I took over. You'll soon pick it up. And it'll only be part time, which will suit us both,' Rachel effused. 'A few hours a day. Ten till two or something like that. We can work that out nearer the time.'

Something still appeared to be worrying Jan.

'It doesn't matter that you can't type,' said Rachel, taking a guess. 'I'll still do all that, and I'll have more time to spend on it if I have help with other things. It's all the other stuff that's weighing me down – the filing, the post and other general office duties. And it would be an enormous help to me if you could do the wages every week once I've taught you how the PAYE system works.'

'You've got it all worked out,' smiled Jan, 'I don't know what to say.'

'Just say you'll take the job,' grinned Rachel.

'I'll take it all right,' she beamed. 'It's such a relief to have that problem sorted. I've been worried sick because I didn't think I'd find a job that wouldn't interfere with the family.' She paused. 'You know how much it means to me to meet Kelly from school and be at home with her in the holidays.'

'I do know, and I shall make sure you're able to do it.' Rachel gave her sister a wry grin. 'Especially as I shall want you to look after mine sometimes.'

'That's settled then.'

'Brilliant.'

'About the other thing,' Jan went on in a more serious tone. 'I'll have to talk to Pete before I give you a definite answer. He's bound to be all in favour, but I'd better tell him about it before I say for certain, out of respect for him.'

'Especially as there's about a year's-worth of DIY involved,' smiled Rachel.

'That won't worry him,' Jan said. 'But I don't want to commit him to something without speaking to him about it first. He's a bit touchy at the moment, blames himself for the mess we're in and thinks he's failed as a provider.'

'Poor old Pete.'

'Yeah, he has been a bit down lately. But doing your house up is just the sort of thing he needs to restore his male ego,' said Jan. 'Because he'll be the one doing the work to get us out of trouble, he can feel good about himself again.'

'There's that to it, too,' agreed Rachel. 'Anyway, as soon as we get the OK from him, I'll put an offer in on the house. I'm really looking forward to being your neighbour.'

Jan wasn't one of nature's weepers but her eyes filled with tears for the second time in twenty-four hours. 'Come here,' she said thickly, opening her arms to her sister. 'Let me thank you properly for coming to our rescue.'

'I've told you, it's an arrangement for the good of us all,' insisted Rachel, hugging her.

'I know, kid,' said Jan softly. 'But thanks anyway.'

Rachel swallowed hard. She was too overcome to reply.

A lot of things happened in the new year. Johnnie started school, Jan started work at the boathouse and Rachel and the boys became neighbours of their beloved relatives when they moved in to number six Ross Street.

Although the house was brimming with potential, it was a positive ruin when they moved in, which they did as soon as the legalities were completed rather than pay rent on the flat as well as mortgage repayments. Initially they seemed to be worse off than they'd been at the flat, because the place was damp, musty and bitterly cold.

But they weren't uncomfortable for long, Rachel saw to that. Having budgeted for central heating, that was her first priority and Pete got busy right away, enlisting the help of a pal – a qualified plumber who owed him a favour and lent a hand with the technical parts of the job. Until the radiators were installed and working, Rachel kept pneumonia at bay with open fires and abundant hot-water bottles. Needless to say, a well-worn path was trodden to Jan's, where succour was always on tap.

For the few first months, Rachel and the boys lived on bare boards and out of boxes because there were no cupboards and every room needed extensive redecoration. Although the boys were still quite small, Rachel talked to them about her plans for the place and let them choose their bedroom wallpaper, managing not to wince too visibly when they chose garish patterns.

With Pete only able to work on the house in the evenings and at weekends, its refurbishment seemed to be taking for ever. There was dust everywhere and they couldn't move without tripping over builder's materials. But despite all the inconvenience, Rachel was certain she had done the right thing in moving into this house. In doing her sister a good turn she had also done herself a favour, because the place felt right for them. It was welcoming, somehow; they seemed to belong here. The only disappointment was that Ben wasn't sharing it with them.

Johnnie occasionally mentioned Ben but Tim never did. Rachel guessed he was trying not to think about him because it hurt to do so. She was trying, unsuccessfully, to do the same thing. The fact that she didn't have time to brood didn't stop thoughts of him coming into her mind, especially in the silence of the night, when she couldn't sleep.

As soon as the weather improved, she spent her evenings and weekends working on the wilderness outside, digging, chopping and raking until her back was aching and her hands were sore. Since she wanted the garden to be somewhere the children could play rather than a showpiece, she wasn't planning any extravagant flowerbeds or untreadable lawns. To make it easy on the eye, though, she planted masses of marigolds, pansies and busy Lizzies.

The boys weren't bothered about the flowers so much as the fact that they could ride their bikes up and down the garden path, which they did with great vigour. Their enjoyment was hers too and she revelled in it.

Slowly but surely the house turned into a home. Walls changed colour, cupboards appeared and the ancient facilities in the bathroom were replaced by a smart new suite in fashionable pale green. Pete was doing a wonderful job.

During the course of this domestic transformation, Rachel had also been busy, acquiring a skill that had been much needed ever since she'd taken over the boathouse. She took a course of driving lessons and when she passed her test in June, she bought a blue Ford Anglia.

It was a legitimate business expense according to the firm's accountant, who didn't think it was expedient to rely on the vagaries of public transport when you were running a business, especially as she was so often out and about representing the company.

Having her own transport broadened her horizons at a personal level too, and in the school summer holidays she took the children on outings to places like Windsor, Runnymede and Chessington Zoo. Naturally Jan and Kelly went along too, and one day they all had a riotous time on a day trip to Southend – cockles, candy floss, the works.

It was the end of August before Pete completed the refurbishments to the house, a year since Rachel had split up with Ben.

'You've done a really good job, Pete.' It was the evening he officially finished and she was standing at the front door seeing him off.

'I'm glad you're pleased,' he told her. 'I enjoyed doing it.'

'You won't know what to do with yourself now, will you?' she grinned.

'I'll soon find something, don't worry,' he smiled thoughtfully. 'I think we could probably do with a few more shelves in our kitchen, you know.'

'Now, why doesn't that surprise me?' she laughed

'Are you suggesting that I'm some sort of a DIY freak?' he protested lightly.

'I certainly am,' she wasn't afraid to tell him. 'And very glad of it I am, too. You've made this place into a little palace.'

'And got my debts sorted in the process,' he said, his tone becoming more serious. 'If you hadn't come up with the idea, Rachel, I don't know where we would be now.'

'All's well that ends well,' she said, making light of it.

'And having Jan bringing in a wage every week helps keep us out of trouble too,' he remarked.

'Having her in the office is a godsend to me,' she mentioned.

'I can't tell you how glad I'll be to have her back at the end of the school holidays. I'm snowed under without her.'

The fact that Jan didn't work in the school holidays suited Rachel in one way because it meant that her sister could look after Tim and Johnnie on the days that Rachel had to go in to the boathouse. But the workload at the office was punishing for Rachel on her own. To alleviate matters a little, Jan came in once a week for a few hours to do the wages and a couple of other jobs. This was arranged to take place when Marge wasn't working at the newsagent's so that she could look after all the children. It was a real family affair.

Pete gave Rachel an understanding nod. 'I suppose you will be glad, having got used to having Jan around.' He paused, glancing towards his own house. 'Well, I'd better be going,' he said, 'so that I can spend what's left of the evening with my other half.'

Rachel reeled from a sudden memory of summer nights spent with Ben.

'Still missing him?' Pete said, surprising her with his sensitivity.

'Is it that obvious?'

'No. Not usually,' he assured her. 'But you did look a bit sorrowful just then.'

'I do still miss him,' she admitted. 'I just can't help it.'

'It's a shame. I was disappointed when you two split up,' he confided. 'He's a nice bloke. I got on really well with him. He was just like one of the family.'

'Yes, he was.' She could feel the pain rising. 'Still, these things happen.'

'See you then,' he said, turning.

'See you, Pete.'

She watched him stride across the road, a large figure with a swaying gait; then she went inside, still thinking of Ben. The thunder of little feet from upstairs, accompanied by giggles, indicated some sort of mischief. Making her way up to read the riot act, she wondered how Ben was getting on now, a year since they'd broken up. She couldn't help wondering if he thought of her as often as she thought of him.

Lorna Smart was sitting indoors in an armchair half listening to a programme on the radio while the afternoon sun bathed the small paved garden with light. Her eyes were dull and lacklustre; her skin was greasy and she wore no make-up; the hair she used to keep well cut and coloured with a tinted shampoo was now mousy brown, long and lank and scraped back from her face with an elastic band.

She glanced towards the open French doors. It was warm and stuffy in here with the sun on the back of the house, a typical humid August day. She didn't have to stay inside, of course. Ben had put a garden chair in a shady corner of the terrace for her before he went to work this morning. But dragging herself out there was just too much of an effort and made her back hurt, especially as she'd put on so much extra weight lately. Anyway, being outside in the sunshine would probably make her even more miserable than she already was, if that was possible.

Moving in with Ben had been a terrible mistake and they both knew it, even though the subject was never mentioned. He was as depressed as she was, though he was at pains not to show it. She loathed being dependent on him, had grown to hate him because of it and detested herself even more for allowing this situation to have come about at all.

But what else could she have done when she came out of hospital? She had no one else and she was certainly in no fit state to live on her own. People at a worse level of disability did manage to live by themselves, she knew that. But it was usually when they didn't have any other choice.

She'd known that Ben wouldn't let her down even though he'd been involved with someone else. She couldn't bear to think about that, the guilt was so overwhelming. He hadn't said too much about the woman in his life, but Lorna knew her name was Rachel and that giving her up had caused him pain.

Until recently, Lorna had not had cause to question her own strength of character; she'd never bothered to wonder if she was a brave or a cowardly person. But having considered the question at length this past year, she had come to the conclusion that she was probably somewhere in the middle, like most people under normal circumstances. But her situation wasn't normal. Constant pain and the relentless grip of depression had made a coward of her; it had made her willing to take desperate measures rather than live on her own.

Despite the cheerful front Ben managed to maintain for most of the time, Lorna perceived his unhappiness and knew he was wishing he was with Rachel; she smarted inwardly from the irritation he tried so hard to hide. He was very good to her, very patient, and did everything he could to make her life easier. He'd made the sitting-room into a bedroom for her to save her having to tackle the stairs; fortunately the bathroom was on the ground floor behind the kitchen, so that wasn't a problem.

She thanked God she could see to her own personal necessities. It was a struggle but she managed. She could even do a few things around the house like making tea and coffee, getting herself a sandwich and so on. But she couldn't stand for long enough to make a meal for them, clean the house, go shopping or any of the other ordinary everyday things she used to take for granted.

Ben did all of that, and never a word of complaint. They talked to each other but never said anything. They might exchange a few words about a television programme they'd watched together or some item of news, but never indulged in conversation of a personal nature. Mercifully they knew each other well enough for silence not to be a problem.

The radio programme was beginning to irritate her. Some self-satisfied man was being interviewed about how he'd overcome crippling adversity with sheer grit and determination. The interviewer was being sickeningly sentimental about his courage. Honestly, it really was over the top. These people who got themselves in the paper or on the radio made recovery seem so easy, as though the cure for all ills was bravery, which wasn't true at all. How many people with a spinal injury such as Lorna had could go back to living a normal life?

According to Ben, she should have persevered for longer with the physiotherapy that had been available to her after she'd been discharged from hospital. He'd even offered to take time off work to drive her to the hospital if she didn't fancy going in an ambulance. He'd been very disappointed when she'd given up. Easy for him to talk; he didn't have to put up with the agony she'd had to suffer at each session until she'd finally stopped going. The pain would have lessened in time, the experts had told her. It was important, apparently, to do the right kind of exercise, to keep active, or everything stiffened up. That was all very well, but the physiotherapist wasn't the one whose back hurt every time he moved, was he? A positive attitude was easy when you weren't the one in pain.

The man on the radio was on a massive ego trip now, she thought cynically. He was banging on about how he'd been through a suicidal stage after his accident. He'd been in a car crash, apparently. Had been in terrible pain and partly paralysed for a while. He still had to use a wheelchair sometimes even now. But he could live with it now. Had learned to accept it.

'How?' she asked out loud. 'Come on, you complacent bugger, how did you get out of it? There's more to getting better than just courage and determination. You can't repair physical damage just by having an optimistic attitude. So what was it, a religious experience? You found someone worse off who inspired you? Which particular cliché are you going to come out with now?'

He'd stopped running away and faced up to things, *really* faced up to them, he was saying. He'd gone *through* the mental and physical torture instead of withdrawing from it. He'd started doing what the doctors advised instead of ignoring everything they said. He'd embarked upon a course of physiotherapy. It had been difficult at first but had got easier in time. He still didn't have full mobility but he was heaps better than he had been. He'd made new friends in a similar position, taken up new interests, had found freedom of a kind, and peace of mind.

Oh, how she longed for some of that freedom; from the pain, from Ben, and most of all from the guilt of making him be with her when it wasn't what either of them wanted. She longed to live in her own place again, with her own things around her; to eat when she wanted and to watch what she chose on the television without feeling that she was imposing. She had had enough of being a lodger.

The interview was coming to an end. The presenter was

thanking Clever Clogs for coming on the show to talk so honestly about his feelings. He was sure it would be an inspiration to others. Oh yeah, thought Lorna bitterly, all over the country people like me are going to become instant heroes just because they've listened to some brave and saintly bloke baring his soul on the radio.

His words lingered in her mind, though, despite herself. Go *through* the pain instead of drawing back from it. It struck a chord even though it hurt to admit it. Drawing back was what she'd done a lot of this past year. She'd withdrawn from life itself because she didn't have the strength to fight back against the appalling fate that had befallen her. She'd chosen to ignore all the experts' advice about perseverance.

She found herself pondering the question. It must have worked for Mr Ego on the programme or he wouldn't have been given air time to talk about it. She felt sure they didn't have frauds on the BBC. Maybe there was something in what he said. She felt her heart lift with hope, only to sink almost immediately with the reality of her own situation. She wasn't like the man on the radio. She wasn't brave, and she had a very low pain threshold indeed.

Almost against her will, she found herself wondering if it might be worth giving the physiotherapy another try. After all, she couldn't be worse off than she already was, sitting here all day feeling sorry for herself. She looked at her watch. Four o'clock. The doctor's would be open for early-evening surgery by now, the receptionist available for making appointments.

She reached over for the telephone placed by her thoughtful husband on a small table next to her. Her hands were trembling, her armpits cold with nervous sweat. She reminded herself that all she was going to do at this stage was make an appointment to see the doctor. She wasn't committing herself to anything more daunting than that. With a great deal of trepidation, she picked up the receiver and began to dial the number.

* * *

Arthur was feeling immensely pleased with himself that same August evening as he let himself into the luxury flat that he and Ella now rented in the better part of the Notting Hill area. They'd gone up in the world quite considerably lately. Oh yes. This was one classy pad, with its fashionable fitted kitchen and coloured bathroom with gold-plated taps. The only reason they were renting a place rather than buying was because Arthur wasn't keen on the maintenance that ownership entailed. There was no point in taking on that sort of responsibility when you didn't have to, in his opinion.

He'd just had an extremely profitable day, having shifted a good few children's novelty watches for under-the-counter resale at the pubs and clubs he visited when he was on his rounds emptying the amusement machines. The watches were a bit of a craze with kids at the moment, and these places were full of men who wanted to please their nippers, which in turn got them on the right side of the missus.

From time to time over the years, Arthur had thought of leaving the collecting job. But staying with it had proved to be a wise decision, because it was an excellent way of selling the stuff he now acquired in bulk from a bloke he'd met in a pub about a year ago.

The man supplied him with a steady stream of the sort of non-perishables that were always in demand if they came cheaper than punters could buy them in the shops: watches, tape recorders, cigarette lighters, fashion jewellery, novelty items. The only condition was that Arthur didn't ask questions. As Arthur had worked on the wrong side of the law for most of his adult life, receiving dodgy gear was no problem at all to him.

So, what with the steady money he was making from the collecting job with its fruitful fiddling opportunities, plus the dough he was stashing away into his back pocket from his profitable sideline, things were really on the up.

'I'm home, babe,' he called out, putting his car keys down

on the hall table, an extravagant little number with a gilt-edged onyx-marble top and legs in fancy white ironwork. It had cost a good few quid and he hoped visitors realised that. Ostentation was second nature to Arthur, who didn't have the wit to realise that classy expense announced itself in a whisper rather than a shout. For him, part of the pleasure of having money was flaunting it, especially when no one could prove how he'd come by it. Lovely, he thought, feasting his eyes on the table and deciding that no one could possibly miss it when they came in the front door because it hit you right between the eyes.

Ella appeared from the kitchen wearing the briefest of mini-dresses. 'Hi, lover,' she said cheerfully, coming close to him and putting her face up to his. 'Had a good day?'

'The best,' he said, kissing her. 'You?'

'Not bad at all,' she told him. 'I've earned some good commission today.'

'That's my girl,' he said proudly.

Ella had moved up in the world career-wise, too. She now worked in a smart dress shop in Oxford Street owned by a Jewish couple. She earned more than she had in the shoe-shop. Not only did she get a basic salary and commission, but she also had a staff discount on any clothes she bought there too. And best of all, there were no smelly feet to deal with.

'Trouble is, lover, we've got nothing at all in the flat to eat.' She was a very casual housekeeper. Sometimes she got around to making a meal but mostly they fetched something from the chippy. 'I didn't have time to go shopping.'

'Don't matter about that, love.' It would take more than a hiccup on the domestic front to rattle Arthur tonight. Anyway, he was used to it.

'Are you gonna take me out for a meal, then?' she asked, her manner slightly kittenish.

'Yeah, let's do that,' he said amicably. 'Where do you fancy going?'

'Depends how flash you're gonna be with your money,' Ella told him.

'I'll be as flash as you like tonight,' he said with an indulgent smile. 'I'm in a generous mood, so choose somewhere nice. After the day I've had, money's no object tonight.'

'In that case, let's go to the West End, shall we?' she suggested. 'I fancy that.'

'Suits me.'

'I'll just have a quick bath then,' Ella smiled, 'and make myself look glamorous.'

'Put on the sexiest thing you've got,' Arthur told her. 'Tonight we're gonna paint the town.'

Slipping her arms around his neck, she looked lovingly into his dark eyes. 'You're a terrific bloke, Art, do you know that?' She fancied him even more when he was doing well. Success was a powerful aphrodisiac to Ella.

'I think I probably do have . . . a certain something.' He moved back slightly and evinced an air of suavity, smiling complacently and wriggling his shoulders.

'You do, you do,' she agreed heartily. 'As a woman, I know about these things.'

'And as a woman, you've got plenty of style yourself,' he complimented her.

'You're right about that an' all.' They were two of a kind. Modesty wasn't in her nature either.

'Go and have your bath then,' he said, giving her bottom a friendly squeeze. 'I'd come and wash your back, but we'll never get out if I do that.'

'We wouldn't,' she giggled.

'I'll sit in the lounge and have a look at the paper while you have your bath,' he said. 'Then I'll grab the bathroom when you've finished.'

'When you do, make sure you slap on plenty of Old Spice,' she told him. 'To put me in the mood for later.'

'Anything for you, darlin',' he said, watching her with

pleasure as she headed off into the bedroom, swinging her hips and humming a pop tune.

This is the life, he thought, stepping on to the deep-pile lounge carpet and pouring himself a whisky at the formica-topped bar that came complete with ice-bucket and tongs. I've got a beautiful wife, a posh pad and plenty of dough in my pocket. What more could any man want?

And to think that he'd been worried about losing that poxy boathouse not so long ago. He had no interest whatsoever in that now. Rachel could stuff it for all he cared. Arthur Banks was a man of substance, successful in his own right. He'd proved that he could do well for himself without the help of that mean-minded git of a father of his.

Chapter Fifteen

Rachel had suspected that her feelings about her birth mother might eventually get the better of her, and in the new year of 1969, the urge to find her became very strong. Being sensitive to Marge's feelings, however, she put the idea to her before taking matters any further.

'I've no objection to your trying to contact your natural mother,' said Marge, though doubt was clearly visible in her soft blue eyes. 'But I'm not sure that it's such a good idea.'

'I'm not certain either,' admitted Rachel with a wry grin. 'But I still feel compelled to do it.'

It was Rachel's lunch hour and they were having a chat over a sandwich and a cup of tea at Marge's kitchen table. Rachel had chosen a day when her mother wasn't working in the afternoon so that she'd have time to give the matter her full attention.

'You could get hurt,' Marge wisely pointed out.

'Nothing could hurt as much as knowing that she abandoned me,' Rachel told her. 'That really toughened me up. Anyway, all I want from her is a meeting.' She gave Marge a meaningful look. 'I'm not looking for a mother, you know. I already have a fantastic one of those.'

'Oh.' Marge coloured up, giving her a half-smile. 'It's nice to hear you say that.'

'I mean it,' said Rachel.

'I know you do, love.' Marge was very understanding, but

she still looked doubtful. 'Even so, it's a very delicate matter you'll be dealing with,' she said.

'Naturally I'll be discreet,' Rachel assured her. 'I don't want to cause trouble for her. Or for you.' She looked at Marge with deep affection. 'My wanting to do this has nothing to do with my feelings for you or Dad. I won't do anything about it at all if you'd rather I didn't. The last thing I want to do is hurt you. That's why I've come to see you first, to make sure you don't have a problem with it. If you're at all unhappy, I won't make a move, I promise. And I want you to be honest with me.'

The other woman lowered her eyes. 'Don't worry about me, and I know I can speak for your dad. You have our blessing to go ahead,' she said, looking up. 'But I'm so afraid you'll be disappointed. She's probably married with a grown-up family by now; she may even have grandchildren. A secret from the past might not be welcomed with open arms.'

'I realise that.'

'Have you thought of the possibility that she might be dead?' enquired Marge.

Rachel nodded. 'Yes, that has occurred to me. But I've worked out that if she did survive the war, she'd still be quite young. If she had me at sixteen, she'd only be forty-five.'

'Mmm.' Marge sipped her tea, looking thoughtful. 'Why have you changed your mind about trying to find her, anyway? You seemed dead set against the idea when you first found out the truth.'

'I don't know the answer to that,' said Rachel, wanting to be absolutely honest. 'I suppose it must be some sort of human need to connect with my roots, to meet the person who's responsible for my existence. Maybe if I actually see her and speak to her, I might be better able to come to terms with the rejection.'

'I'm sorry you still feel bad about that,' said Marge, frowning. 'I'd hoped that knowing you were so much wanted by us would have helped you get over it.'

Rachel drew a sharp breath and reached for the other woman's hand, fearing she might have hurt her. 'As I've said, none of this has anything to do with my feelings for you and Dad.' She was most ardent. 'You are my parents and nothing will ever change that. I love you both to bits.'

Marge's face was flushed with pleasure as she sent a quizzical look in Rachel's direction. 'So why put yourself through all the trouble and trauma of trying to find her, then?' she asked. 'I mean, it isn't as if you don't have more than enough to do with your time, what with the boys and the boathouse and everything.'

'It's something I can't explain,' Rachel told her. 'As I said, I've no intention of making a friend of her or anything like that. I just want to satisfy my urges and find her. But I'm not going to let this thing take over my life.'

'Well,' said Marge resignedly, 'if you really want to do it, I'll help in whatever way I can. I'll have the boys for you while you're out looking for her, for instance.'

'Thanks, Mum,' she responded gratefully, giving Marge's hand an affectionate squeeze. 'You're one in a million and I don't know what I'd do without you.'

Marge turned pink again. 'Mums are good at making themselves indispensable, as you very well know.' She drained her teacup. 'But in all this talk of the emotional side of finding Doris, have you got any idea how you're actually going to do it?'

'I was hoping you might be able to give me a starting point,' Rachel confessed, making a face. 'I know it's a faint hope but I wondered if you might have an address where she used to live. I realise she won't be there now, of course. But at least it would be a first step.'

'She used to live with her family in a back street near Fulham Broadway before she moved in here,' Marge informed her, narrowing her eyes as she struggled to remember more. 'I can't remember the actual address, but I do know the house because I went there once with her to help get the rest of her stuff out when her parents weren't at home. She daren't show her face while they were there 'cause they'd have played merry hell with her. The poor girl was scared stiff they'd come back the whole time we were there, which is why I remember it so well.'

'Would you be able to find the house again?' asked Rachel hopefully.

'I should think so.' She gave Rachel a sharp look, fearing she might raise her daughter's hopes only for them to be dashed again. 'But this was all thirty years ago, love. The street might not even be there now, let alone the house . . . It might have been flattened in the bombing.'

'It might still be there, though,' said Rachel with determined optimism, 'and someone from around there might know where that family is now.'

'Don't forget Doris had been cast out by her family,' cautioned Marge.

'They might have patched things up with her later on,' suggested the indomitable Rachel.

'Yes, they might have,' agreed Marge. 'But even if they did, people move away to different areas, especially in London. It's well known for its shifting population.'

'You and Dad didn't,' Rachel pointed out. 'You've lived in this house since before I was born, and I'm twenty-nine. Maybe they did the same.'

'Yes, there is that,' Marge was forced to admit. 'But many of the old community neighbourhoods of London have been knocked down to make way for new housing. So you must be realistic about this, Rachel. It could take years to find her, and you might never do it.'

'I've prepared myself for that,' said Rachel. 'And I still want to give it a try.'

'I can't say that I understand how you're feeling because I've never been in the same position,' Marge said. 'But if you want to find her, then I want it too.'

'You're a real diamond.' Rachel stood up purposefully.

'I'd better get back to work now, but we'll talk about it again soon and perhaps you'll go with me to Fulham to show me where you think that house is.'

'Course I will, love. When you're ready, just let me know,' Marge said, following her to the front door.

Closing the door behind Rachel, Marge went back to the kitchen and sat down at the table with her head on her fists, her stomach tight with fear and apprehension at the possibility of losing her daughter to her real mother. Rachel had assured her that that wouldn't happen, but how could she possibly know how she'd feel when she actually saw Doris?

Marge had dreaded something like this ever since Rachel's background had come to light. When she hadn't shown any interest in contacting Doris at the time, Marge had hoped they were safe but had known it wasn't certain.

She knew that she had only to say the word and Rachel would drop the whole thing. She also knew that if she did that she would lose a part of Rachel for ever, the part that respected her generosity of spirit. She had to risk losing her as a daughter in order to keep her respect and affection.

The repercussions of this didn't end with Rachel either. There were the boys to take into consideration, too. If Rachel and Doris hit it off, Doris could assert herself as Tim and Johnnie's real grandmother and Marge and Ron would be pushed into the background. In her heart Marge knew Rachel wouldn't knowingly let that happen, but when you raked things up from the past you could never be sure what the consequences would be.

Of course, there was a strong possibility that Doris wouldn't want to know the daughter she'd abandoned. But rather than comforting Marge, that thought worried her even more because of her strong empathy for Rachel.

Whichever way this thing went, there was trouble and heartache ahead; she could sense it. If Chip had had the foresight to realise the complications his bequest would cause, he might have thought again about leaving the boathouse to Rachel.

Still, it had changed her life for the better, and in some corner of her heart Marge was glad that the truth was out in the open. Even apart from the fact that Rachel had a right to know about her origins, family secrets were always a threat. They hung over your life, tormenting you with the possibility of discovery.

Shaking herself out of her reverie, she got up and washed the dishes, hoping that Rachel's search wouldn't end in tears but having a horrible suspicion that it would.

'I don't think you should do it,' was Jan's unequivocal reaction to what Rachel had to tell her when she got back to the office. 'I think it would be completely wrong.'

Rachel hadn't mentioned it to her sister before because she'd wanted to discuss it with Marge first, and now she was somewhat taken aback by Jan's attitude. 'Oh? Why's that?' she asked, her cheeks burning from the terseness of Jan's manner.

'Isn't it obvious?' Jan snapped, a harsh light shining in her eyes. 'Because of Mum and Dad, of course. Especially Mum, because she's the more sensitive of the two and we've both always been closer to her than we have to Dad.'

'It won't affect her,' claimed Rachel, put fiercely on the defensive by Jan's aggression.

'Oh, don't make me laugh.' Jan's tone was uncharacteristically acerbic. 'Of course it will affect her.'

'She's assured me that she doesn't mind,' Rachel was keen to point out. 'Obviously I wouldn't go ahead if she objected.'

'She would say she doesn't mind, wouldn't she?' said Jan, who was standing by Rachel's desk clutching a pile of papers she'd just collected for filing. 'She wouldn't stand in your way because she's a naturally unselfish person. But she's bound to be hurt.'

'You really think so?'

Jan took a loud, angry breath. 'Wouldn't you be if the child you'd brought up, cared for and made sacrifices for suddenly wanted to go out looking for some woman who's had nothing to do with her since the umbilical cord was cut?' she demanded.

'But this has nothing to do with how I feel about Mum,' Rachel protested. 'And I've told her that.'

'You can't possibly know how you'll feel when you actually meet the woman,' her sister proclaimed. 'Do you think Mum doesn't know that?'

'You know perfectly well that I would never deliberately do anything to hurt Mum,' insisted Rachel, determined to stand her ground.

'Prove it, then, by calling off this unnecessary search which can only lead to trouble,' challenged Jan.

'I can't do that,' said Rachel,

'Of course you can,' argued Jan heatedly. 'You've managed to reach almost thirty without meeting the wretched woman; I'm sure you can carry on doing so.'

'I don't expect you to understand,' said Rachel, a knot tightening in her stomach and squeezing so hard it was making her feel sick. 'I'm not sure I understand it myself. But this is something I feel I must do. It isn't just a whim.'

'Why do you want to find her? So that you can see if you've got the same colour eyes as her, or the same kind of smile?' Jan asked with withering abrasiveness.

'It's easy for you to sneer,' retorted Rachel. 'You're safe and snug with parents that you know.'

Jan paused, taking a deep breath as though to calm herself. 'I didn't mean to sneer,' she said, in a less aggressive manner but retaining a firm tone. 'I just think you're going to cause a whole load of trouble for yourself as well as Mum and Dad if you go ahead with your plan.'

'Can't you try to imagine how devastating it is to suddenly find out that your family background has been a lie and the woman who gave birth to you is a complete stranger?' Rachel implored her.

'Of course I don't know how it feels, but I guess it must be pretty weird,' admitted Jan. 'All I know is that Mum and Dad are the ones who were there for you. They sat up with you when you were sick, gave up pleasures of their own so that you could have nice clothes and everything else you needed. We are your family: your boys, Mum and Dad, me and Pete and Kelly. Doris Dunn might have given birth to you, but she has no relevance in your life as it is today.'

'Surely most people are interested in where they came from, aren't they?' Rachel wanted her sister to understand her feelings. 'It's part of the human condition. The reason you're not intrigued by your background is because you know all about it and take it for granted. There's no mystery, it's rock-solid and stable.'

'Yeah, yeah, I suppose you're right,' Jan conceded with some reluctance. 'But honestly, Rachel, I've got a really bad feeling about this plan of yours.'

'You've no need to worry,' Rachel assured her. 'I'll make sure Mum doesn't get hurt.'

'You're not in a position to guarantee that, though, are you?' Jan pointed out sharply.

'No, I'm not.' Rachel couldn't deny it. 'But I'll do my damnedest to make sure it doesn't happen.'

'Well, I'm not going to fall out with you over it at this stage,' Jan told her in a categorical manner. 'But I shall keep a close eye on things and if I see that Mum's upset, then you'll have me on your back in a big way, I can promise you that.'

'Fair enough,' said Rachel. 'But I'm sure she'll be fine. That's why I had a chat with her before making a move, and it's also the reason I'm going to include her as much as I can.'

'I still think you'd be wise to leave it alone altogether, but if you're determined to go ahead, then I can't stop you. Just tread carefully, that's all,' Jan lectured. 'People's feelings are at stake here, not least yours and those of your birth mother.'

'I'll keep it in mind,' agreed Rachel.

'Well, I'd better get on,' said Jan, her manner becoming brisk. 'I've a lot of work to get through before I knock off.'

'Still friends?' enquired Rachel

'Yeah, course we are,' replied Jan, giving her a brief smile before leaving the room.

But Rachel felt uneasy as she watched her sister through the glass partition as she bent over the filing cabinet in the office next door. She and Jan had had their disagreements over the years but had never seriously fallen out. For the first time ever, Rachel suspected that they might be on the verge of doing so. But as much as that thought worried and depressed her, she still felt compelled to have faith in her own decision and pursue her course.

She was so nervous she thought her legs would buckle as she walked up to the front door of the terraced house in Fulham that Marge had pointed out to her earlier that day. The street was different to how Marge remembered it, she'd said. Some of the old houses had gone and been replaced by new flats, which wasn't surprising because Fulham had had its share of bomb damage and there had been a great deal of redevelopment in west London generally since the end of the war. Some of the remaining houses had obviously been refurbished with smart new windows and modern front doors.

There wasn't a front door bell so Rachel used the knocker, which responded with a dull thud. A smartly dressed thirty-something man answered the door and listened to her anxious enquiry.

'Dunn, no, the name doesn't ring a bell with me,' he responded.

'Oh,' she said glumly.

'But we only moved in a year ago,' he pointed out. 'We bought the place to do it up as an investment.'

'Do you know of anyone who has lived in the street for a long time?' she asked.

He shook his head. 'I don't know anyone beyond a passing greeting,' he explained. 'My wife and I are out at work all day so we hardly ever see anyone.' He glanced to the side of him. 'A young married couple live next door: they moved in after us. A lot of the houses in this street have been converted into flats over the last few years, so I've heard.' He puffed out his lips, shaking his head. 'Thirty years ago, you say. Phew, that's a very long time. I shouldn't think there would be many people about who were living here as long ago as that.'

'No.'

'You never know, though,' he said encouragingly, since she looked so disappointed. 'Why not knock on a few more doors? Sorry I can't be more help.'

Rachel thanked him, refusing to be downhearted at this early stage. But by the time she'd knocked on every door in the street and found no one who'd lived there longer than ten years, and not a soul who'd ever heard of any family called Dunn, she couldn't help feeling a bit deflated.

'You knew it wouldn't be easy,' Marge reminded her when she got home. 'You'll just have to think of some other way of getting a lead.'

'I've already called all the Dunns in the phone book in that area,' mentioned Rachel. 'None of them know of anyone with a relative called Doris.'

'And having only her maiden name makes it all the more difficult,' remarked Marge sympathetically. 'Because she's bound to be married and not using that name now.'

'Mm,' sighed Rachel.

They talked about it some more over a cup of coffee until Marge said she had to go.

'Thanks for looking after the boys,' said Rachel. 'I'd rather not ask Jan, as she's so much against the idea.'

'It was a pleasure, love,' said Marge, wisely staying out of the conflict between her daughters. 'I'd only have been sitting indoors on my own tonight anyway.'

'Dad gone out?'

She nodded. 'It's his darts night down at the local.'

'Of course, I'd forgotten it was Wednesday,' said Rachel, who couldn't remember a time when her father hadn't gone to the pub to play darts on a Wednesday.

'It's still the highlight of his week after all this time,' said Marge affectionately. 'Though I think your dad and his mates go for the company more than the game. They've been meeting at the pub once a week for more years than I care to remember.'

Rachel stared at her, a smile forming. 'The pub!' she shrieked excitedly. 'Of course, Why didn't I think of it before? There's a pub at the end of the street where the Dunn family used to live. That's my obvious next step.'

'Yeah,' agreed Marge thoughtfully. 'I think you might have something there. It's certainly worth a try, anyway.'

It proved to be a dead end. The current landlord of the Four Foxes had only been there two years and had never heard of anyone called Dunn. However, he did point out that he knew most of his customers only by their first names. A lot of them were newcomers to the area, though, he said.

She thanked him for his time, finished her drink and headed for the door. She was about to leave when someone tapped her on the shoulder. Turning, she found herself confronting a buxom redhead of middle years; she had bright blue eyes, a large bust, which was pushing its way out of a tight black lurex top, and the warmest of smiles.

'I'm the landlord's wife,' she informed Rachel in a friendly manner. 'My husband tells me you're looking for someone who used to live around here.'

'That's right,' confirmed Rachel. 'But I seem to have drawn a blank.'

'I don't know if it will be any help to you, but I thought it was worth mentioning old Joe who comes in here at weekends,' she told her. 'My husband forgot all about him when he was talking to you. Joe must be eighty-odd and he's lived in this neighbourhood all his life. It's only a long shot but he might be able to help you.'

Rachel beamed. 'That sounds very promising,' she said. 'When's the best time to catch him?'

'He usually comes in on a Friday night, some time after about eight o'clock,' she said. 'If you come and see me, I'll point him out to you.'

'You've been a great help,' said Rachel, spirits soaring. 'I'll make a point of being here on Friday night. And thank you very much.'

'A pleasure, love,' smiled the amiable woman. 'See you Friday, then.'

'You certainly will,' said Rachel.

'Yeah, I knew Syd Dunn. He was one of the regulars in here. His wife's name was Polly,' said Joe, whose withered face was thin and pointed like a greyhound's. He was dressed in a grey tweed cap and a navy blue gaberdine mac that had seen better days. He stooped a bit and faltered slightly when he spoke but seemed to be in good health for a man of his age. He'd left the group of elderly men he'd been sitting with to join Rachel at a table in the corner, where she treated him to a double rum and blackcurrant.

'They don't come in here now, then,' she probed gently.

'Syd passed away a few years ago and his wife moved away from the area soon after,' he explained. 'I heard she'd died an' all.'

'That's a shame.' Rachel tried not to dwell on the fact that the people he was speaking of were her blood relatives. She needed to keep this whole thing under tight emotional control. 'Did you know their daughter, Doris, too?' she asked, waiting for his answer with bated breath.

'I used to see young Doris around but I didn't know her to talk to,' he told her, his eyes glazed in thought. 'Different generation, you see. Anyway, she left home when she wasn't much more than a kid. People said she got herself in the family way and the old man chucked her out.' He drew in his breath, nodding his head thoughtfully. 'Shouldn't be surprised if it was true. He was a hard man and wouldn't have had any truck with that sort of thing. Something like that would have broken his heart, especially as Doris was their only child.' The old man sipped at his rum and blackcurrant, pondering. 'If the rumour *was* true she must have got the problem seen to, because I never saw her with a nipper.'

'You saw her again, then?' Rachel enquired.

'Oh, yeah, she came back after a while. Syd must have forgiven her but he never mentioned it and no one ever dared ask,' he informed her. 'Then she married Billy Finn from Ridgely Street and they moved away.'

'Do you know where they went?'

'I haven't a clue, ducks,' he said. 'No idea at all.'

'Oh, that's a pity.' Having had her hopes raised, the disappointment was all the more difficult to bear. 'I really need to find them.'

'Why not go round to Billy's dad's place?' Joe suggested, lifting her spirits again. 'His mother's passed on but his dad still lives in the same house in Ridgely Street. It's only a few minutes' walk from here.'

'You don't happen to know what number Ridgely Street it is, I suppose?' she asked eagerly.

'I don't know the number but it's the third from the end on the left,' he told her.

It was as much as she could do to stop herself from hugging him, but as he was a stranger, she just thanked him profusely and offered him another rum and blackcurrant.

'That's very kind of you, ducks,' he said, beaming. 'I never say no to a rum and black.'

Given the fact that Mr Finn was Doris's father-in-law, Rachel found it necessary to deviate from the truth when introducing herself. To cover the possibility of a family likeness, she told him she was the daughter of a distant cousin of Doris's who had lost touch with her and was keen to contact her to renew the friendship. She explained that the man in the pub had suggested she come to see Mr Finn.

'Mum and Doris were very close friends when they were girls, apparently,' fibbed Rachel when the white-haired man's wise grey eyes rested on her suspiciously at the front door. 'Used to go out together and that.'

'Couldn't have been that close or they wouldn't have lost touch,' he pointed out shrewdly.

'Well . . .' She was thrown by this for a moment. 'You know how it is when you get married and move away,' she went on, giving him one of her most winning smiles and shivering to illustrate the fact that it was a very cold night. 'You get busy bringing up a family and forget to get in touch with old friends, don't you? Then your parents die and the contact point for distant relatives dies with them. Time passes and you suddenly realise that you've lost track altogether.'

'Yeah, I suppose so.' He seemed to accept her explanation but appeared to become bored with the subject. 'Doris and Billy live over at Brentford,' he blurted out, making as though to shut the door.

'Do you have their address?' she asked, quickly, thrusting herself forward so that he wouldn't shut the door on her. 'I'd really like to have something definite to give my mother.'

'A distant cousin of Doris, you say?' he queried.

She nodded.

He looked at her intently, sucking his teeth. 'Oh, all right, then. You're a bloomin' nuisance but you'd better come in while I find a pen and paper.'

She followed his slow, laborious movements down the hall into a small living room that was old-fashioned and cluttered but very clean and cosy.

'Nice place you've got here, Mr Finn,' she said politely, hoping to engage him in conversation which might contain some information about Doris.

'It suits me,' he told her. 'Not the same since I lost the wife, though.'

'You keep it nice,' she remarked.

'Not me,' he explained. 'The council send a home help 'cause of my arthritis.'

She made idle conversation while he fumbled around on the mantelpiece, finally finding a pencil and piece of scrap paper. 'When is the best time to get hold of Doris?' she asked. 'Is she at home during the day.'

'Not every day,' he informed her. 'She's got a part-time job in a dry-cleaner's shop. She works about three days a week, I think, but I'm not sure which days.'

'Is it far from where she lives?' she probed.

'No, it's in the local parade of shops,' he said, writing the address down with a shaky hand as he spoke. 'It's walking distance; I remember her saying how handy it is for her.'

'Are they on the phone?' Rachel enquired.

'No. But there's a phone number for her at work,' Mr Finn said, becoming more co-operative now that he'd decided to make the effort. 'I ring her there if I need to get in touch with them in a hurry. I'll write the number down for you.'

'Thank you.'

''S all right.'

'Do you see much of them?' she asked casually, as though she was just chatting to be polite.

'They come and see me when they can,' he told her. 'They're good to me. They'd like me to go and live nearer to them, but I'd be like a fish out of water outside of Fulham. You get set in your ways at my age.'

'I'm sure you do.'

'I'm not complaining,' he said. 'There's only one thing I haven't got that I want.'

'What's that?' Rachel asked.

'My missus,' he said sadly. 'She died two years ago.'

'I'm sorry,' she said.

'Me an' all.'

She was bursting to ask him what he thought of his daughter-in-law, to get an idea of the character of the woman she was trying to find, but she decided it would be too intrusive and might worry him. So she made a little more general conversation, thanked him warmly for the information and left, tingling with excitement at this massive breakthrough. She was almost there.

By the time she got into bed that night her excitement had evaporated to grim apprehension. This was much more than just a matter of finding someone. She was about to tread a path of emotional quicksand. Was it morally wrong of her to take it further? Or should she take her sister's advice and leave well alone?

The call of a child interrupted her cogitation and she hurried into Tim's bedroom. He'd woken up and wanted a drink of water. She got it for him and sat on his bed while he drank it, talking to him in whispers so as not to wake Johnnie.

'Has Gran gone home?' he asked.

'Yes, love.'

'She told us two great stories,' he said with obvious affection for Marge.

'From your story book?' she asked softly.

'Yeah, one was from the book . . . but she made the other one up,' he said drowsily. 'She's brilliant at stories.'

'Yes, she is.' She's brilliant all round, thought Rachel, recalling how supportive Marge was being to her in her quest to find Doris. It couldn't be easy for her, however much she seemed to take it in her stride.

'Is she coming to look after us again soon?' Tim asked, rubbing his eyes sleepily.

'She's sure to.'

'I hope so,' he said.

'Go back to sleep now, son,' she whispered, placing a kiss on his forehead and tucking him in.

'Night, mum.'

'Night, love.'

Feeling too wakeful to go back to bed, Rachel went downstairs and sat at the kitchen table with a cup of tea, her thoughts returning to her search for Doris. Given her huge responsibilities with regard to the children and the business, ought she to take it to its conclusion? Lord knew, she had enough strain on her time and emotional resources as it was, without adding to it with something so deeply personal.

She found herself wondering what Ben would advise her to do, and knew instinctively he would not be in favour, given his own background and the filial nature of his feelings for Chip. But she wasn't looking for any sort of bond with Doris. She wasn't sure what she was looking for, but it definitely wasn't that.

As she examined her mind for her true purpose in all this, her motivation became clearer. Perhaps this was all about tying up the loose ends of the past so that she could get on with her life without mystery or resentment. She wanted to get back to normal, to feel as she had before the truth about her background had come crashing into her life.

In retrospect, she could see that the instant she'd learned about her origins, she'd known she would never be free until she tracked her birth mother down. So to pursue her course to its end wasn't an act of self-indulgence but a catharsis, something that would benefit her loved ones as well as herself. After all, if she had peace of mind, she would inevitably pass it on to them. This mission, therefore, must be completed.

She had never intended just to turn up uninvited at Doris' door but planned to contact her initially by letter, to make it easier for the other woman to refuse if she wished. Now she took a writing pad from the dresser drawer and rummaged around in there for a pen.

Sitting back down at the table, she made a start on the most difficult letter she had ever had to write.

Chapter Sixteen

Doris Finn's small face was pinched with cold as she walked home from her shift at the dry-cleaner's. She was an attractive woman of diminutive stature, and she kept herself smart in a cheap and cheerful way. Today she was wearing a red coat and long black boots. A regular customer at Woolworth's beauty counter, she coloured the grey out of her light brown bouffant hair and put a little mascara and eye shadow on her greenish-brown eyes. Taking trouble with her appearance was second nature rather than vanity. It was something she'd always done.

Shivering from the biting February wind, she was warmed inside by the thought that her bus-driver husband Billy was on early shift today so would already be in when she got home. She could confidently predict that he would have lit the fire, set cooking the casserole she'd prepared before she went to work this morning, put the potatoes she'd peeled on to boil and made a pot of tea ready for her. She and Billy were a team and had been for more than twenty-five years. They were utterly devoted.

It was already dusk as she approached the house, where a welcoming light glowed in the bay window of the living room. It was a traditional pre-war-built property in a terrace; quite small, but big enough for the two of them. They'd lived here for most of their married life, renting for many years until the landlord had offered them the chance to buy at a special price because they were sitting tenants.

Now she turned the key in the lock and stepped inside to be greeted by the savoury aroma of beef casserole. Dear Billy, he hadn't forgotten. 'I'm home, love,' she called, taking her coat off and hanging it on a peg in the tiny square hall, then pulling off her boots and putting on her slippers.

'Out here,' he shouted cheerily from the kitchen.

She found him pouring her a cup of tea. They kissed lightly as they always did in greeting. Billy was a burly man with warm brown eyes and a great mass of greying dark hair brushed back from his square-jawed countenance. 'There you are, love,' he said, handing her the cup. 'Everything's under control here, so let's go into the other room and have a sit-down and a chat while the meal finishes cooking.'

'OK, Billy,' she said.

They wandered into the living room and sat down either side of the fire. 'Had a good day?' he asked.

'Yeah, it was all right,' she replied cheerfully. 'How about you?'

'Not bad,' he told her. 'It was bloomin' cold cycling home from the depot, though. My feet were nearly dropping off when I got in.'

'Aaah, poor you,' she sympathised. 'Us women are lucky, with our nice warm boots.'

They chatted for a while, mostly about trivia, until Doris said she would go and see to their meal. 'You stay there and take it easy, Billy.' They were very considerate of each other. 'You put everything on, I'll go and serve it out.'

He shot her a look, seeming suddenly concerned. 'Are you all right, love?' he asked.

'Yeah' she replied guardedly, 'course I am. Why wouldn't I be?'

'Dunno.' He eyed her intently. 'But you seem as though you've got something on your mind.'

'I have,' she said, lowering her eyes just a fraction. 'The casserole. It'll be cooked to a cinder if I don't go and see to it.'

He wasn't convinced. 'Come off it, Doris, it would take more than a bit of stewing steak to put that worried look in your eyes.'

'You'll be black around the eyes in a minute if you don't stop fussing,' she laughed. Doris and Billy were down-to-earth people who didn't go in for sentimental talk.

'All right, keep your hair on . . . I believe you,' he grinned before disappearing behind the *Evening News*.

She left the room smiling, but as soon as she was safely out of sight in the kitchen, her expression changed dramatically. She and Billy were so close, he could sense when something wasn't right with her. They'd always been open and honest with each other, and told each other everything. Except that Doris hadn't told him quite everything. There was one part of her life he knew nothing about, the only secret she'd ever kept from him. And, ironically, it was the one thing she could never ever tell him about that had re-emerged from the past to torment her.

She felt quite ill with worry when she thought of the letter that had arrived this morning and was now stored safely in her handbag because she knew that Billy would never look in there, any more than she would invade the privacy of his pockets; they had respect for each other in that way.

Her husband was a kind-hearted and tolerant man who, she was sure, would forgive her anything, even something for which she was so unforgiving towards herself. But for all that he was understanding, she couldn't tell him about the letter because he would be devastated, and for a very good reason. There was much more at stake here than just the loss of Billy's respect for her over something that had happened many years ago and had been on her conscience ever since. It was much more complicated than that.

It was the early hours of the morning and number six Ross Street was silent, the boys sleeping soundly in their beds. No such luxury was available to Rachel, whose mind was uncomfortably overactive. Bothered by her troubled thoughts, she sat up, switched on the bedside light and took an envelope out of the drawer in the cabinet beside her.

The letter had arrived several days ago and had been read, reread and analysed by Rachel so many times, her brain felt numb with it. She had been so profoundly disappointed, she hadn't even been able to bring herself to show it to Marge, who, until now, had been kept regularly informed of progress because Rachel didn't want her to feel excluded.

Now she took the letter out of the envelope and read it for the umpteenth time.

> Dear Rachel,
> Thank you for your letter. Yes, I am the person you are looking for. But when I gave my baby up to people I knew would give her a decent life, I gave her up for good and on the understanding that there would be no further contact. As far as I'm concerned this arrangement is to continue. I think it's for the best if we don't communicate again. I honestly believe that no good can come from us meeting. I wish you well in your life but I hope you will respect my wishes and not contact me again.
> With best wishes,
> Doris Finn.

The writing was spidery, as though the hand that had written it had been trembling. Choking back tears, Rachel stuffed it back in the envelope, put it in the drawer and turned off the light. How wrong she'd been to think that she couldn't be hurt by this woman again. The anger she had occasionally felt towards her now dissolved into an aching sadness.

'Hmmm,' said Marge thoughtfully when Rachel finally gave her the letter to read the next day at lunchtime. 'I can understand how disappointed you must be.'

'Much more than I expected,' Rachel confessed.

'I know it won't be easy, love, but you'll just have to put the whole thing behind you now,' advised Marge, who had been dreading that Rachel would have to face something like this.

'How could she write such a cold and formal letter about something so personal?' asked Rachel, looking at Marge across the living-room hearth where they were sitting by a roaring fire.

'Because she wants to make sure you get the message, I should think,' suggested Marge.

'But I don't want anything from her apart from the chance to meet her,' Rachel pointed out. 'Is that really too much to ask?'

'She obviously thinks so.' Marge considered it vital that Rachel didn't delude herself about this or the pain would linger. 'Which is perfectly understandable and doesn't make her a bad person. I mean, look at it from her point of view. She's managed to put something painful behind her and make a life for herself . . . then bang, out of the blue, all these years later, it comes back to haunt her. It isn't all that surprising she wants to back away.'

'I suppose you're right,' sighed Rachel.

'If she has other children she probably doesn't want them to know what she got up to when she was a girl,' Marge pointed out. 'Or it could be that she hasn't told her husband and is afraid he'll find out and be angry that she's kept it from him. There could be any number of reasons. You'll probably never know, because you must respect her wishes and keep away.'

'Mmm.'

Marge looked at her sharply. 'Rachel . . . this has to be an end to it. Doris has made it clear.'

'Don't worry, Mum.' Seeming brighter suddenly, Rachel got up, went over to Marge and gave her a hug. 'You've been absolutely brilliant about everything and I think you're great.'

'Enough of the soft soap.' Marge narrowed her eyes on

her suspiciously. 'You're being evasive, which makes me think you're up to something.'

'I have to go back to work now,' Rachel told her, heading for the door.

'You won't write to her again, will you, love?' Marge's only concern was for Rachel, who she believed would create more hurt for herself if she persisted in her quest.

'No, I won't write to her again, I promise,' Rachel assured her, already on her way to the hall to get her coat. 'Must go, Mum, bye for now.'

'Ta-ta, love,' said Marge, looking relieved.

A rush of warm air greeted a shivering Rachel as she entered the dry-cleaner's the next day, the dramatic change in temperature all the more noticeable because she'd been hanging about outside for ages, trying to pluck up courage to come in. She was warmly dressed in a fur-lined red jacket with black trousers and long boots, but she'd still been frozen out there.

She felt bad about deceiving her mother yesterday, even though she hadn't actually lied to her. She'd said she wouldn't write to Doris again, and she hadn't; she'd made no such promise about visiting her personally. Sometimes you simply had no alternative but to disguise the truth for the sake of someone else's feelings. Anyway, she would come clean and tell Marge what she'd done afterwards.

There was a middle-aged woman in a blue nylon overall serving behind the counter when Rachel joined the queue. Rachel wondered if the assistant was Doris and observed her closely as she took tickets and handed over garments, to see if she could spot any similarity. There was no immediate resemblance in this large person with a loud, disapproving voice and big spectacles, though she did have the same colour hair as Rachel.

'Yes,' she said briskly when Rachel's turn came.

'I . . .' began Rachel, her words tailing off nervously as she stared at the woman's face, searching for a likeness to herself.

Noticing that Rachel wasn't carrying any garments to be cleaned, the woman assumed she was collecting and asked her if she had a cleaning ticket.

'No, I don't, I'm afraid,' Rachel was forced to admit.

The woman gave her a fierce scowl, throwing a meaningful glance towards the customers waiting patiently behind her. Rachel found herself hoping that this aggressive person wasn't Doris. 'What's the name and when did you bring the garment in?' the assistant asked brusquely.

'I haven't come to collect anything,' Rachel blurted out through dry lips. 'I'm looking for Doris Finn.'

'She's on her dinner break.' The woman dismissed Rachel by looking past her and saying, 'Next, please.'

'Can you tell me when she'll be back, please?' Having been awake all night worrying about this, Rachel wasn't about to be put off by a hostile counter assistant.

'Does your business with her have anything to do with this shop?' demanded the woman.

'No, it's a personal matter,' said Rachel.

'Oh, I see.' She didn't look pleased. 'She's only just gone to dinner,' was her irritable response. 'She'll be back on duty at two o'clock.'

Rachel took note of the way she emphasised the words 'on duty', making it clear that the staff weren't encouraged to conduct personal business over the counter. 'Would you happen to know where she goes for lunch?' she asked.

'She doesn't go anywhere; she usually eats her sandwiches in the staff room,' the woman told her. 'But today she's gone out to do some shopping first.'

'Thank you,' said Rachel, and left.

Wanting to catch Doris before she went back into the shop, Rachel waited in the doorway of the baker's next door, stomach churning, eyes fixed on every female heading her way – and there was no shortage of them in this busy shopping parade. She had extended her own lunch hour to do this one thing before she cast Doris Finn out of her mind for good.

She planned to approach any woman going into the cleaner's and ask outright if they were Doris. But, as it happened, she didn't have to, because as soon as the woman in the red coat drew near, she knew without a doubt that it was her. It wasn't that they were stunningly alike, but there were definite similarities.

'Hello, Doris,' she said, stepping boldly out in front of her.

The older woman looked startled, and Rachel guessed that Doris knew who she was. 'I asked you to leave me alone,' she reminded Rachel in a breathless, nervous tone. 'Why couldn't you do as I asked?'

'Just ten minutes of your time, that's all I want,' Rachel entreated her. 'There's a café down the road. Will you come there with me, for a chat?'

'I have to get back to work,' Doris said, her small, lined face creased with anxiety.

Anger rose in Rachel. 'Surely you can spare me ten minutes of your time?' she said meaningfully. 'It isn't much to ask in nearly thirty years.'

Doris winced. 'I suppose I deserve that.'

'Ten minutes,' said Rachel as though the other woman hadn't spoken. 'You don't have to be back on duty until two o'clock.'

'You've been in the shop checking up on me,' Doris said, accusingly.

'Don't worry,' said Rachel. 'I didn't give anything away.'

'I hope you didn't,' said Doris anxiously.

'Come to the café with me now,' said Rachel. 'Then I'll leave you alone.'

'Seems to me I don't have a choice if I want any peace,' said Doris, tutting, and the two women walked to the nearby café together.

* * *

'I just wanted to know if you felt anything at all for me when you gave me away,' said Rachel when they were settled at a table in the crowded café, a small, noisy place with an espresso machine and a juke box. Neither of them wanted anything to eat, so they just had coffee.

'Of course I did,' Doris said brusquely. 'Do you think I'm completely heartless?'

'You might be. I don't know anything about you.' Rachel found herself responding sharply to Doris' offhand manner. 'You could be a serial killer for all I know. I've no idea what sort of genes I or my children have inherited.'

Doris' eyes brightened, though her expression remained fixed. 'You have children?' she said.

'Two boys,' Rachel informed her proudly. 'Tim is seven and Johnnie is six.'

'Very nice,' said Doris, in a flat voice. The light had gone out of her eyes as suddenly as it had appeared.

'Yes, I think so,' said Rachel, adding, 'did you have any more children after me?'

Doris didn't reply at once, just stirred her coffee, staring into the cup. 'No,' she said eventually. 'There's just me and my husband Billy.'

At that moment Rachel became acutely aware of the fact that this woman, who had conceived and given birth to her, was like a stranger she could have got talking to in a bus queue. Apart from a slight similarity in appearance, they were poles apart. There was no chemistry between them whatsoever. 'I didn't even know you existed until about three years ago,' she informed her.

'No?' Doris sounded mildly surprised.

'No. It was a shock to find out that Mum and Dad weren't really my parents, I can tell you.'

'I should have thought they would have told you the truth when you got to be an adult,' Doris remarked.

'Uncle Chip didn't want me to know, apparently,' Rachel explained. 'If he hadn't died and left me his business, I'd probably never have got to know the truth.'

For the second time Rachel recognised emotion in the other woman despite her cool manner; she flinched, as though she'd been physically slapped. 'Chip died?' she said.

'That's right.' Rachel told her what had happened.

'Blimey. He wasn't much older than me.' She put her hand to her chest. 'Cor, that's given me quite a turn.'

'It was a shock to us all,' said Rachel.

'I hadn't seen him for nearly thirty years,' Doris went on, staring into space as though she was thinking aloud. 'But you never forget your first love.'

'You did love him, then?' said Rachel, unexpectedly relieved to hear this.

'Of course I did. You wouldn't have happened if I hadn't,' she declared in an emphatic manner. 'It was all just kids' stuff, of course, but very intense at the time.'

There was an awkward silence. Rachel was embarrassed for them both. 'I shouldn't have asked,' she said.

'It don't matter,' said Doris. 'I suppose you're bound to be curious.'

'Naturally.'

'Chip did well for himself, then?' said Doris.

'Very well. He had a boatbuilding business in Hammersmith,' Rachel told her. 'It's mine now, as I said.'

'He was a soldier when I knew him.'

Rachel took a business card out of her handbag and handed it over.

'Banks' Boats,' Doris read aloud. 'Well, well, good for Chip. He was a smashing bloke. He often used to talk about going back to his trade after the war.' She handed the card back to Rachel.

'You can keep it, as a memento, if you like,' she offered.

'Thanks.' Doris didn't enthuse, just put the card in her pocket. 'So, did you have a happy childhood?' she asked.

'Very,' said Rachel, and went on to tell her about the good relationship she still had with Marge and Ron.

'So why go to all the trouble of tracking me down, then?' Doris wanted to know.

'That's something I can't really explain. Some sort of primal urge to get in touch with where I came from, I suppose,' Rachel told her. 'It's only natural to want to meet the person who brought you into the world, isn't it?'

'I suppose so.' Doris didn't sound particularly interested. 'But I shouldn't think you felt very well disposed towards me when you found out what I'd done.'

'I was hurt and angry, of course,' Rachel said.

'Mm.'

'Finding out so late probably made it worse,' she found herself admitting. 'Because my safe little world had suddenly been blown apart. I can't tell you how terrible it feels to know that you were rejected.'

'I couldn't have kept you,' Doris said quickly. 'I was just a kid myself. I didn't have the means.'

'People do keep their babies under those sort of circumstances,' Rachel couldn't help pointing out.

'Yes, they do,' Doris agreed, meeting Rachel's eyes with an air of defiance. 'But from what I can make out, you've done better with Marge than you would have with me.'

'No one could have had more loving parents,' agreed Rachel. 'I've never wanted for anything. My sister and I are still very close to our parents now. I certainly wasn't after a mother figure when I came looking for you.'

There was the briefest flicker of something in her eyes. Rachel wasn't sure what it was. Could it have been pain? Given Doris' attitude, she doubted it.

'I realise that,' said Doris evenly.

Another awkward silence, then, 'Why didn't you want to see me?' Rachel enquired.

Doris stared into her cup again. 'I couldn't see the purpose of it,' she declared. 'I still can't.'

Aware of a dull feeling of anticlimax, Rachel said, 'No, I suppose it is all a bit pointless.'

'Utterly pointless,' Doris confirmed with emphasis. 'I mean, you've got your husband and kiddies to look after, and parents who obviously think the world of you, as well as your business to run. I've got my husband and my job to keep me busy.'

'You're right in what you say, except that I don't have a husband,' Rachel corrected, and went on to give her the basic details of her situation, to which Doris responded politely.

There was more stilted conversation until Doris said it was time for her to go back to work. 'Look,' she said, as they prepared to leave, 'I really am very sorry for what I did to you all those years ago, but I can't change it.' Her small face was brightly suffused, her manner adamant. 'It happened and that's all there is to it. You and me getting to know each other isn't going to alter anything.'

'I know,' said Rachel with a sigh of resignation.

'Anyway, it's turned out all right for you, hasn't it?' Doris said with an urgency in her tone that made Rachel suspect she wanted further reassurance.

'Oh, yes,' nodded Rachel. 'It's turned out fine for me.'

'And us seeing each other could cause trouble with the people we care about. So now that we've met and talked, can you please leave me alone?'

'Yes,' said Rachel, honestly and without hesitation. 'You won't hear from me again, I can promise you that.'

Driving along the Great West Road back to Hammersmith, Rachel reflected on the meeting with Doris. It had been oddly devoid of emotion, and it occurred to her again that there had been nothing more between them than two passing strangers. She recalled Ben's theory about parental bonding. It's what someone means to you that matters, not who they are, he'd said. He was right. Blood was not always thicker than water.

Being realistic, how could it be otherwise? You couldn't expect to feel anything special for someone you'd never met before. For some people there was always the possibility of an instant rapport which could be developed into something lasting, but she and Doris definitely hadn't had any sort of emotional connection.

Something was nagging on the periphery of Rachel's thoughts, though, something she couldn't quite put her finger on. There had been something about Doris' cool, unfeeling attitude that hadn't rung true somehow. The lack of interest in her voice hadn't always matched the expression in her eyes. When Rachel had mentioned the boys, for instance, and when Doris had spoken her husband's name. Rachel didn't believe that she was as hard-faced as she had tried to make out.

Still, the true character of Doris Finn was no longer any concern of Rachel's. She had gone as far as she was prepared to. She'd satisfied her curiosity; she'd met her natural mother and found there was no magic flowing between them, no special warmth or chemistry. Doris was just an ordinary woman trying to get on with her life as best she could. She didn't want further contact and she wouldn't get it from Rachel.

For all that the meeting had been a disappointment, Rachel still felt unsettled, not quite able to draw a line under it. It was strange. Still, there's one person who'll be pleased it's all over, she thought with a wry grin: her sister, Jan, who had made her disapproval clear with increasing intensity. It would be good to get back to their old footing. She hated it when there was a bad atmosphere between herself and Jan.

Doris was too upset to work that afternoon. She went back to the shop, but finding herself distraught and on the verge of tears when she was trying to serve customers, she told the manageress that she wasn't feeling well and would have to go home.

As soon as she got in and closed the door behind her, she went upstairs to the bedroom, sat on the edge of the bed and cried until there wasn't a tear left in her, grateful that Billy was on afternoon shift. She'd had to put a stop to Rachel's interest in her because of what it would do to Billy if he ever found out about her. This was the second hardest thing she had ever had to do in her life; the first, of course, had been giving her baby away in the first place.

She'd hated herself for hurting Rachel by pretending to be cool and uninterested. She'd longed to know all about her, had been hungry for knowledge about Rachel's little boys. *Her grandchildren.* But she'd sensed that the slightest encouragement from her would have had Rachel wanting to pursue matters further.

It gave Doris a very strange feeling to think that the scrap of humanity she'd left in Marge's care all those years ago had turned into such a fine woman, smart, intelligent, attractive. Marge and Ron had done a wonderful job in raising her. It must have been awful for Chip, having her so near and not being able to acknowledge her as his own. She could understand why he'd left his business to her.

Doris had felt proud of Rachel even though she knew she had no right, since she had made no contribution at all to the woman she'd become. Over the years she had shed countless tears for the daughter she had lost; ironically, the only time she was ever to know motherhood.

Rachel would think her cold and unfeeling, which was what Doris had wanted. She couldn't risk the possibility of her coming back, even though it was the thing she wanted most in the world. Rachel had had an urge to find her natural mother, she'd said, something she couldn't explain. But her longings couldn't possibly have been as all-consuming as Doris' had been to see her only child again. The pain had crippled her at times over the years, though she'd learned to live with it and never let Billy see it. Seeing Rachel had brought it all back, and at a more intense level. She'd had to let her only child go for the second time, and it hurt so much it was hardly bearable.

'So this obsession with your natural mother is really all over now, is it?' said Jan when Rachel got back to the office and told her all about her meeting with Doris. It would have been easier for them both not to mention it but Rachel wasn't prepared to lie about where she was when she was out of the office.

'It wasn't an obsession,' corrected Rachel. 'It was a natural human instinct.'

'Well, whatever,' said Jan sharply, 'it wasn't right.'

Rachel bristled. 'You're making it seem like a criminal offence, and it certainly wasn't that,' she retorted.

'No need to be sarky,' snapped Jan. 'You know perfectly well what I'm on about. Anything that hurts Mum isn't right in my opinion.'

'Mum's fine about it,' Rachel insisted. 'She had no reason to be hurt.'

'She's been making out she isn't hurt,' argued Jan. 'But I'm not fooled for a moment.'

Rachel emitted an exasperated sigh. 'Look, Jan. You're entitled to your opinion,' she said hotly, 'but you're not entitled to tell me what to do. I've done nothing to be ashamed of.'

'If you say so,' she said irritably, looking very pale.

'I do.'

Jan held her stomach suddenly, bending over slightly, her face creased with pain. 'All right, let's just drop the subject and get on with our work, shall we?' she said quickly, waving a piece of paper she was holding. 'Quite a few queries have come up while you've been out, phone messages and so on. I'd better go through them with you.'

Rachel gave her a close look, suddenly realising that there might be more to her sister's bad temper than her disapproval of Rachel's search for Doris. Her pallid skin and heavy eyes spoke volumes. 'Are you having a bad time with the curse again?' she enquired, her tone becoming sympathetic.

'This one is a bit of a bugger,' Jan confessed.

'You go home, love,' Rachel suggested kindly.

'Don't be daft,' protested Jan.

'I can manage here,' she assured her. 'Just tell me about the messages and queries and then you get off.'

'I'll be all right, really,' Jan said, not very convincingly. 'It'll probably ease off in a minute. I've taken a couple of aspirin.'

'You need to go to bed with a hot-water bottle on your tummy,' Rachel advised.

'I can't take time off from work just because it's that time of the month,' Jan pointed out. 'I'll be off sick every four weeks, the trouble my periods are giving me lately.'

'It'll soon be time for you to knock off anyway,' Rachel reminded her. 'So go a bit early and tuck yourself up in bed.'

'I have to collect the kids from school,' Jan pointed out.

'I'll do that,' Rachel offered at once.

'But you aren't due to finish early today,' Jan said. 'We'd arranged for me to pick the boys up when I collect Kelly and have them at my place until you get back.'

'Don't worry about that. I'll collect them and take them all round to Mum's,' said Rachel. 'She isn't working today and I'm sure she won't mind having them for a couple of hours, Kelly as well as the boys, so that you can have a lie-down. I'll fetch them from Wilbur Terrace when I've finished here, and bring Kelly home later on. I want to see Mum anyway, to tell her what happened with Doris.'

Jan was obviously tempted. 'I am feeling pretty grim,' she admitted.

Jan had been suffering from exceptionally heavy and painful menstruation for some time. Her periods really pulled her down and made her irritable, because she felt so ill for the first couple of days.

'So give me the messages and I'll run you home in the car,' said Rachel.

'There's no need, honestly.'

Rachel looked at her sister's ashen face. 'It'll only take me a few minutes,' she insisted.

Jan was feeling too rotten to put up any further resistance.

'Thanks, sis,' she accepted gratefully. 'I'll run through the messages with you, then I'll go and get my coat.'

Walking across the yard to the car, a cold wind whipping colour into her cheeks, Rachel had a sudden longing to talk to Ben about the meeting with Doris. He would probably have disapproved of her doing it, but at least he would have been able to view the situation objectively.

Her mother and sister were both far too emotionally involved. She couldn't talk to them about how confused and sad she felt, because they immediately felt threatened when they really had no reason to be.

Oh, Ben, she cried silently as she helped Jan into the car and walked round to the driving seat with the river wind blowing through her hair. Nothing is the same without you, not the job or the atmosphere here at the boathouse. Not the trees or the river, or my life.

'We'll soon have you home,' she said, pushing her own problems to the back of her mind as she started the car.

'I'm being an awful nuisance,' apologised Jan.

'Nonsense,' protested Rachel. 'You're not well. I'm only too pleased to help.'

'Thanks,' said Jan weakly.

A mouth-watering aroma greeted Ben when he opened the front door. It smells like spaghetti bolognese, he thought with zestful anticipation. It was still a novelty to come home from work in the evening to find a meal ready for him, after all the time he'd had to set to and cook for them when Lorna hadn't been able to do it.

'Something smells good, Lorna,' he remarked, poking his head into the kitchen to see his wife busy draining spaghetti at the sink. 'Anything I can do to help?'

'I'm managing, thanks,' she told him cheerfully.

'I'll get myself cleaned up and have a look at the paper, then,' he said. 'Give us a shout if you need a hand.'

'Will do.'

He had a quick wash and went into the sitting room. Settling in an armchair with the newspaper, he glanced idly at a rather bizarre photograph of a long-haired, bearded and pyjama-ed John Lennon and his new wife Yoko Ono in bed in the presidential suite of the Hilton Hotel, Amsterdam, where their honeymoon had apparently become a 'bed-in' for peace.

Thinking of honeymoons reminded him of romance, which led to thoughts of Rachel and a familiar stab of pain. Not a day passed when he didn't think about her, wonder how she was, and want to be with her and the boys.

It had been so long since love of the romantic kind had added richness and colour to his life, he had almost forgotten what it felt like. There was nothing of that nature between him and Lorna at all. Romance never even occurred to either of them, because whatever they'd once had was beyond revival and they both knew it.

Enough of self-pity, he admonished himself. He couldn't have the woman he loved, but life in general had improved considerably for him lately. Ever since Lorna had resumed regular physiotherapy at the hospital last summer, things had got steadily better.

Her movements were still very slow and laborious, but she could now stay on her feet for long enough to satisfy her need to be useful. She was able to cook, and see to a few other light household chores, as long as she took it slowly and sat down at frequent intervals. Whilst he was willing to do it for her, he allowed her to continue because he recognised how important it was to her self-esteem that she make a contribution to their living arrangements.

Her increased mobility had boosted her confidence and the depression had gradually lifted. She'd begun to take an interest in life again. She'd lost some weight, had had her hair cut into a more fashionable style and started wearing make-up again. Some days were better than others, and she still needed to take pain-killers from time to time. But the overall improvement was quite dramatic, and he was delighted for her.

Hearing her call out to him now, he hurried to the kitchen where the food was laid out on the table. The meals were far more interesting than anything she'd cooked when they'd lived together as man and wife, probably because she had more time now that she wasn't out at work all day.

'It's delicious,' he said, tasting it.

'Good, I'm glad you like it.'

'You're getting to be quite a dab hand in the cooking department,' he complimented her, thinking how attractive she looked in a white polo-necked sweater and black ski pants. 'A proper little modern-day Mrs Beeton.'

'Well . . . it's something to take an interest in with my having so much time on my hands,' she remarked modestly.

'I'm not complaining,' he assured her laughingly.

'I should hope not,' she admonished lightly. 'You want to make the most of it while I'm at home all day and have the time.'

'What are you getting at?' He gave her a questioning look, his fork poised.

'I should have thought that was obvious,' she told him. 'I'm hoping to get a job, eventually.'

'That would be great for you, of course, as long as you're sure you feel up to it.'

'Don't look so worried,' she told him. 'I shan't make a move in that direction until I'm certain that I'm well enough. After what I've been through, I'm not likely to risk a relapse through being premature about something like that.'

'No, of course not.'

She twirled spaghetti carefully around her fork. 'Surely you didn't think I was going to stay around the house all day and every day for the rest of my life?' she said, popping the forkful into her mouth and looking at him.

'I didn't know what was going to happen ultimately,' he

confessed. 'I've been taking it one day at a time and not looking too far ahead.'

'That's what I was doing, too, until recently,' she admitted.

'Not so long ago you didn't seem to have much of a choice in your future, did you?' he said.

'No, I didn't,' she agreed. 'Thank God things have changed a bit since then.'

'Mm.'

'And talking of changes reminds me,' she began, giving him an odd look, 'the washing-up is all yours tonight.'

There was nothing unusual in that *per se*, but a note of excitement in her manner suggested a deviation from the norm. 'Is something in particular happening?'

'I'm going out.'

'Out!' He could hardly believe it. She never went anywhere except to the hospital, and occasionally to the supermarket with him for the groceries.

'That's right.' She sounded jubilant.

'You're going out on the town, are you?' he said, teasing her.

'Hardly,' she said. 'I'm only going round to a friend's place, but it'll make a change.'

'Oh?'

'A woman from the office where I used to work,' she explained. 'Some of the others we used to work with are going to be there too. Her husband's going out for the evening, so we're having a girls' night in. A good old gossip, catch up with all the news.'

'How did all this come about?' he asked, because he thought she'd lost contact with all her old friends during the dark days of her depression.

'I thought it was time I had some sociable female company, so I plucked up the courage to ring this friend at the office the other day,' she informed him. 'She invited me round and organised for a few of the others to be there too.'

'Do you want me to take you in the car?' he offered.

'Thanks, Ben, but it won't be necessary,' she told him with the joyful air of someone who now has a choice after a long period without it. 'One of the girls has got her husband's car for the evening . . . she's picking me up here at half past seven.'

'It'll really do you good to get out.' He was genuinely pleased for her.

'It won't do you any harm either, to have the place to yourself for an evening,' she told him.

He acknowledged the truth of this with a slow grin. To have some time at home on his own would be a much-needed pleasure. And he guessed that Lorna was just as relieved to have some breathing space away from him. They both knew from experience how stifling it was to be forced to share your life with someone you didn't want to be with in that situation.

'It'll make a change,' he said.

Chapter Seventeen

One evening in July of that year, Jeff West stood at the bar in a pub in Willesden, drinking beer and mulling over his abysmal situation. He had a boring, low-paid job, he lived in a shabby, overpriced bedsit, ran a clapped-out old banger of a car and had no woman in his life. No wonder he was miserable.

Jeff was a striking man with thick black hair greased into a quiff and worn collar length at the back. His eyes were unusual for someone of his colouring, being a bluish shade of grey. He was six feet tall, but his once slim figure had lost the battle against beer and convenience food, and a paunch now swelled above his jeans, which he wore with a checked shirt, his clothes grubby from a day's work on the assembly line in a cable factory.

It wasn't in Jeff's nature to wonder if he might have been the architect of his own misfortune with his disregard for responsibility and hankering for greener pastures. He preferred to blame other people when things went wrong – his ex-girlfriend, the foreman at the factory, even the government. But it did occur to him now, albeit fleetingly, that if he hadn't walked out on his marriage, his life wouldn't be in quite such a parlous state.

The pub was full of working men straight off the job. Jeff came here most nights when he'd finished at the factory rather than go home to his cramped, badly ventilated attic room which retained and intensified the heat of the day and was stifling on summer evenings like this one. There was a lot of talk among the men in the pub about the men landing on the moon in the early hours of this morning. Some lunatics had stayed up all night to watch it on television. You wouldn't catch Jeff losing sleep over an event of no personal benefit to himself. He had enough problems. He wasn't mad enough to add exhaustion to the list. They could bring in package holidays to Mars for all he cared.

Deeply entrenched in self-pity, he pondered what he had given up for Sheila. He'd turned his back on his wife and children and a comfortable home. OK, so the flat on the Perrydene Estate hadn't exactly been *Homes and Gardens*, but it was a damned sight better than the accommodation he had now. At least he hadn't had to share the lavatory with a houseful of tenants.

That was women for you, he sighed, they overreacted to the most unimportant things. All he'd done was have a bit of a fling with a barmaid at their local and suddenly World War Three had broken out between him and Sheila, leaving him homeless. He'd tried to make her understand that it had meant nothing to him and had only happened a couple of times. But would she listen? Would she hell. She was a female, and every man on the planet knew what weird ideas they had about sex. They just didn't seem able to grasp the fact that men didn't share their sanctimonious attitude towards it, and immediately accused you of not loving them just because you'd had sex with someone else. It was absolutely ridiculous!

Anyway, she'd told him to pack his bags; and as the lease of the flat was in her name, he'd had no choice but to comply. It had been a nice comfortable gaff, too. To think that Sheila had ever seemed worth leaving home for. He'd not been unhappy with Rachel; she was a nice woman, a good wife and mother. But Sheila had been exciting, sexy, smart and independent, with a place of her own. Divorced with no children. The perfect partner for someone who had a low tolerance threshold for babies and toddlers. Little did he know she'd turn out to be such a hard-hearted cow.

He'd been on his own for a year now and he didn't like it at all. Living alone was hard work. He was used to having food appear on the table and clothes washed and ironed for him. Now he had to shop and cook for himself and take his washing to the launderette. He'd even had to buy an iron. He'd have to find someone serious soon. This was no way to live.

'Jeff . . . how are yer going, mate?' said a male voice, as a friendly hand slapped him on the shoulder. 'So this is where you've been hanging out.'

Turning swiftly, Jeff found himself staring at one of his old pals from Hammersmith, a ginger-haired man who lived in Wilbur Terrace near Rachel's parents. Jeff used to drink with him in their local. 'Wotcher, Reg,' he said, pleased to see a friendly face. 'What are you having?'

'That's very civil of you,' replied Reg. 'I'll have a pint of best bitter, please.'

Jeff ordered Reg's drink and paid for it. 'So, what are you doing around here?' he wanted to know.

'Driving a van for a firm of motor factors,' said the freckle-faced Reg, who was wearing a bright blue overall. 'I've been delivering around this way. Just popped in for a quick one on my way home. It's thirsty work, driving a van.'

'You still living at the same place?' Jeff enquired chattily.

'Yeah, me and the wife aren't planning on moving,' Reg told him. 'Once the kids start school and make friends, it isn't fair to uproot 'em, is it?'

'I suppose not.' Jeff found it odd to be regarded as a family man. It was a long time since anyone had thought of him in that way.

'I often wondered where you'd gone to,' mentioned Reg. 'I heard you'd scarpered with some bit of stuff. Never see you around our way now.'

'I steer well clear of the area, mate,' said Jeff, suddenly seeing himself through the other man's eyes as a bit of a jackthe-lad. 'My name's mud around there.'

'Is it?' muttered Reg, noncommittally.

'Oh, yeah, I stepped out of line good and proper.' Jeff wasn't fool enough to admit that he actually kept well away from Hammersmith for fear it would cost him money if he showed his face there. Going off with another woman might give you prestige with the lads when you'd all had a few down at the pub, but not paying to support your kids would be taken a dim view of.

Reg opted for a change of subject. 'You living around here?' he asked.

Jeff nodded.

'A house?'

'A flat,' lied Jeff. 'One of these luxury places.'

'Nice.' Reg drank his beer, looking thoughtful. 'Your missus has done well for herself an' all, hasn't she?' he mentioned casually. 'She's really gone up in the world.'

'Has she?' asked Jeff.

'Well, yeah.' He paused, looking at Jeff quizzically. 'But surely you must know about it. I know you and Rachel split up, but you must still be in touch with her because of the kids.'

Jeff's desire to know about Rachel's upturn in fortune won hands down over his reluctance to admit that he had no contact with his wife and children at all.

'No, we don't keep in touch,' he said.

'Not even with the kids?'

Jeff shook his head, evincing sorrow. 'Rachel and I decided that a clean break would be the best thing for them, rather than have them unsettled,' he lied. 'I pay the maintenance money straight into the court for her to collect.'

'Shouldn't think she needs it now,' Reg remarked.

'What's all this about?' Jeff was dying to know. 'Did she have a big win on the pools or something?'

'Nothing as flash as that,' Reg told him. 'But she did inherit her uncle's boatbuilding business when he died.'

'Chip Banks' place?'

'That's right.'

'Well, I'll be buggered,' said Jeff in astonishment. 'I didn't even know Chip had kicked the bucket.'

'It was a shock to everyone at the time, but it's a few years ago now,' Reg informed him.

'A boathouse, eh?' said Jeff, seeing a wealth of opportunity for himself in the situation. 'She's got someone running it for her, I suppose.'

'I believe she has a workshop manager,' Reg nodded. 'But she runs the actual business herself as far as I know.'

'My wife, running a boathouse?' Jeff burst out incredulously. 'That's the craziest thing I've ever heard.'

'Judging by the way she lives, it can't be all that crazy,' Reg pointed out.

'What do you mean by that?' Jess enquired hastily. 'You don't have a luxury lifestyle when you live on the Perrydene Estate.'

'She doesn't live there any more,' Reg told him. 'She's got a nice little house of her own now. Drives a decent car an' all.'

'Don't give me that,' exclaimed the astonished Jeff, trying to gather his wits. 'She doesn't know the back end of a car from the front, let alone how to drive one.'

Reg puffed out his lips, shaking his head. 'You're well out of date, mate,' he said. 'She drives all over the place in a smart blue Ford. She usually gives me a wave if she sees me. Nice woman, your missus. She's got style.'

Jeff stared at him with a bemused expression. The person Reg was describing didn't sound like the woman Jeff had been married to at all. 'You say she's got a house?' he said.

'Yeah. She's bought a place in Ross Street, opposite her sister,' Reg informed him. 'I get all the gen from her dad when I see him in the pub. He talks about his daughters all the time. He's dead proud of them both. And he's thrilled about how well Rachel's doing. Loves those boys of hers. They're smashing little kids. They were playing outside her mum's when I passed there the other day.'

'Really?' Jeff couldn't picture the squalling, nappy-filling infants he'd left behind as civilised children who went out to play. He remembered them as alien beings who dribbled their food and screamed the place down for no apparent reason.

'The youngest is the dead spit of you,' Reg informed him with a knowing nod of the head.

Jeff's vanity was touched by this, and for a moment he lingered on the pleasant feelings it evoked. But he was far more interested in the boys' mother's good fortune and, more importantly, how he could get a slice of it. This was the answer to all his problems! He and Rachel had been good together once and they could be again with the right incentive. He'd only left her because he'd had a better offer.

Of course, he was in the doghouse with her, and getting back into favour wouldn't be easy. It shouldn't be impossible, though. It would take a little time and a lot of persuasion, but it wasn't beyond his capabilities. He could be irresistible when he needed to be, and she'd been crazy about him once.

Her living opposite her sister was a bit of a stumbling block, though. Jan hadn't had any time for him before he'd left, and would hate his guts now. They were a clannish lot, Rachel's family. He dreaded to think of the extent of Jan's wrath if she spotted him hanging around Rachel's place. She would put a spanner in the works for sure. Once he'd got his foot back in the door with Rachel it wouldn't matter because he'd have regained his power and her sister wouldn't stand a chance. So his wisest move would be to make his initial approach to Rachel somewhere other than at her home.

He had no compunction about his intentions. After all, he was still Rachel's legal husband. If she was doing well in business, he was entitled to a share. He'd supported her once. Not for long, admittedly, because she'd worked up until a few weeks before she'd had their first baby. But he had been the family bread-winner for a while.

The idea of running a business in which he had a part share appealed to him. A position of authority would sit well on his shoulders. It had to be better than making cables all day. There would be other perks, too. A decent car, for instance. Oh yes, he could see it all, and was annoyed that he hadn't heard about Rachel's change of circumstances before. To think that he'd been slumming it in a shabby bedsit when he could have been living the good life.

'She runs the business, you say?' Jeff said.

'That's right,' confirmed Reg.

'Who looks after the kids while she's out at work, then?' wondered Jeff.

'They're at school,' Reg told him.

'School!' Jeff couldn't believe he'd been away that long. He struggled to work out what ages his sons would be now and realised that he didn't have a clue. He would have to do some calculations when he had a few quiet moments.

'Yeah, of course,' confirmed Reg. 'It's what kids do when they get to a certain age. But I think your dad said something about Rachel's sister leaving the boathouse in time to pick them up and looking after them until Rachel gets home from work, if she can't get away in time.'

'Her sister works there an' all?' gasped Jeff.

'Part time, I think Ron said,' explained Reg.

'Quite a family affair, then,' remarked Jeff.

'Seems to be.'

'You're really in the know, aren't you?' said Jeff, miffed because the other man knew things that he himself didn't.

'You know what Ron Parry's like,' Reg reminded him. 'There's no stopping him once he starts yapping about his family.'

'It's a wonder Rachel hasn't got him working for her as well,' Jeff mentioned.

'He hasn't said anything about the possibility of that,' Reg told him. 'But I expect your two boys will join the family firm as soon as they're old enough.'

Their father will be joining it long before that, thought Jeff, but said, 'Yeah, I expect they will.'

They moved on to more general topics, then Reg left, having been asked by Jeff not to mention seeing him. He wanted to catch Rachel off her guard.

Alone again, Jeff ordered another drink and applied his mind to a plan. This was going to take careful handling. But it would be well worth the effort for such rich pickings.

Rachel was making her way out through the workshop one afternoon a few weeks later when the workshop manager Ted Barratt waylaid her.

'I need to put a couple of the lads on overtime for this job,' he mentioned, standing back from a racing boat in the process of construction.

'Oh?'

'The customer's been on the blower asking if they can have it earlier than was originally agreed,' he explained. 'And we can't do it without overtime.'

'You do as you see fit, Ted,' she told him. 'You know I trust you to do what's best.'

'Of course, we'll have to reflect the fact that we're paying overtime rates in the final bill,' he said, his warm brown eyes resting on her seriously. 'I've already mentioned that to the customer. They're quite agreeable if it means they can take delivery earlier.'

'Good.' She looked at the craft. One of the apprentices was busy working on the stern. 'Looks like it'll be a fine boat when it's finished.'

'It had better be,' he said, his weathered face arranging itself into a lop-sided grin. 'I only let the best go out of these workshops. Nothing leaves here until I'm completely satisfied.'

He was a nice man and had settled in well after Ben. 'That goes without saying.' She looked at the framework being crafted from beautiful new wood. 'Why is there such urgency with this one, anyway?'

'They've decided they want it to make its début in the Big River Race next month,' he explained, 'and naturally they want it a few weeks before the race so that they can use it to practise and get the feel of it.'

She felt his words like a hammer blow. 'Oh!' she cried involuntarily.

'What's the matter? What did I say?' he enquired, looking worried. 'You've turned quite pale.'

'It's nothing.' She was struggling with memories of three years ago when another boat of theirs had made its début in the Big River Race. It wasn't the dramatic happening at that race that stuck in her mind so much as the fact that she and Ben had been together at that time. The unexpected reminder had shaken her to the core. 'I think someone just walked over my grave.'

'You'd better get off home to those boys of yours,' Ted suggested amiably. 'They'll soon put the colour back in your cheeks.'

'They will, too,' she said, stepping away from him towards the door, still thinking about Ben. 'I'll see you in the morning, then. Bye for now, Ted.'

'Ta-ta.'

She was too deeply engrossed in her thoughts to pay any attention to the man standing on the river walkway outside the boathouse. There were always plenty of people on the riverside on a summer evening so he didn't stand out. She had turned to unlock her car when a familiar voice said, 'Hello, Rachel.'

She swung around. 'Jeff!' she exclaimed, her legs turning to jelly. 'What the hell are you doing here?'

Waiting for him to reply, her gaze moved over the dark quiffed hair, the chunky jaw, the grey-blue eyes. She'd not realised until this moment just how much Johnnie resembled him.

'You look terrific, Rachel,' he told her, running an approving eye over her pretty face and shiny hair, her trim figure clad in a short summer dress.

'You didn't answer my question, Jeff,' she said, ignoring his compliment. 'So I'll ask it again: what are you doing here?'

'What do you think I'm doing here?' he replied, 'I've come to see you, of course.'

'Why?'

'I'd like to talk to you,' he said.

She had often wondered how she would feel if she saw him again, if perhaps the spark might still be there in spite of what he'd done. It wasn't. Her emotions were mixed. Dislike and disgust for his weakness were the main ingredients of her reaction, though anger at the way he'd deserted his children was also rekindled. She wanted to distance herself from him with all possible speed. 'Well, I don't want to talk to you, so you've had a wasted journey,' she told him.

'Rachel, please,' he said, becoming plaintive. 'I know I've done wrong.'

'Oh, really?' she said with a withering look.

'Please listen to me.'

'No,' she said in an uncompromising manner. 'The only way I will speak to you is through a solicitor.'

'Don't say that,' he said, looking penitent.

'The only reason you haven't had divorce papers through your letterbox is because I didn't know where you were,' she told him brusquely.

'Divorce?' he looked suitably shocked.

'That's right.'

'Not that, please,' he said.

'Don't sound so surprised. It's what happens when people split up,' she reminded him coldly. 'Anyway, I thought you'd welcome it. Or has your fancy woman dumped you?'

'Of course not,' he lied, adding quickly, 'I dumped her, if you want to know the truth. I never loved her. How could I when you're the one I love?'

'Oh, please!' she said acidly. 'Spare me the mushy dialogue.'

'Don't be like that,' he said, looking hurt. 'I want to make it up to you for what I've done. I really do.'

She wasn't normally hard or cynical but she couldn't believe a word he said. 'Oh, for goodness' sake,' she said irritably. 'You sound like a bad actor in a romantic farce.'

'Is that all you can say when I finished work early so that I could get here to see you?' He was full of umbrage. 'I've cut my hours and lost money to come here.'

'I lost a lot more than that when you walked out on me,' she said tersely.

At least he had the grace to look a little sheepish. 'Please just let me talk to you properly,' he begged her ardently.

'I have to go home to my children,' she said meaningfully. 'They need one parent they can rely on.'

'Ouch,' he said, making a face. 'I deserve that, I know.'

'You deserve a lot more than that.'

'If you can't talk to me now,' he continued determinedly, 'could we meet somewhere another time? Tomorrow, perhaps, or the next day?'

She pondered on this, gathering her chaotic thoughts after the shock of seeing him. 'I know what all this is about,' she said, giving him a shrewd look. 'You've heard that I'm doing well for myself and you think there might be something in it for you. Well, you're wasting your time, Jeff.'

'How can you say a horrible thing like that?'

'Because of what you did to me,' she told him. 'I'm surprised you haven't appeared on the scene before. Does the gossip from Hammersmith take a while to reach your neck of the woods, wherever that is?'

'You've become hard,' he accused, full of pique. 'You didn't used to be like this when we were together.'

'That's what desertion does for you,' she said, unlocking the door of her car, wishing her hand wasn't trembling. 'It makes you tough. You have to be to survive.'

'Look, I've admitted what I did was wrong,' he persisted. 'I know I shouldn't have gone off like I did.'

'There's only one thing worse than your going,' she said crisply. 'And that's your coming back. So push off before I get someone to come out here and forcibly remove you.'

Leaving him looking stunned, she got into the car and drove away. She'd been repulsed by him and didn't want him anywhere near her. What a terrible admission to have to make about the father of her children, she thought. But it was his own fault. He had betrayed and abandoned her and her children.

She had a horrible suspicion that she hadn't seen the last of him. Life was never that simple. His turning up out of the blue spelled big trouble, she was sure of it.

She was right. Jeff telephoned her at the office the next day and asked if he could meet her for a drink after work. She refused, with the explanation that she was busy with the boys after work. He asked if he could meet her one lunchtime, offered to take time off from work to come to Hammersmith because what he had to say was really important. Bearing in mind that an address for him would be a useful thing to have when she did go ahead with divorce proceedings, she agreed to meet him in The Dove on Friday lunchtime.

'Be careful,' advised Jan worriedly. 'He'll stop at nothing to get his own way.'

'Don't worry,' Rachel assured her 'I've got the measure of Jeff West.'

'I knew I'd made a mistake soon after I left,' lied Jeff over a light lunch of ham and salad. 'But it was too late to do anything about it by then. Sheila is a very neurotic woman. I was afraid of what she might do to herself if I left her to come back to you.'

'But you've finished with her now, you say?' Rachel said pointedly.

'And I was worried about her for a while,' he quickly cut in. 'But she's come through it all right.'

'Mm.' Once she had believed everything he'd said. Now she didn't believe a word but was oddly devoid of feeling. Even the disgust and anger she'd experienced on first seeing him again had petered out, leaving her irritated and bored with his company.

'I wanted to contact you, but the longer I was away, the more difficult it seemed,' he said.

'Conscience troubling you, was it, because you never once tried to find out how your sons were getting on or sent a penny towards their keep?' she said, reminding herself that he'd never been interested in the boys.

He lowered his gaze, his lashes dark and curling, like Johnnie's. 'That was terrible, I know,' he admitted humbly. 'I always meant to put some cash in the post to you but I never got around to it. I just never seemed to have any money to spare.'

What he was saying was so appalling, she was almost lost for words. 'They should have been your first priority,' she admonished fiercely. 'They're your sons, for heaven's sake. They should have been your first thought when you got your pay packet, not something to consider if there was any loose change left when you'd had what you wanted.'

'What can I say?' He spread his hands expressively.

'You never once stopped to think how they were or how I was managing, did you?' she said, more as a statement than an accusation.

'Course I did,' he claimed.

'It doesn't bother me for myself, but how you could have turned your back on two innocent boys is completely beyond me,' she told him.

'It wasn't that I didn't think about them.' Jeff had experienced only rare feelings of guilt and never allowed compunction to linger for long enough to cramp his style. 'It was just that I . . . well, I'd got myself into a mess, and it was easier to blot them out of my mind. I know it sounds pathetic.'

'It does . . . *very*,' she agreed, determined not to be won over. 'And it's completely unacceptable. There is no excuse for leaving your children, none at all.'

'You're right.' He stared at the floor, looking contrite. 'How are the boys getting on now?' he enquired, because he thought it would impress her.

'They're getting on famously,' she told him proudly. 'A couple of fine boys – no thanks to you.'

'You've every right to be angry,' he said. 'But I've come to my senses and I want to help you.'

'It's a bit late for that,' she exploded. 'I don't need your help now.'

'Oh,' he said, as if he didn't already know.

'But things were very hard for me for the first two years, very hard indeed,' she told him.

He chewed his lip, looking shamefaced. 'I'm really sorry. I feel terrible about it. But I want to make it up to you, believe me,' he entreated. 'I want that with all my heart.'

'And the fact that I have a thriving business has nothing to do with this sudden urge to get in touch with the family you abandoned, I suppose,' she said dryly.

'Of course it hasn't,' he objected, with such vehemence he almost believed it himself. 'I have a job. I'm not the type of man who would sponge off his wife.'

Not much, she thought, but said, 'What exactly do you have in mind?'

'I want you back, Rachel,' he said, his eyes resting on her persuasively.

She didn't reply but turned her attention to her food, though she hadn't much appetite.

'It's taken me all this time to find the courage to come back,' he went on with his well-rehearsed piece of fiction. 'I heard about your uncle's death and your inheritance at the time it happened, from an old mate of mine from

Hammersmith. That kept me away because I thought you might get the wrong impression.'

'Oh, yeah?' He was very convincing but she couldn't believe him. 'So what's made you do it now?'

'About a year ago I decided it was time to sort my life out,' he told her. 'Things weren't going well with Sheila because I couldn't stop thinking about you, so I moved out.'

'Go on.'

'I still wasn't brave enough to come and see you after what I'd done,' he continued. 'But the other day I knew I couldn't stand it any longer. I had to follow my heart and try to get you back.'

Fine words but not the sort that rolled off Jeff's tongue with sincerity; she knew that now. This pack of lies was nothing short of an insult to her intelligence. She said nothing, though, just waited for him to continue.

He reached for her hand across the table. 'I don't expect you to give me an answer right away, but . . .' He gave her one of his most vulnerable little-boy-lost looks. 'But can you tell if there's any chance?'

Unmoved by the physical contact, she removed her hand from his and dabbed her mouth with a paper napkin. 'None at all,' she told him straight.

A fleeting look of fury darkened his expression, before he reverted to a look of humble contrition. 'Aren't you even going to think about it?' he asked.

'There's nothing to think about,' she said firmly. 'You broke my heart once, but it's fully intact again now, I'm happy to say.'

'Does that mean you've got another bloke?' he asked.

'No.'

'Not anyone, in all this time?' he queried.

'There was someone,' she said, her heart twisting again at the thought of how things had ended with Ben. 'But not now.'

'Why not give me a chance, then?' he pleaded.

'I don't want to, Jeff, that's the truth of the matter,' she informed him frankly. 'I'm very happy with my life as it is and I have no wish to alter it.'

'We were good together once,' he tried to persuade. 'And we could be again.'

'Don't kid yourself, Jeff,' was her answer to that. 'Anything we had is too far gone for restoration.'

'You could at least think about it,' he said, becoming sulky now.

'There's nothing to think about because us getting back together is out of the question.'

'I can understand your wanting to punish me, but . . .'

'I am *not* trying to punish you,' she cut in, feeling drained by this meeting now, despite her cool front. 'I'm merely telling you that I don't want you back in my life.' She gathered her handbag and stood up purposefully. 'Thanks for lunch, Jeff.'

And she swung off across the bar, leaving him dazzled by her confidence. Who would have thought that homely little Rachel would become so assertive? Although he found it disconcerting, a part of him was excited by it. He was more determined than ever to get her back now. His motivation was of a practical nature, but her having become so smart and sexy was an added incentive.

But even someone as lacking in depth as Jeff was realised that he wasn't going to win her back with a few soft words. This was a complicated situation and called for a more roundabout route. The only way to the heart of a woman like Rachel was through her children. If he could get them on his side, she would be his again.

It was Saturday evening and Rachel could hear Tim and Johnnie squabbling over one of Johnnie's toy cars in the back garden while she was preparing supper in the kitchen. Any minute now the familiar cry of 'I'm telling Mum' will go up, she thought as she chipped some potatoes.

Sure enough, moments later Johnnie appeared at her side. 'Tim keeps pinching my best toy Jag,' he informed her gravely.

'And Johnnie keeps deliberately getting in the way of my football goal,' defended Tim, looking indignant.

'I'm not doing it on purpose,' countered Johnnie, glaring at his brother.

'Yes you are,' insisted Tim.

'No I'm not,' claimed Johnnie. 'Anyway, you don't own the back garden.'

'Neither do you,' retorted Tim. 'Just because you don't want to play shots, you're trying to ruin it for me.'

'You can't play shots without a keeper,' said Johnnie. 'The ball's bound to go in without anyone to stop it.'

'I'm practising,' Tim told him. 'Anyway, you only stopped playing because you didn't get as many goals as me.'

'I stopped because I wanted to play with my cars,' insisted Johnnie.

'Your cars are stupid,' said Tim.

'Your shots are stupid.'

'That's enough, both of you!' ordered Rachel. 'I don't want to hear any more of this silly bickering. And I don't want either of you in this kitchen. I'll be putting the chip pan on soon and I don't like you to be hanging around me when there's hot fat about.'

'What are we having with the chips?' asked Johnnie.

'Burgers,' said Rachel.

'Yummee!' said Tim.

'We always have burgers and chips on a Saturday night, stupid,' said Johnnie. 'I don't know why you bother Mum by asking her.'

'Don't call me stupid, you thickhead,' retaliated Tim.

'Tell him to stop pinching my cars, Mum,' asked Johnnie.

'Tell him to stop getting in the way while I'm practising shots,' said Tim.

'Right. That's it. One more cross word and there'll be no burgers and chips,' announced Rachel. 'Now go back in the garden, go on, shoo.'

The sound of the doorbell was a welcome distraction. 'I'll

go,' said Tim, and both boys hurried to the door.

Saturday evenings had a special feel for Rachel. She always cooked the boys' favourite tea and let them stay up a bit later, though she'd not been adhering to their usual bedtime anyway during the summer holidays. She took as much time off from the boathouse as she could possibly manage so as to be at home with them during the holidays, but on the other days Jan looked after them for her.

Now she could hear them talking to someone at the front door, then the sound of feet running along the hall.

'There's a man at the door, Mum,' said Tim, looking at her with a mixture of excitement and anxiety.

'He says he's our dad,' burst out the exuberant Johnnie, his eyes shining.

'What?' The potato she was holding dropped from her hand and rolled across the tiled floor.

'Our dad's come back,' announced Johnnie triumphantly. 'Can we tell him to come in?'

'That was unforgivable of you, Jeff,' admonished Rachel a short time later. She'd abandoned the supper preparations and sent the children to play in the garden so that she could talk to her errant husband in private. They were in the living room at the back of the house, a comfortable, homely area with soft chairs, wood panelling, plenty of bookshelves and French doors leading to the garden. 'Springing that on the boys right out of the blue like that. How did you find us anyway?'

'I asked around. I've still got contacts in the area. And I don't see what's wrong with my calling here. I mean, it isn't as though I was telling them lies or anything, is it? I *am* their father.'

'Only when the mood takes you,' she pointed out sternly. 'You should have spoken to me about it first, given me the choice of whether or not to let you back into their lives. I've brought those boys up, I am responsible for their well-being and I make the decisions about what's best for them.'

'Sorry.' He gave a careless shrug. 'It just sort of came out when I saw them standing at the door,' he explained.

'How can you be so irresponsible?' She was furious. 'They aren't babies any more; they're not too little to know what's going on around them. These are growing children who are old enough to be emotionally scarred by parental instability.'

'They seemed pleased to see me, anyway,' he pointed out lamely. 'Especially Johnnie.'

'What else did you expect, for heaven's sake?' she asked him. 'Children like the idea of having a dad, and Tim and Johnnie were too young when you left to feel any sort of resentment towards you about it. But who knows what sort of emotional roller-coaster you've set in motion by coming back.'

'Sorry.' He didn't look it.

'And so you should be,' she told him. 'I mean it, Jeff. This sort of behaviour really isn't on.'

He turned and looked out of the French doors to the garden, where the boys were playing shots at goal, their disagreement apparently forgotten. 'They're great, aren't they?' he said, and this time his words were genuine. 'I just can't get over how they've grown.'

'Children tend to do that,' Rachel pointed out. 'It's all the more noticeable when you haven't seen them for years.'

'All right. Don't hammer the point, Rachel,' he responded with a baleful look. 'I know I've done wrong.'

'Just as long as you don't think a visit to your sons will magically make everything all right again,' she warned.

'I'm not that stupid.' He turned back to the garden and watched his sons in silence for a few moments. 'It seems so strange to see them like this . . . as boys, I mean,' he told her in a subdued tone. 'I remember them as babies, damp and sticky and yelling the place down.'

'Not a very flattering description,' she said.

'I'm just explaining how it was for me,' he said in another rare moment of truth. 'I wasn't comfortable with them as babies, couldn't relate to them.' He stared thoughtfully into space. 'I never looked ahead, never imagined them growing into the fine boys they are now.' Another pause. 'Is it my imagination, or is Johnnie a bit like me?'

'He's a lot like you,' she confirmed.

'Smashing boys,' he muttered to himself, still looking out into the garden. 'You've done a good job.'

'Thank you.'

He turned back to her and cast an eye around the room. 'Nice place you've got.'

'We like it,' she told him.

'A bit different to the old flat, eh?'

She nodded. 'I certainly hope so,' she said.

'It's another world,' he remarked.

'Perhaps,' she said. 'Why have you come here, though? I thought I made my feelings clear to you the other day.'

'You did that all right,' he said with an air of breeziness. 'And I got the message.'

'So why . . . ?'

'I didn't come to see you,' he told her. 'I came to see the boys.'

'I thought you would probably say something like that.' She gave him a warning look. 'You had no right to just turn up.'

'They are my sons,' he reminded her.

'You gave up all rights in that direction when you walked out on us.'

'You wouldn't want to prevent your beloved sons from seeing their father, surely?' he said. 'Their feelings should be taken into consideration, and I think they want to see me.'

'You never considered their feelings before and now you're using them to get at me,' she accused him.

'Rubbish,' he denied, turning to look into the garden. 'I think they're great and I really do want to get to know them.'

Rachel felt a knot of fear pulling tight in her stomach. 'If you're using them . . .'

'Look,' he said, swinging round to face her, 'it's only natural for a man to want to get to know his sons. You can make the rules and I'll abide by them. I'll do whatever you want as long as you let me spend some time with them on a regular basis. Access, I think they call it.'

'Which is usually granted if it's thought to be in the best interests of the children,' she pointed out. 'Being a parent isn't a game, Jeff. It isn't something you can do when you feel like it and give up when you've had enough. The boys are old enough to be deeply affected by things now, especially Tim. He's quite a sensitive child.'

'I'm not a complete moron,' he snapped.

'I didn't say you were,' she protested. 'But you can't deny that your track record as a parent is abysmal.'

'People do change, you know.' He paused thoughtfully, his gaze drawn to the garden again. 'Looking back on it, I think I knew they were too young to be damaged by my leaving,' he informed himself as much as her. 'It's different now that they're older. All I'm asking is to spend a little time with them, to get to know them.'

'I don't know.' She was very doubtful.

'Look, I know I don't have any rights after what I did,' he said, turning back to look at her. 'But I promise I won't do anything to hurt them.'

'If you do, I won't be responsible for my actions,' she told him grimly. 'And that's a promise.'

The conversation was interrupted by the appearance of Johnnie in the doorway. 'Will you come out and be in goal for us, Dad?' he asked eagerly. 'So that Tim and me can both practise our shots.'

Jeff looked at Rachel, and as their eyes met she remembered why she had married him. He still had that same erotic magnetism. It didn't touch her now, but she could see how a young girl would have been susceptible.

'Will you, Dad, please?' begged Johnnie again.

Jeff stared at Rachel, waiting for her decision.

'All right, I suppose you'd better go and be goalkeeper for them,' she said with a sigh of resignation.

'Thanks,' said Jeff, smiling at her, and she had never seen such warmth in his eyes before.

As Johnnie shrieked in delight and rushed back into the garden, she gave Jeff a quiet warning. 'Don't get too excited. It's just a football game. I'm promising nothing more than that.'

Back in the kitchen, watching through the window as the three of them played together, she felt a pang. Tim and Johnnie were obviously delighted to have a father figure around. A father and sons spending time together in their back garden; what could be more natural? But she didn't have the same peace of mind she'd experienced when it had been Ben playing with the boys.

Much to his own astonishment, Jeff was having a wonderful time. He had turned up unannounced this evening because he'd known Rachel would put him off if he'd telephoned first. He'd come here with the idea of gaining favour with his sons merely as leverage back into Rachel's affections – well, into her comfortable lifestyle, to be more precise.

He'd never dreamed that he'd actually enjoy being with his sons, or that he'd feel anything for them when he saw them again. But when he'd first clapped eyes on those fresh little faces looking up at him at the front door and realised they were his, he had felt most peculiar, almost as though he'd wanted to cry. Most unusual for Jeff, who blundered his way through life unscathed by complicated emotions. He could communicate with them now that they were boys and not babies. It was a great feeling.

'Well done, son,' he said now as the ball flew through the space between the two folded jumpers that served as goalposts. He hadn't deliberately let it through to win popularity. He hadn't been able to stop it because he was so unfit. He'd have to get himself into better shape if this was going to be a regular thing.

He was stunned to realise that he actually *wanted* it to be a regular thing. He wanted to spend time with his sons, not just because they were his way back to Rachel, although that was still part of it, but because he enjoyed being with them. This was unlike anything he had experienced before; he felt happy and sort of soft inside. But although he enjoyed these new feelings, they unnerved him because they made him feel vulnerable, and that complicated matters.

At that moment, though – as the shadows lengthened over this conventional suburban garden, with its lilac tree, flowerbeds and child-worn lawn, the damp scent of evening spicing the air and the savoury aroma of cooking drifting out from the kitchen – he knew exactly what he wanted from life. His vague ideas of getting back with Rachel purely for material gain had shifted into place with vivid clarity. He wanted much more than that now; he wanted to be part of their family life, to take his place with his beautiful wife and two fine sons in a comfortable, sweet-smelling home.

It would take time and effort to make it happen, but he was determined all of this would be his eventually. His best bet was to play it cool with Rachel and concentrate on the children – for the moment.

A burst of youthful laughter broke into his thoughts and he became aware that he had let another goal in. 'It's time to change round,' he said matily. 'One of you can come in goal now. I'll show you how to score goals . . . I'll show you how it's done.'

'OK,' said Tim, and changed places with his father.

Magic, thought Jeff. Being a dad is sheer magic. And I want more of it, lots more.

'So you've agreed to let Jeff see the boys again, then?' remarked Jan the next morning when Rachel told her what had happened. Jan had popped over to give Rachel a hand preparing the vegetables for Sunday lunch because all the family were coming. Kelly was in the garden with the boys.

Living in such close proximity meant that the children were equally at home in either house. The easy accessibility was something both sisters valued enormously.

'Yeah,' said Rachel, whisking the batter for the Yorkshire pudding. 'I've said that he can take them out for a couple of hours on Saturday afternoon.'

'You don't sound too happy about it,' observed Jan.

'I'm not,' she confessed. 'It isn't that I think he'll be directly unkind to them . . .'

'But you're afraid he'll get them to like him then drop them when it suits him,' guessed Jan, 'which will be even more cruel in the long run.'

'Exactly,' Rachel confirmed. 'He's already proved how irresponsible he is as a father.'

'I'll say he has.'

'The boys suffered enough when Ben and I split up, especially Tim,' said Rachel. 'I can't let it happen again with Jeff.'

'Dear Tim,' said Jan affectionately. 'He is the more serious of the two.'

'The trouble is,' Rachel confessed, 'I don't think it would be fair to the boys to refuse Jeff access altogether. Do you?'

'Not really,' agreed Jan. 'You'll just have to keep a close eye on the situation.'

'If I thought he was definitely just using them to get to me, I wouldn't let him anywhere near them,' Rachel stated categorically. 'But I can't be certain. He might be genuine about wanting to get to know them. And I can't deprive the boys of their father if that's the case.'

'But he does want you back.'

'So he said, but I squashed the idea right away,' Rachel told her. 'I'm not interested in getting back with him. I think he's accepted it now.'

'Thank God for that,' said Jan with relief. 'I should hate you to get mixed up with him again.'

'There's no chance of that,' Rachel assured her. 'There's

nothing between us any more as far as I'm concerned. The only man for me is Ben. And as I can't have him, I'll stay single.'

'It's a shame about you and Ben,' said Jan, slicing runner beans. 'You two were great together.'

'That's life.' Rachel opted for a swift change of subject to avoid a resurgence of pain. 'You feeling all right today?'

'Better but still very washed out,' said Jan who was still having a bad time with her periods and hadn't been well yesterday.

'The curse really is a curse for you. Perhaps you ought to see a doctor,' Rachel suggested.

'It's probably nothing,' said Jan quickly. 'A lot of women suffer in this way. I think it's quite common.'

'Yeah, but the doctor might be able to help you in some way,' Rachel explained.

'Well, if it gets any worse, I'll go and get some advice.' She looked at the contents of the colander 'And in the meantime, is this enough beans?'

'That'll be fine,' said Rachel.

The children came piling noisily in through the back door.

'Kelly won't believe that we've got a dad and he was here yesterday,' said Johnnie, looking outraged. 'Tell her it's true, Mum. Tell her we're not telling fibs.'

Rachel looked at Kelly, who was now a tall, leggy soon-to-be eight-year-old with long red hair tied back in a ponytail. As usual, she was in competition with her cousins. 'It's true, Kelly,' said Rachel co-operatively.

'See,' gloated Johnnie, looking triumphantly at his cousin. 'I told you so.'

'We're not liars,' added Tim.

'Is he coming here for Sunday dinner with us and Gran and Grandad, though?' the girl asked.

'No,' said Rachel.

'Well, my daddy is,' boasted one-upping Kelly, returning

Johnnie's victorious look. 'If he was your *real* Dad he'd be coming too. So there!'

Rachel and Jan exchanged glances. 'That isn't true, Kelly,' Jan admonished her daughter. 'And if you're going to be horrid to your cousins, you can stay at home. Daddy and I will come for our dinner without you.'

'I only said . . .'

'Well, don't say it again, please,' reprimanded Jan.

'Go out into the garden and play, all of you,' added Rachel. 'We're busy in here.'

As they trooped back outside, Kelly complaining to Johnnie about it being his fault she'd got told off, Rachel said worriedly to her sister, 'Jeff certainly started something when he decided to play father last night.'

'He did indeed,' agreed Jan gravely, rinsing the beans in the colander under the tap.

Chapter Eighteen

It was the fourth anniversary of Chip Banks' death, and the weather was eerily similar. Listening to the howling wind driving the rain against the office windows as she tidied her desk before going home, Rachel reflected on the tragic day that had proved to be a watershed for her. She shivered at the memory of being so cold, wet and windblown in the bus queue outside the factory. Unaware that fate had already taken a hand, she'd been in a state of desperation about finding the money for shoes for the boys, and dreading taking them home from Jan's to their freezing flat on the Perrydene Estate.

She didn't have those kinds of difficulties now. She could afford to clothe and feed them, keep the house warm, and give them regular treats. Not a day went by when she didn't count her blessings and thank the man she still thought of as her uncle for giving her and her children a chance in life.

But her naïve assumption that problems ended along with poverty had proved to be a complete misconjecture. A challenging lifestyle inevitably produced a daily crop of them, not least the emotional conflict involved in mixing a demanding career with motherhood.

Jan had given Rachel a good few sleepless nights lately, too. Obviously not feeling well despite all assurances to the contrary, her sister was miserable and bad-tempered, and would flare up at the slightest thing. If Rachel dared to enquire about her health, she was told in no uncertain terms to mind her own business. Rachel suspected that Jan was still having menstrual problems, but as her low state seemed to be constant rather than a monthly occurrence, she couldn't be sure. It was so unlike Jan not to confide in her. But Rachel couldn't even get her to admit that anything was wrong, let alone talk about it.

Jeff was causing her concern as well. She'd been heartened when he seemed to be taking his paternal responsibilities seriously. Since he'd come back into their lives last summer, he'd seen Tim and Johnnie on a regular basis, usually taking them out on Saturday afternoons, to the park, the cinema, for tea at the Wimpy; he'd even taken them to see Fulham play at home.

He'd kept to the rules she'd set out at the start; he hadn't arranged a meeting with them without speaking to her first about it, and had always brought them home at a time fixed by her. He'd even adhered without a word of argument to her request to slow down on gifts; he said he could see her point about too many being bad for them and had agreed to use the money more sensibly on clothes for them instead.

It was good to see her offspring enjoying themselves. They needed a male influence. Johnnie in particular was very smitten with the whole idea of having a dad. Tim, who was a less effusive child anyway, seemed happy enough to see his father but not so bowled over by it as his brother was.

'Dad never takes us to the river,' he mentioned to his mother one day.

'If you ask him he might,' she suggested.

'I already have and he said he doesn't like water and doesn't know anything about boats,' said Tim.

'He does lots of other nice things with you,' pointed out Rachel, who was wholly supportive of Jeff in his efforts for their children, despite her personal feelings towards him. 'You're very lucky boys.'

'Oh, yeah, I know he's good to us,' agreed Tim dutifully. 'Seems funny someone not liking the river, that's all.'

As time passed and Jeff didn't step out of line, Rachel's confidence had grown. She began to believe that his interest in the boys was genuine and he was no longer trying to engineer a place back in her life.

Until last night, that is, when he'd come to the house uninvited after the boys were in bed, and begged her to take him back. She'd been firm with him, repeated what she'd told him before, that it wasn't even a possibility. He'd eventually seemed to accept what she said, but not before making ardent protestations of undying love for her which she found most disturbing and uncharacteristic of him.

He'd agreed not to raise the subject again and seemed as keen as ever to continue his relationship with his sons. But Rachel had been unnerved. There had been a moment, albeit fleeting, when she'd seen something scary in his eyes. It hadn't been the sorrow of unrequited love; more the wild fury of someone who couldn't get his own way. He'd hastily composed himself but she couldn't forget the chilling nature of that look.

Mulling it over again now as she slipped into her fur-lined coat, she was certain that Jeff had become fond of his sons these past few months. He could relate to them now in a way he never could when they were babies. He obviously enjoyed their company. He wouldn't have the patience to keep it up for this long if it was just an act.

It was just the fact that he wanted her as well that made Rachel uneasy. She trusted him not to be violent or unkind to the boys when he was on his own with them. She no longer suspected that he would drop them when he grew tired of them, because she was sure he would miss them if he didn't see them, especially Johnnie. So what was she worried about exactly?

Nothing she could put her finger on, just a persistent knot of fear every time she remembered that moment of malice in his eyes and the overstated nature of his pleas of love for her. There was something pitiful about him now, a kind of desperation. Even after the way he'd hurt her, she couldn't help feeling sorry for him. Jeff was a loser, a victim of his own selfishness. Deciding that she was probably making more of this than was necessary, she made her way through the workshop and out into the yard.

Battling against the elements to her car, she was again transported back to that other January day when the rain had soaked through the hole in her shabby old boots. A whole lot different to the good-quality footwear she was wearing today, she thought gratefully. Thanks, Uncle Chip, she said silently, as she got into her car and drove to Ross Street to collect her offspring.

Later the same evening, Ben was also remembering that other January day as he walked by the river at Fulham. The rain had stopped but the wind was still ferocious, and it stung his face as it had done in the boathouse yard when Chip had taken that tumble. Ben still couldn't think about it without pain; he missed his old pal dreadfully, even after all this time.

The riverside was deserted on this wild night. Even the indomitable dog-walkers had stayed at home. Ben had been driven to brave the weather by a need to get out of the house, away from the temptation to lash out at Lorna, to tell her how he really felt about being caught in the trap that imprisoned them both.

Her progress had continued to be steady. She still moved slowly, experienced a certain amount of pain and walked with a pronounced limp. But she was heaps better. She had nurtured the friendship of her ex-colleagues since contacting them again last year. She even had a job in a local estate agent's. But she still needed the back-up support of knowing Ben was there for her at home. The strain on them both of their enforced togetherness manifested itself in mutual sniping which left him full of guilt for not being more patient.

Now, finding himself barely able to move against the wind, he turned back the way he'd come. The lights of Putney Bridge arched across the water, a stream of traffic moving over it. He walked along the riverside footpath until he came to the main road, then headed towards home and his mockery of a marriage.

Doris Finn found the wind rather frightening that same evening. 'It's a shocking night,' she said to Billy as gale-force winds whistled around the house. 'The roof will come off in a minute if the wind doesn't ease up.'

'The houses in this street are rock solid, love,' he reassured her. 'They've survived worse winds than this . . . they'll come through this one intact, don't worry.'

'I hope so.' She didn't sound convinced.

'The worst it'll do is blow the garden fence down,' he told her lightly, 'and I can soon fix that.'

'Mm, I suppose you're right.' She paused. 'I'm glad you're not working tonight, though,' she confessed. 'I'd be worried to death, thinking of you out there driving your bus in this wind.'

'I'm glad an' all,' he agreed. 'Home by the fire is the place to be on a night like this.'

She nodded, yawning.

'Are you feeling all right, love?' he enquired. 'You seem a bit peaky lately.'

'I'm fine,' she assured him. 'Just a bit tired, that's all.'

'That isn't like you,' he commented, because Doris was usually a woman of boundless energy.

'This wind is enough to exhaust anyone,' she said, but she knew the weather had nothing to do with her weariness. That was down to the fact that she wasn't sleeping properly at night. Being a heavy sleeper himself, Billy was unaware of the fact that she slipped out of bed in the small hours and sat in the kitchen drinking tea.

'Perhaps you need a tonic,' he suggested.

'You can buy me a few glasses of Guinness down at the pub at the weekend, that'll soon put me right,' she joked. She couldn't tell Billy what was really bothering her.

'Better than anything the doctor can give you, eh, love?' he said, smiling at her.

'And a lot more fun, too,' she grinned.

'Not half.'

Looking across at him in his armchair on the other side of the hearth, she felt tears burning beneath her lids at his concern and limitless affection for her. She longed to share her troubles with him, as she always had done in the past. But any such self-indulgence on her part would hurt him, so she wouldn't do it.

At the same time, though, she knew she couldn't go on as she had been. It was tearing the heart out of her. Pondering on the question and reminding herself that she couldn't ever put things right with Rachel, she found herself wondering if she could, perhaps, make them better. The idea lingered and grew until she decided it was definitely worth a try – and the sooner the better. She would set things in motion the very next day, she thought, enthusiasm rising. She'd go to the phone box in her dinner break and make a call.

Rachel was talking to Ted Barratt in the workshop when Jan called her to say she was wanted on the phone. 'It's Doris Finn,' she announced with unveiled disapproval.

'Oh.' Rachel was taken aback; she hadn't expected to hear from Doris again.

She took the call in her own office and listened as Doris nervously apologised for bothering her at work and explained that she didn't have her home number.

'I was wondering if we could meet somewhere,' she suggested. 'I need to talk to you.'

'I thought you didn't want to . . .'

'I know what I said,' Doris cut in, 'but I have something that I must say to you and I'd rather not say it on the phone.'

Rachel gave the matter some thought. 'I could meet you on Saturday afternoon,' she suggested, 'while the boys are out with their father, or do you work on Saturdays?'

'Only one in two, and I'm off this week,' Doris informed her.

'This Saturday afternoon it is, then,' Rachel confirmed.

'Lovely.'

With a natural impulse to be co-operative, Rachel said, 'Do you want me to come to Brentford to meet you?'

'No, no,' Doris said quickly. 'I'll come to Hammersmith.'

'OK. I'll meet you outside Hammersmith station at three o'clock and we'll decide where to go from there,' suggested Rachel. 'Does that suit you?'

'That'll be fine,' said Doris hurriedly. 'I'll have to go now. I'm in a call box and my money's running out.'

The pips sounded and the line went dead.

Because she liked to be open and above board with her sister, Rachel went next door to Jan's office and told her about the content of the telephone call.

'I hope you told her where to get off,' Jan responded sharply.

'No. I said I'd meet her on Saturday, as a matter of fact,' Rachel informed her evenly.

Jan turned scarlet and shocked Rachel with the vehemence of her objection. 'Well, I hope you're not thinking of asking me to look after Tim and Johnnie for you while you go to meet her,' she stated.

This was the first time Jan had ever objected to looking after the boys and Rachel was stung by it. 'I'm not, actually,' she said. 'I'm meeting her while they're out with Jeff.'

'That's just as well,' said Jan in a temper, 'because I wouldn't do it.'

'Why are you being so horrible?' Rachel wanted to know.

'Because I'm not prepared to help you break Mum's heart by getting friendly with that woman,' she explained.

'I've agreed to meet her, not share my life with her,' Rachel pointed out. 'Mum won't mind.'

'Of course she'll mind,' retorted Jan, her voice quavering on the verge of tears. 'And you should have the common sense to realise that.'

'You're being unreasonable . . .'

'As I've said to you before,' Jan ranted on without letting Rachel finish, 'how would you feel if the child you'd brought up as your own daughter started hob-nobbing with her birth mother? You'd be terrified she was going to get to like her better than you. And that's what Mum's worried about.'

'Mum knows that no one could ever replace her,' asserted Rachel. 'Anyway, this is a one-off meeting. It won't become a regular thing.'

'That's what you said before,' Jan reminded her in a warning tone, 'and here you are doing it again.'

For the sake of her own self-respect, Rachel couldn't allow herself to be bullied over something she didn't believe was wrong. 'I know what I said,' she acknowledged. 'But I'm allowed to have a change of heart. You've no right to tell me what I should and shouldn't do.'

'I have when my mother is likely to get hurt by your actions,' Jan declared, her voice becoming shrill.

Anger and bewilderment invaded Rachel in equal proportions. She could feel this argument getting out of control and she didn't want to fall out with her sister. 'You'll just have to trust me not to hurt her, won't you?' she said.

'If I see Mum so much as frown over this, you'll have me to answer to,' threatened Jan, and Rachel trembled inwardly at the ferocity of her warning.

At that moment she realised that this probably wasn't about her and Doris at all. This explosion was the manifestation of whatever it was that was bothering Jan. 'I realise that,' she said, taking a deep breath and lowering her voice to try and calm herself. Then she went back to her own office in order to defuse the situation.

* * *

'I'll only be gone for a couple of hours,' Rachel told Jeff on Saturday afternoon as she saw the boys off for their outing with him. 'So I'll be here by the time you get back. But if I'm held up for any reason, will you hang on to them until I get home?'

'Course I will,' he assured her pleasantly. 'I thought I'd take them to the West End to see some cartoons. Too cold for anything outdoors today. We'll go for tea out afterwards.'

'They'll enjoy that,' she said.

'Are you going anywhere nice?' he enquired casually.

'Nothing special. I'm meeting a friend in Hammersmith for a cup of tea and a chat,' she explained. Jeff knew nothing about her real origins and had assumed she'd inherited the boathouse because she was Chip's favourite niece. 'I might as well make the most of the opportunity while the boys are out with you.'

'Good idea,' said Jeff, stifling the urge to enquire as to the gender of her companion.

'I'll see you later, then,' she said, kissing the boys on the cheek. 'Be good, you two.'

'I'll soon sort them out if they're not, don't worry,' said Jeff amiably.

'I'm sure you will,' she said lightly.

'See you, then,' he said and hurried out to his car with his charges beside him, swathed in hooded coats and long slimline trousers. The weather was still cold and the sky a sombre shade of grey, but the wind had dropped and the rain petered out.

Rachel couldn't know how delighted Jeff was that she trusted him enough to go out somewhere while the boys were in his care. It made him feel like one of the family. He'd had a bit of setback recently when he'd come on strong to her and she'd turned him down again, but he'd get there in the end if he was patient; he was absolutely determined. He'd have his place by the family fireside eventually. A year ago he wouldn't have believed it possible that he could want anything as much as he wanted this. The bachelor bedsit life definitely wasn't for him.

Having to play it slow was frustrating for someone as impatient as he was. But he had to give this thing time or he could blow his chances with Rachel altogether. He needed to wait at least a couple of months before raising the subject of them getting back together again. Patience was the key to this whole manoeuvre. He simply must keep his head. And in the meantime he had the company of his sons to look forward to. They were great fun to be with, and the more he saw of them, the more he wanted to see. Especially the garrulous Johnnie. Tim wasn't such an extrovert and Jeff was never quite sure what he was thinking.

Doris seemed very tense when Rachel met her at the station, and there was a strained atmosphere between them as they walked to a café in King Street and ordered tea. Neither of them wanted a bun or a doughnut. Doris' agitated manner was making Rachel nervous.

'I'll come straight to the point,' said Doris as they settled at a table by the window and she took off her navy blue chiffon headscarf, her face looking even smaller with her hair flattened to her head. 'I know I hurt you when we last met, and I think you have a right to know why I was so cold towards you.'

'Oh?'

'It was all an act,' she blurted out. 'It broke my heart to be like that to you and I haven't had a decent night's sleep since.'

'You've no need to lose sleep over me,' said Rachel, any feelings of resentment she'd had in the past now dissolving into a surge of compassion for this vulnerable woman. 'I'm a survivor.'

'You've proved that,' Doris pointed out. 'But it wasn't right, the way I treated you when we met.'

'Maybe not. But you *were* right when you said that our getting together is a pointless exercise,' said Rachel.

'I didn't mean what I said,' Doris confessed. 'I was scared, that's all. Still am.'

'Scared that your husband might find out about me?' Rachel surmised.

Doris nodded. 'That's right. But it isn't because I'm afraid he might think less of me,' she explained. 'Billy isn't a narrow-minded man.'

'Why then?'

'Billy and I haven't had any children,' Doris told her. 'They just didn't come along and we've both been to hell and back over it. We learned to live with it eventually, but I don't think Billy has ever got over the disappointment.'

Rachel waited for her to go on.

'We've never known why I didn't get pregnant,' she went on. 'It was just one of those things.'

'You didn't have it looked in to then?' Rachel remarked.

'Ooh, no' Doris replied, as though the idea was abhorrent to her. 'I knew that the fault didn't lie with me because I'd had you. And I wasn't going to suggest that we delve into it and have Billy lose his pride. Anyway, people didn't often get that sort of thing investigated when we were young. If it didn't happen, you just accepted that it wasn't to be.'

'And if Billy got to know about me now, he'd be upset, even after all this time?' suggested Rachel.

'Yes, he would. But mostly, I suspect, because I've kept it from him,' Doris said. 'We've always been so honest with each other, you see.'

'Why weren't you honest with him about this, then?' wondered Rachel.

Doris shook her head slowly. 'It was a major disgrace back in the days when I first met Billy, so I kept shtoom at first for fear of losing him,' she explained. 'By the time I realised he wasn't the sort of man to hold something like that against me, some time had passed and I was afraid he'd be hurt that I hadn't told him before. Then, when we started to realise that we couldn't have kids, there was even more reason to keep quiet about it, so that he wouldn't blame himself.' She sipped her tea. 'And now of course it's unthinkable. I can't even bear to imagine how devastated he'd be if he found out that I'd kept something like that from him for all these years.'

'You can hurt people more by keeping something from them than by the actual thing itself,' was Rachel's opinion. 'At least, that was how I felt when I found out that Mum and Dad had kept the truth from me for all those years.'

'I take your point,' Doris said. 'But I know Billy, and believe me, it's kinder this way.'

'Keeping the truth from him is hurting you, though, isn't it?' Rachel pointed out. 'So maybe it would be best to bring it out into the open.'

Doris' face tightened, her lips set determinedly. 'No, I couldn't do that to him,' she said, shaking her head.

'That's up to you, of course,' Rachel told her, 'and if you're worried that I might spill the beans, you can put that right out of your mind, because I won't come anywhere near you. I'm only here now because *you* contacted me.'

'I know that, dear,' Doris acknowledged. 'I just couldn't live with myself any longer. It suddenly seemed vital that you know the whole truth; that's why I asked you to meet me.' She paused, giving Rachel a close look. 'And the truth of the matter is that having to hand you over to Marge damn near destroyed me.'

Rachel swallowed hard, emotion welling up inside her.

'When my mother first found out that I was pregnant, she wanted to drag me off to a back-street abortionist so that my father need never know,' continued Doris. 'But I wasn't having that. Oh no. I knew I wouldn't be able to keep you, but I wasn't prepared to do what my mother wanted. So I left home before she could make me.'

'I see,' said Rachel in a small voice.

'I did the worst thing a woman can do, Rachel,' Doris went on with tears in her eyes. 'I abandoned my child, and it took me a long time to get over it. I don't think I ever did get over it, not really. Barely a day has passed that I haven't thought about you, wondered how you were getting on. But I comforted myself with the thought that what I did was the best thing for you.'

The small woman looked so achingly forlorn that Rachel reached across the table and gave her hand a comforting squeeze. 'Yes, I believe it was too, so you've nothing to reproach yourself for.'

'It's very hard to come to terms with not having children, you know,' Doris went on.

'I'm sure it must be,' said Rachel, from the heart.

'I bet you're a good mum,' remarked Doris.

'It isn't for me to judge that,' Rachel said modestly, 'but I adore the boys and don't know what I'd do without them.'

'It must be hard for you, bringing them up on your own, though.'

'It hasn't always been easy, especially when they were small and I was so hard up,' she admitted. 'But even then I enjoyed every second of being their mum. They're my life.'

Doris wanted to know more about Tim and Johnnie, and Rachel never needed a second bidding to rave about her offspring.

'They sound smashing,' said Doris after Rachel had entertained her with a few favourite anecdotes.

'They are.' Rachel sipped her tea thoughtfully. 'Did you and Billy never think of adopting a child?'

Doris nodded. 'By the time we gave it any serious thought, we'd gone past the age limit,' she explained. 'We couldn't bring ourselves to give up hope of my becoming pregnant, you see. And when we finally did, it was too late.'

'That's really sad.' Rachel's heart went out to her.

'Yeah, it is. Still, we're happy enough, just the two of us,' Doris said with determined cheeriness. 'And you didn't come here to listen to my troubles.'

Rachel assured her that she didn't mind, and they went on to talk about other things. Doris seemed keen to know all about Rachel, so she gave her an insight into her life and told her about her doubts about Jeff coming back into the boys' lives. 'Which reminds me, I must be going,' she said, 'or they'll be waiting for me on the doorstep.'

'Thanks for letting me put the record straight,' said Doris.

'I've enjoyed it,' said Rachel, realising as she spoke that it was true.

'Me too.' Doris put her chiffon headscarf back on, tying it under her chin. 'I feel as though we've barely scratched the surface, though. There's so much more to say . . . thirty years to catch up on.'

Rachel nodded.

'Perhaps we could meet again?' suggested Doris, giving Rachel a cautious look.

Agreeing to this could cause serious family problems for Rachel, especially with Jan. But she felt sorry for Doris and would like to get to know her better, purely as a friend. 'What about Billy?' she enquired.

'On Saturday afternoons we usually do our separate things anyway,' she explained. 'If he isn't on duty and Brentford are playing at home, he goes to see them; if not, he watches the sport on television. If I'm not working I go for a look-around the shops. He'd just assume that's where I was.'

'You'd still be deceiving him, though, wouldn't you?' Rachel pointed out.

Doris sighed. 'I know, it's awful. But this way he can't be hurt by it.' She paused, looking at Rachel persuasively. 'And I really would love to see you again.'

'OK,' agreed Rachel, making a sudden decision. 'I'll meet you in here on your next Saturday off then. Will three o'clock a fortnight today suit you?'

Doris' face lit up. It was the first time Rachel had seen her smile properly and she was transformed completely, her eyes glowing with warmth. 'I'll look forward to that.' She made a wry face. 'I know I don't deserve it.'

Rachel made no comment about that, and they left the café

and went their separate ways. Having pointed out to Doris the error of keeping secrets, Rachel decided with a great deal of remorse that she wasn't going to tell Marge or Jan about her future arrangement with Doris. To steal a phrase from Doris, it was kinder this way.

Lorna told Ben she wanted them to go out for a drink that Saturday evening. 'It'll make a change for us to go out socially together,' she said.

This was perfectly true. Usually on a Saturday night she went out to the cinema with a friend from work and he went down to the pub for a pint.

As they settled at a table in their local, she with a gin and tonic, he with a pint of bitter, Ben thought how attractive she looked. She was wearing a black polo-necked sweater and tight trousers which showed off her figure. It was nice to see her back on form again, taking an interest in her appearance and full of life.

'It was a really good idea of yours for us to have a night out together,' he remarked, taking the head off his pint.

'Actually, I do have an ulterior motive,' she informed him, giving him a sheepish look.

'Oh, really?'

'Yes.' She knocked back her gin and tonic. 'I have something to tell you, and I thought it best if we were in a public place so that you can't argue about it.'

'Sounds to me as though you're about to tell me you've met someone new,' he suggested.

'I've met a lot of new people since I've been back at work,' she said. 'But that isn't it.'

'What is it, then?'

'I'm moving out, Ben,' she announced with a note of triumph in her voice. 'Getting out from under your feet. Getting a place of my own.'

'You mean you're going to live alone?' he said with predictable wariness.

'That's right,' she told him brightly. 'I thought you might have doubts about it.'

'Surely you didn't think I'd object, though?' he said. 'The way things are between us.'

'No, of course not,' she was quick to point out. 'But you're the sort of bloke who'd feel duty-bound to try and talk me out of it, however much you want your own space back. Because you'll be afraid I'll find it hard going on my own.'

He didn't disagree, just waited for her to go on.

'A ground-floor flat has recently come on to the books at the office,' she explained. 'It's dead convenient, just around the corner from work.'

'Sounds perfect,' he said.

'I think so,' she told him. 'It's only a one-bedroom place, but it's big enough for me. Anyway, I've made an offer and it's been accepted.'

'Can you afford it?' he asked.

'Yeah. I'm going to use the money I had put by from the sale of my old place for the deposit,' she explained, 'and I can afford the repayments now that I'm working again.'

Ben was consumed both with relief and with guilt for being so pleased about her imminent departure. 'Are you sure you're up to living alone?' he asked her.

'Yeah, I'm pretty certain I'll be all right,' she said.

'What's made you decide to do it?' he enquired. 'I hope you've been comfortable at my place.'

'A bit too comfortable, I'm afraid,' she admitted with a wry grin.

'Oh?'

'You've been wonderful, letting me stay and looking after me for more than two years,' she said, leaning over and touching his hand briefly. 'You couldn't possibly know how much I appreciate it.'

The sudden release from the burden made him feel emotional. 'I think I do,' he said with a lump in his throat.

'Unfortunately, I got used to the security of knowing you

were there for me,' she confessed. 'I got scared to make a move.'

'You don't have to move out. You can stay for as long as you like,' he said, ardently hoping she wouldn't change her mind.

'I know that, Ben,' she said, 'but you need your space and I need mine.'

'I can't deny that,' he agreed. 'Just as long as you're sure you can manage on your own.'

'It's time I gave it a try anyway. I've been reliant on you for far too long.' She gave him a grin. 'And don't pretend you're not pleased, because I know you are.'

'Well . . .'

'If I hadn't been in such a pathetic state when I came out of hospital, I would never have lumbered you like I did,' she said. 'But I felt so damned weak and helpless, and you were the only person who was there for me to turn to.'

'I know.' It was so much easier to be sympathetic now he knew she was going.

'I should have moved out sooner than this,' she admitted. 'I've been able to manage for some time.'

'It doesn't matter.'

'I just couldn't pluck up the courage to strike out on my own,' she said.

'But now you have, and I'm proud of you,' he smiled.

'Oh.' She coloured up. 'That's nice.'

'I mean it.'

'Well, when this place came up, I knew I had better make a move now or run the risk of relying on you for the rest of my life,' she admitted.

He shook his head. 'I don't believe that,' he said. 'You'd have found the courage sooner or later.'

'Be that as it may,' she continued, 'once I've got settled into my new place, perhaps we should think in terms of getting a divorce . . . It would tidy things up.'

'Maybe it would be best.' There was no acrimony between

them over this final step. They both knew it was the right thing to do. 'But in the meantime, I hope it works out for you.'

'I'm going to make sure it does.' She was very positive.' I've got a job and a few friends; I'll be all right.'

'Well, if you're sure it's what you want, I can only wish you well,' he said.

'Thanks, Ben,' she replied, brushing his hand with hers again. 'So, how about getting some more drinks to celebrate us both getting our lives back?'

'Sure.' He gave her a questioning look. 'Same again?'

'Please.'

As he walked over to the bar, he felt quite light-hearted about Lorna's decision. But he couldn't help thinking that the return of his freedom had come too late in one important respect. He'd already lost the woman he loved.

Chapter Nineteen

It was most unusual for Doris to be late for her meeting with Rachel. She was always at the café first. Guessing that she'd probably had to wait longer than usual for a bus, Rachel ordered some tea and settled down to wait for her, mulling over the situation in general.

It was now March, and she and Doris had been seeing each other every second Saturday afternoon since January. Rachel enjoyed Doris' down-to-earth company, and their mutual interest in each other's lives meant the conversation never flagged. They got on so well, Rachel even confided in her about Ben and Jeff and all the various complications.

In retrospect she could see that they had advanced from being strangers with a guarded expectation of each other to friends with a growing rapport. Her pleasure was somewhat diminished by the fact that she hadn't told her family she was seeing Doris, something that had been possible only because their meetings took place when the boys were with Jeff.

Her own hypocrisy appalled her. She was doing something she had condemned her parents for: protecting their feelings by keeping a secret. She'd been weak; she'd allowed Jan's attitude to influence her judgement. She knew there would be all-out war if her sister got to know about the meetings, so to keep the peace, she had said nothing.

Now Rachel frowned at her watch. Where was Doris? She was nearly an hour late. Rachel would have to go soon so that she was at home when Jeff brought the boys back. But Doris looked forward to their meetings; she wouldn't let Rachel down unless there was a very good reason. What *had* happened to her?

Rachel waited a bit longer then left. She went to the nearest phone box and got through to the dry-cleaner's, thinking that perhaps Doris had had to go in to work unexpectedly. The woman who answered the phone said briskly that Doris wasn't working today. Telling her that she was a friend of Doris', Rachel explained what had happened, guessing that the voice on the other end was that of the sour-faced counter assistant she'd encountered when she'd called at the shop.

'It isn't like Doris not to turn up,' said the woman in a more helpful manner. 'She wouldn't let anyone down unless something important had come up to detain her.'

'That's what I thought.'

'Perhaps you should go to her house,' the woman suggested.

'Yes, I'll do that,' muttered Rachel worriedly.

'I hope she's OK.'

'Me too,' said Rachel and hung up.

A visit to the Finns' residence was not a prospect she relished, because it would send Doris into a panic and mean more lies if Billy was at home. But she couldn't rest until she knew what had happened, though she'd have to go home first because of the boys. How she hated all this deceit, she thought, as she walked around the corner to her car parked in a side street.

'Where are we going, Mum?' asked Tim from the back of the car as they headed along the Great West Road to Brentford.

'To see a lady called Doris.' Rachel had had to bring the boys with her. Asking Jeff to look after them hadn't been a sensible alternative, because he would undoubtedly have mistaken such a request for encouragement.

'Who's Doris?' enquired Johnnie chattily.

'Just someone I know,' Rachel told him.

'Is she your friend?' probed Tim with the relentless compulsion children have to ask questions.

'Yes, that's right.' It wasn't the whole truth, but at least it wasn't a lie, she told herself.

'Is she your best friend?' asked Johnnie, who always wanted the details.

'Grown-ups don't bother about that sort of thing as much as children do,' she explained.

This provoked a discussion between the two of them about the merits and otherwise of their own friends at school, which kept them entertained for the rest of the journey. Rachel located the Finns' house and parked outside. Telling the boys to wait in the car, she hurried up to the front door and rang the bell. As well as being in a state of anxiety about Doris, she was also filled with nervous apprehension about entering into forbidden territory.

A big man with a lot of hair and a warm smile opened the door. 'Yes, love?' he said.

'Is Doris in?' she enquired.

He frowned. 'She's in,' he told her, 'but she's laid up at the moment.'

'Laid up?' repeated Rachel, looking worried. 'She hasn't gone down with that horrible Hong Kong flu that's still hanging around, has she?'

'No. Nothing like that,' he informed her. 'She's had a bit of an accident, as it happens. Missed her footing on the garden path when she was hanging some washing on the line this morning and took a tumble.'

'Oh dear,' exclaimed Rachel, 'poor Doris. Is she badly hurt?'

'Not seriously, thank goodness. She's got a few bruises and a sprained ankle but nothing's broken,' he explained. 'So she should be all right after a few days' rest. But she can't get about at the moment.'

'Ah, what a shame,' sympathised Rachel. 'Still, at least she didn't do any serious damage.'

'And that's a blessing,' he agreed. 'But what am I doing keeping you outside in the cold? Come on in. Doris isn't in bed. I've made her comfortable on the sofa downstairs and I'm sure she could do with a spot of company.'

'I won't bother her if she's poorly,' Rachel told him, hoping to avoid more deception. 'I only called on the off chance.' She looked towards her car. 'I've got my two little boys with me. I don't expect she'll want a couple of boisterous kids around when she's not feeling well.'

'I'm sure she'd love to see you all,' he insisted. 'Just pop in to say hello. It'll cheer her up.'

The warmth of his welcome was irresistible. So Rachel went to get the boys.

Despite the tense undertones – of which Billy seemed happily oblivious – a pleasant air of friendliness reigned over the gathering in the Finns' living room. A fire crackled in the hearth, the lights were on, and bright multicoloured curtains covered the gathering dusk outside. Doris rather cautiously held court from her bed on the sofa and Billy produced tea and biscuits, apologising for having no squash or pop for the children to drink and explaining to them that he and Doris weren't used to having little ones around. He and the boys struck up an instant rapport. An ardent Brentford fan, Billy teased them about being Fulham supporters.

There was only one really bad moment for Rachel, who'd been introduced by Doris as a cousin far removed.

'I don't remember you mentioning a cousin called Rachel,' remarked Billy when Rachel was about to leave, 'though I can see the family likeness.'

'It's a very distant connection,' fibbed Doris. 'Rachel's the daughter of a second cousin of mine, so I don't know how many times removed that makes us.'

'Well, it's been lovely to see you, Rachel, however distantly you're related,' said the unsuspecting Billy.

'We've enjoyed ourselves too,' responded Rachel,

checking that the boys' coats were properly fastened. 'But we'd better be going now. My parents are expecting us for tea.'

'We hope you'll come and see us again,' said the sociable Billy. 'Don't we, Doris?'

'Yeah, that would be lovely,' agreed Doris, who was looking very strained. Fortunately, thought Rachel, Billy was putting this down to her accident.

'We'll get something arranged when Doris is feeling better,' suggested Rachel, careful not to make any commitment.

'Mind how you go now,' said Billy, seeing them off at the door.

'We will,' she assured him.

Hurrying out to the car, still glowing inwardly from Billy's friendliness, Rachel could understand why Doris didn't want to upset and risk losing a gem of a man like him. But now that she had actually met him, Rachel also wondered if Doris might have underestimated the limit of his capacity for forgiveness and understanding.

'I'm fed up with all this deception,' declared Rachel, two weeks later, when she and Doris were in the café having a post-mortem about Rachel's visit to her house. 'It's bad enough keeping our meetings secret from my family, but I felt really terrible actually telling lies to Billy. But what else could I do? I had to find out if you were all right.'

'I appreciate your concern,' Doris told her. 'I was worried to death about letting you down, but I had no way of letting you know what had happened as I couldn't get out to the phone box.'

'Never mind,' sighed Rachel. 'It turned out all right in the end, didn't it?'

'Yeah, it did.' Doris raised her eyes, tutting. 'But I nearly had a fit when you walked in,' she said. 'I was dying to tell Billy who you really are.' She gave a helpless shrug. 'But I daren't.'

'Don't you think you might feel better if you were to be honest with him?' suggested Rachel.

'Maybe I would, but I'm damned sure he wouldn't,' was Doris' answer to that.'

'Oh well, it's up to you what you do about that,' said Rachel with an air of decisiveness, 'but I've decided to come clean with my family about these regular meetings you and I are having. I can't stand all this secrecy.'

'You've not told them, then?' Doris hadn't realised.

'I thought it would be better not to,' Rachel admitted ruefully. 'My sister is dead set against my making a friend of you. She thinks it will hurt my mother's feelings. But I can't bear all this hole-and-corner stuff, so I'm going to do what I should have done at the beginning and tell them.'

'Marge has nothing to fear from me, you know,' Doris assured her.

Rachel seized the opportunity to make certain the other woman was fully apprised of the situation. 'I've known that all along, Doris,' she said, determined to make things clear. 'And the reason I've been so sure is because Marge is my mother and always will be, despite the biological situation. No one can ever take her place.'

Doris' eyes filled with tears. 'Yeah, I understand what you're saying,' she said thickly. 'I'd be lying if I were to say that I've never hoped it could be different between you and me. But I don't expect anything from you. Just to see you now and again for a chat is all I ask.' She gulped, lowering her eyes momentarily. 'But I realise I have no right even to that, and I'll understand if you feel you must stop doing it. The last thing I want is to make trouble for you with your family.'

Rachel stared hard into her tea cup, struggling with a lump in her throat. 'If Mum would rather I stopped seeing you, then that's what I'll do,' she said with necessary candour, 'because she really does mean everything to me.'

'I know,' said Doris sadly.

* * *

On Monday morning Rachel told Jan that she would be out of the office for a couple of hours and left the boathouse before her sister had a chance to ask questions. She headed for Wilbur Terrace, knowing that her mother would be on her own.

Sitting at Marge's kitchen table, Rachel bared her soul. She told her the reason for Doris' initial coldness, and that she'd been seeing Doris and had grown to like her. Nothing was left out. 'I didn't tell you I was seeing her because I thought you might be hurt,' she told Marge.

For the first time, Marge was completely honest with Rachel about her feelings. 'I wasn't so much hurt as terrified that I'd lose you to Doris when you said you were going to try and find her.'

'You didn't seem to mind at the time,' Rachel mentioned.

'I didn't want to stop you doing it,' she explained. 'I knew it was something you had to do before you could be at peace with yourself. I lived in hope that Doris wouldn't replace me.'

'She could never do that,' Rachel assured her ardently. 'What you and I have is very special to me. No one else could even come close to it. I've told her that.'

'I'm so glad you've come to me and told me the truth,' Marge said.

'I've hated deceiving you,' Rachel told her. 'I've been feeling dreadful about it. But I felt so sorry for Doris. She seems so vulnerable somehow, despite her chirpy attitude.'

'Does she?'

'Yeah. She has a really good marriage, but not having children has left its mark on both her and Billy,' Rachel explained. 'I just wanted to be a pal to her, that's all. Never anything more than that. She has Billy, of course, but she seems to need a woman friend.'

'And you must carry on being a friend to her, dear,' advised Marge.

'And you won't mind? Because I'll not see her again if you do,' Rachel told her.

'No, I don't mind. I know I've nothing to fear.' Their unity was so strong, it was a tangible thing. 'Now that you've opened your heart to me, I know that our relationship can withstand anything. You go ahead and bring a little happiness into Doris' life with my blessing. Let her see her grandsons every so often too.'

'Oh, Mum,' said Rachel, her eyes brimming with tears, 'you really are a diamond.'

'Go on with you.' Marge was being affectionately dismissive but she was close to tears herself.

Rachel guessed that Jan wouldn't take the news as well as her mother had, and her stomach churned nervously on the way back to the boathouse. Before she had time to lose her nerve, she asked Jan to come into her office, closed the door and got on with what had to be said. She told her sister where she'd just been and repeated what she had told their mother.

'Why, you sly cow,' said Jan accusingly. 'Sneaking off to see that woman without telling any of us. Poor Mum.'

'Mum is fine about it.'

'Fine, my arse,' proclaimed Jan.

'She really is, Jan.' Rachel was determined to stand her ground over this. 'She knows that Doris is no threat to her.'

'It suits you to believe that so that you can keep in contact with her with an easy conscience,' said Jan, trembling with rage, her eyes bright with angry tears. 'You make me sick.'

'I know,' said Rachel wearily. 'But I'm not going to let that stop me seeing Doris.'

'Aren't your real family enough for you?' asked Jan.

'Of course they are,' said Rachel. 'If only you'd let me explain.'

'What is there to explain?' Rachel had never seen Jan so furious. She was more than just angry; she was deeply distressed, almost manic on this subject. 'You obviously think more of this Doris Finn than you do of the woman who's been a real mother to you, or you wouldn't hurt Mum by persisting with this relationship.'

Jan's unreasonable attitude was beginning to take its toll on Rachel's patience. She could feel repressed anger building inside her. 'You really are out of order on this one, Jan. You're my sister, not my keeper,' she blurted out. 'It isn't your place to tell me who I can and can't see.'

'Oh, so I'm just your sister and my opinion doesn't count,' she raged. 'Well, I'm the one who's looked after your kids for you whenever you've needed it. It was me who gave you moral support by the bucketload when your husband walked out on you. It's me and Pete and Mum and Dad who have always been here for you, not Doris Finn.'

'I know that, Jan,' said Rachel, lowering her voice to a murmur. 'And I'm sorry I'm upsetting you so much.'

'Not half as sorry as I am,' interrupted Jan, her neck and face suffused with scarlet, eyes blazing. 'You can stick your excuses and . . .' She paused for a moment. 'And you can stick your job.'

Before Rachel could say another word, Jan rushed out. Rachel followed her into the other office, where she was already putting her coat on with sharp, angry movements.

'Jan, don't go like this, please . . .'

'Just get out of my way,' said Jan. 'I'm not staying to work out my notice, I'd sooner lose the money.'

'Listen to me, Jan . . .'

Jan turned to face Rachel for her parting shot. 'Don't say another word, just keep out of my life.' She paused, her breath coming in short bursts, the blood seeming to drain from her flushed face. 'You can collect your own kids from school this afternoon. Not only do I quit the job here, I quit as general dogsbody as well.'

Rachel realised the futility of rational argument while Jan was in this unreasonable mood. Bruised by that blistering finale, she stood back and let her go, questioning her own behaviour. Had she been wrong to make a friend of Doris? Had she taken Jan for granted? Standing there in the small general office, she searched her conscience.

She'd been wrong to hide her meetings with Doris from the family. Yes, she accepted that. But she couldn't truthfully castigate herself for wanting to be a friend to Doris. And as for treating Jan like a dogsbody, that just wasn't true. She'd always insisted on paying her for any child-minding, even when she'd been hard up. She paid her more than the going rate for her services at the boathouse, let her be as flexible as she liked with the hours, and looked after Kelly whenever Jan needed her to, for whatever reason.

Jan wasn't being fair, she told herself as she went back into her own office and sat down at the desk, still trembling with reaction. Her sister was barely recognisable as the woman she knew and loved. Until recently, she'd always been such an easy-going, jolly kind of person. Nowadays she didn't seem to like anyone. Even poor little Kelly got a scolding for the slightest thing. Rachel lingered on the suspicion she'd had before: that her friendship with Doris wasn't the real cause of Jan's fury and was merely an outlet for something else.

Forcing herself to work, she typed some estimates and dealt with several phone calls, but her mind wasn't on the job. As well as the personal anguish of a split with her sister, there were the practicalities to consider. She couldn't bear to replace Jan in the office, but neither could she run the business efficiently without help. Jan was very good at the job and when she was her normal self they worked well together.

Rerunning the altercation in her mind, she sieved through every painful word. And then she heard it, loud and clear. Somewhere beneath all that rage was a cry for help.

She shot up, grabbed her bag and dragged on her coat en route for the workshop. Telling Ted Barratt she had to leave on urgent family business, she hurried out of the boathouse.

'What do *you* want,' asked Jan when she answered the door to her sister, her face blotchy from crying. 'I thought I told you to keep out of my life.'

'That's what came out of your mouth,' replied Rachel, 'but

I don't believe it came from your heart.'

'What are you rambling on about?' Jan said with seething impatience.

'Are we going to discuss this on the doorstep or can I come in?' Rachel wanted to know.

Scowling, Jan moved aside to let Rachel into the hall. 'Do you want a cup of coffee?' she asked grudgingly, walking down the passage towards the kitchen.

'No, not really,' said Rachel, following her.

'I'm making one for myself,' Jan informed her, still sounding miserable but seeming calmer suddenly, as though all the fight had gone out of her, leaving her drained.

'OK, I'll join you then,' said Rachel, sitting down at the table while her sister put the kettle on.

'I hope you're not expecting an apology,' stated Jan, giving her sister a withering look, teaspoon poised over the coffee jar.

'I'm not that much of an optimist,' Rachel told her straight, 'but I am determined to find out what's going on.'

'Going on?'

'What's behind the foul mood you've been in these past few months,' she said.

'You know how I feel about you and Doris Finn,' Jan replied, spooning coffee into the cups. 'Just hearing her name is guaranteed to put me in a temper.'

'Your black mood has nothing to do with Doris Finn.' Rachel raised her hands in a halting gesture as her sister seemed about to let rip. 'Oh, I know you don't approve of my seeing her, but this violent disapproval is only happening because you're worried sick about something else.'

'I'm sure I don't know what you're talking about,' denied Jan haughtily.

'What is it, Jan?' Rachel asked in a gentle tone. 'What is it that's getting you into such a state?'

'Your determination to break up our family, that's what's upsetting me, as you very well know,' Jan insisted.

'Are you still having menstrual problems?' persisted Rachel. 'Is that it?'

Jan swung round. 'No, it isn't!' she blasted.

Rachel knew she was lying, despite the vehemence of her denial. 'I'm sure something can be done to help you,' she went on, ignoring Jan's reply.

'No, there's nothing, not with this.' Realising she had given the game away, Jan put her hand to her head. 'Oh God, Rachel, why can't you keep your big nose out of my business?'

'In the same way as you keep yours out of mine, you mean?' retorted Rachel pointedly.

'That's different,' Jan protested. 'The Doris Finn business affects us all.'

'And your change of personality affects us all,' Rachel pointed out, 'not least young Kelly.'

'I hope you're not about to start telling me how to bring up my daughter.' Jan's voice had risen to a shriek and Rachel braced herself for another verbal attack. But instead her sister's face crumpled and she collapsed into tears, head bent, the spoon she was holding dropping to the floor with a clatter. 'Oh, my Lord, Rachel, what's happening to me?'

Rachel was on her feet, her arms around her sobbing sister. 'There, there, love, what is it?'

'I don't know what's the matter with me and that's the truth,' Jan confessed through heaving sobs. 'But I do know it's probably something serious.'

'You sit down while I make the coffee,' instructed Rachel, leading her sister to a chair, 'and you can tell me all about it.'

'Having heavy and prolonged periods has probably made you anaemic,' suggested Rachel as the story unfolded. 'That would account for your being under the weather, which in turn caused the bad temper.'

'Everything has got on top of me because I'm feeling so washed out,' admitted Jan, who had finally stopped crying and was noticeably less tense. 'I knew I was being hellish but

I haven't been able to stop myself.'

'I thought not,' said Rachel in an understanding manner.

'I'm sorry I've given you such a hard time about Doris,' Jan went on. 'I'm not happy about it and that's a fact, but it's got out of proportion inside my head. It's as though it's someone else flying up in the air over the slightest little thing. I've been out of control. What with feeling so worn out the whole time and worried to death about what's causing the symptoms, my nerves have been in shreds.'

'I take it you've not been to see the doctor,' guessed Rachel.

Jan shook her head, looking sheepish. 'I've been feeling as guilty as hell about that, too, because I knew I should go. But I kept hoping it would clear up. And it would seem better for a while, then all hell would break loose again. They've been coming so often I've been more on than off.' She lowered her head, looking at Rachel from beneath her lids. 'The truth is, kid, I'm a coward. I'm scared stiff of what they'll find out is wrong with me. That's why I wouldn't tell you what was happening. I knew you'd nag me into going to see the doctor.'

'You're right about that,' Rachel told her. 'The sooner you get medical advice, the sooner something can be done about it. You can't go on like this. You must get an appointment with the doctor right away.'

'I know,' muttered Jan, sounding none too sure. 'I'm just so scared.'

'If there was anything wrong with Kelly or Pete, you'd have them at that surgery before they knew what was happening to them,' Rachel reminded her. 'You owe it to them to do the same for yourself.'

Jan nodded. 'You're right, of course,' she said.

'I'll go with you to the doctor's,' suggested Rachel.

'To make sure I do actually go, eh?' said Jan.

'Yes,' admitted Rachel frankly, 'and also to give you some moral support.' She finished her coffee and stood up in a purposeful manner. 'And the sooner the better. I'll get on the phone to the surgery right away and fix you an appointment.'

'Thanks, Rachel, I needed someone to give me a shove,' Jan said.

'And I won't let up now,' Rachel made it clear.

'All those things I said this morning . . . I didn't mean them.'

'Forget it. The important thing is to get you well again,' Rachel said, and went to the telephone in the hall.

Whether or not it was Rachel's influence Doris couldn't be sure, but that same day she decided she couldn't live any longer with the secret she had kept from Billy.

So, over their meal that evening, she told him everything. He listened in astonished silence until she had finished the whole story. Her heart beat wildly and she was praying silently as she waited for his reaction.

'I can't believe you've kept something like that from me all these years,' he said at last.

'I can hardly believe it myself,' she admitted.

'I've always thought our marriage was based on honesty,' he told her in a bitter tone.

'And it has been,' she assured him.

'With a secret like that between us?' was his curt reply. 'I don't think so.'

'That's the only thing I've kept from you, Billy.' Her hopes that he might take the news well were fading fast. He was obviously very upset. 'I swear to you.'

'You have a grown-up daughter and two grandchildren that I knew nothing about,' he said, shaking his head as though mystified. 'I can't take it in.'

'I didn't know about the grandchildren until recently myself,' she pointed out.

'Even so . . .'

'Anyway, Rachel isn't my daughter and her sons aren't my grandchildren,' she pointed out. 'They are already very well catered for in that department.'

'They're still your flesh and blood,' he reminded her grimly.

'But they're not mine. You've known for all these years that it was my fault we couldn't have children and you've never said a word.'

'We don't know that for sure,' she mentioned.

'Yes we do,' he insisted gruffly. 'You've had a child, so there can't be anything wrong with you in that direction.'

'Maybe some women only conceive at a certain time in their life,' she suggested without managing to sound very convincing. 'It could be that I developed some fault later on that stopped me getting pregnant, or that I just wasn't as fertile later on.'

'That's a load of rubbish and you know it,' he stated categorically.

'Not necessarily . . .'

'That's why you didn't tell me you had a daughter, isn't it?' he continued, as though she hadn't spoken. 'Because you didn't have the courage or decency to let me know that I wasn't a real man.'

'Oh, don't be so ridiculous, Billy, of course you're a real man,' she contradicted fiercely. 'But I knew that would be your attitude towards it, so, yes, that's why I didn't tell you when it became obvious that we weren't going to have any children.'

'And before that?'

'Common sense told me to keep it to myself when we first got together, given the attitude to that sort of thing in those days,' she explained. 'I meant to tell you later on, when I trusted you not to hold it against me. But by then I was afraid you'd be hurt because I hadn't told you before . . . then there was the thing about my not getting pregnant, and, well . . . it just never got said. I really was trying to spare you, Billy.'

'I'm not a child who needs protecting, or some weakling without the guts to face up to his own failings,' Billy retorted bitterly. 'If you'd told me the truth, at least I would have come to terms with it, eventually. We could have talked about it. But now . . . I mean, how do you think it feels at this stage in my life to find out that you have a daughter by someone else, when I couldn't give you any children at all? To know that all these years you've been blaming me, probably even pitying me for not being a proper man?'

'I have never done either of those things,' she stated firmly. 'Surely you know me better than that.'

'I thought I knew you, but apparently not,' was his terse reply. 'You could have been thinking anything for all I know. You were very disappointed that we didn't have kids, you can't deny that.'

'Yes,' she admitted, 'I was *very* disappointed. We both were. And yes, I did think the problem probably didn't lie with me. But I *never, ever* blamed you. I accepted the fact that we weren't meant to have children. You have always meant more to me than anything else. I married you because I loved you as a man, not as a provider of children.'

He shook his head slowly. 'Rachel . . . your daughter,' he muttered, as though he still couldn't believe it.

'Only technically,' she pointed out. 'Rachel and I can never be more than friends.'

'That's beside the point.' Billy had pushed his plate away and was leaning on the table, his brown eyes resting on her coolly. 'If Rachel hadn't turned up out of the blue, I probably would never have got to know about her.'

Doris ran her tongue over her dry lips. Now that she had wiped the slate clean, she didn't want there to be any more lies between them. 'I can't possibly know whether that's true or not,' she admitted, 'but I do suspect it's her influence that inspired me to tell you.'

'Because you were scared she might let the cat out of the bag?' he accused her.

'No, that isn't the reason, Billy,' she denied. 'I knew she wouldn't say anything to you. I've told you because I didn't want this one secret to be there between us any more. It's troubled me for long enough.'

He didn't reply, seeming lost in thought. 'You even got her

to lie about who she was when she came to the house,' he said, looking up bleakly.

'Yes, I did,' she admitted shamefaced. 'I'm not proud of it, but it seemed the only thing to do at the time.'

'It isn't your having had a baby before we got married that hurts me,' he told her grimly. 'It's the fact that you didn't trust me enough to tell me about it from the start.'

'I did trust you,' she cried emotionally, 'but things were different in those days, you know they were. I've told you why I kept quiet.'

'All these years, Doris,' he went on, as though her explanation hadn't made any impact on him at all, 'and I could have sworn you were on the level with me.'

'I have been about everything except that one thing, honestly,' she insisted.

'I have no way of knowing that, though, have I?' he told her, sounding very troubled. 'You could have deceived me about other things, too.'

'I haven't though,' she said, reaching for his hand. 'Please forgive me, Billy.'

He pulled away and stood up. 'It isn't a question of my forgiving you,' he declared. 'I feel so betrayed, Doris. I don't know if I can learn to trust you again.'

'Surely you can't doubt that, after all the years we've been together,' she entreated. 'This is me, your wife Doris. OK, so I made a mistake in not telling you this one thing. But I thought I was doing right at the time.'

His hands were clamped tightly to his head. 'I'm going out,' he informed her coldly.

'Don't shut me out, Billy, please,' she begged him. 'We have to talk about this.'

'We've done quite enough talking,' he told her. 'I need to be on my own now.'

'Where are you going?' she asked.

'I don't know.'

'I'll come with you,' she suggested in desperation.

He looked at her, his eyes hot with rage. 'I want to be by myself, woman, can't you understand that?' he growled.

Doris had never seen him like this before. 'Billy, please ...' she began.

'Just leave me alone.'

His reaction was an emotional body blow which left her reeling. She sank weakly down on a chair, leaning her elbows on the table, and listened as he got his coat from the hall. As he left the house, the slam of the front door pierced her heart. Rather than bringing them closer together, confessing to Billy felt like the worst mistake of her life.

The doctor's waiting room was packed with patients, every seat taken. People were coughing and sniffing, babies were crying, the receptionists answered a constantly ringing telephone. The room smelt musty, the air heavy with a sickly mixture of antiseptic, cough mixture and stale clothes.

'Perhaps we should come back another time,' said Jan in a hushed voice, 'when the doctor isn't so busy.'

'Oh, no.' Rachel was firm. 'You can forget any ideas about getting out of it.'

'We'll be here all day at this rate,' said Jan, who had a serious case of cold feet.

'You've got an appointment with the doctor and we are not leaving here until you've seen him,' Rachel was adamant.

'My appointment was for ten o'clock,' Jan said. 'It's quarter to eleven now. I think we should go.'

'Since when did a doctor's appointment ever happen on time?' Rachel pointed out.

'I still think I should come back another time,' Jan went on as though her sister hadn't spoken.

'Stop worrying,' Rachel advised her.

The conversation came to an abrupt halt when the doctor poked his head around the door and read Jan's name from a file he was holding. She didn't move and Rachel thought she was going to lose her nerve completely and make a run for it.

She gave her sister's arm an encouraging squeeze. Jan eventually got up in a rush and followed the doctor. Rachel was inwardly trembling herself.

To take her mind off Jan's problem, she tried to interest herself in an out-of-date women's magazine from a well-thumbed pile on the table. But she couldn't concentrate, so she occupied her mind with thoughts of the office and all the work that would be piling up while she wasn't there. Thank God Jan had retracted her resignation. The thought of managing without her added to the tension knots already pulling tight in her stomach. She was passing the time by wondering how many queries would be waiting for her when Jan reappeared. All else left Rachel's mind when she saw the look on her sister's face.

'Well?' she said, as they walked out of the surgery together. 'What did he say?'

'I've got to go into hospital, Rachel,' Jan said, whey-faced and grim.

'Oh.' Rachel tried to sound calm, to hide her instinctive feeling of panic. 'Did he say what they're going to do?'

'They've got to scrape my womb to find out what's causing the problem,' she explained nervously.

'I know women who've had that done,' said Rachel to reassure her. 'It isn't a major operation.'

'I'm not bothered about that,' Jan said. 'It's what they'll find that's worrying me. If there's anything untoward, I'll have to have more surgery.' She paused, looking tenser than ever. 'Could be even worse than that.'

Rachel knew exactly what was on Jan's mind. 'You're letting your imagination run away with you,' she advised her. 'It probably won't be anything sinister at all. And the sooner they know what the trouble is, the sooner they can put it right.'

'Yeah, I know,' Jan uttered through dry lips.

'Did he say how long you'll have to wait?' asked Rachel.

'That's the scary thing,' she said shakily. 'He wants me to

go in right away. He's going to try to get me a bed in the next couple of days.'

'That's a good thing,' encouraged Rachel, linking arms with her sister. 'You don't want to be kept hanging about.'

'He must think it's something serious, though,' Jan said, 'to be making it a priority.'

'He's just being careful.' Rachel was determinedly positive. 'Doctors always cover their backs.'

'I hope that's the reason,' said Jan. 'But even apart from the worry of that side of it, I can't just drop everything and go into hospital, can I? I have a child to look after and a job to go to. I told the doctor all that and he just said I'll have to make arrangements.'

'And he's right. Don't worry about a thing,' Rachel assured her. 'I'll take care of everything.'

'How can you when you've a full-time job yourself?' Jan asked worriedly.

'Mum will help out and I'll take some time off if necessary,' she announced firmly.

'How will you manage at the office?' Jan wanted to know.

'I managed before and I'll do it again,' said Rachel. 'I'll get a temp in to cover for you if you're going to be away for any length of time . . . then your job will be waiting for you when you're ready to come back. And between us, Mum and I will look after Kelly, so you can go into hospital with an easy mind and make the most of being waited on.'

'Thanks, Rachel.'

'A pleasure.'

Rachel was careful not to let her sister know just how concerned she was. But the truth of the matter was, doctors didn't send people into hospital this quickly unless there were serious implications – not National Health patients anyway.

Chapter Twenty

Jeff was drowning his sorrows in his local pub after paying Rachel a surprise midweek visit that hadn't gone well. He was getting nowhere with her. For more than two months his conduct had been exemplary. He'd proved how devoted he was as a father without so much as a whisper to her of a romantic nature. But still she refused to allow him his rightful place in the family.

Earlier this evening his impatience had got the better of him and he'd turned up on her doorstep and begged her to take him back. She'd repeated what she'd said before, that it wouldn't work out, and asked him not to bring the subject up again. She'd been pleasant enough but immovable on the subject in this new assertive way she had of carrying on.

As if that wasn't enough, she'd informed him that he couldn't see the boys on Saturday this week because they were all going to the river to watch the University Boat Race with Rachel's family. Everyone was going to her place afterwards to make a day of it; a regular thing now that the boys were old enough to take an interest, apparently. He wasn't invited to join them, he noted blackly. In the mood he was in, the fact that he didn't want to go anyway because he couldn't stand his in-laws didn't stop him feeling sulky about his exclusion.

It was all so frustrating. Everything he wanted was within his grasp – a comfortable home, a share in a family business, a beautiful wife and two fine sons – and he couldn't get his hands on any of it because Rachel had become so stubborn. She wasn't the woman he remembered at all. She'd known her place when he'd been with her, he'd made sure of that.

In all honesty, he couldn't claim that he got nothing from the situation as it stood at the moment, because he'd grown to love his sons and enjoyed seeing them. But a few hours of their company each week wasn't enough. He wanted to live with them in his proper role as their mother's husband and head of the household. And Rachel just wouldn't have it.

The more he thought about it, the angrier he became. He ordered another double whisky to calm himself. It had the opposite effect, so he ordered another. He carried on drinking in search of oblivion. By the time he left the pub, he was staggering and beyond coherent thought. But even in his inebriated state, his determination to get Rachel back stood, however long it took.

Arthur was in a pub that night, too. But far from drowning his sorrows, he was celebrating his good fortune, having just purchased a high-quality car at about a thousand pounds less than the retail price. This wasn't just a car, it was a white Mercedes with a soft top, a status symbol, proof that Arthur Banks was a man of means. He already lived in classy accommodation and wore smart clothes; now he had the motor to complete his image.

To add to his enjoyment was the fact that he'd conned the vendor of the car so effortlessly. The poor sap hadn't stood a chance against someone with the nous of Arthur Banks. That was the good thing about dealing with the general public, they were so wonderfully gullible. A professional car dealer wouldn't have let him get away with such a ridiculous offer. But the man had been looking for a quick sale, and Arthur had had the advantage of being able to pay him in cash. No cheque to clear, no complicated hire-purchase.

Who else in this pub could produce three thousand

smackers immediately? Nobody, if he was any judge. That was what came of having good contacts and a lucrative sideline in dodgy gear. He declared what he earned from the legitimate side of the collecting job; the rest went under the mattress.

He smiled at the thought of how pleased Ella would be with their new transport. He hadn't said anything to her about it yet because he wanted to surprise her. Suddenly eager to share it with her, he finished his drink and left. A thrill ran through him as he walked towards the classy white vehicle in the car park.

Getting talking to that bloke in the pub the other night had proved to be a real stroke of luck. The man had wanted to raise some cash quickly and Arthur had been in the market for something special. And now this glorious beast was all his, he thought, as he got in the car and rolled away, the engine hardly making a sound.

'They're coming, they're coming,' shrieked Tim excitedly, peering towards Hammersmith Bridge from the boathouse balcony. 'I think Oxford are in the lead.'

'I think they are too,' yelled Johnnie. 'Come on, Oxford . . . come on.'

All eyes turned towards the bridge for their first sight of the participants in this, the 1970 Boat Race. The riverside was clamorous with excitement, the crowd's noisy support divided between the two crews on this spring day of fresh breezes and intermittent sunshine. It was a colourful scene, observed Rachel, as the sun appeared from behind the clouds, gleaming on the water and enriching the trees along the bank, some not yet in full leaf, others already lush with fresh green foliage. The seagulls looked silver in the sun as they rose to the sky.

Rachel and her party were all shouting for Oxford and sporting dark blue rosettes.

'I hope that isn't just wishful thinking,' was Ron's response to the boys' comments, because Cambridge had beaten Oxford in the two previous races.

'Oh, you of little faith,' laughed Jan.

'Jan's right, Dad,' Rachel joined in light-heartedly. 'That isn't the spirit we want here today.'

There was quite a gathering on the balcony. As well as the family, some of the boathouse staff were also taking advantage of the view of the race from here. Rachel had bought a supply of drinks and savoury snacks to add to the party atmosphere. The whole family had supported Oxford for as far back as she could remember. She wasn't sure why, and thought it was probably because they preferred the darker shade of blue of the supporters' favours. It certainly wasn't because they had any allegiance to one university or the other, since such temples of learning were unknown territory to them. Taking a keen interest in the Boat Race was a tradition in the area where Rachel had grown up and it simply wasn't done to be neutral.

Today, Rachel's enjoyment of the occasion was enhanced by the knowledge that Jan's illness was not terminal. She did have to have a hysterectomy and the usual long period of recuperation afterwards, but the cause of the trouble was fibroids. She had been assured there was no malignancy.

Although Jan wasn't quite her old self because she still had to face major surgery, now that her worst fears had proved to be unfounded she was much less tense and more even-tempered. As yet she didn't have a date for the operation and was continuing with her job at the boathouse.

Unaware that she was being observed from the crowded river walkway, Rachel was entering into the spirit of the occasion with gusto. The tension and excitement grew as the two boats came into view, moving smoothly, the blades striking the water with an easy rhythm, a conflicting roar of encouragement rising from the bank.

'Can we go down to the bank, Mum?' asked Tim as the racing boats sped by, followed by the official launches, leaving a wash behind them. 'It's more exciting down there.'

'Yeah, can we?' enthused both Johnnie and Kelly.

There was a short discussion among the adults as to who should accompany the children. 'I'll go with them,' Rachel offered. 'You lot can stay here and finish your drinks.'

She didn't receive any argument because they were all enjoying the view from the balcony.

'Be back soon,' she said, and hurried through the boathouse and down the stairs after the children.

Ever since Ben and Rachel had parted, Ben had studiously avoided places where he might see her because he knew it would be painful for them both. Before he'd left the firm she'd agreed that he could continue to moor his boat at the boathouse moorings, but he only ever went near it in the early morning or late evening when he knew she wouldn't be around; he paid the rent on the mooring annually by post.

After Lorna's departure, he'd ached to see Rachel, to tell her that he was now free and that he'd never stopped loving her. But he'd decided it wouldn't be fair, might even be seen as insulting. After all, it was nearly three years since they'd split up. She probably had someone else by now.

But on Boat Race day, his good intentions deserted him. Guessing what she would be doing on this day, and that he could probably catch a glimpse of her on the boathouse balcony, he drove to Hammersmith, parked his car in a side street and mingled with the crowds on the river walkway. Just to see her, that was all he wanted. He had no intention of making his presence known or intruding in her life in any way.

Making himself inconspicuous among the crowds a little to the right of the boathouse, he glanced up at the balcony, his heart leaping as he caught sight of her in the centre of the group gathered there. She was as lovely as ever, in a bright blue sweater and jeans, her hair blowing in the wind as she peered in the direction of the oncoming boats, the boys by her side. How they'd grown! A lump rose in his throat at the sight of them, and his heart overflowed with love for her. As he watched, she bent her head to speak to the boys, then they turned and went inside the boathouse.

Being so engrossed in events on the balcony, Ben wasn't paying attention to what was happening around him. But as the crews drew level with where he was, people began running along the towpath, cheering and shouting messages of support, photographers madly snapping. In all the riotous activity, he found himself swept along by the human tide so that he was outside the boathouse before he could do anything about it.

Moving back from the jostling crowds, he was about to make a hasty exit when he heard a high-pitched childish shout. 'Ben! Look, there's Ben, Mum. It's Ben, it really is.'

And before he had time to gather his wits, Tim had thrown himself against him, wrapping his arms tightly around him, his brother close behind.

'Hello, Rachel,' he said.

'Hi, Ben.' Her tone was matter-of-fact despite a thumping heart and a sensation of intense joy at seeing him again. 'How are you?'

'Fine.' His gaze rested on her rosy cheeks and lustrous wind-blown hair. 'You're looking well.'

'You too.' He was thinner than she remembered and had gained a few furrows on his face. But he was still as gorgeous as ever, hair untidy in the breeze, shoulders strong and broad beneath a navy blue sweater.

'Come on,' urged Tim, grabbing Ben's hand and pulling him. 'We're going up there to see if we can get a last look.'

'Look where you're going, you two,' called Rachel as Johnnie and Kelly rushed on ahead, shouting support for the Oxford crew. Rachel and Ben hurried along behind them, with Tim dragging at Ben's hand.

'I have to see you, Rachel,' Ben blurted out when Tim ran on ahead to join the others.

'Well, here I am,' she said, deliberately misunderstanding him, her casual manner concealing her tumultuous emotions. She daren't lose control. It had taken an enormous amount of self-discipline to build a life for herself and the boys without him. She was determined that that wouldn't be destroyed by an impulsive response because she was so delighted to see him.

'You know what I mean,' he told her. 'I need to talk to you on our own.'

'I don't think so, Ben,' she replied evenly. 'There's no point in harking back to the past. Everything's been said.'

'Please, Rachel.' His manner was ardent, his face tight with anxiety.

'No, Ben,' she refused firmly. 'I'm not having the boys upset. Even if you were to come to the house after they were in bed, they might hear you.'

'Meet me somewhere then,' he suggested.

She shook her head. 'I've a problem with baby-sitters at the moment. Jan isn't very well so I don't want to ask her.' It was just an excuse, because her mother would willingly sit with the boys.

'What about lunch, then?'

'Won't lunch be difficult for you as you don't work around here?' she mentioned.

'I'll take an extended dinner break, or an afternoon off.' He was pleading with her now. 'But I *have* to see you.'

'OK, but just one meeting, that's all,' she agreed, managing to retain an even tone. 'I'll see you in the Old Ship at one o'clock on Tuesday.'

'Wonderful,' he said, visibly brightening.

She gave him a sharp look. 'I'm only agreeing to have lunch with you,' she pointed out, keeping her head. 'It's nothing to get excited about.'

'Seeing you is cause for excitement,' he said.

'Just as long as you don't make more of it than it is,' she told him crisply, though she was melting inside. 'Now let's catch up with those children before one of them falls in the river.'

'I think I'd better disappear,' he suggested. 'I know you're with the family and I don't want to complicate things for you.'

'Yes, I think that's probably best,' she agreed, though all her instincts cried out for him to stay.

'Can you tell the boys I'm sorry I had to rush off?' he requested of her.

'Yes, I'll tell them,' she agreed.

They sat at a table near the window, eating cottage pie and looking out at the river, which was at low tide. A soft, persistent rain was falling; the waters were dark, the river bed muddy. A light mist shrouded everything, making the riverside seem bleak despite an abundance of new spring growth.

For a while they had a rather stilted conversation, mostly about the Boat Race on Saturday, and the fact that Cambridge had won yet again. Then Ben put things on to a more intimate level by telling her what had happened between him and Lorna and going on to speak of his feelings for Rachel. She listened with mixed emotions. Although she was thrilled to hear that he still loved her and wanted her back, the fact that she couldn't accept his proposal was a matter of enormous sadness to her.

'This isn't just a simple matter of us getting back together because you happen to find yourself free again,' she said.

'You're making it sound as though it's a casual thing on my part, and that couldn't be further from the truth,' he told her fervently. 'There was no point in my approaching you until I was free. And even then I stopped myself because I didn't want to intrude. Until today, when I just couldn't keep away any longer.'

'I know it isn't a casual thing for you,' she accepted. 'But it's complicated.'

'Is there someone else?' he wanted to know.

'No,' she stated firmly. 'No one else.'

'So, will you just think about giving me another chance?' he entreated.

She emitted an exasperated sigh. He'd thoroughly unsettled her. 'I've just said, there are too many complications,' she told him.

'Divorce proceedings are already under way between Lorna and myself,' he informed her to strengthen his case. 'It was a mutual decision. So the way is clear on my side.'

She reached over and put her hand on his in a brief halting gesture. 'No, Ben,' she told him. 'I can't take you back.'

'Are you saying you don't love me?' He looked stricken.

He couldn't know how she'd longed for this moment. Not a day had passed during their separation when she hadn't thought about him, wanted to be with him. 'I didn't say that,' she corrected.

'If it isn't that, and there isn't anyone else, why . . . ?'

She looked intently into his face, tanned as ever from being out in all weathers. 'I was utterly devastated when you went back to Lorna,' she began. 'I know that it wasn't your fault, and it was the only thing you could have done under the circumstances. But that didn't make it any easier for me to bear, or for Tim and Johnnie. We were all deeply hurt by it, and I can't take the risk of anything like that happening again. It isn't just a question of what I want. I have my children to consider. Their well-being is far more important to me than my own personal happiness.'

'But nothing will go wrong this time, I promise you,' he said. 'There was nothing except friendship between Lorna and me when she was staying with me.'

She couldn't pretend not to be cheered by what he said, even though it was irrelevant to the choice she had to make. 'I wondered if perhaps the spark might be reignited when you were together so much.'

'No, definitely not.'

'But the fact that it wasn't doesn't make any difference to

my decision,' she went on to say. 'As I've said, I don't have just myself to think about.'

'You know that the last thing I'd ever want to do is hurt the boys,' he pointed out.

'Yes, I believe that you don't *want* to hurt them,' she said, 'but you still went ahead and did so, didn't you?'

'Oh, Rachel . . .'

'I know I sound hard,' she cut in determinedly. 'But I'm their mother and it's my job to protect them. When I saw how upset they were after you left, I vowed I'd never risk having them hurt in that way again. And I intend to stick to it.' She paused, looking at him thoughtfully. 'As a matter of fact, their father has come back on the scene and I'm dreading that he will let them down in some way.'

'Jeff's back?'

She explained the current situation with Jeff. 'I think initially he was just using the boys to get his foot back in the door with me. And he still is doing that to some extent. But I believe he has grown genuinely fond of Tim and Johnnie.'

'Is there any chance of you two getting back together again?' Ben asked.

'None at all,' she stated categorically. 'I've told him that until I'm tired of saying it, but he still pesters me about it every so often. He's getting to be a nuisance, to be perfectly honest, though I can't help feeling a bit sorry for him.'

'Sorry for him?' Ben said incredulously.

'Yeah. I know that what he did to me and the boys was unforgivable, and that he lost what he had through his own selfishness, but he doesn't seem to have much of a life now,' she told him.

'Sounds to me as though you've let him get to you,' he observed.

'Only in that I pity him,' she made it clear. 'I wouldn't let him near the place if it wasn't for Tim and Johnnie. But he is their dad when all is said and done, and they need a man in their life. They took an awful knock when you left, especially Tim.'

'I've never forgiven myself,' Ben said with genuine contrition. 'It was a terrible blow for me too. I've missed you and the boys so much.'

She gave him an understanding nod.

'I thought they would have forgotten me by now, but Tim obviously hasn't.'

'Not Tim,' she confirmed wholeheartedly. 'Johnnie hasn't forgotten you either, but he is more inclined to take things and people in his stride. It certainly didn't take Jeff long to win him over.'

'It's only natural, I suppose,' Ben said.

'Mm.'

He reached for her hand. 'Please let me back into your life,' he begged. 'I promise I won't let you down.'

She held his hand in both of hers, feeling the long, strong fingers, the rough texture of the skin from physical work. 'I don't believe that you'd ever purposely let anyone down, Ben. But if something beyond your control were to happen, like it did last time, you'd be off. And I'm not willing to take that chance.'

'You want me back, though, don't you?' he told her. 'I can see it in your eyes.'

'There's nothing I want more,' she admitted. 'But we can't always have what we want from life, can we? Not when we're responsible adults, anyway. I'm sorry, Ben, but there it is. You and I have always been honest with each other and I want that to continue.'

'But . . .'

'Please don't put pressure on me to change my mind,' she said. 'It won't help and it will upset me.'

'I've no choice but to accept what you say, then, have I?' he said sadly.

'Not really, no.'

The tension was unbearable. Their eyes met and they both

laughed nervously. She was given a vivid reminder of how good they'd once been together.

Neither of them could finish their lunch, so he paid the bill and they left. They stood outside, paying no attention to the rain, dreading the parting but wanting it over. She asked him not to contact her again, planted a kiss on his cheek and turned and walked away towards the boathouse.

Tortured by what she'd just done, she turned to see Ben walking away in the other direction. Doubts consumed her. She loved him and knew he was loyal. Why tell him not to contact her again and close the door forever? In desperation, she began to go after him, but reminded herself of her responsibility to the boys and turned and walked sadly back to work.

All afternoon she agonised over her decision. When she went to bed that night she was still thinking about it. In her eagerness to do right by the boys, maybe she had done the wrong thing for them all. She'd rejected Ben for a less serious reason than he'd originally rejected her. But it was done now. She couldn't expect him to take her back after what she'd put him through this afternoon. She'd been so sure she was right, she must stand by her decision, even if it was the wrong one. The night was almost over before she finally fell into a troubled sleep.

The rest of the spring and the early summer was so hectic for Rachel she didn't have time to brood on personal heartache. Jan had her operation and was out of action. So what with hospital visiting, teaching the temp Jan's job and running her sister's household as well as her own, she never seemed to have a minute to herself. But the operation was a success and that was all that mattered to Rachel.

Between them, she and Marge looked after Kelly, and when Jan came out of hospital they made sure she was able to have the rest and recuperation she needed at home. They took it in turns to do her housework, as she wasn't even allowed to lift a duster, and Rachel did her shopping.

'You've been brilliant, sis,' Jan mentioned to Rachel one day when she got back from the supermarket, having worked her way through her sister's weekly shopping list. 'I don't know what I'd have done without you.'

'I'm only too pleased to help,' Rachel assured her. 'And you'd do the same for me if I ever needed it.'

'I was really out of order,' began Jan, taking this opportunity to mention something that had been on her mind for a while, 'when I was giving you a hard time about Doris. I hope you've forgiven me.'

'Yeah, course I have,' Rachel told her. 'That's all past history.'

The mention of Doris set Rachel's nerves on edge, because she was worried sick about her. The woman she had grown fond of had been in very low spirits lately when they'd met at the café, and it was hardly surprising given that her rock-solid marriage was in trouble. Rachel couldn't help feeling partly responsible, in that she had suggested that Doris tell Billy her secret. She wanted to do something to help but was at a loss to know what. It wasn't wise to interfere in someone else's private affairs, but some sort of intervention would be necessary if things didn't begin to improve for Doris soon.

'Life's too short for harbouring grudges,' Rachel said, helping Jan to unpack the shopping.

Jan changed the subject. 'I could get quite used to this, you know,' she said jokingly as Rachel lifted a heavy carrier bag on to the worktop for her. 'Having everyone running about after me.'

'You wait till you're back at work,' laughed Rachel. 'I'm going to work you into the ground.'

'I'd like to see you try,' said Jan.

Rachel smiled. She was so glad to be on good terms with her sister again.

It was with a great deal of trepidation that Rachel rang the

Finns' doorbell one Saturday afternoon in July. Her heart did a horrible somersault when the door opened and she found herself face to face with Billy.

He observed her coolly. 'Doris isn't in,' he informed her.

'I know she isn't,' she told him, having ascertained that Doris was on duty at the dry-cleaner's this Saturday. 'It isn't her I've come to see. It's you I want to talk to.'

'You've got a nerve, showing your face round here,' he snapped, 'after coming here pretending to be someone else.'

'I'm sorry about that, Billy, I really am,' she apologised with feeling.

'I should think so an' all.'

'Can I come in for a few minutes?' she asked. 'I just want to talk to you.'

His reply was a scowl, which seemed incongruous on the face of a man she knew to be warm-hearted.

'Just hear me out, please,' she begged him.

'I don't know why I didn't realise that the two of you were closely related,' he muttered gloomily, 'since you're so much like Doris, especially when you want your own way about something.' He stood aside and opened the door wider. 'You'd better come in.'

She was shown into the living room and offered a cup of tea, which she refused. 'I'll come straight to the point, Billy,' she said, perching on the edge of an armchair. 'I know how hurt you must be because Doris didn't tell you about me. I, too, was devastated when I found out that my parents hadn't told me the truth about my background. Even though I realised that they had behaved with the very best intentions, it was still painful. It took a while to get over it, but I'm all right about it now.'

'It's none of your business what happens between Doris and me,' he declared.

'You're right, it isn't,' she agreed, 'but I feel responsible for your present difficulties because it was me who sought Doris out, not the other way around. If I'd left well alone . . .'

'I might never have been any the wiser,' he cut in.

'Exactly. And probably all the happier for that,' she suggested. 'I know that I went through a period of wishing I'd never found out the truth about myself, but now I'm really glad I got to know, because Doris and I have become friends. We got off to a bit of a rocky start but I think I can safely say that we're pals now.'

'You're mother and daughter,' he corrected sternly.

She shook her head vigorously. 'We'll never be that. My mother is someone called Marge.'

'Fine words,' he mumbled. 'But all that psychology stuff is too deep and complicated for me. I'm just an ordinary bloke who thought he had a good marriage.'

'You *do* have a good marriage,' she cried ardently. 'Doris is breaking her heart because you've turned against her. She thinks the world of you.'

'She's no right to discuss our personal affairs with other people,' he objected.

'No, and I don't think she would have done normally,' she told him, 'but she needs someone to talk to now that you won't even give her the time of day.'

He sank wearily into an armchair, emitting a heavy sigh. 'I hate the way things are between us now,' he admitted. 'I'm as miserable as sin, to tell you the truth.' He pressed his fingers to his temples, closing his eyes for a moment. 'But I just can't forgive her for not telling me about you, for keeping something as important as that secret from me when we'd always vowed to be honest with each other. Every time I think of it . . .' he paused, pointing to his heart, 'it gets me right there.'

She decided to take a gamble. 'Could it be that you can't forgive yourself for not being able to provide her with the family you both wanted so much, and you're taking it out on her because she's the person you love most?' Seeing his face work as though she had physically slapped him, she was filled with remorse. 'I meant subconsciously, of course, Billy. I wasn't suggesting that you would deliberately try to punish her for your own sense of failure. But I shouldn't have said it at all. It isn't my place to get personal.'

He didn't answer for a while, just sat very still, staring gloomily at the floor. 'It's obviously what you're thinking, though,' he said at last. 'And you're probably right. Pathetic, aren't I?'

'Of course you're not,' Rachel disagreed. 'It's perfectly understandable that you would want to hit back after the shock you've had.'

'Is it?' he said miserably. 'I'm no expert on human behaviour. I just do what comes naturally.'

'I'm no expert either, but because I'm on the outside of this thing between you and Doris, I can see what's happening more clearly than you can,' she explained.

'Maybe,' he agreed half-heartedly.

'And I'm going to chance my arm here and say that I think it's time to let go of something you can do nothing about,' she went on. 'OK, maybe Doris should have told you about an indiscretion in her past, in the same way as my parents should have told me who I really am. But they didn't, and you and I both have to live with it. It doesn't make them lesser people. They were only doing what they thought was right for us.'

'Hmm,' he grunted.

'Ask yourself, Billy,' she continued doggedly, 'would you have told Doris if it had been the other way around?'

'I'd like to think I would,' he replied quickly.

'But you can't be absolutely certain of that, can you?' she pointed out. 'Especially if it became a matter of sparing Doris from the painful fact that she was the one who couldn't have children. Personally, I think you'd have done exactly the same thing as Doris did.'

'You don't mince words, do you?' he said.

'Not when it's something as important as you and Doris getting yourselves sorted out,' she told him. 'I can't bear the thought of the two of you splitting up.'

'Who said anything about splitting up?' He looked shocked.

'Nobody. But I believe that's what will happen ultimately if you let the situation go on as it is,' she warned him gravely. 'And you've an awful lot to lose if you lose Doris. Wives don't come more devoted than she is to you.'

'You really think I'll lose her?'

From the way he spoke, Rachel got the impression that he hadn't thought this thing through. 'Well, yes. As devoted as she is, even Doris can only take so much,' she informed him. 'The way I see it, one of you will have to leave if things aren't put right. I don't see how you can live in a state of war forever. It's not doing either of you any good. It's really getting Doris down. She's very unhappy.'

'I'm so confused,' he confessed, wringing his hands. 'I'm angry with Doris, angry with myself.'

'But you're not confused about your feelings for Doris, are you?' she mentioned. 'You know that you love her?'

'Course I do. There's never been any doubt in my mind about that,' he stated.

'That's all that matters in the long run, then, don't you think?' Rachel suggested. 'The rest can be worked out between you.' She paused, wondering if she should interfere any further, and deciding she must for the sake of both Doris and Billy, however angry it made him. 'I wouldn't leave it too long, though. Don't let things get so out of hand that they can't be put right.'

He didn't reply.

'Anyway, I've said what I came to say. Now it's up to you what you do about it,' she said, rising with a purposeful air. 'I must go. The boys are out with their dad this afternoon, but I like to be home when they get back.'

He showed her to the front door, looking thoughtful. 'Does Doris know you've come to see me?' he asked.

'What do you think?' she said with a wry grin. 'She'd go mad if she knew I was here.'

'Do you want me to keep quiet about it?' he asked.

She was about to reply in the affirmative but had a sudden change of mind. 'No, you go ahead and tell her, Billy. Keeping things back has caused enough trouble already. That's what secrets do.'

He nodded, and she perceived that his mood had changed since her arrival. 'Truth be told, I'm pleased Doris has someone besides me to look out for her,' he said. 'Thanks for coming.'

'A pleasure,' she said. 'I hope you can work things out.'

'Me too, but it isn't a simple matter,' he told her, his expression hardening again.

She reached up and kissed him lightly on the cheek. 'You must do what you think best for you both. See you, Billy.' She turned and hurried out to her car.

'See you, Rachel.' He stood at the door, watching her until the car was out of sight. Doris' daughter, he thought, with a mixture of joy and sadness; the daughter he had always wanted.

Later that same afternoon, knowing that Billy would be at home, Doris had tension knots in her stomach as she approached her front door. How could something that had once been such a joy to her now fill her with dread? She remembered the glowing anticipation she used to feel coming home to Billy. The welcome, the simple pleasure of being together had been priceless.

But that was before her confession four months ago. Since then life had been hellish. The warm and loving man she had been married to for more than two and a half decades had become cold and aloof. They only spoke when it couldn't be avoided, which meant meal times were torturous, so much so that she was relieved when he was on late shift and they didn't have to eat together.

For weeks after the confession she'd begged him to forgive her, pleaded with him, tried to persuade him to see the thing from her perspective. But he'd refused to talk about it, and had withdrawn into himself. After a while her remorse had become tinged with irritation and a sense of injustice at his lack of understanding. After all, no one was perfect.

With every day that passed, the atmosphere in the house became even more unbearable. Worse than strangers, they were like sworn enemies. She still cooked and kept house for them but things had reached a stage where she felt uncomfortable in her own living room. There was no teamwork any more, no companionship. They went through the motions of daily living in a mood of bitter resentment. She didn't know how much more she could take.

So now it was with a trembling hand that she put the key in the lock and turned it. Stepping into the hall she was greeted by the unmistakable aroma of steak grilling. They always had steak on a Saturday night, as a treat. Apprehensively, she headed for the kitchen door and saw Billy coming to meet her.

'Steak under the grill, chips in the pan, everything under control,' he said, giving her an uncertain look.

'Why are you being so nice all of a sudden?' she wanted to know. 'What's happened?'

'I've come to my senses, that's what's happened,' he explained. 'I'll tell you all about it while we eat.' He made a wry face. 'That is, if you're willing to talk to me after the way I've been behaving lately.'

'Oh, thank God, Billy,' she said, her voice loud and warm with relief. 'Thank God!'

That same afternoon, Arthur and Ella had been shopping in Kensington High Street and were feeling extremely pleased with themselves as they loaded their purchases into the boot of the car. They'd been buying new things for the home – table lamps for the lounge, bed linen, cushions, ornaments – and a plentiful selection of new clothes for them both.

'I can't wait to get home to have a proper look at it all,'

said Ella excitedly as Arthur closed the boot.

'Me neither,' enthused Arthur. 'We'll have a good look through then get ourselves dressed up in our new clothes and go up the West End for a meal.'

'Smashing.'

'We'll have a drink at our local on the way to show off our new gear,' he suggested.

'Ooh, yeah,' she said with a giggle in her voice. 'Eat your heart out, pop stars . . . Ella and Arthur Banks are going out on the town.'

Walking round to the driver's door, Arthur noticed a police car parked across the road. The two officers inside were looking in their direction. 'I hope those bobbies aren't planning on doing me for parking,' he said to Ella. 'I've piled loads o' money into that meter.'

'We'll soon put 'em right if they do,' she said, her eyes flashing angrily. 'They're coming over.'

'Good afternoon, sir,' said one of the policemen, while the other walked around the car and appeared to be examining it.

'Afternoon, Officer,' replied Arthur with a complacent smile. He was just waiting for one of them to accuse him of something he hadn't done so that he could have the pleasure of putting them in their place.

'Is this your car, sir?' enquired the constable.

'It certainly is,' said Arthur proudly. 'I bet you wish it was yours, don't you?'

The policeman ignored Arthur's suggestion and asked to see his driving licence, which he checked and handed back to him. The constable then exchanged a look with his colleague, who proceeded to open the bonnet of the car.

'Here, what's your game?' demanded the outraged Arthur, striding round to the front of the car and looking over the policeman's shoulder. 'You can't do that. You've no right to interfere with a member of the public's personal property.'

Ignoring him, the policeman peered inside the bonnet,

referred to a piece of paper he was holding, then nodded at his colleague.

'I'm afraid we're going to have to take possession of this vehicle,' announced policeman number one.

'Over my dead body,' exclaimed Arthur cheekily. 'If you want a quality car like this, you'll have to change your job for something that pays better than the one you've got now.'

The wisecrack appeared to go unnoticed by the officer. 'This car is on our list of stolen vehicles,' he informed Arthur evenly.

'Don't make me laugh,' he snorted. 'This car was bought and paid for, all legal and above board. I've got the logbook and everything. It's fully taxed and insured.' Arthur was truly enraged. For once in his life he'd bought something in a legitimate manner, and here he was in trouble with the law. 'There's nothing dodgy about this bit of gear.'

'We'll be needing to see the papers, sir,' said the policeman calmly.

'I haven't got 'em with me at the moment,' Arthur told him irritably. 'They're at home.'

'In that case, you'll have to take them to your local police station as soon as you've found them,' the man said in a tone of quiet authority. 'Now, if we can have your name and address, please, you can take your belongings out of the car and we'll arrange to have it picked up.'

'But you can't take our car,' Ella chimed in. 'My husband paid good money for that.'

'Where did you buy it, sir?' asked the law officer.

'From a bloke in a pub,' Arthur told him.

'His name?' the policeman enquired, pencil poised over his notepad.

'Bob, I think he said,' supplied Arthur.

'Can you give us his full name and address, please?' asked the policeman patiently.

'Not off the top of my head, no,' Arthur informed him furiously, 'but it'll be written down in the logbook.'

'Yes, so if you can take that to your local police station as soon as possible, the details will be checked out. And your name is . . . ?'

'What's my name got to do with anything?' Arthur was seriously affronted.

'You're in possession of a stolen vehicle, sir,' explained the policeman. 'We'll have to check a few things out.'

'Look here,' objected Arthur, white with temper, 'I bought that car in good faith, you've got nothing on me.'

'We're not suggesting that we have.' The policeman was being patient but firm. 'So if you could give us your details, then we'll get the car returned to its owner.'

Arthur could hardly speak he was so angry. 'I've told you, I'm the car's owner,' he uttered at last. 'I paid good money for it, which makes it mine.'

'Yes, of course, sir,' said the officer, with chilling politeness. 'Now, if we could have your name and address, we'll give you a lift home with your packages.'

'I'm not going home in a police car,' Ella intervened. 'I wouldn't be seen dead in one of those things.'

'As you wish, madam,' said the policeman, an edge to his voice. 'Now, can we have your name and address please?'

Shaking with fury, Arthur gave the officers what they wanted.

'Three thousand pounds!' exclaimed Ella in the taxi on the way home. 'You chucked away three thousand quid of our money on a dodgy motor?'

'I didn't know it was dodgy, did I?' he defended. 'And the book price on that model is four thousand, so I saved us a grand.'

'A fat lot of good that is to us now,' she ranted. 'Anyway, if you'd had any sense, you'd have wondered why it was so cheap.'

'I did ask about that,' he retorted. 'The geezer said he was only selling the car because of a cash-flow problem. He seemed genuine enough to me.'

'And you didn't even bother to check him out?' Her tone was fearsome. She didn't often get angry with her beloved husband, but she was absolutely steaming now.

'There didn't seem to be any need,' he said guiltily. 'I mean, he had the logbook and everything seemed to be in order.'

'The papers were probably forged,' she guessed.

'How would an ordinary member of the public be able to get something like that done?' he queried.

'Honestly, Arthur, you can't half be dim when you want to be,' she rebuked. 'He obviously wasn't just a bloke who happened to want to sell his car. He'll have been an experienced villain working territory where he isn't known.'

Arthur still couldn't accept that he'd been taken in so easily. He was much too astute. 'I'll find his address on the logbook when we get home and make him give me my money back,' he told her.

'Don't make me laugh,' she scoffed. 'You've seen the last of that money, and you'll be lucky not to get done for nicking the car yourself.'

'Thanks for having such confidence in me,' he said sarcastically.

'Well, *really*, I don't know how you could have been so dumb,' she told him.

'We all make mistakes,' he pointed out.

'Yeah, well, you've really dropped a clanger this time,' she grumbled. 'It won't half set us back.'

'We'll come through it,' he assured her. 'We always do.'

'I know,' she said with a sigh of resignation. 'But I could really kill you for this, Art.'

She'll get over it, he thought. But he did wonder if he was losing his touch. And a few days later, when he was charged with being in possession of stolen property and subsequently fined fifteen hundred pounds, he began to seriously question the way he earned his living. This mistake had cost him four and a half grand, counting the money he'd spent on the car itself.

There was something else beside the financial aspect, too. He'd never admit it to anyone, not even his darling Ella, but appearing in court had scared him witless; it had made him realise that prison was a possibility when you broke the law, and he'd hated the feeling.

Maybe his luck was running out and he'd be wise to stick to the legitimate side of the collecting job, for the time being anyway. It would mean a drastic drop in their standard of living, but better that than a stretch inside. And it would only be temporary. He had no intention of sticking to the straight and narrow permanently. He hadn't lost his nerve to that extent.

Chapter Twenty-One

'Why can't you take no for an answer, Jeff?' sighed Rachel, weary of his relentless persistence. 'I'm not going to change my mind about having you back, so there's no point in your continuing to pester me about it.'

His eyes narrowed with resentment. 'You're being very selfish,' he accused. 'You're not the only one to consider in this. The boys need their father around all the time, not just once a week.'

Angered by his effrontery, she responded heatedly. 'That's rich, coming from someone who deserted them without a second thought, and didn't even bother to find out how they were for five years.'

'Yeah, well, I've told you I'm sorry about that,' he mumbled. 'How much longer are you going to carry on punishing me?'

'I'm not trying to punish you,' she told him for the umpteenth time. 'I'm saying no because I don't want us to get back together. And don't tell me I should do it for the sake of the children, because it would be wrong for them too. I wouldn't be happy and that would have a bad effect on them.'

This conversation was taking place at her front door on a glorious autumn Saturday afternoon, the sun spreading a honey glow over everything and adding splendour to the scarlet potted geraniums that flourished around the shiny red doorstep. Jeff had come to collect the boys, who were waiting for him in his car. She guessed he'd sent them on ahead so that he could badger her some more about the subject he refused to leave alone.

'It wouldn't have a bad effect on them if you really made an effort,' was his tenacious response. 'You could be happy with me if you tried.'

'Don't use them to get your own way, Jeff,' she opposed him. 'I won't have it.'

'Well, how do you think I feel?' His voice was leaden with self-pity. 'With the three of you living here in comfort while I'm stuck in some little place on my own.'

'Is that what this is *really* all about?' she suggested. 'You wanting to improve your situation?'

'No, I love those boys,' he hastened to correct. 'I love you all, and I want us to be together.'

She believed the bit about him loving the boys, anyway. 'If it's money you want so that you can move into more comfortable accommodation, you should look for a better job and start saving. I'm not taking you back, Jeff. In fact I think it's time we thought about getting a divorce.'

'Never.' Panic at the thought of losing all hope of a better life quickly turned to anger. 'I'll *never* give you a divorce.'

'I don't think I actually need you to "give" me a divorce, since your desertion and adultery would be sufficient grounds for me to proceed,' she pointed out. 'But this isn't the time to discuss it, not while the boys are waiting for you to take them out.'

'Perhaps we could get back together for a trial period, to see how it goes,' he suggested, desperate now. 'I wouldn't make any demands on you, not until we knew if it was going to work out.'

Rachel felt bruised and brow-beaten by his tenacity but was determined not to give in. 'Will you please stop this, Jeff?' she begged him. 'This is the boys' time; don't use it all up trying to get at me.'

He fell silent, a savage look in his eyes. Then he affected a dramatic change of mood. 'Yeah, you're right. Sorry. I have been getting a bit heavy lately. I'll watch that in future.' He glanced towards the car. 'I'd better get going. They want me to take them down to the river.'

'So they've been telling me,' she said, relieved that the assault on her patience seemed about to end, for the time being anyway. 'I know the river isn't really your thing. But you've a lovely day for it.'

He nodded, looking towards the sky and shading his eyes with his hand.

'I hope you manage to enjoy it anyway,' she told him.

'I'll do my best,' he said. 'What are you going to do with yourself this afternoon?'

'Tidy up in the garden, ready for the winter,' she told him. 'It gets very messy at this time of the year, with all the fallen leaves, and everything dying off.'

As gardening was unknown territory to Jeff, he just said, 'I'll leave you to it, then, and see you later.'

She followed him into the street to see them off, feeling strangely disturbed as she watched the car disappear around the corner, the boys peering bright-eyed out of the back window, grinning and waving madly at her.

Ben was in his back garden, sweeping up the fallen leaves, having dug over the flowerbeds in preparation for winter. It was only a small area and mostly paved, but the few beds that he did have demanded a certain amount of attention. The fallen leaves were endless in autumn. It often seemed to him that the screening trees shed more than were ever on the branches.

The sun was low and heavy, the shadows lengthening with the advancing afternoon. The air was still; not a breath of wind anywhere. He felt a stab of aching nostalgia as he remembered another autumn, the year he'd fallen in love with Rachel. The weekend of the Big River Race and the sinking of their much-vaunted boat had had the same sort of weather, the air as sweet as the scent of cinnamon, autumn earthiness pervading everything. He smiled as he remembered telling her for the first time that he loved her.

He paused, broom in hand, frowning at the memory of meeting up with her again in the spring, and how disappointed he'd been when she wouldn't have him back. Looking back on that last meeting with a fresh eye, something became glaringly obvious to him; he'd been much too easily defeated. If he wanted her that much, he should go after her and fight to get her back. Not tomorrow, or next week, but now, this very moment.

With a sudden and acute sense of urgency, he dropped the broom and hurried inside. He got washed, changed out of his gardening clothes into a pair of jeans and a sweater, and rushed from the house.

'Why are we stopping, Dad?' Tim enquired.

'I need something from the shops,' explained Jeff, pulling in at a small parade in the back streets of Hammersmith.

'Are you going to buy us some sweets?' suggested Johnnie hopefully. Their father was a soft touch when Mum wasn't around, and Johnnie exploited it to the hilt.

'Yeah, if you like.' Jeff was in a foul temper after the conversation with Rachel, and was finding it difficult not to let it show, something he daren't do if he was to keep the boys on his side. 'I won't be a minute. You stay in the car.'

'Can we come with you and choose what we want?' nagged Johnnie.

'No, not this time,' said Jeff, getting out of the car and making a beeline for the off-licence.

When he got back and handed each child a Mars bar, Johnnie asked what was in the bottle Jeff was having a swig from.

'Gin,' Tim informed his brother, reading the label. 'And it smells horrible.'

'Can we have a taste?' requested Johnnie.

'You wouldn't like it,' Jeff told him.

'How do you know I wouldn't like it?' Johnnie wondered.

'I just know, believe me.'

'Doesn't it taste nice?' Johnnie persisted.

'A child wouldn't think so,' replied Jeff.

'Why do grown-ups like it, then?'

'They like the way it makes them feel,' Jeff explained, struggling to stay patient.

'It'll make you drunk,' disapproved Tim. 'And you're not supposed to drink that stuff when you're driving a car. I heard them talking about it on the telly.'

'A little drop won't hurt,' Jeff assured him. 'You want your dad to be in a good mood while we're out, don't you?'

'I thought that seeing us was supposed to put you in a good mood anyway,' said Tim. 'That's what Mum said. She said it's the highlight of your week.'

'Yeah, she did say that,' added Johnnie.

'It is,' said Jeff, unable to stop himself adding, 'it's your mother who's spoiling things.'

'Why?' Tim wanted to know.

Jeff wanted to give full vent to his anger by uttering the invective about Rachel that was rattling around in his head. But knowing that it would damage his relationship with his sons, he just had another swig from the bottle and said, 'Never you mind.'

'Mum doesn't spoil things for anyone,' defended Tim. 'She isn't like that.'

'No, she isn't,' Johnnie piped up supportively.

'If you say so, boys,' sighed Jeff, turning on the engine and heading for the river.

She told herself she was being ridiculous. It was only four thirty. They might not be back for another half-hour or so yet. But as the sun sank low and a chill crept into the afternoon air, Rachel's feeling of unease turned to panic. There was no logical reason for her feelings, just something about Jeff's mood when he'd left with the boys that lingered in her mind.

The sudden change from resentful pleading to resigned acceptance hadn't been genuine. There had been rage simmering beneath his amiable manner that was only discernible in retrospect.

He wouldn't knowingly hurt the boys, no matter how angry he was with their mother. She was sure of that. But still her uneasiness persisted. In a torment of anxiety, she paced from kitchen to living room window, longing for the sight of Jeff's car or the sound of the doorbell. Jan and Pete had gone out, or she'd have run across the road in search of moral support.

She was in the kitchen, moistening her parched mouth with yet more tea, when the front doorbell echoed into the silent house. Thank God for that, she thought, hurrying to the door to let them in.

'Ben.' Her emotions were confused. Other than her children, there was no one else in the world she would rather have seen at that moment.

'Whatever's the matter, Rachel?' His purpose in being here was pushed to the back of his mind by the stricken look on her face. 'You look worried to death.'

She ushered him inside and told him about her fears. 'It's nothing definite, just a feeling,' she confessed. 'But they're usually back by now on a Saturday.'

'They'll have forgotten the time, that's all it'll be,' he said encouragingly. 'But get your coat on and we'll go out looking for them to save you wearing the carpet out here in the house. We can leave a note on the front door to tell them where we are in case they come back while we're out.'

She hastily scribbled a note on the jotter pad by the telephone in the hall, tore the top sheet off and secured it under the knocker before grabbing her anorak from the coat rack. 'Thank goodness you're here, Ben. I've never been more pleased to see anyone in my life,' she told him. 'It must have been telepathy that brought you to me in my hour of need.'

'Not telepathy,' he said.

'What did bring you here, then?' she wondered, zipping her coat.

He made a wry face. 'This probably isn't the right moment to mention it, given the situation, but I might as well come right out and say it. I came to tell you again what I told you when we met in the spring: that I love you and want you back.'

She'd regretted her decision with increasing intensity since the spring. Now that he was here, she never wanted to lose sight of him again. 'Oh, Ben,' she said, throwing her arms around him, 'I was mad to turn you down.' Anxiously she combed her fringe from her brow with her fingers. 'I was being overprotective of the boys, but I can see now that they're losing out by not having you around. I love you, Ben. I've never been more certain of that than I am at this moment.'

He smiled and held her tight. 'First things first, though, eh?' he said, taking control of the situation. 'Let's go and find out what's keeping those boys. We'll go in my car so that you can look out for them while I drive.'

As they hurried out to his car with his arm around her shoulders, their closeness was as strong as ever, despite such a long time apart. He'd immediately tuned in to her problems and accepted them as his own. Her worries were his too, and vice versa. He was the one for her.

Everything was so much easier when you'd had a drink, Jeff thought, as he steered *Nipper* back towards Hammersmith, having managed to get as far as Kew. Actually he must have had a bit more than just a drink, he decided, taking another hefty swallow from the gin bottle and realising that there wasn't much left.

He felt pleasantly benign, drowsy but confident in himself. Rachel was the one who was losing out by rejecting him, a man who could turn his hand to anything. Here he was cruising along the Thames, dazzling his sons with his competence. Young boys admired a man who could do things. That was why, when he'd noticed the little boat moored at Rachel's boathouse and realised how accessible it was, he'd offered to take them out on the river. It was the perfect opportunity to impress them.

Getting the craft started had been surprisingly easy, after some instruction from Tim, who knew *Nipper* well, apparently. The boy was very well informed about boats for someone so young. He'd told Jeff to use the cord to start the outboard motor, and away they'd gone. Steering hadn't been any trouble once he'd been shown how to use the rudder.

Now, through the mists of alcohol, he realised that Tim was speaking to him. 'Shall I steer the boat, Dad?' he suggested a little desperately.

'How can you steer a boat?' asked Jeff in a slurred voice. 'You're just a kid.'

'I can steer and I think I should,' said Tim, his voice rising with panic as the boat swerved off course dramatically. 'We're heading straight for the bank.'

'So we are,' said Jeff, letting out a roar of drunken laughter but managing to steer the boat away from the side. 'But we're right back on course now and no harm done. Your old dad knows what he's doing.'

'I can handle this boat,' Tim wanted his father to know. 'Ben taught me how to do it.'

'Ben . . . that was your mother's boyfriend, wasn't it?' Jeff asked in a slow, sleepy voice.

'Yes, but he was our friend too,' Tim informed him.

'Maybe he was,' muttered Jeff, blinking to focus his eyes, 'but you don't need him now, because you've got me. I'm your father . . . your friend . . . everything.'

'We're gonna hit another boat in a minute,' cried Tim, his eyes wide with horror as *Nipper* swerved crazily.

'You'd better let Tim take over at the rudder, Dad,' put in Johnnie, also very frightened now. 'As you're not feeling very well.'

'What d'ya mean, I'm not feeling well?' Jeff objected, swaying. 'I'm feeling fine.'

'You're drunk,' accused Tim.

'Not drunk, son,' he denied thickly. 'Just a bit happier than I was when we left your place.'

The boys stood either side of him, their faces ashen against their bright blue anoraks. They were both shivering with a mixture of fear and cold, the temperature having dropped with the setting of the sun. A mist was hazing the banks, which were beginning to look deserted with the onset of evening.

'Please let me take over, Dad,' Tim was begging now. 'You're all over the place with the boat, honestly. You'll cause an accident in a minute.'

'Shut up.' Jeff was belligerent now from the booze and pushed Tim away, his impaired judgement causing him to do it rather more forcefully than he had intended. Tim fell to the deck. As he scrambled to his feet, Jeff asked if he was all right.

'Yeah, I'm OK,' said Tim, but he was shaken.

'Sorry about that,' apologised Jeff squiffily. 'I didn't mean to hurt you. The last thing I want to do is hurt either of you. You do know that, don't you?'

Neither of them replied. They stood close together in a state of horror.

'Answer me when I speak to you,' Jeff demanded, becoming aggressive.

'Yes, we do know that you don't want to hurt us,' said Tim in a quick, dutiful voice. 'But we'll all get hurt if you don't keep the boat on course.'

'OK, so I've had a drink or three,' he said, ignoring Tim's warning. 'It's your mother's fault. She's driven me to it. She's such a selfish cow.'

'Don't you *dare* say that about our mother,' said Tim, his cheeks flaming.

'No, don't,' added Johnnie.

'I'm only saying what's true, son.' Jeff was no longer in control of word or deed, all earlier thoughts of caution and tactics wiped out by a surfeit of gin. 'She won't let me come back home to live so that I can be with the two of you. Even young lads like you must know that isn't right.'

'You left us,' reminded Tim, who wouldn't hear a word against his beloved mother. 'Why should Mum have you back?'

'She should have me back, my dear old son,' he was hardly able to articulate the words now, 'because I'm her husband, and the father of her children. Thinks she's Lady Muck now that she's got a few bob. Too good for her own husband.'

'I want to go home,' said Johnnie, on the verge of tears.

'That's where I'm taking you,' said Jeff, as they took a zigzag course past Chiswick Eyot. 'Home to your lovely house that I'm not allowed to live in because of that bitch of a mother of yours.'

'Don't call her a bitch,' warned Tim.

'You mustn't say bad things about our mum,' said Johnnie, sobbing openly now. 'Because we love her.'

'That's it, close ranks against me,' complained Jeff, his voice so slow and heavy as to be barely comprehensible. 'She's turned you against me, the bitch.'

'I've told you not to say things about her,' shouted Tim vehemently, tears streaming down his cheeks. 'And I mean it. Stoppit, stoppit.'

'Oh, blubbing now, are we?' said Jeff. 'I didn't realise I had a couple of sissies for sons.'

'I hate you,' wept Tim, wiping his eyes with the back of his hand and struggling to stem the flow of tears.

Jeff was entering into the maudlin stage of inebriation. 'Sorry son,' he muttered sluggishly. 'You don't really hate your old dad, do you?'

'I do when you say nasty things about my mum,' Tim told him solemnly.

'I haven't said anything bad about her, have I?' Jeff said, his brain so addled as to be blank about what he'd said or thought just seconds before.

'Yes you have. You know you have,' declared Tim, biting

back tears of anger and fear, his lean body quivering. 'And I won't have it, do you understand? I won't let anyone say anything bad about our mum, because she's brilliant.'

'She is too,' agreed Johnnie, less brave than his brother but just as ardent.

'I'm sorry, I'm sorry, I won't say anything else bad, I promise,' said Jeff in a slow, laboured manner, his face red and blotchy and gleaming with sweat.

'We're going home,' said Tim, boldly pushing in front of his father and grabbing the rudder to straighten the craft, which was careering towards the middle of the river into the path of an oncoming cabin cruiser, provoking angry shouts from the crew.

'Let Tim steer the boat, Dad, please,' begged Johnnie, terrified and bitterly disillusioned by his father's behaviour.

'Go and sit down, Dad, for goodness' sake,' ordered Tim, concentrating on the job in hand, 'and let me get this boat home.'

Johnnie was an easy-going little boy who had welcomed his father into his heart without reservation, even though he'd been a stranger. Now he stared at him, terrified, as Jeff stumbled about the boat before collapsing on to the bench and dealing the final blow to the boy's illusions by throwing up all over the deck.

In Jeff's drink-crazed mind there was a burning need to put things right with his sons. Too drunk to realise the stupidity of his actions, he got to his feet with the intention of resuming his place at the rudder and taking the boat into its home moorings, the triumphant father. But his co-ordination was out of synch and he couldn't keep his balance, so he staggered hopelessly around the small deck, emitting a string of expletives.

Trembling from head to toe, Tim bravely steered the boat on its homeward course.

'That's odd,' said Ben as he and Rachel approached the

boathouse moorings. 'My boat isn't here.'

'Oh.' She was puzzled too. 'Might one of your mates have taken it out?' she suggested.

'No one has asked me if they can use it this weekend.'

They stared at each other with a single thought. 'He wouldn't have, would he?' said Rachel, biting her lip. 'He knows nothing about boats. He'll drown the lot of them if he has.'

'You're letting your imagination run wild.'

'Oh, Ben, supposing he has?' she said worriedly.

'It's an easy enough boat for even a novice to handle, but I'm sure he wouldn't have,' he said to reassure her. 'It's funny that it isn't here, though. I mean, nobody would bother stealing an old buggy like *Nipper*. That's why I'm never too worried about security.'

'Some youngsters looking for devilment might have taken it, perhaps?' she suggested hopefully.

'Possibly,' he agreed, 'but I'll sort it out later on, when the boys are home.'

There were only a few people about now the sun had gone down – the odd walker and cyclist; none of the regulars who moored their boats along here – so there was nobody they could ask if they'd seen anything.

'There's no sign of Jeff and the boys along here,' Rachel mentioned, looking around.

'We've probably missed them on the road,' Ben suggested. 'But let's take a walk, just in case they're further along.'

As they began walking upstream towards Chiswick, they were frozen in their tracks by what came into view. 'Oh my God,' gasped Rachel as *Nipper* appeared around the bend in the river. They could just make out two small figures in blue anoraks at the rudder. 'Jeff *did* take the boat, and he's got Tim steering.'

'What the hell's the man playing at?' said Ben as they watched Jeff moving about the deck.

'Drunk, by the look of it,' said Rachel. She and Ben ran

along the walkway in the direction of the boat, waving and shouting.

As the craft drew closer, they could see what was happening on board. Jeff was staggering about, Johnnie was screaming and gripping the handrail, and Tim was hanging grimly on to the rudder. Numb with horror, Rachel and Ben watched as Jeff lost his balance and fell flat on his face. After a few agonising moments, he got up, holding his head and looking dazed. Even from the bank they could see the blood on his face. Still very unsteady, he seemed to catch his foot on a rope and stumbled towards the side of the boat, hitting his head on the bench. He got up again and tried to grab the handrail. But his body crumpled suddenly and he toppled over the side. There was no struggle, no arms raised or calls for help. He just seemed to sink like a stone.

While Rachel tore towards the mooring into which Tim was skilfully steering the boat, Ben's coat was off and he was in the water, swimming towards the spot where Jeff had fallen in.

Rachel jumped on to the boat, secured the mooring rope and swept the boys into her arms. They were both silently weeping and shivering. 'Well done, Tim,' she said. 'You're a clever boy to bring the boat into the mooring like that. And you helped him, Johnnie. I'm proud of you both.'

'What about Dad?' asked Johnnie fearfully. 'He fell and hit his head, then just sort of slipped over the side.'

'Has he drowned?' Tim's face was wet with tears.

'I don't know, love.' She wanted to protect them but knew they trusted her to be truthful.

'He wouldn't sit down,' sobbed Tim. 'He was drunk. I couldn't stop him falling over the side. He just went over. There was nothing I could do to stop him.'

'Of course there wasn't anything either of you could do, darling,' said his mother, holding them close. 'We all know that.'

'We kept telling him to sit down,' explained Johnnie

thickly. 'But he wouldn't take any notice. He was acting really weird. Like he was mad.'

'Ben's got him,' she said, watching Ben swimming on his back with Jeff in a life-saving grip, his head above the water. She heard a passer-by shouting about having called an ambulance so knew that that was under control. She soothed her sons, wiping their tears and putting herself between them and what was happening on the bank, as Ben dragged Jeff out of the water and attempted mouth-to-mouth resuscitation. They'd been through enough; they could be spared that. 'Ben's looking after him and the ambulance will be here in a minute.'

Much later that same evening, Rachel sat between Tim and Johnnie on the sofa in her living room. Ben was in an armchair nearby. They had both just got back from the hospital, having collected the boys from her parents' place on the way.

'Is Dad in heaven?' Johnnie enquired.

'I should think so,' said Rachel, deeply shocked by Jeff's death.

'Is he or isn't he?' asked Tim, who always wanted things made definite.

'No one knows for sure where people go after they die,' she told him gently. 'But wherever he is, he's at peace now. And he didn't feel any pain at all when he died; they told us that at the hospital.'

'He's never coming back, is he?' said Johnnie.

Rachel exchanged a look with Ben. 'No, darling,' she said, smoothing the boy's hair back from his damp brow. 'He isn't ever coming back.' She cuddled them both to her. 'But we'll think about him lots . . . he won't be forgotten.'

Jeff had been dead on arrival at the hospital despite Ben's attempts to revive him. The doctor said that he'd been unconscious before he'd even hit the water so wouldn't have known anything about it. That explained why he didn't struggle. They couldn't say for certain until after the post-mortem, but a severe blow to the head was almost certainly what had killed him, probably sustained when he fell. He'd obviously been very drunk so wouldn't have felt much pain.

Tim looked across at Ben, who had been keeping a diplomatic silence while Rachel spoke to her sons. 'You're not going to die or go away again, are you, Ben?' he asked.

'No, Tim, I'm not going away,' Ben quietly assured him.

'I hope you never do,' said Tim.

'Me too,' added Johnnie.

'Will you come and sit over here with us?' asked Tim gravely.

'Course I will.'

They all moved up to make room and he parked himself beside Tim. The four of them sat very close together, needing each other, wanting to be together. Rachel was aware of how much these children were going to need both her and Ben in the days ahead as they came to terms with the traumatic events on the boat as well as the loss of their father.

She felt very sad at a personal level too. Jeff had almost destroyed her in the past, and more recently had become a source of annoyance. He had had a self-destructive streak and it could be said that he'd brought his early death on himself. But that didn't make it any the less heart-rending.

February 1972 was a bleak month for the people of Britain, as the miners' strike caused havoc with power cuts over virtually the whole country. Homes and offices were plunged into cold and dark for long periods each day. Shop assistants worked by candlelight and hundreds of thousands of factory workers were laid off work as electricity supplies to industry were cut off. An official three-day week was introduced as the crisis deepened.

But upstairs in the functions room of the Blue Anchor, during an electricity blackout one Saturday evening at the height of the crisis, the atmosphere was far from gloomy, as friends and relatives of Rachel and Ben gathered for their wedding reception. The pub had plenty of candles in stock and they burned brightly, spreading a warm, undulating glow around the room.

The speeches were over and Rachel and Ben were mingling with their guests. 'I think the candlelight is really romantic,' said Rachel as they managed a few quiet words to each other. 'It adds a certain something to the party.'

'It's different, anyway,' laughed Ben.

'It would still be the happiest day of my life even if the place was pitch dark,' said Rachel.

'Mine too,' he said.

It was an informal party with a cold buffet and small candlelit tables set around the room. Some people were sitting down, others standing around chatting in groups. Neither Rachel nor Ben had wanted a big do, especially as they'd been living together as a family for some time. Ben had moved in soon after Jeff's death, partly because they both felt they'd waited long enough to be together, and also because she and the boys had needed him so much at that tragic time.

His reassuring presence in the house gave Tim and Johnnie some added security when they were feeling so vulnerable. Their father had had very little to do with them until the end of his life and they hadn't been closely bonded. But the dramatic nature of his death had left them reeling.

Taking on two growing boys was no small thing, and Rachel was constantly impressed by Ben's patience with them. He was kind and gentle but not afraid to risk his popularity with discipline when necessary. As much as Rachel adored her children, she knew they weren't always easy to deal with. They were noisy, exuberant and downright naughty if the mood took them.

It was the normally carefree Johnnie who'd been most affected by Jeff's death. He'd been exhaustingly difficult for a while, stamping about the house angry and embattled, blatantly disobeying any form of adult authority. Although Tim was usually the more sensitive of the two, he had never taken to Jeff in quite the same way as his brother had, and was more able to cope with his loss.

However, it wasn't in Johnnie's genial nature to dwell on things for long, and he eventually reverted to normal, after strong words and sympathy in equal measure.

But now the day Rachel had waited for for so long had come and they were a real family at last. Because Ben's divorce had already been underway when he and Rachel had got back together, they hadn't had to wait as long to get married as they otherwise might have done. But it had still felt like for ever.

'Did I tell you that you're looking gorgeous today, Mrs Smart?' Ben was saying now as he cast his eyes over her radiant face, glowing against a cream winter suit with scarlet accessories.

'Several times.' She ran an approving eye over her new husband. Ben was normally a casual dresser, and it was strange to see him in a suit. But he looked good, his white shirt gleaming against the dark fabric, his thick blond hair brushed back from his tanned face. 'You look smashing too.'

'I thought I'd better make a special effort,' he said. 'Didn't want to show you up.'

'You could never do that,' she said, her tone becoming serious. 'We're partners, you and me.'

And they were, in more ways than one. Soon after their reconciliation, he'd come back to work at the firm, as a partner. She'd insisted on it. As they were going to share their lives, she thought it appropriate that their equality was established in the workplace too.

'That's a nice thing to say,' he said, kissing her lightly.

'That's enough, you two . . . there'll be plenty of time for that later on when you're on your own,' joked Jan, appearing in front of them with Pete, both looking well and happy. Jan was now fully recovered from her operation and enjoying better health than she had in years.

'You having a good time?' enquired Rachel.

'Not half,' said Jan. 'There's nothing like a bit of a do to make you forget all about the doom and gloom. The power cuts can do their worst and they won't worry us, not today.'

'Are you sure you'll be able to cope with the boys while we're away?' asked Rachel. Tim and Johnnie were going to stay with Jan and Pete for a few days while Rachel and Ben took a short honeymoon in a luxury hotel in the country.

'Course we're sure,' said Jan. 'When have we not been able to cope with a couple of lads?'

'They'll be no trouble at all,' added Pete. 'They're as much at home at our place as they are at yours, and Kelly will have a whale of a time bossing them about.'

'Where are the kids, anyway?' Ben wondered.

'They were talking to Doris and Billy the last time I saw them,' said Pete.

Glancing across the crowded room, Rachel caught Doris' eye and smiled at her. Now that Billy had entered into the equation, Rachel's friendship with them both had become a valuable part of her life. The couple clearly enjoyed seeing Rachel and Ben and adored the boys, but were careful not to impose. Rachel made a point of inviting them over regularly; she knew they wouldn't take the initiative because they were afraid of overstepping the mark. If she were to analyse her feelings for them, she supposed she would regard them somewhere between just friends and a favourite aunt and uncle. She still never thought of Doris as her mother.

But now the people she did think of as parents joined the group. 'Well, they all seem to be enjoying themselves, don't they?' remarked Marge. 'Despite the blackout.'

'It'll take more than a power cut to stop us lot having a good time,' commented Ron.

'I'll say it would,' agreed Marge. 'You've waited long enough for this, love. I'm sure a bit of disruption won't spoil the day for you.'

At that moment the lights came on, accompanied by loud cheers and whistles.

'We really must start mingling now that we can see where we're going properly,' suggested Ben as people began blowing the candles out.

The bride and groom moved slowly among the guests, making casual conversation. It wasn't a huge crowd, but everyone Rachel cared about was here, the staff from the boathouse and their wives added to relatives and friends. Two family members were missing, though: Arthur and Ella. Rachel wouldn't have known where to send the invitation even if she had wanted to invite them. She'd heard rumours about Arthur appearing in court for being in possession of a stolen car a year or two ago. He'd been heavily fined, apparently, and had had to move out of his posh flat.

But he was still ducking and diving, so she'd heard. She couldn't imagine him doing anything else. Fortunately, she never heard from him now.

'Having a good time, Doris?' asked Rachel as they reached the table where she and Billy were sitting with the children.

'Lovely, dear, thanks,' said Doris.

'Billy?'

'Smashing,' said Billy, who had grown fond of Rachel. 'You've put on a good do, and in such lovely surroundings, too.'

Rachel glanced towards the big glass doors which opened on to a balcony overlooking the river. The curtains weren't drawn, and through the glass she could see that darkness had already fallen and the waterfront lights were shining on the river. 'Yes, it is a nice spot,' she agreed. 'Any of the pubs along this stretch of the river would be an appropriate place for us to have our wedding reception.' She smiled up at Ben. 'It's along here that we got to know each other; it's where we've been happy. Where we belong.'

Ben replied by slipping his arm around her.

'Yuck,' complained Tim, now in his eleventh year and at an age to be appalled by any tendency towards sentimentality.

'Oh no, they're gonna start kissing again,' Johnnie chimed

in. 'Come on, kids. Let's go and see if there's any grub left. I like those little chicken things.'

'I want some more of that trifle,' said Kelly, a tall, pretty ten-year-old with long red hair and freckles. 'It's really yummy.'

'You two are always scoffing,' admonished Tim, now tall and slim, his features changing as he headed towards adolescence.

As the three of them disappeared, Rachel emitted a wistful sigh. 'They're growing up so fast I sometimes wish I could turn back the clock,' she said.

Doris, looking smart in a bright blue suit and matching hat, nodded. Rachel couldn't possibly know what it meant to her to have been invited to this wedding. She felt so proud of this warm-hearted, intelligent woman who had made a friend of her, despite what she had done all those years ago.

It warmed Doris' heart to see her grandsons now and then, and to be included in family occasions. She always held back, was careful never to encroach upon Marge's territory. She kept a certain distance from Rachel because she knew she wanted it that way. They could not be more than friends; her common sense accepted that.

But her heart was less compliant. She would never embarrass Rachel by telling her, but she loved her like a daughter; she worried about her and empathised with her. You couldn't turn off your feelings just because they weren't appropriate. Human nature didn't work that way.

All she could do was value Rachel's friendship, be there for her but make no demands; to visit if invited and look after the boys if asked. This was all that was wanted of her. It was too late for anything more.

She looked across at Marge, who smiled and waved. Marge had done a good job in raising Rachel and was entitled to the rewards. Doris guessed that she saw no threat to her being around because she was utterly confident in Rachel as a daughter.

'Yes,' she said now in reply to Rachel, 'I think most of us wish we could turn back the clock at some time in our lives.'

Rachel knew exactly what she was referring to and experienced a moment of aching poignancy. Doris' heartache wasn't something they ever talked about, but it was as certain in Rachel's mind as the filial feelings she had for Marge. Nothing could change the way things were, but Rachel comforted herself in the thought that she could make the best of what she and Doris had. She touched Doris' hand in silent acknowledgement of what the older woman was telling her. Then the bride and groom moved on.

'Are you enjoying yourself, Doris?' asked Marge, appearing at Doris' side.

'I'm having a lovely time, thanks, dear,' said Doris. 'Billy's gone to get some more drinks.'

'Yeah, I noticed that you were on your own, so I thought I'd come over and have a word.'

'Oh?'

'I just wanted to say that I'm glad you came,' explained Marge warmly.

'We were thrilled to be invited,' smiled Doris.

Marge liked Doris. She thought she was a warm-hearted soul. She guessed that Doris envied her relationship with Rachel, even though she never showed it. Doris had never tried to get back what she had given up all those years ago, and Marge respected her for that. She doubted if she and Doris would ever become bosom pals, but it was rather nice having her and Billy on the edge of the family circle, another set of grandparents for the boys, who had no one on Ben's side.

'I'm glad we've all managed to stay friends after everything that's happened,' said Marge.

'Me too,' said Doris.

Noticing the other woman's eyes brighten with tears, Marge gave her hand a comforting squeeze to let her know that she understood. 'Here comes Billy with the drinks,' she said as he approached. 'I'll leave you two to enjoy yourselves.'

And she went to find Ron, her own eyes feeling moist.

When they'd done the rounds, Rachel took Ben's hand and led him towards the balcony doors, closed on this winter's day. She opened them and they stepped out into the night air, arms entwined, looking out at the black Thames illuminated by the lights of Hammersmith Bridge. There was a cold, nocturnal beauty about the scene, the stars crystal clear in the navy blue sky.

A little further upriver was the boathouse that had changed her life and brought her and Ben together. It occurred to her briefly that if her Uncle Chip had lived out a normal lifespan maybe it wouldn't have happened. But she knew deep down that they would have found each other somehow.

This area was embedded in her heart. She didn't want to live or work anywhere else. Words weren't necessary between her and Ben at that moment. They were at one with each other and their surroundings.

A sudden movement at her side made her realise that the boys had joined them, and for once their cousin Kelly wasn't in tow. She put her arm around Tim, and Ben did the same with Johnnie. The four of them stood there, close together, silently observing the scene. Even the boys didn't speak. Rachel could feel the bond between them like a living thing. It was wonderful.

Predictably it was Johnnie who broke the spell, prattling on about what a glutton Kelly was for eating so much trifle and making herself feel sick, and it served her right too for being so greedy, whereupon Tim said that Johnnie had been a pig too and it was a wonder he hadn't made himself ill.

As the squabble gathered momentum, Rachel turned to Ben and they burst out laughing. Everything was reassuringly normal. They went back inside, smiling, closing the balcony doors behind them against the chilly winter evening.